W9-AQX-348

OBEY THE MOON

Also by Vicky Martin:

Tigers of the Night
Changing Partners
The Windmill Years

OBEY THE MOON

VICKY MARTIN

ST. MARTIN'S PRESS
NEW YORK

 For information, address St. Martin's Press, 175 Fifth Avenue, New York, N.Y. 10010.

Library of Congress Cataloging-in-Publication Data

Martin, Vicky.
Obey the moon.

I. Title.
PR6063.A731502 1989 823'.914 88-29881
ISBN 0-312-02624-2

First published in Great Britain by New English Library.

First U.S. Edition
10 9 8 7 6 5 4 3 2 1

This book is dedicated to my parents,
Jean and Lance Martin.

I would like to acknowledge the generous assistance given to me on the technical aspects of this book by certain eminent London ship-owning friends.

OBEY THE MOON

Chapter 1

When Robert Stoner emerged from the lift and walked across the room towards Eliza Marland's desk, Eliza watched his approach with a feeling of deep relief. She had spent the previous week in a state of apprehension, holding her breath in a way she hadn't done since her teens. All day her tension had increased. She had known about Robert for four years and had wanted to meet him ever since she became involved with personnel. In these first few moments before he reached her desk, she seized an impression of a powerfully built man with dark red hair and a fighter's face who looked uneasy in his grey suit. He was not a disappointment. The face fitted the legend. It was all right. Relief, sweet relief, made her smile.

He did not return the smile. He was frowning slightly. "My name is Robert Stoner. I have an appointment with David Otterwood at five fifteen." The voice was deep, with a slight northern accent. He looked at her intently, eyes moving slowly from the dark brown hair, caught back with combs from an unusual face, down to the bright yellow dress. The final choice. Everything Eliza possessed had been tried and rejected that morning.

Eliza suppressed the urge to say, "I know exactly who you are. I know that you sailed with Otterwoods as a master for three years and that is the only reason you have been granted this appointment. David expects absolute loyalty but in return does not forget even ex-employees."

She lifted the telephone, carefully making her face and voice serious.

"Mr Stoner is here to see you, Mr Otterwood."

There was a short, irritable acknowledgement and Eliza bit her lip at the curtness of the voice, guessing that David was still infuriated by the article in *Lloyd's List*, circled with blue pen by the PR department, that she had taken in with his cup of tea an hour earlier. She had read the article that morning. Everyone had read it! And it certainly wouldn't help Robert Stoner get whatever it was he had come for, she thought, looking across to the tall window where Robert stood while he waited, head bent forward thoughtfully, feet apart, hands in his pockets. She would have liked to warn him that he had arrived at a most unfortunate time but, although she had known about Robert for four years, he was a complete stranger and she didn't know how to begin.

"Will you come with me please?" she said formally, but as Robert paused with her outside the solid mahogany door of David Otterwood's office, she whispered impulsively, "Good luck!" Robert smiled as she knocked.

David Otterwood took his eyes reluctantly from the newspaper and removed his glasses. He had read the piece three times. He knew it by heart.

The strength of the Otterwood family has always been their ability to produce generation after generation of able heirs and, every few generations, a man of outstanding brilliance such as David, the present chairman. It was a little later that the journalist began to bite. *David's son, Harry Otterwood, after an undistinguished career at Harrow is currently at St Andrews University where, rumour has it, his engaging character compensates somewhat for his lack of academic success. But could it be that in this, the seventh generation, the Otterwood knack of producing the right type of man to run their empire has at last failed them?* Bitch!

"Good afternoon, Mr Stoner. Please sit down." They exchanged token handshakes and Eliza reluctantly left them, walking slowly back to her desk. The walls were so thick in this old building which housed the London head office of Otterwood Shipping that no sound would escape to satisfy her curiosity, but still she listened intently, narrow body erect and head tilted with concentration, drumming her long fingers against the desk in a restless rhythm.

David sat back. Automatic good manners would make him give this man a hearing but his expression was grim. "You were master on the *Peacock* for three years, weren't you, Mr Stoner, before you left the company? I remember your brief interlude of fame when you were made master at sea. What can I do for you now you are no longer with Otterwoods?"

Robert paused. This interview was extremely important to him and yet he was able to leave a short silence. He looked round this comfortable room with its oil paintings of Otterwood ships and the framed copy of Kipling's poem 'If' which hung above David's desk.

"On the *Peacock*, we had delivered cement to Lagos for four years. I made friends there. When the port came to a standstill I was well placed to set up on my own, by-passing the jam by renting a jetty up river and getting hold of a couple of war-surplus landing craft. Otterwoods have certainly not lost out. I imagine it suits you very well to have your ships unloaded promptly."

David nodded rather impatiently.

"My years with Otterwoods, watching from the inside, have shown me that there are times when a small operator who can move quickly can do very well indeed. I've seen another such opportunity in Venezuela."

"Yes?" Again the distinct hint of impatience.

"The lack of deep-water loading terminals means that small tankers are in great demand. I want to buy a small Norwegian tanker to carry light Nigerian crude oil to Brazil for refining and bring back the heavy oil from Venezuela that the Nigerians need so badly. I am confident I can operate it profitably but I cannot raise the fifteen per cent I need to put down on the Norwegian ship. I have prepared some figures." He held out a sheet of paper.

David liked this man's firm voice with its traces of a northern childhood. He had a file which told him that Robert was the son of a merchant seaman, that he had started with nothing and elbowed his way through school and his years at sea until he saw his chance to change sides. David sensed his energy and a certain ruthlessness. In some ways Robert reminded him of himself two decades ago. He projected a confidence he had no possible grounds for, a hunger to succeed. The words of the article, painful because they were so true, repeated themselves in David's head. *The Otterwood knack of producing the right type of man.* This was the right type of man, if he didn't sail too close to the wind. Robert would probably succeed with his proposal but David had made up his mind before Robert entered the room that he did not want Otterwoods involved. This interview was merely a gesture.

"You must be well aware of the troubled state of shipping at the moment. Nothing is moving. I'm sorry, Mr Stoner, but it's not the time to gamble on what appears to be a risky operation, however small." His voice was flat, polite and cold.

"Surely there is no wrong time to exploit a good opportunity?"

"That's a matter of opinion. Although I may not be on what you call the inside, I do hear things. A man was stabbed at your jetty a few weeks ago. Ship-owning is a small world. I don't want to be involved in Venezuela if it connects me with Nigeria and my advice to you is to get out of Lagos with what you have made before it turns sour."

Robert squared his shoulders. In the few minutes he had been in David's office he felt the beginning of intense dislike for this large man but he hid his anger as best he could. "It seems there is no more to be said."

David looked up and read the disappointment and anger behind Robert's expression and he remembered the excitement of an idea which promised success and the raging frustration when it was baulked. For the first time in several years he remembered how it had felt to really want to deal. Otterwoods was so big now that no one deal mattered that much. His eyes dropped, against his will, to the newspaper article.

"How is Harry?" Robert said as he stood up.

David frowned in surprise.

"I met him when he was fifteen. You had him sail with us on the *Peacock* for a week. He got on well enough when he stopped being sick."

"Of course." Quite suddenly Robert moved categories, changing from an ex-employee who wanted finance onto another more personal level. "That's why your name is so familiar. It wasn't just the boat people. I remember now. You gave Harry a lot of your time. More than you had to. He liked you. He talked about you a lot." For the first time since this interview began, David's voice held some expression.

"Is the article fair?"

David shrugged. "Is any newspaper article wholly fair or unfair? It's one person's opinion, that's all." He crossed the room slowly and paused at the door. "Look, I don't want to finance you myself but I can think of a couple of people who might be interested. I imagine you wouldn't be here unless the banks had turned you down." He frowned for a moment and then said, "If you want to come to my house in Hampshire tomorrow evening there will be a gathering of shipping people. I'll introduce you to two men in particular who like a gamble and you might strike lucky. If you want to come, my secretary Eliza will give you the details." He opened the door and held out his hand. "Good afternoon, Mr Stoner."

As the door closed Eliza looked up at Robert sympathetically, her hands tightly interlocked. He stood with his back to the solid door.

"No luck?"

"He can be a patronising bastard, can't he? He gave me a brief lecture on the depressed state of shipping and finished off by telling me that he didn't want to get involved with an operation like mine anyway! To hell with him. His great-great-grandfather wasn't too sensitive about ethics when he started this whole circus."

"That was in 1825," Eliza said gently.

"Correct. And being such a well-informed secretary you'll be aware that Harold Otterwood founded his fortune on opium, shipping it from India in clippers and stopping along the way to seek out new provinces full of potential addicts. The profits were immense. Later on he became very respectable, built himself a castle in Scotland and went into politics." Robert walked towards her desk. "Not that I'm condemning old Harold. If I had lived then I might well have done just the same. It's the holiness of the subsequent generations that's so bloody hard to swallow. The sanctity that money endows. Despite that, I admire success in any form and especially in this family, I admire the way they keep producing sons who are clever enough and tough enough to expand rather than squander old Harold's legacy."

Eliza said nothing and Robert looked at her enquiringly. "Or is Harry turning out to be a disappointment? Is the article true?"

"There is an element of truth in it," Eliza said carefully.

"That's a pity. Anyway, I may not have got the money I came for but he's asked me to his house tomorrow evening to take my chance there. I must say, it surprised me. I had the impression he wouldn't care if he never saw me again, but I'd be a fool not to go even if I don't like him. Can you give me the address and tell him I'll be there?"

Eliza wrote an address and a time on a piece of paper. "They change for dinner when they have this sort of party."

"They may. I don't. I haven't got a dinner jacket." He took the piece of paper from Eliza. "You know a lot about them, don't you? What's your name?"

"Elizabeth Marland."

"I hate long, elaborate women's names."

"My friends call me Eliza."

"Liz would be better." He sat on the opposite side of her desk, looking at her intently with dark blue eyes.

"I hate being called Liz."

"Eliza then. Come for a drink, Eliza, and tell me about them all?"

The blatant attempt to use her made Eliza look away. She didn't want him to be like this, sharp and opportunist. She wanted the man to fit the hero's image she had embellished over the past few years. She wanted an impossibly strong, quiet man. Anyway, this couldn't be happening so easily; for years she had pretended around the image of Robert Stoner she had built up. This was much too quick, too smooth.

"I'm sorry, I can't," she said, before she had even thought about the words.

For several seconds he stood and looked at her and she looked back, wanting him to ask her again but he merely shrugged and turned towards the door. "Not my day, is it? Everyone's turning me down. Goodbye, Eliza."

Eliza watched him go with a sense of panicky regret which made her want to call him back. She sighed angrily. The office was suddenly very quiet. An ache of discontentment made her hurry to one of the tall windows and look down at the street which was shimmering with heat on this brilliant afternoon in mid-August. The street surprised her. In the air-conditioned silence there was no sense of summer. She put her face close to the glass and watched for Robert Stoner, wondering if she would recognise him from five floors up. *Why the hell didn't I go with him? I've wanted to meet him for four years! Why am I like I am?* The glass was cool against her cheek.

She sighed again and turned her back to the window. *It doesn't matter. This is enough.* She raised her chin, defending herself to herself. *I could have married Paul.* It had taken a long time to convince him that she did not want marriage and children, that she loved her work, that the affair which she had entered into only out of loneliness had matured on her part into a kind of love but not the kind she would marry for. He had been so hurt. She had tried to explain that there must be a different way to feel. A stronger, undeniable attraction. She had mentioned excitement, mentioned Robert. Paul was justifiably infuriated to be rejected for what he called childish hero-worship. He had taken her dreams apart, realising too late he was only strengthening her decision with his brutal common sense. In the end she had been in a panic to get away. At twenty-four, apart from her father there had been only one man in her life that Eliza had loved. Only Paul, and he had not been allowed too close. She had never stayed all night but had always gone back, however late, to her own bed in her own flat in the wide road that slanted down to Lupus Street, to wake on home ground. Safer to be alone, to pretend around some distant image she would probably never meet.

But I have met him. And I turned him down.

She straightened, sighing angrily. It was nearly six. Eliza had created an ordered framework to live within and she hated to stay late unless there was a definite reason. She moved towards the door of David's office and knocked.

He was speaking on the telephone and Eliza stood and waited, looking at the photograph of Celia Otterwood as she often did. Could any man be unfaithful to a woman with such a gentle, intelligent face and the kind of uncontrived beauty that Eliza envied more than any other? There were many rumours about this big, rather arrogant man whose high forehead and pale blue eyes were so characteristic of the Otterwoods; a man who had been born into a powerful family and who had used his advantages to increase his inheritance enormously.

"Mr Stoner would like to have dinner with you tomorrow," she said, when David finished speaking. "I gave him the address and asked him to be there by eight."

David nodded. "I rather thought he would accept," he said dryly. "Thank you, Eliza. Nothing else, is there? See you on Monday."

As she stood in the lift, Eliza anticipated the solitude of her flat and the weekend ahead with mixed feelings. It was strange, after two years, to have no one to make plans with. In one way she relished her complete freedom with all its potential, and in another she dreaded it. Without Paul, she had lost her best excuse for not going home occasionally and home was a bruise which, after all these years, still hurt if she touched it. She was frowning as she crossed the tiled hall of the new annexe with its atrium full of enormous magnolias and stepped outside, into a rush of hot air quite unlike a normal English summer evening.

Robert Stoner was standing in the street. "You took your time. I keep thinking of things I want to ask you and things I should have said to him. I should have told him that in two hundred years when Otterwoods are a distant legend like the East India Company is today, Stoner's will be handling vast amounts of inter-galactic cargo on a fleet of space shuttles! I don't know why it is but I always find it much easier to talk to women I don't know. The better I know them, the less I want to say. Change your mind about a drink?"

I don't believe this, Eliza thought, feeling a reaction as he touched her arm and held her back until the traffic parted and they could cross the narrow street. Robert was a man of medium height, who appeared shorter because of his wide shoulders and she was surprised, as she walked beside him, to find he was slightly taller than she was. He pushed open the door of the first pub they came to and found a table near the window and Eliza sat down and glanced out at the grey-suited army and brightly dressed secretaries beginning the homeward struggle.

"Well?" Robert asked.

"Well what?"

"Have you changed your mind about having a drink?"

"It looks as though I have."

He smiled and pulled off his tie and unfastened the top button of his shirt. He hung his jacket over the back of his chair. "Dressing up didn't do me much good, did it?"

"On the contrary, he probably wouldn't have asked you tomorrow night if he hadn't liked the look of you. You have to play by his rules and give an impression of confidence. I thought when I left you alone together that you couldn't have two more different men in the same room. Everything about David Otterwood is distilled, subtle to an extent that you rarely know what he's thinking. Control like a mask, even with his friends. And yet he can be surprised into laughter and into intense anger and if all the rumours are true, he must be a passionate man."

"Know him fairly well do you?" Robert asked, the words heavy with suggestion.

"If I do it's only because I've watched him. I was with him temporarily last year while his secretary was on holiday and I was summoned again on Friday as she was taken ill. Much as I'd like to stay on, it will probably only be temporary again this year, so I'm no good to you as a friend at court." She sat back, making her wide mouth small and prim. "Do you still want to buy me a drink?"

Robert laughed. "Yes I do. If only to find out what you

think about me. You've given him all the strong points. Obviously I'm going to be described as the brash, unsubtle seaman whose rugged face shows everything he's thinking. What do you want to drink?"

"Vodka and tonic with a lot of ice, please.

"I remember all the excitement in the press when you were made master at sea after Gerald Hassock became ill and the subsequent dramas with those boat people," she said, when Robert returned with two glasses.

"Yes, the press loved it. In fact it was greatly exaggerated. There was nothing heroic about it. There were only five rather pathetic pirates and the boat people might well have escaped without our intervention but it suited us to bring them to safety."

"With very good press for Otterwoods!"

Robert smiled wryly. "And the chance to consolidate my position as master. It was bloody lucky. I joined the company at seventeen and had my Second Mate's certificate at twenty-four. Had my progress followed the normal pattern I would have been First Mate for another ten years, I imagine."

"Where will you try next for your money?" Eliza asked. "And what do you want it for?"

"I'm not sure where I'll go next. I've tried most other sources. David Otterwood is not the first man you think of approaching when you need cash." He frowned as he drank. "Also, time is short. I have to go back to Lagos very soon. I have to watch things there. I have some good Nigerian friends but you can never be complacent in Africa and I run the whole operation with the help of an engineer I've known for years and two sailors. I need a base here, an office to give me respectability. Somehow or other I'm going to get in, Eliza. I know how it all works. I know how they think. You have to be fast on your feet and I am. Somehow I'll get in." He drank deeply from his glass of beer. "And what about you? Are you just filling in time before you find someone to marry and give you a warm little house and kids?"

The irony of his words made her deny it emphatically. "No. I'm not interested in getting married for a long time yet. I shall buy my own house. I think I'm very good at my job and I want recognition and responsibility. I'm quite determined to leap the gap from the secretarial side to the management side." When Eliza spoke passionately her brown eyes shone and she sat very straight.

"In something as big as Otterwoods?" Robert said. He found her air of determination rather touching and suspected it hid a complicated vulnerability. The really hard women he had known seldom explained themselves. "You'd stand a better chance in a smaller company, surely?"

"Perhaps." She leaned back against the plastic seat, hating this particular pub for its ugliness. It was crowded now. "Look at all these people, unwilling to go home without a couple of drinks to blur whatever it is they're going back to. I never want to feel like that. I need to go home tired but satisfied, exhilarated by the thought of the next day and believing I have achieved something."

"Not another bloody idealist," Robert smiled. "What's wrong with simply making money?" He leaned his elbows on the table, studying her intently. His face was very freckled. "Why did you refuse when I offered you a drink the first time?"

She looked down, disconcerted by the question.

"Partly because you seemed to assume I'd accept and I hate being taken for granted and partly because I have been in the habit of refusing for so long that it's almost automatic."

"But not any more?"

"No. Not any more."

He sat back. "I suppose the same applies to me," he said wryly.

"It takes some getting used to, doesn't it?"

"Yes."

Robert looked at his watch and then back to Eliza's face. For a moment he studied the wide cheekbones and pointed chin, the eyes that were such a dark brown they gave nothing away. Strange, attractive face. "Fairly soon I have to go and make some phone calls but later this evening I shall go out and eat. Nothing fancy. Where do you live?"

"Pimlico."

"Shall I come and pick you up, around nine? I'm going back to Africa in a couple of days so there'll be no waiting around outside the doors of Otterwoods another time."

Eliza smiled and her eyes went paisley-shaped. "I'd better say yes, then."

She watched Robert join the crowd round the bar a second time and she thought, *It's so extraordinary to have reality smash through imagination. Like going back to a place you have loved in the past that has changed terribly but is not ruined. Just so different from your memory.* She thought, *Six weeks since I last saw Paul. Hardly a decent interval of mourning to leave after two years, is it?* Robert turned and looked at her, making a grimace of impatience and pushing one hand through his short red hair. Only two men in Eliza's life who had counted. Looking at Robert Stoner and feeling the nervousness and excitement which signalled the beginning of sexual attraction, feeling intense curiosity about the man and his life, and wariness, almost a reluctance to become involved, Eliza had a conviction she had just met the third.

Chapter 2

Alice Marland knew every paving stone in Seagull Avenue, the pattern of cracks in between and the way, each spring, a gradual invasion of dandelions and grass grew where the paving stones met the walls which enclosed the front gardens. She had walked home this way every evening since she began work and before that, every school day of her life apart from an occasional afternoon when, despite her mother's obvious disapproval, she went to a friend's house. When she came home from visiting a friend, her mother would treat her as if she had been contaminated, as if even her clothes smelled of strangers, and if Alice asked a friend back, afterwards Jane Marland would slowly and thoroughly pick the girl to bits, the way she picked meat from a cooked chicken carcass. A widow for eight years, Jane Marland chose to despise the outside world in order to justify her isolation. Eight years to spin a web with herself and Alice at the centre. Now, at nineteen, Alice was so used to their solitary life, she found that other girls gave her a sad, uncomfortable feeling as if, the moment she left, they would laugh about her. Other girls talked almost entirely about the way they looked and about men. They were constantly changing themselves whereas Alice looked complete.

"Your face makes no definite impact at first," Eliza had told her once, "but the more you look at it the more you want to. It's a satisfying sort of face. I wish I had it!" Hair the colour of honey that grew back strongly from her forehead and waved around her head in a way that did not need changing. Definite eyebrows above long, pale blue eyes. Her body was small and strong with not much change between waist and hips but a definite bosom. There seemed no point in trying to alter the shape of her body and, being adopted, she could not complain about having inherited some unfortunate characteristic from her parents.

As Alice walked, she was frowning. She was oblivious to the beauty of the afternoon as Paddy's words repeated themselves in her head. "I may have to sell up, Alice love. Temporary financial embarrassment. If the shop were in London, it would be a different matter. As it is, it's only the tourists who keep us going." She shivered unhappily despite the heat. Alice loved her job, hid in it, wrapped it round her like a cloak while she waited. She hid her shyness behind a perfectly normal, if rather remote exterior. People who were silently, miserably shy, who blushed and stammered and even burst into tears, were eventually broken through to and formed intense friendships but people like Alice seemed to like being alone. No one except Eliza guessed at the complicated blend of relief and restlessness Alice felt each afternoon as she walked alone up Seagull Avenue. It was just a question of waiting. As with her body, so with her life, Alice did not believe she could alter things. She had been taught from early childhood that, despite the slavish observance of hundreds of small superstitions which served Jane Marland in place of religion, fate would control her life. She might make a cross in the salt but the bad luck would strike anyway.

Seagull Avenue ended at a crossroads where it was intersected by a similar wide and quiet street and a few hundred yards beyond was the sea with its neat fringe of bathing huts. Such a tame sea, that stripe of water along the coast of Hove between the sky and the shingle. Not a real sea like the one that battered the Cornish coast or the wild Scottish waters, but this dozing ocean did attract summer visitors and the four big bedrooms at the front of the house were nearly always occupied between May and September. Bed and breakfast families and sometimes they booked for an evening meal. Alice lumped them together in her mind. These summer families were not very real to her. They were necessary to help pay for this big Edwardian house with its square walled garden and high-ceilinged rooms. Many of the other houses in the street had fallen to an invasion of doctors and dentists and private nursing homes. Was it worth all the work, Alice wondered. What were they keeping the house for? When her father had been alive and Eliza had been home, the house had been a frame for a family but now it was just a small, clean hotel.

Alice let herself in through the back door, knowing the house would be empty. Once a month Jane Marland visited a cash and carry at Shoreham with her sister. The two families who had been staying had left that morning and the new people were not expected till seven. Alice sighed, trying to prepare herself for the ordeal of welcoming total strangers. Although she had done it so often, it was never easy for her. She closed the back door and breathed in the familiar smell of this big, tidy kitchen, sighed at the safety of it all, and then she saw the note leaning against a jar of sweet peas. *Bramsdens not coming till Sunday. Car trouble. Salad and ham in the fridge. Back about nine thirty. Mum.*

A slow delight spread through Alice as she anticipated several hours of totally unexpected peace, a Bramsden-free evening, a wonderfully empty Saturday. She threw her bag down on the table, hunching up her shoulders in a tight bunch of pleasure as she made herself a drink full of ice which she carried out into the back garden, kicking off worn sandals and pushing her bare toes into the grass. She settled herself in one of the old garden chairs and shivered with contentment as she drank. The second time she dipped her mouth into the icy liquid the front door bell rang.

It never occurred to her to ignore it. With a moan Alice got out of the chair and walked barefooted through the cool house to unlock the heavy front door.

Halfway down the wide mosaic path, facing the gate as if he were about to leave, stood a tall man in baggy blue jeans and a T-shirt. He turned as he heard the front door open and Alice had a first impression of a young face, big features, a frown, very straight shaggy hair as dark as Eliza's. He came towards her and she saw he was probably a little older than herself and that his nose had a bump on it as if it had once been broken.

"I saw the sign. Have you a room free for tonight?"

"Just one night?"

"Yes." A deep, very English voice.

Jane Marland had one rigid rule: Never take a single man. They drink or try and bring a woman back to the room at night.

He stood with his head slightly bent and he looked exhausted and dishevelled. A dirty red open-topped car was parked by the gate, radio still playing. In the awkward silence he rubbed his chin as if apologising for the fact that he was unshaven. "Shall I pay in advance? Is that what you want? How much is it?"

"Five pounds for bed and breakfast. An evening meal would be extra. Cash please," Alice said solemnly, heart thumping as she gave in to an impulse to alter the endless repeating pattern of her life.

He frowned and she knew he was mentally counting his money. "I don't want an evening meal, just somewhere to sleep." He pushed his hands into both pockets and pulled out crumpled notes, two of them with an unfamiliar Scottish pattern. He counted out the fifth pound in silver and he was thirty pence short.

"That doesn't matter," Alice said quickly, embarrassed for him, and he looked up and laughed suddenly, making her smile in return, although she had no idea what he found so funny. He went back to his car, still laughing, and took out the key and turned off the music. As he followed Alice into the house he said, "My name is Harry. What's yours?"

"Alice." She went ahead of him up the stairs, aware that he watched her bare legs beneath the loose cotton dress. When she glanced behind her his eyes swept up quickly and he smiled, the expression lighting his angular face for a moment before it settled back into a frown. She ran up the last few stairs, opened the door to the blue room and went in.

"You can use the bathroom next door." Automatically

she opened the big sash windows as the room was airless, checked the basin for soap and towels.

"Where is the sea from here?" He had thrown his holdall on the bed and was at the window, holding aside the clean net curtains. The deep voice was too old for him, Alice thought.

"It's two minutes' walk on over the crossroads but it's not worth looking at."

"Why not?"

"It's so dull and calm."

"Is there a beach and icecream and things?"

"Yes."

"But you don't like it?"

"I've lived next to it all my life. There are better beaches you can go to when it's very hot but I hardly ever do."

"Where do you go, then? What will you do tonight?"

"Nothing much."

"Tomorrow?"

"I have to work every other Saturday. I work in a little shop in the Lanes, in Brighton."

He nodded and he moved away from the window and dropped onto the bed, looking up at Alice again and this time keeping his eyes on her face. Quite often people looked at Alice like this a second time, surprised that they hadn't noticed at once the way her features belonged so perfectly. Nothing to change. He looked exhausted and he rubbed his forehead roughly with his fingers, hiding his face. His whole attitude expressed desperation.

"Would you like some tea?" Alice asked, cautiously, because she could think of nothing else to say.

He hesitated.

"It's free."

"Do you read minds?"

She shook her head. "I know about people not having money. You get an instinct. We always ask them to pay in advance but sometimes they want to stay on." She moved out of the open door into the passage and because the part she had been playing, the capable part she always played with the guests, seemed such a waste with him, and because there was nothing to put in its place, the shyness began to rise. "I'll take the tea into the garden at the back."

"Okay." This time he did not smile and his face slid into an expression of serious bitterness which was shocking. She looked back from the top of the stairs. He had made no attempt to shut his door. He was unzipping the holdall and Alice saw him take out a bottle and drink deeply from it.

She made tea in the small pot they kept for themselves and put it on a tray with a few scones. She carried the tray out into the garden. Only this was sacred, kept from the visitors, this garden of buddleia and roses and the big square of vegetables and fruit bushes. Even if the visitors were out, Alice would come here to escape the careful neatness of a house that was run for guests. The garden was a tangle of different scents and colours, embroidered with butterflies. She sat on one of the faded canvas chairs and poured herself tea and wondered if he would come or if he would stay in his room and drink what was in the bottle instead. They had had several like that, who looked okay when they came, putting on a big effort, hiding their shaking hands, and then not appearing for so long that eventually Jane would have to steel herself and go up and knock. Women on their own were suspicious. Jane much preferred families but sometimes, if they had not been busy, she couldn't afford to turn anyone reasonable away. Alice had already thought up her explanation. "It seemed silly to say no, with all the rooms empty. It seemed a waste." Jane must not know he had been allowed into the garden. The garden was sacred.

As he came out of the house, Alice looked up at him and felt an excited lightness that was quite new to her, as if she would laugh soon. He hesitated before he came and sat down. She gave him a cup of tea.

"Thank you. It's hours since I had any nourishment. I take meals for granted, assuming that they will be provided by other people, I mean."

"Where have you come from?" Alice asked, as if he were one of the normal summer people.

"Scotland. I was in Peterhead yesterday. On the east coast. It's small and orderly and grim as hell. North Sea supply ships. And there's a fishing fleet. The harbour is the only part of the town with any sign of life. I went to look at the ships and finally convince myself that none of it is for me. Then I just turned south and drove. I slept in the car for a few hours and then drove again all day, right through London. I just kept going till I was sick of the music and I knew I must have nearly reached the sea. I wanted to drive from coast to coast, north to south. From the heights to the depths." He rubbed his face wearily with bony hands. "I'm not going back to St Andrews. I have just scraped through the exams. I worked like a slave for that rotten third. What's the point? It's just too difficult. I've struggled for years with exams and now I'm giving up and they will all have to accept that I will never go into the company. It doesn't interest me and I can't do it." He dropped his head into his hands, voice muffled. "God, I can see it now, the carefully concealed disappointment that will change into anger, the amazement that they've produced something as stupid as I am." He drank deeply from his cup and held it out for more, his other hand taking a scone which he ate in one mouthful. "I'm sorry. All this means nothing to you." He leaned back in the chair. "I have so little time. They have expected me back since mid-July. I have to go home and tell them soon."

"What were you reading?"

"History." His eyes came to rest on Alice's face. "My father's subject. My father is not just clever but unusually brilliant and shrewd, as is my sister, as my grandfather was, as they've all been, right back to old Harold, and they can't understand anyone who isn't like them. Are your parents clever?"

"I've no idea."

"What do you mean?"

"I don't know who they are. I'm adopted."

He rocked forward again, his face alive with interest. "God, what a marvellous bit of luck. No one you have to compare yourself with, no standard to measure yourself against and constantly fail, and no previous generations hanging over you like so many stuffed stag's heads, staring down unbelievingly with glassy eyes at the latest unworthy heir."

Alice clenched her hands, sudden anger at this flippant misunderstanding sweeping the shyness away. "Luck? Is it lucky to have no one else who looks like you, just slightly, no one with any similar characteristics? No one to tell you that you are like your grandmother, to tell you what she did, what they all did, the pyramid of people who came before; no real mother to tell you the story of your birth, exaggerating her moments of pain and triumph. No background. Just me. Like Eve. Do you know what my sister said once when she was angry? She said, 'Just think, some of these people who come and stay could be your relations.' I've never stopped thinking that. I pick some of the ones I like the look of and pretend they are mine. I'm always looking at people to see if they look like me." She stopped abruptly and blushed.

"You must know some things. Aren't there rules?"

"Yes. But only if you know your real name. You have to start somewhere. I think I was born in Ireland, in the south. My mother must know something about me but she won't talk about it. My adopted father knew more but he died very suddenly eight years ago."

Harry sat back and folded his arms. "I envy you more than you can possibly know. You will never be able to fail your family."

"No, but they have failed me! I won't have anything to bring to my children, if I have any, except myself."

"You have a home. An adopted family."

"I know that. I know I'm lucky. You were going to say that next, weren't you? Everyone always does." She wanted to tell him much more about it but she had never discussed her sense of isolation with anyone but Eliza before and was amazed that she had said so much now. The shyness washed back and, in her silence, Harry began to talk about himself again.

"God knows I've tried hard enough. I have had more special coaching than anyone can possibly justify. I've worked through the holidays . . . It just isn't in me! They can't understand anyone who hasn't got it. I hate ships. I'm seasick. I hate the whole ghastly City thing. There is no end to it. It goes on for ever, more ships, more deals, more money. I think my mother may realise how I feel. She isn't particularly clever." He was talking to Alice as if he'd known her for years, a constant passionate explanation of his feelings. "I could have given up years ago. Why did I have to be born into this position? And it will only get worse if I let it go on." Alice watched his wide mouth and his anguished face and tried to understand. "You see it's such an enormous thing, the company, with banks and ships and thousands of people. Why do they want me, for God's sake? I just can't do it!"

She said very little. She wasn't required to. His life sounded quite unreal but she could have sat and listened and watched his face forever. She had no sense of time. The sun moved behind the roof of the next-door house and the garden seemed to grow hotter as the shadows deepened and the scent of the flowers was as strong as incense.

"What time is it?" Harry said at last. "I'm starving."

His words broke the spell.

Alice was surprised into smiling by this sudden change of subject. "It's seven-thirty. I could make some sandwiches." Harry had eaten everything on the tray. "No extra charge!"

He stood up, pushing the chair back. "No, let's go out somewhere. Show me round. We can drive along to Brighton. I've never been there. I haven't got any money but there's petrol in the car and I've got credit cards. I may never come here again in my life. I often think that about places and people, do you? That I may never see them again. I always want to try everything I can. Just this one chance. Like life itself. One chance only. Why should the company have me? Come on."

Alice stayed where she was, looking up at him, with one hand on each wooden arm of her chair. The sudden change panicked her. She never did things on the spur of the moment and she was afraid of impulses. "My mother will be back soon and she expects me to be here."

He frowned and the eager look left his eyes. Harry was used to people taking up his suggestions instantly and enthusiastically. "Surely you're allowed out? Aren't you a little old to be so cautious?"

Alice flushed. "You don't understand. She would worry. I should be here to help with everything." How could she begin to explain about her mother and herself? Why should she? Should she tell him that the night of her father's funeral she had moved into the empty bed in her mother's room and had slept there ever since, every night for eight years.

"But there aren't any other people here."

"No. They cancelled. But there will be so much to unpack and put away when she comes."

Harry's face took on a bitterness which was extraordinary on such a young face. Then he crouched down to her level, put out his hand and touched her wrist, moving his fingers lightly against her skin and sending shock waves through her whole body.

He gripped her wrist tightly. "Please come. I feel desperate. I've never felt like it before. Normally I ignore my feelings but I can't ignore this."

Alice looked into his eyes and thought that nothing he could talk about would destroy him but she heard Eliza's mocking voice in her head, "You can't let her have you all your life. You've got to get out some time."

He released her wrist and his fingers had left a white bracelet of pressure on her skin.

"All right. I'll leave a note. But can't we just walk?"

"If you want." He frowned. "Is it better to walk?"

"Yes."

They walked down Seagull Avenue to the shingled beach and wandered out towards the sea. Harry took off his shoes and let the waves lap at his feet. He bent and tasted the salt water. "The sea. The cause of all my troubles. Why couldn't my family have been farmers and spent the last hundred and fifty years struggling to keep their land, getting steadily poorer instead of building ships and getting steadily richer?"

They walked towards Brighton and the evening was so hot there was an almost Mediterranean atmosphere. Whole families were paddling. At a hamburger stall Alice used some of the money Harry had given her and there was some trouble with one of the Scottish pounds. Harry, who had talked so much earlier, now hardly spoke. Occasionally he took the bottle out of his pocket and offered Alice a drink and then drank himself when she refused. They wandered along the second pier, looking down between the slatted boards to the sea far below. It was like walking back in time, Alice had often thought, to pass the peeling white Victorian buildings with rusted iron supports and the elaborate fretted wood, until the roar of the amusement arcade dragged you back into the present time.

Later, Alice led him away from the sea front, into the warren of streets that lay between the sea and Eastern Road. They went to a small restaurant in Dukes Lane and had coffee and icecream and the five pounds was reduced to a few pence.

"Thank you for coming with me, Alice. I was desperate, but I'm beginning to feel different. A change has come over me. I've made a decision to stop. Well, not so much a decision as a realisation of hopelessness. As from now, I've given up hoping for a miracle!" It fascinated Alice to watch him persuade himself out of his desperation, to watch his mood change as the alcohol he was drinking so steadily took effect. She felt that half the time he didn't know she was there. She felt as if she had walked in her sleep and woken here, swaying down a narrow street and stopping to listen to a busker who played a guitar and a mouth organ at the same time. As they were listening, she felt Harry's arm along her shoulder, his hand turned her face towards his. She could smell the alcohol as his mouth closed in on hers. She stiffened as she always did when she was kissed, waiting for the wave of disgust, but it never came. In the past she had always thought that mouths, close up, looked and felt like the dark, shiny jellied things that clung to the edges of rock pools, but now she felt timelessness, pleasure at the warmth of his mouth. There was tension in his fingers against her face as if he wanted to grip too hard, to hurt her. When he kissed her again, it was much more roughly and for longer and he pushed his hands against the loose cotton dress until she managed to free her mouth enough to tell him to stop.

"Why?" he looked surprised, slightly hurt.

"Because it's late. Because you've had a lot to drink. Because it was different before but now it doesn't seem as if you know it's me you are kissing."

Harry frowned, leaning away from her. "Of course I know it's you. I just don't know you very well and this is one way to find out." And he leaned forward once again and touched her lips with his and she felt his mouth stretch into a smile against hers. "I'm trying to believe in you. You're like a miracle."

They sat on a seat in front of the bathing huts just opposite the end of Seagull Avenue and Harry fell asleep against her. She sat stiffly, supporting the weight of his head until her back ached unbearably and when at last she moved he woke without comment, as if he had slept for a few moments instead of nearly an hour. They talked until dawn and it seemed to Alice, when at last they walked back, that time had moved in leaps and pauses not in a smooth flow. They passed Harry's car and she imagined how it would have sounded, roaring up a sleeping street and mocking the disapproving silence of the consulting rooms and nursing homes.

It was after four when Alice unlocked the back door and Jane Marland was sitting at the kitchen table, a mug of coffee in front of her, fingers fidgeting with Alice's note and her shoulders hunched up stiffly. The terrible disasters she had imagined befalling Alice burned in her eyes.

"Alice, it's so late!" The words burst out of her mouth. She had obviously been waiting to say them for hours. "It's so unlike you. I couldn't think where you were, who the friend was. Who is he?"

Harry swayed forward, made a small bow, hand held out and his voice blurred with drink. "Alice said you wouldn't want her to go but I persuaded her. My name is Harry Otterwood."

Jane's expression of bewildered distaste was snatched

from her face. "Otterwood? Are you related to David Otterwood?"

"Yes. Unfortunately he's my father. Do you know him?"

"Eliza, my elder daughter, works for Otterwoods." Jane stood up, her face expressing disbelief. "At the moment, because your father's regular secretary is ill, she's actually working for him. Surely Alice told you?"

"Alice never asked my second name."

This, at least, Jane could accept. Alice was extraordinarily vague about social details as well as many other things. "I don't believe in coincidences like that! You must have known we lived here. Do you know Eliza?"

"Yes, I know Eliza. I thought I might find her house and that she might be here. In a way, I wanted to see her. She helped before when I was trying to get my father to lend me enough money to go to Australia, which he wouldn't. I wanted a year off before I started at St Andrews. I thought it was the only time in my life I might be able to do nothing. He didn't agree. My mother would have bought me a ticket but I didn't want to start the family row of the century so I gave in and went to Scotland." he sighed. "I like Eliza."

He knows exactly how appealing he looks, Jane thought, *knows how to raise his eyebrows in a way that is quizzical and imploring, how to use his marvellous mouth. Why has Eliza sent him here?* Then she looked at Alice, saw how Alice watched him with her head slightly bent; Alice, who normally gave nothing away, had a bright light in her eyes and pink cheeks. Her face was quite changed. Jane felt fear when she looked at Alice's face.

"Would you mind if I went to bed now?" Harry said. "Last night I slept in the car. Thank you for showing me round, Alice." He stood awkwardly, feeling the tension even through the alcohol, seeing that Alice had retreated into a shell. He had great difficulty keeping his eyes open but he managed to look quizzically at Alice, tried a small smile, wanting a response, but her face was stiff and wary as she said a formal "Good night."

Chapter 3

Celia Otterwood stood on the warm grass outside the open doors of the dining-room, looking up at the stray wisteria spray which had flowered out of due season and trying to shake off the inertia which filled her. She had swum forty lengths of the pool and she longed to lie in the sun and smooth everything from her mind except warmth and peace and the scent of her garden but it was after eleven and there were other things she should do instead. She sighed. Her total disenchantment with these large business dinners that David organised had increased steadily over the past few years. Once she had enjoyed planning them, embellishing the beautiful dining-room in this dignified old house with lovely china and silver, with lace table mats and elaborate glass. In the beginning she had felt that she was helping David as he fought to stamp his identity onto Otterwoods. She had been far busier then when the children were small, her days intensely varied. Much less time and yet she had taken far more trouble, agonising over the menus and the seating plans. Now she did not care very much. These dinner parties were routine, well-practised events and all David's battles were won without her help. Looking up at the delicate purple cluster of flowers above her head she suddenly remembered a summer evening ten or twelve years ago when she had gone to kiss Julia good night and Julia had been sick all over her, just as the front door bell rang. Then she had cried. Now she laughed as she remembered.

Rebelliously, Celia walked into the dining-room with damp, bare feet. The table was laid for twenty-five although twenty-four was the most they could manage comfortably. David had sprung an extra man on her yesterday evening. "Robert Stoner," he had said, pouring himself a drink after the ritual kiss he always gave Celia when he came in and went out. For appearances' sake, she knew. To preserve a normal façade, wherever his affections might be entangled at that particular moment. "I asked him on impulse and I regretted it the moment I'd done it. He came to try and get me to back some rather shaky scheme and he reminded me that Harry spent some time on the *Peacock* when he was first mate and liked him. Can we squeeze him in somewhere? Better keep him away from the Russians. I'll do the seating plan later."

David always did the seating plan now, putting on either side of Celia men she was required to be charming to. It was quite easy for her, or it had been until the last few months. Last night she had looked across the room at David, seeing him as if he were a man she knew very well but someone else's husband. A big, tall man, light hair receding above a handsome enigmatic face, a man who made people wait until he spoke. His silences were sometimes menacing, always considered, but, until recently, Celia had believed that he still confided in her, no matter what else was going on, telling her about Otterwoods and any other problems he might have, telling her everything except why he needed other women in his life. Last night she had looked at his face and thought, *Is this all there is? Just the organised outer layers of marriage with a void inside?* Last night she had thought, and thought again now, *In a few months I shall be forty. David and I have been married for twenty-one years. The children are almost grown up. What was it for? What was the point? Over half my life used up, given to David. Will he have it all?*

Throughout this summer Celia had been growing increasingly restless. She listened to herself when she spoke as if she were listening to another person and often she found this other person boring. Celia was tired of the opinions she had formed years ago and never bothered to change. *What have I done with my life? Is this just fear of being forty, a whisper of old age I have overheard?* She walked round the long table, feeling soft old rugs beneath her feet. *Or is it that, having more time now the children are older I want more of David, not less?* Little shreds of dried grass were left in a trail where she had walked. The roses in the centre of the table smelled strongly. *I have lived my life at one extreme or the other, pushed backwards and forwards as David moves in and out of his affairs, questioning everything about myself when he is being unfaithful, overwhelmed with relief and triumph and resentment when he swings back to me. As he always has. But will it always be like that?* She turned and caught her reflection in the huge looking-glass above the sideboard and saw her face brutally naked after swimming, dark hair wet against her head, skin tanned, long narrow neck. One of her good friends had said yesterday, "Celia, that straight blunt hair is starting to make you look older than you are. When are you going to change it?"

Oh God, Celia thought, moving in closer and seeing the delicately mapped out lines, a blueprint of old age beneath her eyes and each side of her wide mouth and on her forehead, *am I going to have to start worrying about how I look? Really worrying? It's always been so easy.*

She went through the flagged hall into the kitchen where Maria, her cook for ten years, was piping meringues onto large baking sheets. The kettle was hot and Celia made herself a coffee. "Twenty-five," she complained. "I hate being squashed. Is there enough smoked salmon?"

"More than enough, as usual!"

"It's just David and me for lunch unless Josie gets up, so I'll take a salad and some cheese and ham down to the pool." She took her coffee and the newspapers and went into the hall, listening at the bottom of the wide staircase for any sound of her youngest daughter and, hearing nothing, made her way out to the garden again, granting herself another half hour of peace. In a few moments, coffee and newspaper forgotten, she was crouched down by the rockery, weeding happily, and totally absorbed in her garden.

Harry had woken much later than he had intended in the unfamiliar room and the dread which waited for him each morning was miraculously soothed a few moments after he remembered it by the peace of his decision. Energy flooded through him. He remembered Alice and he got out of bed, dressing quickly, wanting to see her. His head ached. The whisky bottle was almost empty.

Jane Marland was in the kitchen making pastry and Harry watched her for a few moments from the doorway, watched her hands making little stabbing dives into the brown mixing bowl. A tall woman with grey hair and a stern, sad, creased face, he could see little likeness to what he remembered of Eliza. When she looked up her expression was one of irritation.

"You're very late. I can't do a cooked breakfast now."

"I never eat cooked breakfast. Can you do coffee?"

"Of course. And toast if you want it."

"Just coffee, please." He stayed in the doorway, unsure whether to enter the room or not. He was bewildered by her attitude. Harry was unused to hostility from strangers. Most people liked him at once. Cautiously, he asked, "Where's Alice?"

"At work."

"Of course. She said. I forgot." Last night she had shown him the small shop with its window full of antique lace bedspreads and nightgowns and napkins, her voice lighting with pride as she said, "I do most of the buying now. We do quite well in the summer and photographers' stylists come in and buy or rent our things to use as props, but still it barely pays its way."

After a brief, awkward breakfast alone in the dining-room, during which he felt as if he was on stage with no lines to say, Harry escaped thankfully to his car. He sat yawning, stretching long arms above his head as he tried to shake off the weariness and the feeling of unreality caused by two nights with little sleep and too much whisky, and he tried to decide whether to go home now, while he still felt determined, or to go and find Alice. He was half afraid that his recollections of Alice were coloured by whisky and exhaustion and dreams. He tried to visualise her as he had first seen her, standing in the dark doorway, hair a light halo round her head, bare legs with narrow ankles, bare feet beneath the long white cotton dress. The polite enquiring face. He recalled her mouth, the tantalising hint of the shape of her body. He groaned. Knowing he couldn't face disappointment with a headache like this and unsure of the strength of his decision to go his own way, he decided it was better to go home while he still felt courageous. Once they were told it would be irrecoverable.

When Celia looked up and saw Harry walking towards her, her face lit with surprise and pleasure. She came to kiss him.

"Darling, we didn't expect you today. How lovely." She stood back from him a little. They were so alike, tall and dark, their hair growing up from their foreheads with slight widow's peaks, their faces appealing in their gentleness, often anxious.

"Was it next week? I didn't think I said exactly. It seems so long since I was here and all my friends have gone on holiday and there are things I want to tell you."

Celia sat on the sunbed again, one leg each side. It was a typically ungainly position. All her movements had a youthful abruptness. She looked at Harry and her heart began to beat hard as she anticipated bad news.

"I'm not going back to St Andrews. Even though I scraped through, I made a hash of the exams. I worked as hard as I could. I couldn't do any better. And I'm not prepared to do any more. It's so humiliating to keep struggling and failing. I'm wasting my time. I want to do something entirely different. I don't know what, but I'm going to take a few months off and think about it." He lifted his head and looked at her, mouth a straight line, eyes uncertain.

Celia said nothing. She could not speak as she registered a feeling of absolute dread, of things destroyed.

"I know Dad will say I should come into the company, start at the bottom. At first he'll try and be nice and tell me a university degree doesn't mean a lot and a great many people work their way up, and then, when he realises I don't want to do that, he'll turn nasty, won't he?"

"Harry, you must think of it from his side too. He is so proud of the long history of Otterwoods and the continuation of the family in it all. He is building everything up for you to take over. He always has done."

"No, he hasn't. He's done it because he's good at it, he loves success, he loves winning and he hates not getting his own way. And he would never let me take over. He would never let go. For the next twenty or thirty years I'd be a puppet, constantly apologising and despised by all the able men in the company who aren't called Otterwood. If it's the name he wants, he's got Julia. She's longing to get in there." Harry sighed, hands deep in his pockets. "Most of all I'm sorry because it will cause trouble for you."

Celia sat upright as she felt the enveloping misery, the compulsion to escape from the trouble to come. Pretend it isn't happening. Look the other way. She thought aloud. "You look absolutely exhausted. Have you come straight down from Scotland?"

"No. I left on Thursday and drove all day and stopped for a few hours and then drove on again to Hove. Have you been there? It's next to Brighton. I arrived there almost by chance." He looked up and smiled, a wry enchanting smile that Celia loved. "I went from coast to coast. I spent last night in a bed and breakfast place in Hove, but I didn't get to bed till after four. I sat on a seat by the sea and talked to a girl I met. And then I woke too late for breakfast so it wasn't a very good deal! She is a most unusual girl, though, if I remember her right."

Celia smiled and it was the same expression that she loved on her son's face. "You always say they are unusual."

"Do I?" Harry dropped his head into his hands, fingers buried in his thick hair. "Party tonight, is there?"

"Just one of Daddy's business things."

"Awful time to talk then. I'll come back tomorrow, shall I?"

"Can't you stay? Daddy will be back for lunch. You don't have to eat with us tonight if you don't want to. In fact I can't get you round the table, anyway. Josephine would love it if you had supper with her. She's had a difficult summer. She came home from school a week early with suspected glandular fever and has been rotten ever since. They say now it was just very bad flu."

"Will you tell him first, so that he's prepared?"

"Do you want me to?"

"I don't really know." He went into one of the changing rooms which had been converted from old brick dog kennels and came out wearing faded trunks. He dived into the pool, shattering the surface of the still blue water and sending shock waves lapping the sides from end to end in a gesture that Celia thought was wholly symbolic. She watched him swim and then closed her eyes, listening to the sound of the water as she tried to think of the best way round things. It seemed she spent her life in the middle of them all, trying to think of ways out, excusing one to another, excusing David to herself; she lay back and put her arm across her eyes. Harry was right about David's reaction. David refused to consider the idea that Harry might not join Otterwoods.

Harry pulled himself out of the pool and lay on the very edge, one hand in the water as he felt the healing heat on his wet body. He wished his father was here. Then it would have started. Now he would have to go through the preparation again.

At twelve-thirty, Celia went back to the house and changed and found David in his study. She stood in the doorway and waited until he finished speaking on the telephone. "Harry's here. I thought we'd have lunch by the pool at about one."

"Fine." David frowned. "He wasn't due till next week, was he? Anything wrong?"

Celia had already closed the door, anticipating the question and not wanting to answer it. David forewarned, she knew, was even more formidable than David surprised. His initial reactions were generally gentler than his considered ones.

Josephine Otterwood, kneeling on the wide chintz-covered window seat in her bedroom saw her mother go down towards the pool carrying a tray, leaning backwards to balance the weight, and guessing there would be salad and cheese, perhaps raspberries. Josephine was hungry for the first time in weeks. Being ill, she had discovered, was an acceptable alternative to ordinary life and especially to school. The first week of a high temperature had left her feeling exhausted and slightly unreal but she was enjoying the reverence with which they still treated her, the care with which her wishes were considered. She was in no hurry to recover. She stood up and stripped off her cotton nightdress, examining her body in the long mirror for some time before she collected her discarded clothes from the floor. At fifteen, she was four inches taller than her older sister Julia and a very different shape, narrow like her mother and Harry, her face a blend of both parents, promising an elfin beauty. The suddenness of her movements made her feel rather weak again and she sat down on the window seat to recover, tracing the familiar lily of the valley pattern and loving the distinctive smell of the chintz she would not allow Celia to change. Josephine hated rooms to alter. Hated anything to change. She looked out of the window again and saw her father walking down towards the pool and almost called out to him but something in his attitude made her change her mind. She was clever with her father, knowing exactly how and when to approach him, and she watched her mother's clumsy approaches and withdrawals with a combination of panic and impatience.

Harry had fallen asleep. He opened his eyes suddenly when he heard his father's voice and sat up and then stood and the combination of sleeping in the sun and the hangover made him feel rather sick. All the carefully rehearsed explanations deserted him. He wanted to say it straightaway before David had a chance to say anything more than hello. He took one quick look at Celia who was setting out a meal on the wooden table and then said, his voice flat and loud, "I'm leaving St Andrews. I tried as hard as I could for that bad third and I'm not prepared to try again. And I don't want to come into the company and work my way up, always being the Otterwood who didn't have the brains. I want to break right away."

"That's impossible," David said softly after a silence during which he and Harry looked at each other from opposite sides of the pool. "Someone has shown you the article in *Lloyd's List*, I imagine?"

"Yes, but that's incidental. It's also true."

"Of course it's not true. You don't have to stay at

university. Exams are useful but not essential. It's common sense and experience and a certain amount of luck that you need, and the Otterwood blood in your veins. We have been going for a hundred and fifty-six years, always controlled by a member of the family."

"Julia can join."

"I want you, not Julia."

"Well for once in your life you can't have what you want because it's just not in me. I can't be what I'm not and I'm fed up with trying."

Josephine walked slowly down the long, sloping lawn, feeling the prickle of dry grass under her bare feet, spreading her toes with each step, and at first the voices were just a murmur, but as she got closer they became a blur of angry noise from which she gradually picked out separate voices and then actual words. She stood still behind the thick beech hedge, not wanting to go in amongst it all, listening to her mother trying unsuccessfully to stop her father and Harry shouting. When Harry came past her, striding up the lawn towards the house, he was so preoccupied he never even saw her.

Alice was moving more slowly than usual. Like a being under water, she swam through the amazement of living in the same world as Harry Otterwood. She recalled, again and again, every minute detail of the previous evening. The pressure of his hand on her arm, the sensation of being kissed by him. She had hardly slept. The bedroom had been hot and very light and the little patches of sleep she did achieve were full of sharp-edged dreams. It had been a relief to get up at six-thirty when Jane's alarm rang and she had left the house even earlier than she needed to, pausing for a little while outside the silence of Harry's door.

Even now, late in the afternoon, she was overwhelmed by the total unexpectedness of him and of her feelings. Her hands sorted through a hamper of old white linen, Victorian christening robes and tablecloths and antimacassars, sorting and folding, enjoying the cool feel of the materials, noting tears and iron mould, thinking she would probably never see him again and that she had only been granted his attention for one evening because of his unhappiness. One evening to set a standard of feelings that she would try and match for the rest of her life. She picked up a delicate lawn baby's dress and looked up as the bell on the door rang and Harry came in.

He closed the door carefully. It was cool in the small shop. He stood and looked at Alice for a few moments and there was a barrier of shyness he had not expected but to his great relief she looked as he remembered.

"I had difficulty finding this shop again. It's such a maze of little roads and squares and I thought it was much nearer the sea. I've been wandering round for half an hour. I couldn't remember what the shop was called or anything except that it sold old clothes."

Alice stood up and the neat pile of clothes on her lap fell to the floor. She looked down at them and smiled. "I've been sorting those for an hour."

"I'll help you pick them up."

"It doesn't matter. It was just something to do. Where have you been?"

"I went home. I sat outside your house this morning trying to decide what to do and finally I thought I would rather get it over with, so I drove home and told them and it was exactly as I expected but rather worse. My mother said very little but basically she understands how I feel and my father is going to make a God Almighty fuss and be no help at all with anything else I want to do. Which is probably a good thing. Whatever I do will be entirely my own doing. Even if it's nothing. I should have stayed and gone on arguing but I couldn't. He'll never give in." Harry sighed. "Could I have a coffee or tea or something?"

They sat in the tiny paved yard behind the shop on the wooden seat, the back door open so that Alice could hear the bell if it rang, and the late afternoon sun picked out every different colour in the old bricks of the walls. There was one apple tree and a few tubs of neglected, leggy geraniums. "Are you going to stay at Seagull Avenue again tonight?" Alice asked.

"Can I? I've stuck one of my plastic cards in a slot and

got hold of a bit more money so we can go out properly." He smiled, turning his head sideways to look at her. "Not that I didn't enjoy last night or what I can remember of it, it's just that I'm bloody hungry!" He took her hand. "It's such a fantastic feeling to have made the first move. I can't explain it. It's like being told you are cured of some terrible disease you have suffered from for years. All my time and attention have been taken up with struggling to pass exams and I have no idea what to do instead. I don't know anything about myself. I have never been allowed to speculate about life outside Otterwoods. Even as a small child I was shown ships and offices and told I would run it all one day. Now I've abdicated." Very cautiously he moved his face close to Alice's and kissed her. "I'm so glad I remembered you right."

As Alice locked up the shop at six and walked with Harry to his car and as they drove back to Hove along the wide road that followed the sea, they thought up occupations for Harry and laughed most of the way back. The wind caught their hair and tangled it and when they came in at the back door of Seagull Avenue they were dishevelled and still laughing.

"Icecream salesman!" Alice said.

Eliza, sitting at the table with a glass of wine in her hand, swung her head up sharply as she heard the voices.

"Good God! The prodigal son!"

All the laughter left Harry's face. "He can't have tracked me down already! Why are you here, Eliza?"

"What a ridiculous question. My mother and my sister live here. Why shouldn't I come?" Eliza sat upright, folding her arms. "Don't try and pretend you didn't know. It can't be a coincidence. And yet I never told you where I lived, did I?"

Harry's face regained some of its animation. "You told me you came from Hove and my father talked about you once or twice at home."

"Why should he do that?"

"Occasionally my mother asked him about his temporary secretaries as a kind of defence mechanism, as if by making a joke of his susceptibilities she can stop it happening. And as far as I know he has never bothered with anyone he employs. He made you sound as dull and unattractive as possible. 'Very efficient. About twenty-three. Flat-chested. Comes from Hove where her mother runs a boarding house for summer visitors in a street called Seagull Avenue.' We laughed at the name."

After a short pause, when Eliza remembered the way David had looked at her last year, she laughed too.

Alice watched Eliza curiously, knowing what an ordeal it was for her to come home at all, let alone on a summer Saturday evening when she must have expected to find the house full of summer families. Eliza had broken free so suddenly and brutally after their father's death that she could never be comfortable here again. She had left on the night of the funeral when the bitterness of seventeen years as the outsider, seventeen years of war with Jane, had boiled up and overflowed and there was no Gerald to intervene when Jane had told Eliza to go. "That's what you've always wanted, isn't it? Now he's gone you get rid of me and have Alice all to yourself." The horror of that night would stay with Alice forever.

Eliza read Alice's curiosity plainly. Alice couldn't know that London had become intolerable on this hot Saturday evening. The telephone a silent enemy. Robert had rung her at nine last night, cancelling dinner, explaining that he had problems and would be on the phone for hours. Her disappointment had amazed and infuriated her. He had hinted he might ring at some other time over the weekend but by noon she knew she could not sit and wait. Hove had seemed the only possible alternative. She drank deeply from the glass of white wine, looking from Harry's face to Alice's and back again, wanting to be drawn into this new and unexpected turn of events, to distract herself.

"It's good to see you again, Harry, now I've got over the surprise." She looked at her mother and her eyes danced maliciously. "What have you been doing for the past year? I understand you had to settle for Scotland rather than Australia in the end."

"Yes and now I've finished with all that. I've made a clean break." Harry crossed the room and stood by the sink where Jane was washing lettuce. She had barely looked round when they had come in. "I want to get myself organised, you see. Mrs Marland, I'd like to take the small bedroom at the back of the house for a week. I know you don't often let it because it's so small but I'd be quite happy to pay the normal rates or even a bit more. I'll be out of the house all day."

Jane did not look at him. "I don't often let that bedroom because I feel it makes too many people for the one bathroom on that floor, especially as the small room doesn't have a basin. The Bramsdens have three children."

"I don't need to wash. I'll swim in the sea occasionally and grow a beard." There was not a trace of amusement in Jane's face and Harry retreated to the table and looked at her angular back. She wore a navy cotton dress with a narrow white belt. White sandals on her feet. He thought how well she dressed for a woman of her age and then wondered what her age was? Mid-forties? He had not yet succeeded in making her smile, much less laugh, although he had heard her and Alice laughing that morning and the hum of their voices. Jane turned and dried her hands and he felt her disapproval like a weight on him. He searched about for another incentive and suddenly thought of money. It was so natural to him that he often forgot its effect on other people.

"Is it fifty pounds a week?"

"Thirty-five," Jane said softly, feeling a stab of fury that this boy should use money like a bribe. What had he ever done to deserve his money? She was aware of Alice's round, pleading eyes and of Eliza's straight mouth.

"I'd be happy to pay fifty."

"You could stay in an hotel for that."

"I don't want to stay in an hotel. I want to stay here." He realised too late that to have pleaded poverty would have been far more effective, if rather hard for her to believe. His rueful expression was as ineffectual as rain on glass. He changed his approach. His voice was flat. "Look, I want to stay here because I feel safe here. I need a refuge for a few days."

"There must be a lot of friends you could stay with."

"Probably but not in Hove and I'd like to see Alice."

"You won't see much of Alice. She helps me in the evenings and we will be very busy with five guests here. Five beds to make in the mornings, five lots of breakfasts to cook . . ."

"Five lots of washing-up and extra rooms to clean," Eliza interrupted.

"Alice leaves for work at eight-fifteen," Jane went on as if Eliza hadn't spoken.

"I'll help with the breakfast. I'm quite a good cook and I'll play cards with the children in the evenings."

"Has Alice told you exactly what to say?" Jane asked angrily. "Have you rehearsed every line?"

Suddenly Eliza couldn't stand any more. "What do you want from him?" she snapped. "Has he got to go down on his knees and beg for a few nights in that rotten little room?"

"I knew you'd have to get involved," Jane said bitterly.

"Please?" Alice shouted and it was so unusual for her to shout that there was complete silence after the single word.

Jane gave a small shiver. "All right."

Harry's face changed as if he had taken off a mask but Jane was quite untouched by the enchantment of his smile. Everything appealing about him made her dislike him more. Her eyes went back to Eliza.

Harry walked towards the door. "I'll telephone them and let them know where I'm staying. I left in rather a rush, you see. I'm not hiding. Now that I've made the break I feel quite benevolent towards them. I just need to stay away from home for a little longer." He sounded as if he were trying to convince himself. "I'll use the call box in the hall," he said, and Alice followed him out of the room.

"Don't ruin this for her," Eliza said softly and when Jane turned to look at her she saw the anger blazing in Eliza's eyes and knew they were going to fight the same old battle.

"What right has he to descend on us, waving his charm and his wealth like banners? She is quite defenceless."

"Does it matter? Isn't it the most marvellous piece of luck? She has to start somewhere. She has to have her own life. If you don't let her go gradually she will go horribly like I did in the end. And you have to have your own life too. Why should you both be tied to this place?" Eliza sighed, anger being replaced by the old helplessness of trying to help someone who did not want anything from her. She tried again. "If you sold it you'd have quite enough money to live on and to buy a small house or a flat. You would have time to do things. You could travel a bit. You might even marry again if you went out into the world. You're only forty-seven, for God's sake. Do you really want to spend the rest of your life in rubber gloves?"

Jane's bitter answer was cut short as Harry and Alice came back into the kitchen, asking to borrow ten pence coins, but she and Eliza both knew the anger would surface again later. The only relationship they had was this ritual of Eliza attacking, trying to free Alice and Jane from what she considered to be the prison Jane had built, and Jane defending the life they lived.

Chapter 4

Celia dressed that evening in a narrow black silk dress which showed her brown arms and back, fastening at the front of her neck the diamond clasp of the three rows of pearls David had given her when they became engaged. Her hands were still shaking slightly. She could not get the events of the morning out of her mind. The worst thing was not knowing where Harry had gone, and she blamed David for the fact that he had gone at all. They could have sat and eaten lunch and talked if only David had not been so aggressively unreasonable. The angry sentences ran over and over in her head as she went down to the drawing-room. David came in a few moments later.

The anger she felt had driven away for the moment the resigned emptiness, destroyed her usual way of dealing with unpleasantness by pretending it hadn't happened. She looked at David and felt a sudden intense longing to change things, to go back to the time when she had been the woman he had wanted so badly, to a time when he would have done almost anything to please her. She remembered the bewildering strength of his willpower. She remembered how it had felt to be loved.

They had met at a dance when she was eighteen and coming out, quite unsure of her own attraction, amazed and flattered at the attention of this mature man of twenty-four. David had just come down from Cambridge, and had started with Otterwoods. He was far more obvious then, already in conflict with his father who was resisting the changes that David wanted to make. In those days his ruthlessness had showed. Celia adored him. Two months after they met they were lovers and only her virginity had made him delay so long. By Christmas they were engaged.

She began to walk towards him. Their marriage was a

chess board and there were squares of scar tissue onto which she could not step, whole areas she could not speak about. She took a breath, not even sure what it was she wanted to say to him. He was not looking at her. He was frowning at his own thoughts.

"David." As she said his name he looked up, surprised, and smiled slightly. For a moment she thought, *It is still there, underneath. He can still look at me gently.* "David, all afternoon I've been thinking about Harry and you and about you and me. You have to be different, especially with Harry. If you are so implacable you'll drive him farther and farther away."

She saw the anger come into his face but before he could answer they both became aware of sounds from the hall and they turned automatically to welcome the first guests. Too late. Almost at once, Celia was involved in introductions, being careful to remember people she had met before, careful with names; checking their drinks, catching the eye of Maria's husband, Carlos, in his white coat, if he had missed someone. She had had so much practice that it was easy for her to talk for a few moments, establish a conversation and then gracefully slide away, eyes always on the doorway, looking for newcomers.

It was as she took one of these swift glances at the door that she saw a strongly built man with dark red hair hesitate in the hall before he came in. His grey suit was conspicuous among the dinner jackets, and because he fitted no particular category and because she had never seen him before, Celia guessed he must be Robert Stoner. She was a long way from him and David, who was nearer the door, approached him before Celia could.

"I'm glad you could come," David said untruthfully and as he looked at Robert he guessed the tension Robert must feel, the determination to make the most of any potentially useful contact. He introduced Robert to a group of four men, two of whom might possibly be interested in Venezuela, and after a few moments' conversation, he withdrew, thinking that now Robert had his chance, any kindness he had shown Harry had been amply repaid.

For the next half hour as the room gradually filled, Celia

watched Robert Stoner, sometimes coming quite close to him and hearing his voice. There was an air of authority about the man, she thought, and wondered how old he was. He intrigud her. At one point she was about to introduce herself, but he was deep in conversation. Instead, on impulse, she went into the dining-room and changed the place names, putting Robert Stoner on her left and condemning Claus Svensen to a place between two shy English wives who would be hard work. Claus was an old friend of David's and Celia had never liked him.

By eight forty-five they were in the dining-room and settling into their seats. As Celia came to her own place Robert held her chair for her.

"We haven't met, Mrs Otterwood. My name is Robert Stoner. It is an unexpected honour to sit by you. I was surprised to be asked here at all but I certainly didn't think I'd be sitting at the top of the table." He had expected a very different type of woman, older and more aggressively glamorous. Something in Celia's gentle face as she looked up at him made him angry. He didn't want such a vulnerable woman to be David's wife. Why should David Otterwood have this lovely woman as well as everything else?

Celia was surprised and disappointed by his obvious hostility. It was so unusual for anyone to be even slightly rude to her. She tucked her thick dark hair behind her small ears in a schoolgirlish way and the pearl earrings swung. Weariness overwhelmed her. She felt she had not enough composure left to deal with a man who obviously had a chip on his shoulder. Why the hell had David asked him? She sighed without realising it. "We may not have met but I know who you are. I remember your name from that boat people episode."

"That was exaggerated ridiculously." Robert had brought his unfinished whisky with him. He drained the glass. "I don't think I would have picked you out as David's wife although you look different from most of the other women in this room. I don't suppose you've ever had a job, have you? If so you'll be the exception, I imagine."

"I think I'm pleased that I'm not type cast and you are

quite right that, like most of the other wives here, I have not worked in the sense that you mean it, although David and three children and three homes do take a little organisation." She cut a piece of smoked salmon. "I had such a hopeless education I don't think I could have worked. I went to one of those small English girls' boarding schools, full of the daughters of my parents' friends, and I learned nothing. Then I went to France, then I learned to cook a bit, then I did the Season and then I got married. It sounds rather slight, doesn't it?" She smiled at Robert, wondering why she was bothering. "I think you'd better call me Celia if we're going to sit next to each other for a couple of hours. Perhaps it will stop you disliking me so much."

After a few moments Robert's face relaxed and he smiled back, a wide, apologetic smile. He thought she was one of the loveliest women he had ever seen and he was deeply surprised by her lack of affectation and by the underlying reserve he sensed. He liked her and he wanted her to like him.

"I'm sorry. Really. I'm not usually so bloody rude. My only excuse is that I've had a rough three-quarters of an hour."

"Was it better at sea?"

"In many ways it was. I was happy, anyway."

"Harry talked a lot about you. He hated being on the *Peacock*. He was acutely embarrassed at being thrust onto your ship. He hates being David's son in many ways. But he liked you. I always meant to thank you but I never knew how."

"I liked Harry once I got over the annoyance of having him thrust onto the ship as you put it. It wasn't my ship then. Not till the next year did I become master."

"I remember that. Harry said he thought you had probably arranged the master's illness so that you could take over. He said you were so impatient."

Robert laughed. "He was right about the impatience but I didn't arrange Hassock's heart attack. Harry will never come into the company, will he? He's too straightforward and far too gentle."

"Yes, he is." She looked at him, wishing she could talk to David about Harry like this.

"You look so like your son. Are you like him? How well do you fit in?"

"What an extraordinary question. Are you asking me how well I fit in to my own life?"

"Yes."

"Well I suppose the answer is, not as well as I used to."

"Is it no longer enough?"

"Is what no longer enough?"

"All the things you listed, your husband and three children and the house in London and the castle and this lovely place? Is it what you wanted out of life when you were at the small boarding school, learning nothing?"

"I didn't know what I wanted until I met David and then I wanted to marry him and all the rest followed on." She kept looking at Robert's face, seeing, now he was so close, the very blue eyes and the wide mouth. A strong face, she thought.

"And now that you have it all, is it enough?"

Celia thought, *It could have been more than enough.* Then, quite suddenly, she was angry, with Robert and with herself for talking so openly. "You can't expect me to answer a question like that in a genuine way. I don't know you. Why should I discuss my life with you?"

"No reason at all." Robert ate his smoked salmon in five or six brisk mouthfuls and then tasted the dry white wine as Celia spoke to the Frenchman on her right in fluent French, regretting her impulse to put Robert next to herself. He made her uneasy. Even with her back to him, she was acutely aware of him. She turned to face him again when the plates were being cleared.

"I'd like to know every man in this room," Robert said slowly. "Every one would be useful to me in one way or another. Tell me, who is the tall Norwegian sitting near your husband?"

"Lars Jorgen. He sells ships to the Russians. He deals only in gold, they say. What line of shipping are you in, Mr Stoner?"

"Robert. I'm hardly in it yet but I intend to be. I sailed

with Otterwoods for fourteen years, three of them as master on the *Peacock*, sailing to Nigeria most of the time. Before that I was on the *Swallow*, a small chemical tanker, making runs to Ireland. But I expect you know all that."

"Not any more. I used to know most of the ships and quite a lot about what was going on but the company has become so enormous now it's beyond me."

Her instinct had been right after all. Now that he had dropped his hostility, Celia began to enjoy talking to Robert in a way she had almost forgotten. She found herself thinking about the things she said, discarding the automatic answers. He made her aware of herself and she forgot, for a short time, Harry and David and the nagging misery that today's scene had dragged to the front of her mind. For a while she was totally engrossed in Robert Stoner, as he talked about his plans and his life, and the situation she had been in so often, in this room and at this table and only the faces different, was changed. She neglected her duties, turning only occasionally and guiltily to the Frenchman and the woman beyond him, but always turning back, with pleasure, to Robert. *How strange and sad*, she thought, *that I should have forgotten something as simple as sexual attraction*. She laughed a lot. Towards the end of the meal, ridiculously at ease, she looked at him and his expression was so obvious she said, without thinking, "Don't look at me like that."

"Why not?"

She thought, but didn't say, *Because I am nearly forty, although I can't understand how I became so old without realising it was happening*.

"Why not?" Robert asked again.

"David used to look at me just like that once." She nodded her head as if realising an obvious truth. "You are the same kind of man, aren't you?"

"Perhaps, but with one enormous difference. He is at the top and I am at the bottom."

"Ah, but you have fifteen or twenty years to catch up!"

Celia became aware that David was trying to catch her eye and get her to take the women away so that the men could drink their brandy and smoke their cigars and do some business. She stood up and Robert stood too and his hand brushed her arm. The contact echoed all through her body. As she turned towards the door, leading her small obedient flock of women with her, she looked at Robert with a serious face and he made a mockingly grim expression.

"Can I look at you like this?"

Celia was laughing as she went towards the door.

"What an extraordinary custom this is," a tall Norwegian girl was saying loudly as they crossed the hall. "Like the Australians, keeping the men and the women apart!"

"I rather like it," Celia said soothingly. "It gives me a chance to catch up on the gossip that I certainly wouldn't hear in front of the men."

"I like men's gossip better! And while we are on that subject, who was that man you kept next to yourself, Celia?"

"Robert Stoner."

"He's very attractive. Who is he with?"

"Himself, I think. We didn't talk much about shipping, strange as it may seem."

She led them up the stairs to her bedroom, showing them where the bathrooms were and excusing herself to go along the corridor and see Josephine for a few moments. She would have liked to sit on Josephine's bed and laugh for a little while about the people at dinner, to take refuge with her youngest daughter, but Josephine was asleep. With a sense of disappointment, Celia turned out the lamp and stepping over the discarded clothes, made her way back to her bedroom where her guests were brushing their hair and reapplying lipstick and scent. *He's wrong,* she thought, looking at the expensively dressed throng. *Some of them have worked, some of them work now. It's just that they don't look as if they could.*

She was impatient for the men to come back into the drawing-room but it was nearly forty minutes until they did, wandering in for coffee in twos and threes. She watched Robert as he walked across to her and her smile came easily. He accepted a cup of coffee and sat down rather awkwardly on the edge of a small antique chair.

"Have you made any useful contacts?" Celia asked him, aware of a feeling of satisfaction that he had come back to her. He was so different from the other men in this room. To look at him stirred in her long-forgotten memories, a sense of recklessness.

"Oddly enough, yes. I'm going to see someone on Monday. He was sitting on my left. I'd really given up hope earlier on. It seemed that most of them were suspicious of the small amount of money I need. They talk in millions and I talk in thousands."

Celia smiled, thinking that after all it was a good thing she had changed the place names. "I hope it all works out for you."

"It will. In the end it will. And if it doesn't I can always go back to sea." He finished the tiny cup of coffee in one mouthful and he met Celia's eyes. For a moment they both acknowledged the attraction.

Robert put down his cup. "I hope you won't think it rude if I go quite soon."

Celia interrupted, before he could give his reasons. "I know. You've been dressed up for long enough and you've got the contact you came for so there is no point in staying on."

"You're right but I wouldn't have put it quite so bluntly. Look, I'm sorry I was so hostile at the beginning. Put it down to a sense of inferiority."

"I know that's not the reason. Quite the opposite, probably."

Her face gave him intense pleasure to look at. It was difficult not to reach out and touch her. "I have enjoyed meeting you, and the dinner, of course, was delicious."

"Oh, I had nothing to do with that."

A feeling of depression enveloped Robert. It felt so natural to sit and talk to this lovely woman and he sensed her restlessness and her anxiety and he wanted to know far more about her. He looked into her speckled eyes and saw they were a mixture of green and brown and grey, and then he watched her withdraw, wrap her position about herself again, look round the room as she played the hostess. He got abruptly to his feet. He would probably never see her again and he didn't want to stay any longer. Although Robert attracted a lot of women, on the whole he did not need them, choosing, very often, to ignore the invitation.

"Please don't get up, Mrs Otterwood. Goodbye and I hope all goes well for you in the future."

Before she could answer he had crossed the room and was saying goodbye to David and several other men. As Celia watched his back she stifled an impulse to go after him and say goodbye again. When Robert Stoner left the room all the life was drained out of it and she was acting again, playing the same old part in the stale repetition of a scene she had lived a hundred times. A sharp sadness filled her. Robert Stoner had had a disturbing effect on her. It was as if he had uncovered with his careless questions layers that she had carefully buried.

She stood up and circled the room, seeing who needed more coffee, pausing here and there to join in conversations but relieved when, just after one, they all began to leave. When she and David were finally alone she felt she could not start talking to him again that night. She had no strength left to counter his anger and no defence for Harry except her love for him. David poured himself another brandy and wandered towards the french windows that opened onto the lighted terrace and the darkened garden beyond.

"Harry rang earlier, while you were changing. He's staying somewhere in Hove for a few days."

"I wish you had told me before. I've been worrying about him all evening."

David turned and looked at her and she leaned back, her expression strange. Anger flared in him. "You did Stoner a disservice by changing the place names. I put him within reach of two men who might have backed him." He turned back to the garden. "But perhaps it was just as well. He might have irritated them. Luckily Claus can look after himself. He particularly didn't want to talk to Bob Teo. Please don't interfere with the placings again." Without looking at Celia, David stepped out into the garden, leaving her to go upstairs alone.

Chapter 5

Robert woke on Sunday morning after a restless night and lay for a few moments registering the stillness. After so many years at sea the stillness of land disturbed him if he let it. The land felt dead. The air in the small hotel room was warm and stale and he wanted the great blocks of wind, the smell of diesel, the hum of a ship. He nurtured his background longing to return to the sea. If everything failed he would have an escape that he would almost welcome.

He got up and made his way down a silent corridor to a white-tiled bathroom with a frosted glass window. The water was very hot, scalding away the effects of too little sleep and complicated dreams. Celia Otterwood's presence seemed to have been imprinted in his memory. Not so much her face as a blend of feelings about her and about the previous evening. He thought how David Otterwood had introduced him to the first group of men and then stood back, face impassive, listening for a few moments as Robert began, as subtly as possible, to put his case. It had counted for a lot, that introduction from David. Why should he bother? It seemed the reputation that everyone had accepted in Otterwoods was far too simple. He had been known as a cold man who had only two interests in life, both of which he pursued ruthlessly: the continuing success and expansion of Otterwoods and all its subsidiaries and a constant variety of women.

Robert was relieved that David had not witnessed the humiliating lack of interest with which the two men he had been introduced to responded to his proposal. They had not bothered to conceal their indifference. Robert had come into the dining-room in a mood of angry frustration. He had found in Celia a quite unexpected distraction and it was only after the women had left the dining-room that he had turned to talk to the bald-headed man on his left and, in answer to Michael Copper's questions, had explained his business. He had been surprised by Michael Copper's interest. Robert knew he would spend the time between now and his meeting with Michael tomorrow, rehearsing how to put his case in the best possible way and he had the particulars of four offices which he intended to look at from the outside, as much to counter his restlessness and to distract himself as to find himself premises. He stood up, turning the shower attachment to cold and gasping as the shock of the icy water over his head and body tore away the last traces of sleep and he cursed the small, mean towel which was quite inadequate to dry his strong, freckled body.

He usually stayed in this little hotel behind the Cromwell Road when he was in London. It was comparatively cheap and the food was reasonable. He drank his third cup of tea out of a solid white china cup and he thought back again to Celia Otterwood and that long dining-room table; to the way she had watched him cross the room after dinner as he came to sit by her. He smiled, thinking how unlikely it would be if, after all, it was through his connection with Otterwoods that he finally got his finance. David had been the last resort. *And yet,* he thought, *Otterwoods have had me at their disposal since I was seventeen. Why shouldn't I get a favour in return?*

When he had finished his tea, Robert went back to his room to make several telephone calls and an hour later, having contacted Lagos and changed his flight of the following day to the evening, he got into the Escort he had hired and drove towards the City with the sheaf of office particulars on the seat beside him.

Robert disliked all big cities, especially London, and yet on this soft summer Sunday morning which hinted of real heat later on, he found the city clean and pleasantly quiet. There were clusters of map-reading tourists but little traffic. He drove slowly, intending to follow the river to the City, and realising a few moments later that he was in Pimlico, he thought of Eliza. He didn't particularly want to be alone all day and the recollections he had of Eliza were appealing. She would probably be out of London for the weekend, he thought, but at a red light, he consulted his map and drove to Lupus Street, parking outside a small block of flats in the wide road where Eliza lived. He looked down the list of names until he found E Marland and pressed the bell.

Eliza was not expecting anyone and her voice over the answerphone was suspicious. "Who is it?"

"Robert Stoner. Can I come up?"

She hesitated as amazement was followed by a chain reaction of feelings, elation which made her literally bounce and then horror at being caught without make-up, her hair tied back at the nape of her neck like a thick paint brush. But she could think of no credible excuse to keep him waiting and she certainly didn't want to send him away.

"Yes, come on up." She pressed the buzzer and had thirty-five seconds to look at her face and put lipstick on her mouth before she heard him outside the door.

She seemed smaller, Robert thought, and looked down at her bare feet. Her face was different too, less sophisticated and younger. Or was he setting her against the other image in his memory? He closed the door behind him and looked round the large, pale living-room, seeing how tidy it was. He liked it. It was the room of a confident woman not a chaotic girl's flat. The pictures interested him and he was surprised and rather pleased by the silence. It seemed she did not crave background music.

"I'm sorry about the other night. I meant to ring you yesterday."

"I wasn't here. I went to Sussex. I came back early this morning."

Eliza was nervous and it was a feeling she hated. It made her hesitate, it slowed her normal wit. She registered again the presence Robert had, the energy she had felt the first time she met him, as she tried to believe he was really here, in her flat, uninvited.

"Do you prefer to spend hot summer Sundays in London?"

"Not usually." She looked at Robert, her face rueful as

she tried to explain. "It was just that I couldn't stay any longer in Hove. I've never learned to keep my temper. Most of the time, especially with strangers or at work, I disguise it, but not with people I know well. My mother and I had one of our usual arguments last night and this morning I wanted to disappear before any of them woke up. I didn't want to spoil my sister's day. My sister is about to fall in love for the first time in her life and with Harry Otterwood of all people. It's certainly time she broke away from the black widow but I wish she could have picked some local boy with fewer problems. She's adopted and my mother is terribly over-possessive about her." She made herself pause and forced herself to speak more slowly. "Do you think that Harry has inherited his father's need for a lot of different women? I can't help liking him although I try and tell myself he must be spoiled and arrogant. But I like his smile and he makes me laugh and I'm sorry for him. I liked him the first time I ever met him."

"So did I. His father dumped him on my ship for a few days when he was fifteen. We could have given him hell but everyone liked him. If he ever does control Otterwoods it will be a very different set-up."

"Harry will never run Otterwoods. I doubt if he'll even work for the company. He hates the whole thing." Eliza faced Robert directly, still frowning as she finished speaking.

"Why do you look at me like that?"

"Because I know you are thinking how different I look from the efficient woman at the office. I wish I had known you were coming."

Robert laughed. "I wasn't thinking that at all and I didn't know I was coming myself until I found I was driving through Pimlico and I remembered your address. If you have nothing else to do, come and give me your opinion of a few offices in the City and we'll have lunch in a pub somewhere."

"Okay. But give me five minutes to change. Do you want some coffee while you're waiting?"

"No, but I'll read your papers if you have any."

"I have them all!" She went into the bedroom and threw

out a thick pile of unopened newspapers. "I love Sunday papers. I read them all week and on Saturdays I make a desperate sprint to finish them off before the next wave." As she spoke she was changing into a bright yellow cotton boiler-suit. She knotted a scarf round her neck and knelt on a stool, face close to the glass as she began to make-up her eyes.

"Who is the black widow?" Robert asked from the next room.

"Just an affectionate nickname for my mother."

"Are you also adopted?"

"No. To save you bothering to speculate, I will admit now that, as the real child, I have always been jealous of my parents' devotion to their adopted daughter and, since my father's death, my mother's selfish smothering of Alice has frenzied me, although I know that I am unsatisfactory and quite unwilling to be what my mother wants, whereas Alice has been loving and docile and has flourished like a chick hatched under a vulture." She heard Robert laugh. "The thing is, Alice is the only person left in my family that I care about. From the moment she came I wanted her to be mine, to love me best. She was an adorable baby and I was a plain, unpleasant five-year-old. I loved my father very much and when he died I couldn't stay to watch the black widow devour Alice."

Even now the memory of that night after the funeral appalled her. Unfair or not, she had blamed her mother for her father's death. Jane had never understood him, never loved him as he should have been loved, flamboyantly and generously, had stifled Gerald with her disapproval and shut him out as she had shut Eliza out. *When he was alive, my father was alternately apologetic or defiant. Without him there was nothing. She told me to go and I went because I couldn't help either of them. Alice understood.*

Eliza emerged from the bedroom, hair looped back with black combs, mouth a brilliant pink. "A transformation and my life history all in five minutes," she said, laughing to hide the embarrassment she felt because she had talked so openly to a man she hardly knew. "Do you often have this priest-like effect on people, making them pour out their lives without a thought?"

"Sometimes," Robert smiled. "Go on. I was just getting intrigued."

She shook her head. "I must have something left for later."

They drove to the City, parking Robert's car in one of the deserted streets and examining the buildings which housed the offices on the particulars; Eliza knew the City very well after five years of working there and she showed him short cuts, leading him between tall modern buildings and narrow, ancient alleys, through this maze that was wholly dedicated to the making of money. Robert disliked the two premises he could afford.

"I suppose I don't really need to be in the City," he said. "It would be ideal if I was so well placed that I could walk to anyone I needed to see but I won't be here all the time and obviously the rent I can afford is going to condemn me to something small and dilapidated. What I need is a telephone, a secretary and a reasonable address."

As they turned in disgust from the last possibility, Eliza suggested, "You could try the West End. It should be cheaper, especially if you can get the end of a lease. How urgently do you need a place?"

"I'll tell you the answer to that tomorrow."

"I could look at offices for you in my lunch hour if you tell me exactly what you can pay and the amount of space you need. Then when you come back to England, you could go through a short list of real possibilities."

They walked past the enormous unreal mass of the Tower of London and along beside Tower Bridge into St Katherine's Dock with its collection of small boats moored in the little harbours which were bounded by long walkways and narrow bridges. They looked into the big windows of the now-closed shops and offices which had been built in the disused warehouses; vaulted brick ceilings and black-beamed spaces now housed yacht chandlers and a flowershop and souvenirs and Eliza led Robert towards the Dickens Inn, its many windows decked with flower boxes. They sat in the cobbled yard that overlooked the dark still water of this inland pool which no real wave ever ruffled and they ate French bread sandwiches and drank a bottle of wine. The sun freckled the brown water, spattered through the trees onto the table, onto Eliza's hands and head. She gave a small shiver of contentment.

"I love it here although it's all been prettified. I still feel I have come back to London's roots. The City was spawned here by the water. It all grew from this. Looking at the Tower, you can almost taste the past."

Robert smiled. "This little puddle is no good to me. Or these silly little boats. I expect someone to pull the plug out at any minute!"

"I'd love to live on one of these silly little boats. At night it would be wonderfully quiet and I could walk to work in the morning. Perhaps you should have your office here?" She sat back a little, at last asking the question she had been considering for hours. "Did you make any useful contacts last night?"

"Could be. Someone called Michael Copper. Runs a company called Copperline. Most of the time he manages other people's ships but he likes to diversify. He sounded interested." Robert sat forward, a small cigar between his fingers, and the sun blazed in his red hair."

Eliza lifted her wine glass. "Good luck."

"I don't think luck comes into it. The man will back me if I can put myself across well enough and if he thinks he can profit from the deal."

"And what if he fights with his wife that morning or misses his train or wins on a premium bond? Won't those things affect him? Isn't that luck?"

Robert shook his head. "None of that will matter. He will judge my proposal on its merits."

"And if you happened to be his brother or if you had saved his life, wouldn't that count for something?"

"Depends on the man, I suppose. If the situation was reversed and he was my brother it wouldn't matter to me. Every man for himself."

"Have you got a brother?"

"I have three. They all live near Newcastle and I am much the youngest."

The coffee came and Robert lapsed into a preoccupied silence, frowning through a thin stream of cigar smoke. Eliza leaned back and closed her eyes, letting the warmth wrap round her body. Occasionally she opened her eyes and looked at Robert and felt such exhilaration, such pleasure that they could sit in silence like this, that to register her feelings scared her. She remembered her intense disappointment when he had cancelled that first evening and cautioned herself. The few people she had loved in her life had caused her nothing but suffering, whether by their fault or her own. She closed her eyes tightly. *Be careful. Tomorrow he will go back to Africa. Out of my life.* She felt she had not really touched him, that she was merely useful. But at least there was now. She anticipated an afternoon spent with him. An evening? A night?

When he suddenly said, "Eliza, do you know anything about Michael Copper or Copperline?" she felt relief and disappointment in equal parts. Of course. Information. That was what he wanted.

She left a small pause and when she spoke again her voice was cold. "A little. He's been in to see David recently. I understand Copperline bought an Otterwood ship a few months ago. North Sea supply, I think." She sat forward. A small breeze inflicted patterns on the water of the dock and she let the anger she felt build up through the silence until she said, "I'd like to be back by about three thirty, Robert, if I could."

He raised his eyebrows and his expression was one of genuine surprise. "Must you? I was going to suggest we drove out of London and had supper in Windsor or Marlow. I have nothing to do. I'm sick of thinking about my interview with Mr Copper and I would enjoy your company." He took her hand and turned it over, uncurling the long fingers.

Eliza looked into his eyes and she heard her own voice, nagging at Alice, urging her to get out and take chances, to live in the world not hide from it. She made herself keep silent for some moments as if she were considering several options. Then she shrugged her shoulders and smiled and her face was transformed, every part of it touched by the smile. "I prefer Marlow."

"Tell me what you are trying to do?" she asked as they drove.

"I'm trying to set up a small shipping company. Something that can skip from one operation to the next. One success to pay for the next idea. As you probably know, you only need fifteen per cent to put down on a ship and the rest you can borrow if you have reasonable security and if you have trade for the ship that is good enough security. So, see an opening, raise your fifteen per cent and you're rolling." He took a sideways glance at Eliza as red traffic lights held them. "Would you be able to find out any more about Michael Copper for me early tomorrow morning before I meet him? I would be very interested to know how healthy his company is."

A coldness in the pit of her stomach again quenched the exhilaration. *Information,* Eliza thought. *I keep forgetting. It is almost a relief. At least I know exactly where I stand.*

"I might be able to, but I won't tell you anything that isn't generally known. I am not a spy."

"That's fair enough." The car started again. He frowned as he said, "You hate me asking, don't you? You might as well realise from the very start that at the moment I put the success of Stoner Shipping above everything else. Never say I pretended to be anything other than single-minded. You have met me at my worst, Eliza, on the floor trying to fight my way up. Perhaps, in a few years' time, I shall play the gentleman like David Otterwood, but underneath the façade he is exactly the same as I am." He looked at her again in surprise. "Why are you smiling?"

"Because this morning you saw me at my worst, after a terrible night, ashamed of my temper and feeling bloody. Things can only improve." But the real reason she was smiling was because his words implied a beginning of something. "From the very start," he had said. The start of what?

They drove for an hour and then walked by the Thames, drinking expensively in a smart hotel by the river and eating cheaply in the bar of a small pub. A whole long afternoon and evening through which Eliza lost some of her wariness, tried to be natural with him. His laughter came easily and they found the same things funny. She loved the way he listened to her; she enjoyed the sound of his laughter and the distinctive way he stood, feet a little apart, stooping slightly as if bracing himself for whatever was coming. It was eleven when he stopped his car outside her flat and kissed her mouth in a brief good night.

The start of what? Eliza thought, watching the small car move away. Her heart pounded steadily in her chest, as if she were far more alive than she had been yesterday. She felt softened and warmed. It was no use thinking she could ignore the effect he was having on her. It was too late. She anticipated the morning and the thought of his voice on the telephone eagerly. She would not go away again if she thought there was a chance of seeing him. As she turned to go in, she laughed at herself and the strength of her feelings affectionately, as she might tease a friend, and as she let herself into her flat she answered her own question. *The start of a complete change in my life and in what I am aiming for.*

Chapter 6

Michael Copper pushed back his chair as Robert came in and held out a small, plump hand. "Good to see you again, Robert. I've been thinking about your proposal and I think we may be able to come to an arrangement. As I told you, just at the moment things are rather quiet."

He sat down behind the cluttered desk that gave an impression of great activity and motioned Robert into the opposite chair. "Coffee?"

"No thank you." Robert hated the social preliminaries of business, the greetings and the drinks and the ritual waffle before getting to the point. In Africa it was far worse. Sometimes it was impossible to get to the point at all until money was produced. Robert opened his flat briefcase and took out several sheets of paper and he thought of what Eliza had told him on the telephone that morning. "Michael is an old friend of David's. His company is small but somehow he has managed to survive the recession. Copperline bought a North Sea supply ship from us last year rather cheaply, I understand, which could have been because David wanted to do him a favour but it's much more likely that it was losing money and David wanted to get rid of it. Most of Michael's business is managing other people's ships for them. Michael and David were at school together. They are the same age and their wives are friends. In any case, ship-owning is a small world. I overheard David discussing Michael Copper on the telephone when I worked for him last year. As I remember, he said that Michael is far tougher than he looks but very impulsive. Appearances are deceptive, he said."

Michael's telephone rang and he answered it and spoke for several minutes, occasionally raising his eyebrows at Robert and moving his hands in a gesture of impatience. "One of our ships has lost its anchor and we have to send a notice to all ships to check theirs. And we lost a man overboard on Friday. The ship was in Aberdeen. The man came back drunk and vanished and police divers found the poor devil under the ship two days later." He pressed his intercom and asked for coffee and lit a cigarette and rocked back slightly in his chair. "Now, to get down to business."

The door opened and a middle-aged woman brought in coffee and a letter for Michael to sign. Robert felt a pulse of impatience beating steadily but he kept his face expressionless.

"Now, tell me about Lagos," Michael said as his secretary left the room.

"I want to talk about Venezuela."

"And so do I, but I want to know about Lagos too. I like to know exactly who I am dealing with. If you are shipping oil from Venezuela to Nigeria you want to be on a good footing in Lagos before you start."

"I realise that and I feel the Lagos end is well taken care of. At the moment we are a very small operation with two ancient landing craft. Mick Morris, an old friend who is an engineer, runs things with the help of two seamen." Robert outlined the operation for him as briefly as he could and then went on, "My ambition is to have a small, highly mobile company always on the lookout for good opportunities and with ready access to finance for them. If Venezuela is as profitable as I expect, I have three other schemes in mind."

"This Norwegian ship. How much is involved in the down payment?'

"Sixteen thousand."

"By when?"

"As soon as possible. Every day that goes by gives someone else a chance to see the opening and exploit it."

"And why do I need you? What's to stop me moving into Venezuela on my own behalf?"

"The Venezuelan end might be all right but Lagos would not. You don't know the port, you don't know the people, especially the two or three vital people. It's a long way from home and I would make life extremely difficult for you if you tried to cut me out." Robert's eyes were almost black as he stared across the desk at the deceptively gentle round face. "Either you do it with me or you don't do it."

"Well, that answers my question," Michael said dryly. "And the cement?"

"It will wind itself up shortly. Too many people are doing it now."

The two men talked for half an hour. Robert found Michael Copper disconcerting to deal with. Michael had a habit of suddenly changing the subject. He chain-smoked and the office was unpleasantly warm. At the end of half an hour there was a long pause and then Michael stood up.

"Okay. I'm in. I'll have my lawyers draw up some papers."

Robert stood up. His exhilaration showed in his face.

"And where can I contact you, Robert?"

"I'm in the process of getting some offices and probably a flat but at the moment I'm in an hotel." Robert wrote the telephone number on a piece of paper. "I shall be flying back to Lagos tonight. I'll give you a number there, although, as you probably know, the telephones are very unreliable. I'm usually on the move but a friend of mine, Sophia M'habela, or her secretary, will take messages in office hours."

"Any relation to Michael M'habela?"

"His daughter."

Michael Copper's face twisted into an exaggeratedly knowing expression. "You've made a shrewd contact there, Robert. Chief M'habela goes from strength to strength, I understand, and his past seems to have been conveniently cancelled out!"

"He's certainly a powerful man. I've known him for six years. We've done a lot of business over the cement. I should be back in London in about ten days and in the meanwhile I'll open serious negotiations with the owner of the Norwegian ship." As they approached the door he said, "It was a piece of good fortune that we met on Saturday."

"More fortunate than either of us realised! I was

speaking to David this morning and I mentioned that we had talked at his house and that you were coming to see me. I asked him if he deliberately placed us together at the table and he said that, on the contrary, Celia had taken a fancy to you and switched the place names!" Michael Copper laughed. "Nothing like a friend in high places! Funny, I never thought Celia felt the slightest interest in any other man, even to talk to. She is the least flirtatious woman I've ever met but I always thought that someday she'd start playing David at his own game." He winked at Robert. "Still waters, Robert. Still waters!"

Although he knew it was ridiculous, Robert felt a possessive distaste at the way Michael spoke about her. In the doorway, he turned just as he was leaving. "If you can't contact me in Lagos, and the phone system *is* pretty hopeless, you can always leave a message for me with David's secretary, Eliza Marland. I shall be keeping in touch with her while I'm away."

"How useful it must be to have all these women on your side," Michael said dryly as they shook hands.

Robert came out into the brilliance of the street and paused for a few moments to give himself time to accept what was happening. He loosened his tie and he looked across the street to a florist's shop, the window displaying bowls of lilies and long-stemmed roses, stocky chrysanthemums and a great central arrangement with a single fountain of water in the middle. He dodged through the traffic and went in to the damp, scented atmosphere and ordered a bouquet of yellow roses to be sent to Celia in the country.

"And the message, sir?"

"Just put, 'Thank you. Robert.' And I'll take a dozen of those small pink roses with me."

When Eliza looked up from her desk just before one thirty and saw Robert advancing towards her with a wide smile and a bunch of flowers she pushed back her chair and came round her desk towards him.

"It worked!"

"Yes. It worked. These are for you and you were right. Luck did come into it." He leaned towards her and kissed her mouth in an utterly natural gesture. His exhilaration was irresistible. His presence lit the dignified office like a firework display.

"Come and have lunch with me. I want to celebrate and I leave from Gatwick this evening so it has to be now. I told Michael Copper to leave any messages with you, that I would be keeping in touch with you while I was away. That background you gave me this morning helped. It gave me confidence. I felt I knew a little of the man I was dealing with." As he spoke he had picked up Eliza's bag and tossed it to her, tucked his arm through hers and was walking her to the lift. There was no point in her speculating if she wanted to go or not.

Eighteen hours later Robert looked out of the oval aircraft window as they descended towards Lagos, at the distant port and the oil tanks of the Terminal and the sprawl of shacks between the airport and the city itself, and although the long flight had blunted his first triumphant exhilaration he was still a very happy man.

Looking down at the City he recalled Sophia M'habela's words when they had first met.

"Lagos was blown up like a balloon with the coming of oil, everything built so hastily that nothing really works. Nothing was thought out properly. Lagos was plucked from a hundred years of obscure decay and bejewelled with the wealth the oil brought. It is a chaotic and bewildered city, typical of the difficult mingling of tribes that make up Nigeria. The Ibo from the east and the Hausa from the north and the Yoruba, the south-western tribe from which I am descended, and an immense Army control this totally tribal country. In Lagos you will find small estates which the many foreign companies have built for their employees, self-sufficient in everything and patrolled by guards; some hotels, some apartments, some shops in the city centre which was a consumer's paradise gone mad in the seventies when the wealth first took hold. Lagos has a modern telephone exchange that is badly maintained and constantly failing, frequent electricity cuts and a drainage system that is virtually non-existent."

As he had grown to know the city, Robert realised what a remarkably accurate portrait Sophia had painted, leaving out only the extreme corruption. Very few Nigerians were optimistic enough to imagine this tangle of peoples working easily together, or brave enough to attempt to drag this country forward a hundred years in a generation. But there were a few exceptions and Sophia M'habela was one of them.

Thinking of her brought Robert a complicated blend of feelings that he did not want to analyse. It was finished. He came through customs and approached the main doors, stepping out of the comparative coolness of the airport building into the wet equatorial heat, and although he had informed Mick about his change of flight, he was very surprised to see Sophia's scarred white car waiting for him. It was impossible to drive in Lagos for more than a few weeks without being involved in an accident and to constantly repair cars seemed a waste of time and money. Robert opened the door and tossed his bag onto the back seat and the car was full of Brahms.

Sophia turned, leaning against the door and considering him, as if she too were surprised to find herself here, her face with its delicate Nilotic features, serene and intelligent.

"I'm glad you were on time. I'm due in court in an hour." She made no move to kiss him, and to cover the awkwardness she started the car.

"I didn't expect you to meet me."

"I didn't expect it myself but I had time."

"What footing are we on now?"

"A wary and disillusioned footing." She took small curious glances at him. "I can feel that you have had success in London. There is a suppressed excitement about
you. I suppose I should be happy for you."

"I wish you wouldn't read my thoughts so easily. It makes me feel rather simple."

"I would be the simple one if I didn't know you after all these years. So you have got the money you needed. Will your success take you away from Lagos?"

"Yes. I'll be here intermittently for the next few months as there is a lot to arrange, but I want to establish a base in

London if I can and eventually I hope to leave Mick in charge here." He looked at her profile, the long neck and the cropped black hair. "I shall be glad to get out. No one in their right mind would live here if they had a choice. Except you."

"That is the crucial word, choice. My work is here so I must stay here." Sophia braked violently to avoid a collision. Her hands gripped the wheel tightly and almost against her will, she said, "My father wants you to go for a meal tonight. Do you know it's exactly five years since he first brought you back to the house with him? I remember looking at you and wondering what he wanted from you, what bribe you were offering for what service." And she remembered many other things about that first meeting and about subsequent days and nights.

"You're always so hard on him. He does a lot of good."

"Only if it pays well. You know he is totally unscrupulous. It amazes me the way his past appears to have been absolved now he is in government."

Robert smiled. "He always tells me how relieved he was when you moved into your own house. It must have been like living in court when you first came back here."

"Actually we are getting on quite well at the moment. Since he became a minister, he is pretending to have reformed. There is a truce between us."

Liar, she accused herself, almost before she had finished speaking the words, *I both love and despise him as I love and despise you.*

"I have left your number with several people in London," Robert said. "Will you still take messages if anyone should want me?"

"Of course. I am not so petty as to cut myself off completely, but as I told you when you left last time, I have finally accepted that your path and mine are different. You are too like my father and I cannot accept your ideals." She paused. "You have blood on your hands and you do nothing about it."

"Don't be ridiculous. That was one unfortunate incident. I wasn't even in the country. You know your own city, Sophia."

"Yes. And I see that you have sunk down to the worst part of it and that your set-up, which I pretended was merely opportunist, is corrupt and, far worse, protected from the law. Mick should come to trial. He killed a man. Whatever the circumstances it should be brought into the open."

"You know very well it was self-defence. You know Mick."

"I know that because of my father everything is being glossed over and it sickens me."

Robert straightened angrily, pushing a big hand through his thick red hair in a gesture that was so familiar, Sophia flinched.

"I think it would be better if I didn't come tonight," he said.

"I won't be there to harass you both, if that's what you think."

She ran the gauntlet of the city centre traffic, dropping Robert outside the house he shared with Mick Morris. As Robert got out of the car the smell of Lagos and the wet heat wrapped itself around him and England with its gentle summer seemed quite unreal. *If I was deaf and blind*, he thought, *I would know I was back.*

He came round to Sophia's side of the car, feeling the need to say something else. She wound down her window, brown eyes hard and sad in the dark beauty of her face. "How long are you here for?"

He shrugged. "I don't know."

"Well, enjoy yourself tonight." She raised her hand in a small stiff wave, thinking how awkward it was to greet or leave Robert without the kiss which had been automatic for so long. It was the first time he had mentioned leaving Nigeria without urging her to come too. It seemed that the break she had so deliberately engineered was now real.

Chapter 7

Harry came to the shop with Alice each day of that hot week in August, and his presence changed every part of her life, the early mornings and the days and the evenings; over and over again she had to convince herself that he was real. During those first days, trying to evolve a natural way of behaving, she watched him so closely that she could have described the way he looked and moved and spoke and his unpredictable extrovert behaviour and lapses into deep silence in the most minute detail.

He had woken early on the Monday morning and come down into the kitchen, cautiously offering to help prepare the Bramsdens' breakfast. Grudgingly, Jane allowed him to serve the food. The Bramsdens were from Yorkshire and nothing was quite right for them and Jane and Alice, after years of experience, resigned themselves to a difficult fortnight.

"They're bloody rude," Harry said, coming back into the kitchen, "and absurdly fussy. They can't all have their eggs cooked differently and if they don't like the cereals they needn't eat them. God, they should have seen the breakfasts I ate at school."

"Don't talk so loudly," Alice said. "They'll hear you."

"I hope they do. 'Happen I like my tea stronger than this, young man.' Happen you'll get it down your neck tomorrow, you old crow!"

He drove Alice to the shop and all the way he talked Bramsden. "'I can't sleep under one of these du-vets, Mrs Marland. Sheets and blankets is what I like.' How can you stand them?"

"Because we have to and because we've had people like them before. The only way is to humour them and they usually get nicer. Argue with them and they become more and more bloody-minded."

"Your mother can't enjoy it. She's not the type. She hates them."

"Yes, she does, but we get our revenge at night, whispering about them. And we need the money. It's as simple as that."

Harry parked in the narrow street beside the shop and Alice unlocked the door and began to set out the low tables of bits and pieces which passers-by liked to pick through. Since her early teens, Alice had spent any free Saturday mornings wandering the Lanes and small back streets of Brighton and she had discovered Paddy's shop not long after it opened. She loved the soft white lace-trimmed clothes which suited her rather old-fashioned looks so well and when, one Saturday morning, there had been a postcard on the door advertising for part-time help, after several nervous journeys back and forth past the shop, she had gathered her courage and gone in. She had started working there three days a week as soon as she left school and six months later, realising that Alice was far better at running the shop than he was, Paddy Armstrong had employed her full time.

At ten, Paddy wandered down the narrow stairs from the floor above where he lived, a mug of coffee in his hand. He was a small man in his late forties, an actor who had never worked more than a few months in any year and who survived by doing voice-overs for commercials and a pantomime season. For the past three years he had also had a regular income from a series of detergent commercials in which he played the long-suffering father of a chaotic family and it was the possibility that this contract might be coming to an end which was causing him to talk about selling the shop.

He sat on the stairs and nodded as Alice introduced Harry. "There's a country house sale this weekend near Basingstoke which should be worth going to, Alice. Huge old Victorian place. Viewing on Friday afternoon, sale all day Saturday. I can lend you the car if you want to go over Friday and take a look." He tossed Alice a fat catalogue. "I'll be here all weekend to mind the shop. Of course, it'll mean getting a weekend pass from Jane. You've met the formidable Mrs Marland have you, Harry?"

"Yes, I think she hates me."

"Join the club, but Eliza says it's fear, not hate. D'you know I once plucked up my courage and asked her out. Jane, not Eliza that is, chiefly because I know she thinks all male actors are gay and although she wouldn't come she tolerates me now so perhaps Eliza is right."

Alice went out onto the narrow pavement and pulled out the faded awning. She hated to discuss her mother. It was pointless. It was so much simpler than anyone understood but there was no point in talking about it because Jane would never change. Whatever Eliza said, Jane would never sell the house in Seagull Avenue. The calm, strict routine of her life with Alice enclosed them safely.

"Bad news about the contract, Alice love," Paddy said, as Alice came back in. His voice was resonant, full of meaningful pauses and never quite natural. "My agent rang last night and they're definitely finishing next month. The company want a new image entirely and there's not a bloody thing on the cards except a bit part in 'Doctor Who'. I shall probably have to put this place on the market but if I do sell, you can have all the stock cheaply. You could start up on your own, just doing the leasing. You seem to have that taped."

"Have you ever thought about starting on your own?" Harry asked her as they drove home.

"Yes, ever since Paddy first mentioned selling up. I've kept the names and addresses of all the photographer's stylists who've come in. I would drop the old clothes side and concentrate on leasing but I couldn't possibly afford any premises."

"Suppose you could, would you stay in Brighton or be in London?"

"I've never even thought of London, but of course it would be a far bigger market. You'd get more film trade, not just stills."

They were sitting in Harry's car in Seagull Avenue, bracing themselves to face the Bramsdens. Harry rested an arm along her shoulders. "I've been thinking. I could take you to view the sale on Friday and we could spend the night at my home. It's about thirty minutes from Basingstoke." He touched Alice's forehead where she was frowning. All day he had wanted to touch her, to help himself believe in her.

"I feel so guilty about going away when we have visitors, especially people like the Bramsdens."

"Oh, they'll mellow," Harry said airily, "and you have to go to the sale as part of your job. You're the one who's been impressing me about how essential it is to take work seriously."

"You change things round to come out the way you want them to," Alice said and she was as close to being angry with him as was possible in this state of mind.

Each day that week, Harry got up a little later, but was always in time to take Alice to work. He relished the long, quiet days in the shop and the exhilaration of his new life, going out to buy fruit and hot bread from the baker three shops down, making incessant cups of coffee. On Thursday Eliza called in unexpectedly, explaining that David was at a conference in Brighton. "They will be hours over lunch," she said, "so I thought I'd come and see you." She wandered the shop, her eyes dancing with curiosity, and Alice knew she had been unable to resist the opportunity to see how things were going. Neighbouring shopkeepers came to try and discover Paddy's plans and there was an uneven flow of customers and once or twice a day a photographer's stylist looking for props to buy or hire, but most of the time they were alone, delighted with each other's company, exploring each other, moving into the chaotic secrecy of the stockroom to kiss each other.

Harry enjoyed everything about the shop. He liked talking to people and if he sold or hired an article, however cheaply, he was thrilled. "I love taking the money," he said and Alice knew exactly how he felt, remembering the beginning and the feeling of playing shop. The only awkwardness between them was Harry's insistence that she spend Friday night at his home. In just a week, Alice thought, he had changed her life completely, bringing with the intense happiness the feeling that she stood between Harry and her mother, one hand stretched out to each and that both pulled. But when she told Jane on Wednesday evening, quickly, without quite meeting her eyes, she was surprised at Jane's calm reaction. It occurred to her that her mother was so uneasy, watching her with Harry, that perhaps she would rather see neither of them.

Harry and Alice left Brighton at two on Friday afternoon and drove towards Basingstoke. "You're a very quiet person, Alice," he said as the traffic caught them.

"Am I? I suppose I spend a lot of time on my own. Do you mind?"

"No, I love it." They moved out of the slow-moving tangle of traffic on the coast and went inland, cutting across the rich farmland of southern Hampshire. It took an hour and a half to reach Basingstoke and another fifteen minutes to find North Lodge, an immense Victorian house in beautiful grounds with a large white marquee in the garden and all its lower rooms full of sale goods. Alice had marked the catalogue. She spent an hour sorting through neat bundles of linen, cardboard boxes of lace and table mats, folds of curtains and old clothes while Harry browsed happily through a room of weapons and framed photographs of immense fish and stiffly triumphant fishermen and wondered who would want to buy the shoes and black umbrellas.

"It's definitely worth coming tomorrow," Alice said. "The prices will depend on whether it's just curious locals out for a sentimental bid or dealers. But I'd like to be here by two when they start on the afternoon lots." They were walking back towards Harry's car and when they reached it, Alice stood by it, her hand on the door, without attempting to get in. She put on her white cotton sun hat. "Harry, are you sure we should go to your home?"

Harry looked surprised.

"Are they expecting us?"

"No, not definitely, but I half promised my mother I'd come home at the weekend."

"It's Friday, not the weekend. Are you sure we can just arrive? I'm so bad at talking to people I don't know. I haven't got any smart clothes. They may not want to feed two extra people."

Harry frowned. "You don't understand. I could turn up with ten people and they would be fed. My house is a hotel, run for Otterwoods by my mother, a cook named Maria, her husband, a housekeeper and a collection of cleaners and gardeners. I have to go back some time. I haven't spent more than a couple of nights there the whole of this summer and I owe it to my mother to turn up. Last summer was so different. I had masses of friends to stay. I really thought I'd make it to Australia and I was happy and I know she wanted this year to be the same. And most of all, I want to spend time there on this new footing. I want to face my father again. I was hoping you'd come with me, to distract them slightly and to give me moral support." As they got into the car he leaned across and put his arms round Alice. "I'm far more nervous than you are." He watched her face intently, trying to guess her thoughts, his hazel eyes flecked with many colours.

Alice sat in a frightened silence for the thirty minutes it took to reach Harry's home, a dignified three-storey Queen Anne house with a long gravel drive. Harry turned left down the side of the house and drove under an archway that connected the house to a bricked stable yard where he parked.

Reluctantly, Alice got out of the car, smoothing her creased dress, and she followed Harry through the open door into a kitchen which surprised her. Here were no perfectly matched wooden units along every wall but instead a large painted dresser, a long wooden table and, at one end, a stainless steel cooking area that could have come from an hotel kitchen. Copper saucepans hung in orderly rows from metal hooks and a tiled windowsill was crowded with pots of herbs. Fresh pasta hung in a long, creamy fringe from a drying rack. Music throbbed out of a cassette player and two girls sat on the table, eating biscuits. They smiled at Harry and looked curiously at Alice who was wearing one of the white cotton and lace flounced petticoats from the shop that served her as summer dresses.

"My sisters," Harry said. "Julia and Josephine. The bigger one is the smaller one, if you follow me. This is Alice Marland." Harry left Alice standing awkwardly between the door and the table as he went and kissed the girls, hugging the tall, thin one who was so like him. "Are you better, Josie?"

"Sort of."

"Of course she's better. It's just that she likes being ill now!"

Josephine ignored her sister. "What happened last Saturday? I was coming down for lunch and I heard terrible shouting."

Harry shrugged. "I finally gave in my notice. Stand by, Julia. The way is clear for you."

Julia grimaced. "There is just the small matter of Dad being adamantly opposed to women getting very far in his company."

"You'll get round him."

"At the moment she can do no wrong," Josephine said dryly. "Her A level results came yesterday. Three Grade As. Her place at Cambridge is assured."

Harry and Julia looked at each other, both aware of the irony.

"Well done," Harry said.

Julia's voice was soft. "You can't really get away, Harry. It's unthinkable. You'll have to work for some part of it."

"I'm not going to." Harry opened an enormous fridge, bent down to study the contents and then selected a slice of ham before shutting it again. "I'm never going to put myself in a position of working for my bossy little sister. I feel great. I'm free for the first time in my life."

"Mummy's very worried about you," Josephine said severely. "What about her? She has to cope with it all. He hasn't stopped thinking about your abdication all week. He's only mentioned it a couple of times but you can tell it's in his mind. Mum's packed this weekend with people to try and distract him. She's even rung the Macphersons and asked them to come so he'll have to play tennis and exhaust himself. And Julia and I will have to play with the twins and they're so bloody good it's embarrassing. Have you brought a racquet, Alice?"

"I can't play tennis."

"Not at all? Or are you just saying?"

"Not at all."

"Lucky you!" She looked at Alice intently, her blue eyes almost luminous in her pale face and underlined by dark shadows.

"I'd better go up and tell Mum we're here if she's got a lot of other people coming," Harry said, and he went out into the hall.

There was a silence. Alice looked desperately round the room and because she couldn't go on standing still, two hands holding her big tapestry bag, she walked towards one of the windows and looked out over a vegetable garden as neat as a sampler.

"I like your dress," Josephine said. "I love those droopy Victorian-looking things. Where did you get it?"

"I work in a shop which sells them. In Brighton. We have shawls, too, and baby clothes and tablecloths and everything."

"I would look awful in something like that," Julia said flatly, "but it suits you. I hate clothes. Or rather, I hate the way I look in them. It's especially annoying when Mum and Josie look fantastic in anything."

As she spoke, Alice studied them discreetly, thinking that Harry and Josephine were obviously related but that Julia was quite different, with her high forehead and short, square build. An intelligent cat-like face, small-nosed and round-cheeked, her light brown hair tied back in a bunch as if she couldn't be bothered with it.

"How did you meet Harry?" Josephine asked, leaning on the table now and tracing with one fingernail the long grooves in the wood.

"He came to our house." Alice felt warmth in her cheeks and her voice became slightly defensive. "We take people in for bed and breakfast in the summer. He came last Friday evening."

"In a terrible state?" Julia said quietly. "Was he drunk?"

"No. Just exhausted I think."

"Raving about how he couldn't do it, that too much was expected of him, etcetera, etcetera?"

"Yes."

"He'll never get away, whatever he thinks. What else can he do? He is the heir to the kingdom. I don't count. However well I do, it doesn't matter. My father is convinced that men will not work for a woman. He thinks he knows all about men and women but in fact he judges all men by himself and he only knows about women's bodies. He will have Harry stuck up there like a figure-head whatever Harry says." She folded her arms, round blue eyes blazing in her face. "What he doesn't realise is that I don't give a damn for his absurd ideas."

Harry looked round the half-closed door of his mother's room. Celia was lying on her bed, eyes closed, one arm thrown up over her face. Beside her lay her tapestry and dozens of skeins of wool, as if she had been choosing colours. Harry went in and closed the door behind him. He sat heavily on the bed and she opened her eyes.

"I've come back for the weekend and I've brought a friend. Is that all right?"

"Of course." Celia's eyelids were heavy, and, beneath the tan, he could see deep shadows under her speckled eyes. Her voice was uncharacteristically dull. "All summer I have been looking forward to you and then you came and went in such a state." She half sat up. She saw Harry's anxious expression and touched his face with the fingers of one hand. "I'm quite all right. Just tired. The Russians stayed until Monday afternoon and they exhausted me."

"Then why not have a quiet weekend, for God's sake? Why ask the Macphersons? They are far worse than the Russians."

"How do you know? You've never played tennis with the Russians!"

They laughed and leaned inwards and embraced.

"Things will get sorted out," Celia said lamely. "I suppose you couldn't start with Otterwoods, just for a few months? You could work on a ship."

"I'm seasick."

"What will you do then, Harry? He won't leave you alone. Why don't you say you want to spend a year in France, at Grenoble or somewhere similar? It would give you a breathing space and it's something he would accept. You could ski every weekend."

"It would just be putting off the break. I want to get a job, although God knows what as."

"You'll come to Scotland in October as usual, won't you, Harry?" Celia asked, the anxiety straining her voice, and then hated herself for being possessive.

"Probably," Harry answered vaguely. "I've brought Alice Marland for the night. She is Eliza Marland's sister. You know, the secretary Dad has at the moment. It's her house I've been staying in all week. She has to go to a sale at Basingstoke tomorrow afternoon so I said I'd take her. I'd better go and look after her. She's rather shy and she's scared of you all."

"Is she the unusual girl?" Celia asked, smiling.

"Yes." He laughed. "It's not smart tonight, is it? She's worried that she hasn't got the right clothes."

"Not at all smart. Just us and the Macphersons and two business couples of Daddy's." Celia put her arms round her knees, her mood lightening in Harry's presence. "D'you know what I used to long for, Harry? I use to dream of going to Scotland with just ourselves. Just the family. No business people. Perhaps just a friend for each of you three children. Two weeks of peace and rain and fishing and long walks."

"Did you ever suggest it?"

"Yes. He looked at me as if I were mad. He said, 'But I do more business in the castle in two weeks than I do in two months in the office!'"

Harry frowned. "I can't imagine how it would be to have him on his own, not trying. I think we need the other people to distract him."

"Yes." There was a short silence and then Harry opened the door. Almost at once a loud burst of voices and laughter rose up from below.

"The Macphersons!" Celia and Harry said in unison.

* * *

Harry took Alice up narrow back stairs, along a pale-carpeted corridor to a wide landing and up another flight of stairs. He showed her into a room with dormer windows and a single fourposter bed dressed in a delicate flowered material. Alice had never seen such a pretty room in her life. The walls were a pale pink. There was a tapestry rug on the floor.

"The bathroom is through that door. There's always hot water. You don't have to change, it's not smart." Harry looked at his watch. "We eat at eight thirty. I'm going to have a bath as I never got round to swimming in the sea and I'll be down in about an hour." He kissed her, arms round her, his hands meeting in the small of her back and the feel of him and his warm distinctive smell made her feel weak. Then he broke away, abruptly, as if remembering something urgent and he left. Alice rocked forward slightly, as if she had been leaning on him.

She put her bag down in several places. It looked wrong in this room. Everything about her felt and looked wrong. She opened the bathroom door cautiously and the bathroom matched the bedroom and as there was no other entrance she guessed it belonged to this room alone. It was, as Harry had said, a small hotel. Knowing just how difficult it was to keep rooms as clean as this, she tried to guess how many cleaners they must employ.

To use up some time, she ran herself a bath and poured highly scented bath oil into the water, watching the drops turn the clear water milky. She pushed her hair into a bath hat and tried to enjoy the silence and the warmth but she kept thinking of Jane, coping alone with the Bramsdens' complaints, and the terror of the evening to come. Although Harry had told her not to change, she did put on what she considered to be her best dress, a nineteen-thirties relic with beads sewn on and a hem that dropped in four points, the dress hanging straight from the shoulder. She had no lipstick but she darkened her eyelashes and dabbed a little of the bath oil on her neck in place of scent. She brushed her thick hair into a fluffy halo and, feeling sick with fear, she forced herself to leave the safety of the flowered room and go downstairs into the hall with its mellowed black and white tiled floor and a round polished table bearing an immense vase of heavily scented lilies.

There was no sound except a grandfather clock ticking thickly. The elaborate hands said seven thirty and after standing in the hall for some little while, trying to look unconcerned in case anyone appeared down the stairs or from one of the many doors, Alice decided they must be in the garden. She went out of the open front door and walked round two sides of the house until she came to a paved patio with heavy white wooden furniture and a dozen people talking. She was so nervous her legs moved stiffly and she felt swollen. She licked her lips. There was no sign of Harry and Alice would have retreated again had Josephine not seen her and waved and come to meet her drawing her into the group of people. "This is my mother and Mrs Macpherson and Ginny and Vera Macpherson. Alice Marland. Harry's friend."

There was a slight, mischievous smile on Josephine's mouth. At first, because she was so scared, Alice registered nothing, not their names or their faces. She stood and smiled and a drink was put in her hand and she answered a couple of questions and then stood in silence, thinking, as she listened to Julia talking, how very self-possessed she was. It seemed she would be at home anywhere. The confidence came, Alice supposed, from having been brought up with all this. Was Josephine the same? Gradually, as Alice recovered, she looked at them all, especially Celia, thinking how like his mother Harry was, seeing the same smile on Celia's mouth, the same swift movements. It was easy to talk to Celia. She had a quiet way of making conversation flow. She asked about Hove, about the summer, but every now and then in a pause or when someone else was talking, Alice thought she sensed Celia's tension, a tension that increased when her husband joined the group.

"David, this is Alice Marland. Eliza's sister. She is staying here tonight. She and Harry are going to the auction at North Lodge tomorrow.'

"The Elliotts' place? Not much worth having there, I

shouldn't think," David said. "Are you in the antique business, Alice?"

"I'm interested in the linens and fabrics and the clothes."

David nodded his big head. He looked down at her intently. "I suppose you hear this all the time but you're quite unlike your sister."

"I'm adopted."

"Really?" Interest flickered in his eyes. "And do you know anything about your real family or don't you care to discuss it?"

"I know nothing about them at all. I wish I did."

"Aren't there ways of finding out now?"

"If you have something to start with. I have nothing."

"Is the dress you're wearing one of your acquisitions?" David asked, smiling a little.

"Yes." Alice blushed but she managed a smile and she had the satisfaction of seeing him look at her again, as if memorising her face.

"I like your dress," he said. "It's unusual. Celia dresses far too simply. I'm always telling her."

Alice became aware of Harry beside her, heard him acknowledge his father with a sound that was not exactly a word, saw David return the greeting coldly and then move away.

"Sorry I was so long. I fell asleep in the bath. Are you all right? I'm much more nervous that you are, I promise. This whole place is like a volcano and I'm sitting on the top. My mother looks as if she hasn't slept for a month and my father is horribly calm, like a tiger stalking a kill. Thank God the Macphersons are here, much as I hate them. Sit next to me at dinner. I'll get a drink and then we'll go and fiddle the places."

Harry swallowed a glass of champagne in one swift movement and then held out his glass for more.

"If you're going to drink like that, Harry," the man called John Macpherson said, "I should go onto beer."

Harry flushed. "I thought it was pale beer in the wrong glass," he said, and linked his arm through Alice's and led her into the dining-room. "It's all right, she's put us together."

The meal was fairly simple but Alice drank too much because her glass was constantly filled. Josephine sat on her left and was an easy companion. Opposite, Alice was aware of the icy stare of one of the Macpherson twins although she couldn't tell which. They appeared identical, with such very pale blonde hair they were like twin dolls. She understood from that continuing hostility that whichever twin it was, she resented Harry bringing Alice. Now she understood Josephine's expression when she had introduced Alice earlier. The Macphersons did their utmost to talk about places and people and events that Alice knew nothing about but Josephine, well aware of their tactics, countered every new subject, the wicked smile never far from her mouth. By the time the pudding came, Alice felt she had a friend.

She was almost enjoying herself and the eruption Harry had predicted occurred so gradually that she had no warning at all.

"I hear you've done very well in your A levels, Julia," John Macpherson said loudly so that the whole table was drawn towards him, towards his topic. "Well done, god-daughter. Two of them at university, David. You must be pleased."

"We are very proud of Julia," David said softly.

"And how's St Andrews, Harry?"

Unlike Alice, Harry had been waiting all evening for something like this, drinking steadily, almost in silence. Still he hesitated. It was so tempting to answer non-committally and let the cup pass. He could feel Celia's eyes. He lifted his head and looked at his father and knew that if he did not tell them, David would.

"I'm not going back there. I did very badly in my exams and although I just scraped through and I could go on for a second year, I have decided it's a waste of time. I shall let Julia excel in that department."

"So you're going straight into the company, are you?"

"No," Harry answered shortly.

"Harry is thinking of spending a year at Grenoble," Celia said. "It will give him time to get organised and his French could do with some practice."

"Harry's decision not to go back is very new," David said softly. "Just last weekend, I think, it came over him. I'm hoping he will change his mind. I remember feeling the same myself after my first year, that life was passing me by."

"I won't be changing my mind. It's the first time I've ever made a decision for myself. I'm not likely to change it." Harry looked down at the pale lump of peach icecream and disembowelled it with his spoon. He was aware of a silence that was hot and heavy and Celia broke into it, talking about Scotland, about the castle, about the lack of salmon for the past three years. Under her tan her cheeks were flushed and her eyes were very bright.

They took their coffee into the garden where clusters of moths besieged the outside lights and it was very warm. Alice and Harry sat on a long painted seat and Harry dipped his hand absentmindedly into a dish of chocolates.

"When did you think of Grenoble?" David asked, leaving his group to Celia.

"I didn't. Mum did. At least, I have thought of doing something like that but it's such a waste of time you see." He sighed. He looked up at his father and then stood up. David was two inches taller and far broader than his son. "I wish you could understand that for twelve years or more I have tried my utmost to be what you want me to be. I can't go on all my life. It's so humiliating to keep failing, especially when I am surrounded by people who don't fail. I can't come into Otterwoods." Harry pushed back his hair with a swift, nervous gesture. "I'm going to start a small business with Alice. I'll tell you about it later when things are more definite. I would only damage Otterwoods."

"Of course you wouldn't damage it. You're not entirely stupid. You could learn if you wanted to. There are so many aspects to the company. If the shipping side doesn't interest you, you can start with the transportation – the property company – insurance. Few people are offered such a choice."

"It's all the same thing. It's not really a choice. My life would be one long humiliation. I won't do it."

"Oh yes you will." David's tone and expression caused Alice to shrink down on the seat. She looked up into David's face and she understood in that moment exactly what Harry was up against.

"Julia is everything you want. She will get a brilliant degree. She will be wonderful for Otterwoods."

"A woman cannot run the company. However clever a woman may be she is still subject to distraction by marriage, children, emotional changes."

"Were you never distracted by your marriage or your children, then?" Alice said bravely into the silence.

David glanced at her impatiently. "Only once. We had a child who died. A baby boy, born four years after Josephine. His death affected me."

"Probably because it was one of the few times you didn't get your own way," Harry said and, as if aware of the brutality of the remark, he stepped backwards. "Well this is another time." He turned and walked off into the darkness beyond the circle of light.

"Harry always ends an argument by walking off," David said dryly as Alice stood up. "Usually in the middle. It's rather unsatisfactory." He looked down at Alice. "If you have any influence with him, Alice, try and make him realise that he hasn't a hope on his own. When he is twenty-five he will come into some money from his grandfather but not enough to keep him in the style to which he is accustomed. I don't think he has any idea what life is like on the outside, how difficult it is to earn money and how easy to spend it. I don't know what business he has in mind but I will not subsidise him. He will get nothing from me."

"I don't think he wants anything from you. It's you who want so much from him."

As David's eyes blazed with anger Alice flinched, feeling his fury as a physical threat. The moment passed and David laughed, "Perhaps you had better retreat as well," and she turned and almost ran into the darkness, in the direction that Harry had taken.

Chapter 8

Before I knew Harry, Alice thought, *I never waited impatiently for anything. I existed. He has changed everything. He looks at me as if he were seeing someone quite different, not the person I know I am. Before there was no hurry because each day was roughly the same. No urgency to answer the telephone every time it rings, no reason to look up when the bell of the shop door announces a customer, just in case. No one to dress for. No one. Half alive, as Eliza always said.* She was waiting for Harry now in a mood that was becoming familiar, a restless excitement with an undertone of fear in case he didn't come. September rain distorted the shop window in long slow rivulets as she waited to close the shop.

In the two weeks since she had stayed in Hampshire with Harry she had seen little of him. Paddy had definitely decided to sell the shop and Harry had seized on this news, convinced that Alice must take the opportunity to start up on her own. If she said very little during the discussions they had, Harry didn't notice. He saw a shop as an ideal way of seeing a lot of Alice and gaining time for himself. He was taking her to London with him that afternoon to look at possible premises. The idea, with all its attendant parts, terrified her. She had tried to put him off the idea, to explain that there was no fortune to be made. She tried to explain again, after the first onrush of joy when he arrived, as she locked the shop and followed him to his car.

"There are a number of places in London which hire out props for films and television; there are specialists who deal only in costume, only in china; there are even places where you can go and say, 'I want an authentic nineteen-thirties washing line' and they'll supply all the clothes that could have been hanging there, I am not so ambitious. My idea is just to hire out linens for photographs, mostly cookery photographs. I would keep all the old bedspreads and shawls and the napkins; they are very popular. But I'd have to buy a lot of modern table linen too and lengths of cloth and table mats; I need more big damask cloths and they're expensive. Then I'd have to let people know I exist. It's going to cost a lot of money, Harry, and I have nothing. It's impossible."

"Don't worry about any of that yet. Come and see these houses I've found. They are both near the Portobello Road. That is an ideal place, isn't it? It's about five minutes' walk from Notting Hill tube. I parked my car and walked it. Just to check."

Alice laughed. "They'll come by car, Harry. They're not going to take armfuls of tablecloths and curtains on the tube and they will have been collecting other props all over the place."

Harry was silenced. He frowned. Alice had begun to realise how he hated to have his ideas laughed at, however gently. If he could not be the light-hearted version of himself he liked to project, the alternative was a mood of angry depression. The depth of his insecurity meant that sometimes being with him was like walking on a minefield. But today he shook off the mood, determined not to be discouraged. "A friend of mine works for Hartford Hollis. He looked through endless particulars. One house is freehold. The second has a short lease and it's a mess so it's fairly cheap. I'm sure I can persuade the trustees to buy something for me. I must be allowed somewhere to live. If they are difficult, I will hint that I am going to work for the company and need a base in London. I've thought it all out."

"But surely they will check with your father?"

"He can't stop me spending money on something that the trustees consider reasonable. A house in London is a very good investment. We'll get one somehow."

Alice tried to let his enthusiasm carry her although she was afraid his eagerness was all part of establishing a life for himself outside Otterwoods, making an imprint that did not have the shape of the family. Harry was singing with the radio. She had noticed before what a lovely voice he had, deep and tuneful.

"I've got tickets for *Evita*, tonight. Why don't we stay in London and go down early tomorrow morning? You could be in the shop by nine if we left at seven thirty.

Stay away? The initial reaction was to refuse. Impossible. How to tell Jane? But gradually the first reaction was weakened as Harry took a lot of little sideways looks at her. "Where could we stay?"

"Lots of places. With Eliza if you like. Don't you sometimes stay there?"

"About twice I have but it was always arranged."

He laughed. "Well, this could be arranged, couldn't it?"

They picked up the keys from the Hartford Hollis office in Kensington High Street and then got lost in the maze of curving streets between Notting Hill and Westbourne Grove. "It was far easier on foot," Harry said when at last he found the first house, an immaculate and fully furnished property which they were shown by the owner. Alice couldn't imagine living in anything so chillingly smart. The second house was very different, a narrow, four-storey building in Pembridge Gardens, its peeling white paint almost hidden under an immense vine.

Harry parked on a yellow line and went up a narrow path and several dilapidated steps to the front door. He found the right key on the large bunch and they stepped at once into a narrow hall which led, via an archway, to a room which occupied the whole ground floor. Big sash windows at the front and the back let in a lot of light. There was a Victorian cast-iron fireplace with a few broken shelves each side but otherwise the room was empty.

"The showroom," Harry said. He led the way down to the basement kitchen and a small room which adjoined it. "This room could be for the repairs and washing and whatever." Downstairs was very dark and smelled damp and cold. Alice shivered with the chill and with excitement, peering through the cracked glass panes in a back door into the tiny garden.

"A cloakroom on the half landing," Harry read, "and two floors above, one with a living-room, bedroom and bathroom, the top floor with two small attic rooms." He went ahead of her, running up the stairs. The banisters shook as Alice touched them and the wooden floor moved like a house in a nightmare. The windows were blind with dust like beggar's eyes. Alice went slowly, looking into the series of small rooms. It was like a neglected doll's house, waiting to be restored. At the very top, the attic rooms were warm and seemed dry, the ceilings sloping so steeply that Harry had to bend his head. "Well?"

"Empty houses are frightening, aren't they? I expect to find something horrific each time I look into a room. I can't imagine it any different. But with curtains and rugs and furniture I suppose it would be fine. And the big room downstairs is the right size. And it is a good area. But I can't believe I would come here every day. It's impossible."

"Why?" Harry said gently. "We don't need much furniture. Some friends of mine at St Andrews furnished a house they were renting just by going to secondhand furniture shops. It was fine. You'll need a room as an office and I could have the floor with the bathroom as my living quarters. You can have these rooms at the top as you can actually stand up in them. Another bathroom would be good. I'll find out how much it would be to make another bathroom."

He turned at the top of the narrow stairs, putting his arms round her, leaning away and smiling down at her. He breathed deeply and his arms tightened, his body tensed. "You look so scared. Why do you look like that, as if I were suggesting a suicide pact or something. What do you think of the house? Forget all the problems."

"How much is it?"

"That's not an answer."

"I don't want to think if I like it until I know how much it is."

"Well, I'm not telling you how much it is until you tell me if you like it."

"It would be very good and when I got used to it, I

would like it. It's just that I have never thought of anything like this. Even when you talk about it I don't really believe it and now it's real, dusty and damp and perfect and so far away from everything I know about."

"It's a seven-year lease and it is thirty-five thousand."

Alice broke away from him. "But that's ridiculous! How can you even think of spending so much money? Why did you bring me here at all?"

"It isn't impossible." Harry said patiently. "The trust has hundreds of thousands of pounds. It was started when I was born by my grandfather and increased when the girls were born. They have been putting money in for twenty years. Have you any idea how much well-invested money has increased over the last two decades?"

"No."

"Nor have I!"

They laughed and came together again. "I don't understand money like that," Alice said. "Ever since my father died we have been short of money. We manage until some unforeseen horror occurs like the roof leaking. There is no spare money. Nothing saved. Eliza says she can't understand why not. When he died, Dad had a reasonable job with a firm of chemists but there was nothing saved. No insurance. Just debts." She faltered. It was so impossible to describe to Harry the humiliation of unpaid bills, the terror of everything collapsing and being taken away, the ecstasy of relief when the situation was somehow resolved. In the first year after her father died her mother had cried over bills. Harry could never understand. She turned back to another problem, her face and voice both serious. "You may get tired of putting money into something that could take several years to get going. You might lose money. And what if you wanted to go and work abroad, would you be prepared to leave me here, running things? And how can I pay you a proper rent or buy the stock I need when I have no money? How can I start?"

"I will put up the money for the business and you will supply the expertise. We will own half each."

Alice shook her head with doubt. "You talk as if it were simple. There are so many problems, Harry."

"I know."

"My mother."

"My father."

"We can't laugh at everything."

"Why the hell not?" They returned the key and drove to Eliza's flat, waiting outside until half-past six when she arrived.

The previous two weeks had been strange for Eliza. The Sunday she had spent with Robert and the jubilant lunch the following day seemed, when she looked back, quite unreal. She had invented so many situations around the image of Robert before she met him that it was hard to believe the meetings had actually happened, especially as she had heard nothing of him since he left for Nigeria. David had been extremely busy and Eliza had been working late most evenings, happy to be so occupied and watching without resentment the last of the summer weather displayed but out of reach. David was taking possession of a new ship the following week and Eliza had been in charge of all the arrangements to do with launching. Numbers constantly changed. Hotel and train bookings had to be altered. As she walked down the street and went up the shallow steps she was so involved in her thoughts she didn't notice Harry and Alice until Alice called out.

Eliza swung round. "What brings you two here? Have you been waiting long?"

"About fifteen minutes," Alice answered, joining her on the step. "We've been to see a house which Harry's thinking of buying. He thinks I could run a linen hire business from there but it's all so improbable!"

"I can't see why." Harry followed them into the characterless hall and up two flights of stairs to Eliza's flat. When she had opened the front door, he looked round admiringly as Robert had done. "I like the way this place looks, Eliza. Do you live alone?"

"Yes." Eliza kicked off her shoes and then scooped them

up and put them neatly side by side. "What can I give you? Coffee or tea or a glass of wine?"

"Tea," they said together and Alice went into Eliza's small red kitchen to boil the kettle. The kitchen was immaculate. Eliza inherited so many things from Jane although she chose to deny them all. Even the superstitions that she so despised still clung about her. She would always draw a cross in spilled salt and touch wood to keep luck or God on her side.

"Are you still working for my father?" Harry asked.

"Yes. I can hardly believe it myself. Poor Sheila, who I have never met, gets sicker and sicker."

"It's an ill wind . . . " Harry said and Eliza groaned at the awful pun.

"I think if it's obvious she's not coming back, they'll look for someone permanent from higher up in the company. I work very hard but I have made the odd mistake. Your father is really very frightening when he's annoyed. For the past few weeks he has been far more ruthless with everyone. It must be your fault, Harry. And yet he can be very considerate in small matters. He has good manners even when he's furious. It makes it worse. He's just much more alert than most people."

"Christ, you're not sleeping with him, are you?" Harry said bluntly.

"Don't be ridiculous! He isn't the slightest bit interested in me. Nor I in him. But it's fascinating to watch him in action and as I know I'm only there temporarily, it gives me a slight advantage. I stand up for myself because I have another job to go back to. He really has to win, doesn't he, in everything? He knows he is right. I've never met anyone so confident. They are all afraid of him, whatever impression they give. He won't let anything go by."

"You don't have to tell me. I've lived with him for nearly twenty years. These past few weeks are the first time in my life I have ever felt free of his presence. I'm staying at a friend's flat at the moment, sleeping on the sofa; it's very uncomfortable but I wake in the morning smiling and wonder what it is and remember. Life is one long celebration with little cold patches when I'm afraid I am still entangled and an awful feeling of guilt when my mother rings. I feel like a defector. I have had to leave my family behind but it's still wonderful to be free. One long party!" He threw his arms wide open.

And, for the moment, Alice is at the same party, Eliza thought.

"Eliza, if I stay the night, would you ring and explain that I will go straight to work tomorrow morning and be back tomorrow evening? I can't bear to hear that dull sad voice she uses when I'm doing something she dislikes."

They both knew Jane would not like to be told by Eliza. When they had left to see *Evita,* Eliza was surprised by her own feelings. For so long she had nagged at Alice to move into the world, for so long she had blamed her mother for cocooning Alice, and now that Harry had arrived, Eliza felt uncertain. Alice had been so safe at home, so enchantingly vague. What would happen, now she was awoken, when Harry tired of her and moved on? She was afraid for Alice. *So I am just as bad. Just as over-protective. Or is it plain old jealousy? Did I want her to come here, to be with me?* She rang her mother, making her voice as friendly as possible, making it easy for Jane. Jane received the news coldly.

When, ten minutes later, Eliza got out of the bath to answer the telephone, standing on her towel so that she wouldn't make wet footprints, she expected it to be her mother, checking Alice's plans once again.

"Eliza?"

Robert's voice drew her from her thoughts of home, made her straighten, push back her damp hair with one hand and smile, made her admit in that moment that for all this time she had been waiting for a call.

"I'm back."

"Yes, it sounds as if you are close by."

"Any luck with offices?"

"I think I've found some you will like. In Holborn. A narrow little street but they have their own parking for two cars. They are the size you want, nice inside and the right price. I said you might look at them next week."

"I shall be away for a few days next week. I'd like to see them tomorrow."

"I'm sure I can arrange that."

"Thanks." He paused, picturing Eliza's face. "How about dinner this evening? There are some things I want to discuss with you. I'll pick you up about nine."

Eliza dressed carefully, changing her mind twice about what she would wear, which was unusual for her, and still she was ready long before Robert came. She wandered her flat, impatience hammering in her. She felt that the carefully constructed card house of her life had been flattened and shuffled. She was breaking her own rules. She wanted him. She was letting him in too soon, too much. She knew that, in the past, her appeal to men had been a combination of the interest she could show and a genuine self-reliance. Work had come first. Now her conviction that above all she wanted success in her work, dignity, her own house, was being attacked. She tested herself. *If it was a choice between seeing Robert and going somewhere for Otterwoods, not essential but somewhere which would score points, which would it be?* She was still weighing the answer when Robert rang her bell. The moment he stepped into her flat even the question seemed irrelevant.

Robert kissed her mouth very lightly. He refused her offer of a drink. "I'm too hungry to wait any longer for food. We'll go somewhere near. That Italian place in Pugh Street." He moved quickly, arm through hers, the night warm and damp round them. They were shown to a small table at the back, the restaurant was crowded and smoky. Robert lit a little cigar, rolled up his sleeves and leant his elbows on the table. He ordered a carafe of wine and filled two glasses. "I'm having Parma ham and then tagliatelle and salad," he said to Eliza. "You?"

Eliza laughed and put down the menu she had had no time to look at. "I'd better have the same."

"Good." He grinned. "I hate women who spend hours reading the menu and then end up choosing prawn cocktail and rump steak."

"Especially if they have elaborate names!" Eliza said dryly.

"I wouldn't have taken them out at all in that case."

Instinctively Eliza drew nearer to his smile, leaning on the table too. "What's been happening to you?"

"A great deal and very fast but so far I'm keeping up. The Norwegian ship is crewed and is operating. The cement is virtually closed down. I seem to be spending a small fortune on air fares but I find things go so much better if I see to them in person. Talking to people face to face is essential, especially in Africa and South America. I've made some good friends but I have to work at keeping them. And there are so many interesting rumours about. I have always believed that if you want something badly enough you can get it but you have to really want it."

"And luck?"

He smiled. "Although, as I remember so airily telling you, I don't go much by luck, it did occur to me the other day that my life has taken a decided turn for the better since the afternoon I met you."

Eliza smiled. "I wonder if I can say the same?"

He leaned away again, eyes narrowing slightly. "I hope you will be able to, in time." He was watching her intently. "I have a proposition for you. When we first met you told me that you wanted to be much more than a secretary. Well, quite soon I shall need someone to run my office here. I hope to expand rapidly. To start with the money may not be spectacular but you will be in at the beginning. You can help shape it all."

"How do you know I am capable of doing that?"

"For several reasons, the most telling of which is that David Otterwood would not keep you in his office for ten seconds if you weren't extremely good."

"So I owe this offer to David?"

"Indirectly, yes. Has he asked you to stay on with him?"

"No, he hasn't." She looked at him, her face mischievous. "A pity. Much as you'd like to employ me yourself, I would be even more useful to you if I went on working for David permanently, wouldn't I?"

Robert grimaced. "Not at all. You are the wrong kind of person. Too loyal to be much good as a spy."

The food came and for a while they spoke little. Robert

ate with all his concentration, as if he hadn't eaten for days, every now and then smiling across at her, filling her glass, asking a little about the offices she had found. Neither of them wanted a pudding and while they waited for coffee, Eliza reached out and took one of the small brown cigars from his packet. "I don't need to be paid a fortune. As long as I earn enough to pay my rent, run my car, buy food and some interesting clothes, I shall be happy. But what I really want if I am to leave Otterwoods and my secure future, is a share in the business."

Robert frowned. "I'm not sure I want to give away part of something I don't have myself yet."

"Just a small part. Otherwise I won't come."

She leaned forward towards the lighter he held out. The cigar smoke was rough in her lungs. She so rarely smoked. The coffee was strong, cancelling out the taste, and she watched Robert and waited for his answer.

"Why should I bother? I can hire a secretary anywhere, any time, who will meekly take the salary I offer."

Eliza shrugged. She looked down into the impenetrable blackness of the coffee cup and pretended she didn't care at all.

"On the other hand," Robert said, "I need all the luck I can get, now that you've alerted me to the stuff."

"Fifteen per cent."

"Five."

"Ten."

"That's ten per cent of nothing but a name and a few good ideas. It could be ten per cent of failure and a resulting loss of money."

"It's ten per cent of you."

Robert sat back. He was contented and well fed and the second carafe of wine was half drunk. He looked across at Eliza and smiled, thinking how unusual it was for him to really like a woman that he found attractive. "Which particular ten per cent are you interested in?"

She gave a small, smiling shrug. "I'm just starting with ten per cent. I hope to work up to a lot more."

Robert parked his car outside her flat, turned off the

engine and looked at her expectantly, surprised at how much he had enjoyed the evening. He felt happy in Eliza's company. In the dim light her face was enigmatic.

"Can I come in and have that drink now?"

"Just for half an hour."

Robert put his hand under her hair, moving his fingers against her neck. She felt the full weight of his attention and leaned away a little.

"My sister and Harry are spending the night."

He smiled. "Half an hour."

Eliza unlocked her front door and was aware of semi-darkness and absolute stillness, of Harry and Alice sitting on the sofa and looking expectantly towards the door. Eliza laughed at their expressions.

"You look like two surprised owls! Robert, this is my sister Alice. You know Harry, don't you?"

Harry stood up. "The *Peacock*. That was the first time I knew for certain that I could not go to sea. God, I was so sick. I thought I would die." He took a step towards Robert and held out his hand. "And you must have wished to God he hadn't picked your ship to dump me on."

"I did at first, but we got quite attached to you in the end when you stopped throwing up. You were about a foot shorter then, weren't you?"

"Yes. It was almost exactly five years ago. I shall never forget it. Are you still with the company?"

"No. I have set up on my own. Stoner Shipping. But I went back to Otterwoods a few weeks ago. I went to your father for finance."

At the mention of David, all the interest left Harry's face. He sat down on the arm of the sofa, long legs sprawled outwards, pushing back his shaggy hair with thin fingers.

"Did you like *Evita*?" Eliza asked.

"Loved it. Especially the sets. Alice has been humming 'Don't cry for me, Argentina,' all through dinner." He looked over his shoulder at Alice affectionately.

Eliza made four coffees and carried them into the sitting-room, folding herself onto the floor, heels tucked beneath her, and Robert, in the armchair behind her, put a hand on her shoulder and pulled her back until she leaned against him. She was aware of every part of his leg that touched her back as if she were naked. He stroked, occasionally, the narrow nape of her neck where her hair parted as she leaned forward. The music from the souvenir cassette of *Evita* which Harry had bought, sang to them.

It was one of those simple moments of happiness which seemed to cancel out all that had been before or would come after. Complete in itself.

I wish, Eliza thought as she drank her coffee and leaned her head back against Robert's knees, *that it could be like this. Alice and me, both with someone to love.*

Chapter 9

There is always some magic about a launching, Celia thought, standing in the mid-morning commotion at King's Cross and watching David's secretary, Eliza, hand tickets and itineraries to the group of Otterwoods employees who were to attend the launch that evening in Hull. It was a cold afternoon. Apart from the few very hot weeks in August, summer had never seemed serious this year and now, in late September, seemed to have abandoned the year to autumn almost overnight. A cold wind gusted through the station as Celia watched the thin, dark girl in her brilliant red coat, a butterfly amongst the grey suits of the Otterwood men and the sensible green and brown winter coats of their wives. Eliza wore a black felt hat, the brim caught up on one side, and she looked quite at ease in it. Her face was solemn with concentration, her mouth a scarlet line. *Is she the sort of girl David wants?* Celia thought. He had mentioned that while Sheila, his comfortable middle-aged secretary, was recuperating from a hysterectomy, Eliza had been asked to stay on for a while. "She's good," he had said. "Dull but efficient." Celia thought dull was the last word she would have used for Eliza. She burned with energy. Her walk was swift and graceful and Celia was aware of a reluctance to meet her, talk to her, to face yet another possible threat. Having seen this intriguing girl, she did not want to know her and yet, because of the link with Alice, Celia longed for news of Harry.

"Your ticket, Mrs Otterwood."

Eliza handed Celia a neat package of ticket and and publicity material on the *Kingfisher*, the latest Otterwood ship, a North Sea supply vessel, and introduced herself, fascinated to meet, at last, the person who belonged to the photograph. Celia looked just as lovely in real life but far less resilient and slightly older.

She looked unhappy. Eliza wanted to talk for a few moments, to make an impression.

"We have a whole carriage to ourselves with forty-eight seats, arranged in groups of four with tables. Mr Otterwood has chosen who will sit where. You will find names at the tables." She smiled, apologetically. "It's the first time I've organised anything like this. I hope it goes smoothly. The numbers kept changing. Also, the menu for lunch is very ordinary but Mr Otterwood said he would rather have something simple, well done, than an elaborate mistake. He chose the wine, of course. The train will leave at twelve thirty and they will serve lunch at half past one."

"Thank you." Celia put the folder in her bag. She tried to shake off her wariness and respond to Eliza. "I met your sister a couple of weeks ago; Harry brought her to stay with us. They were on their way to an auction sale."

"Yes, she told me. She did very well at that sale. No one else was interested in the things she wanted except the Indian silk shawls which went for ridiculous prices."

Celia made no move and Eliza sensed that she wanted to ask about Harry.

"Is Harry still staying at your mother's house sometimes?"

"I don't think so. It was just for that one week."

Celia nodded. She was wearing a long coat of such fine grey suede that it moved like silk. "Well, I suppose I had better go and rehearse my speech. I never get used to speaking in public." She turned and climbed into the carriage, making her way to a table at the far end where she was to sit. In the centre of each white-clothed table was a small arrangement of flowers and as she sat down, Celia leant forward and smelled the yellow rosebuds and thought of the bouquet she had received from Robert Stoner.

The idea of Robert and the memory of that evening had been clear in Celia's mind for the past few weeks, surfacing again and again above the tangled unhappiness. He was something quite different to think about, interesting and intriguing, a brightly coloured memory to counter the anxiety. She had seen very little of David. He had been in

America for ten days and before that Canada, returning only two days ago to write Celia's speech. The girls were gone, Josephine back to school with extreme reluctance, ringing most evenings to tell Celia that she was unhappy and worried about the work she had missed when she was ill, and Julia had gone to stay with friends for a week before she went up to Cambridge. Celia was possessed by a mood of melancholy dissatisfaction which she hated but could not shake off.

The train drew out of King's Cross at exactly twelve thirty and drinks were served. Celia talked to Otterwoods' chief engineer and the publicity director and his wife as they left London and moved at speed through the flat heart of England, towards Hull. At one thirty lunch was served by skilful waiters who seemed unaware of the occasional violent lurches of the train. Celia liked to travel by train. It seemed safe and reminded her of the excitement of childhood journeys, to or from school, and the very different emotions tied to each. She ate melon and roast lamb, apple pie and cheese, surprised at her hunger, while the two Otterwood men talked earnestly about the state of the North Sea and the publicity director's wife sat in a silence so dense that after half a dozen attempts to hack her way in, Celia gave up. She sipped black coffee and looked out of the window, through complicated reflections; she watched the boat-yard as they passed it and the new Otterwood ship was pointed out to her in its raw orange paint, silhouetted with tall, slanting cranes against a white sky and fast-moving clouds. At three thirty they came into Hull station.

The entire party were booked into the Station Hotel, a far grander establishment than its name suggested, with twin curving staircases and immense urns of flowers in the mirrored hall. When they had been shown their room, David went down again to have tea with several of his employees, leaving Celia to unpack her dress and coat and hat and order tea in her room. She sat on the window seat, drinking from a pretty flowered cup and looking out over this solid city and she played a game of suggesting ideas to herself and seeing which comforted. Only Scotland held any allure. It was so far from the rest of her life. She remembered when David had first taken her there, just after their honeymoon. It had bewitched her then and she would never tire of it.

She was still on the window seat at six when David came back. "There will be a coach at seven to take us to the dockyard for a short reception and the launch is at eight. Are you happy about your speech?"

"As happy as I will ever be. You know how much I dislike making speeches."

He shrugged. "Very few people enjoy it. This is your third launch. I should have thought you would be used to it by now." He went into the bathroom and the sound of running water and traces of steam issued through the open door. Celia sat hunched up. His deliberate lack of understanding hurt her until she hardened the feeling into anger. She followed him, leaning in the open doorway and watching David take off his clothes and fold them over a chair. He was fanatically neat.

"David, ever since this thing with Harry started you have hardly spoken to me. If I am to be relegated to being merely part of the company you could at least treat me with the consideration with which you treat the rest of your employees." She watched him get into the steaming water. She had spoken these words in her head again and again but aloud they sounded stilted and pompous. Her voice faltered. "Harry's behaviour is not my fault."

"Harry's defection may not be your fault but I know you don't support me. You could use your influence."

"But I think you are wrong. You want the impossible." She came into the room and closed the lavatory seat and sat on it. "Have you any idea what Harry is really like? Do you ever try to consider things from his angle? He genuinely feels he can't do what you want. As he says, he has tried for years."

"What has he tried for years? To pass exams. The whole point of the exams was to equip him to take up a position in Otterwoods. If he can't manage the exams, I'm prepared to let him work his way up. He is perfectly able to do that. He can't possibly reject the company without even trying it."

"Why don't you try a different approach? Why can't you back him in something, let him get some confidence in himself? Then he could come in to Otterwoods from a position of strength. You're so obstinate and impatient that you're driving him farther and farther away." She paused, aware that in her anger she was at last saying what she felt to David, that the coldness had gone. She looked at David expectantly.

"He will come into the company."

Celia stared at him. Hopelessness replaced the anger. He gave her the impression that she was not a person of flesh and blood; she felt that he could see through her, walk through her if he wanted, that nothing she could say would touch him. What was it that he wanted? All summer she knew he had been involved with someone else. He became more passionate, not less, when he had a new mistress. His love-making drew her, against her will, down into a whirlpool of pleasure that left her hating herself and him. "Why can you never imagine yourself in someone else's place? You must have imagination or you couldn't run Otterwoods as well as you do."

"Of course I can imagine myself in Harry's place or yours or anyone's but it makes no difference to what I want."

Absolute helplessness flooded through Celia. She leaned forward, putting her head in her hands and her voice was muffled. "I used to feel that, despite everything, our lives together were a success. In the last few months everything has disintegrated. Nothing is right now."

David raised his eyes and looked at her as if he were seeing her properly for the first time, frowning at the desolation in her voice. He sat up. "Look, I realise that you have been unhappy recently. If I've been away too much, I'm sorry. This American take-over was important. Shall we have a big party for your fortieth birthday?"

"No," Celia said. "I don't want to think about it. It's months away," and she thought, *How convenient. He has convinced himself I am unhappy about my age.*

"Four months." He sat up, pouring shampoo into his hand and rubbing it into his hair. "You don't look forty."

She didn't answer.

"Celia, it's not too late to have another child."

Celia sprang upright. She opened her mouth. Eventually the words came. "Another son, is that it, as an insurance policy? Because the children I have given you are not turning out to be exactly what you wanted, you would like some more? I told you after Christopher died I could never go through that again."

"You wouldn't have to. Obstetrics has improved vastly in the past twelve years. Think how many of your friends have babies in their late thirties and early forties. You are strong. You wouldn't notice a pregnancy. I know you're not happy. Another child could take you back to the time when things were simpler. It might be a girl. I'll take that chance. But I feel it would be a boy. I've thought about it a lot."

"There is no question of it." Celia stood up unsteadily and lurched through the door, crouching back onto her window seat, arms wrapped tightly round herself. Was there nothing left of the David she had loved in the hard, opportunist man she was married to? She rocked herself and through the uncurtained window she saw the pale crescent of a new moon and shivered, remembering the superstition of her childhood.

The reception was crowded. Traditionally the launching party was given by the shipyard and they were inclined to ask not only the new owners of the ship but other prospective clients as well. They drank champagne for half an hour and then went out into a cool, damp night and walked round the puddles of the dockyard to the flight of wooden steps that led up to a raised platform under striped awning. The ship stood in front of them, fantastic in the darkness, its immense smooth orange bows slanting upwards, close enough to reach out and touch. Below in the floodlit yard little clusters of people stood watching, the ship-workers and their families. The platform was crowded. Photographers nudged their way forward. Flash lights flowered.

Celia shivered in her thin coat and the feathers on her pretty, silly hat were teased by the wind. She grasped the bottle firmly on its long ribbon. There was an expectant silence as the manager spoke. He finished by saying, "And Mrs Otterwood has kindly agreed to launch the ship."

Celia took one step forward. "I name this ship *Kingfisher*."

Her voice was clear as she drew back the bottle. "May God bless her and all who sail in her." She swung the bottle hard and it travelled the short distance and smashed against the orange hull. Flashlights everywhere. The ship did not move. Down below there was some activity as the pneumatic hammer was used and after a tense couple of minutes the *Kingfisher*'s enormous hull began to slide down the wooden ramps and into the dark water, drifting slowly out into the estuary. The figures on the deck cheered and there was some cheering from the shore but it seemed to Celia too muted for such an extraordinary occasion. She had seen dozens of launches in her life and every time she was impressed and moved but this was the first time she had launched a ship into darkness.

They began to descend the wooden steps to go back to the coach and she was aware of the friendly curiosity of the ship-workers and their families as they stared at her dress, at the frivolous hat. Celia knew she would never enjoy being someone who was looked at. The coach was waiting to take them to dinner and at the thought of her approaching speech she felt herself grow narrow with nervousness and she experienced a moment of loneliness more intense than ever in her life before. *He doesn't know what I do for him, what I go through. Has he ever known? I know him so well. Does he know me at all?*

The private dining-room at the Station Hotel had been decorated for the occasion, with one long table and numerous other smaller tables. At every place lay a glass paperweight with the *Kingfisher* engraved on it. Celia ate very little as she waited for the moment when she would have to speak. The meal seemed endless. David, on her right, barely spoke to her. At last the master of ceremonies rapped for silence and Celia stood up, the words on four sheets of white paper. "Ladies and gentlemen . . . " David had written the speech. It praised the shipyard, it dealt a little with the future of the ship, it congratulated the ship-workers on finishing before time. The speech lasted three minutes and she ended by thanking them for the exquisite diamond brooch, trying to sound as if she were surprised, when in fact she had chosen it. The etiquette of a launch was as elaborate as that of a wedding. She sat down amid applause with a huge sense of relief and drank a glass of wine in several swift gulps as David got up to speak. He smiled down at her and made a series of affectionate remarks about the ships his wife launched having a good start in life. The contrast between this public affection and the private coldness made her feel sick, made it almost impossible for her to smile as she was expected to.

The words of the remaining speeches washed over her. She was thankful when it was time to get away from the table and walk towards the crowd of people who now clustered round the bar. David had vanished. Celia stood on the outside of a large group of people and experienced again a terrifying loneliness such as she imagined a person would feel when death was inevitable.

"Launches are always unreal, romantic occasions, aren't they? Especially at night."

She felt a touch on her arm. She turned reluctantly.

"Robert Stoner, in case you've forgotten."

"Of course I haven't forgotten." She felt surprise and intense pleasure, both emotions ridiculously strong. "The flowers were lovely."

"Well, it seemed I had you to thank for my meeting with Michael Copper."

"I wondered if that worked out for you. For some reason I haven't seen Michael and Betty or I would have asked."

"It worked out very well."

It seemed so long ago. The misery of the present overwhelmed her again. Her voice was dull. "It seems a pity they can't always launch at night but I suppose they have to obey the tides."

"And the tides obey the moon." He smiled. "Although I shouldn't admit it, having been a seaman, I can never really understand what actually starts the ship sliding. If it is so ready to go, why doesn't it go too soon?"

"This one nearly didn't go at all. I felt I should lean out and push it. Why are you here?"

"The shipyard director asked me. I've known him a long time and there is just a chance that I may be interested in a support vessel in due course . . . Quite a lot has happened in the weeks since we met. My fortunes have changed for the better. Can I get you a drink?"

"Yes. I'd like a whisky please. With ice."

They moved to a corner and sat at a deserted table. The noise from the bar increased. There was a small orchestra playing in the hall.

"You look sad," Robert said softly.

Celia drank deeply from her glass of whisky and heard herself laugh. "I can't think why I should. I like it here. It's old-fashioned and slightly unreal, as if we had slipped back fifty years. If it was hotter, I'd feel the waiters should wear turbans and there should be huge fans on the ceiling. I've been here before but I'd forgotten how I felt about it. I sat on the window seat for hours this afternoon and looked out at the city." She paused. All the time her eyes had been on his face and now, into her mind, uninvited, came an image of Robert and herself walking up one of the wide curved staircases into the big, deserted bedroom and making love.

"Then, why do you look so sad?"

"That's as bad as telling me I look tired or ill or old."

"You don't want to talk about it?"

She shook her head.

"I liked your speech. It almost sounded as if you meant what you were saying. That rather charming blend of confidence and shyness must have taken years to perfect, or did they teach it at your school?"

"David wrote it but I did mean it. I do care about the ships. More than any other part of the company."

"I have a ship now." He smiled, deliberately letting

the pride come into his voice. "An ancient Norwegian ship that is already working out of Venezuela. Thanks to Michael Copper. And you. And David, of course." He looked up as he spoke to where David stood, talking to the tall blonde wife of one of the Norwegians.

Celia knew all her husband's expressions. She saw he was being charming, impressive, reasonably interested. What was it that they thought they would get from him? What was it that she had been drawn to? Some undercurrent of power that spelled safety. That unshakable confidence of success and wealth? She moved her gaze back to Robert and her eyes were clouded with misery or anger. Instinctively he used the moment.

"Are you often in London?"

"Yes. It's only in the summer that I spend most of my time in the country. We are in London until October the seventh when we go to Scotland for two weeks."

"Would you have lunch with me next week?"

"Lunch? Why?"

"Because I'd like to see you. Just a way of showing my appreciation that you arranged such a successful introduction."

For a few moments, Celia let the idea take root. She would like to know him better. Because he knew so little about her, she felt she could be different with him, leave behind, if only for a few hours, the coldness of her life. He was looking at her again as David used to. She had forgotten how it felt. Damn them all! She felt fury rise up in her. She tore up the idea as if it were a written invitation.

"You must be mad." She stood, pushing her chair back and finishing the whisky all in one angry, ugly movement. "Good night." She walked swiftly towards the arched doorway.

Eliza, glass in hand, stood on the edge of a little group, smiling enough to seem as if she were listening but taking regular glances, like deep breaths, at the table where Robert and Celia were sitting. Curiosity pulsed through her. She had seen Robert at the far side of the room at the pre-launch party, had been seated on the opposite side of the room at dinner; he had not mentioned that he was coming; she had watched the changing expressions on Celia's face, saw the anger just before she stood up; she watched Robert get to his feet rather slowly and look after Celia's retreating figure. He stood, feet apart, head forwards, his strong body looking poised for sudden movement if necessary. Murmuring something, Eliza went towards him, quite slowly, but he turned as she was approaching and came towards her, taking the glass out of her hand and putting it down.

"Come and dance with me, Eliza, to this ridiculous band, not that I can remember these dances very well." And he led her quickly into the hall. They were in time to see Celia at the top of the wide staircase.

They danced very gently so that they could talk.

"You never mentioned that you were coming here."

He shrugged. "I never know myself what I will be doing until a day or two beforehand. Ralph Miller, the director of the yard, is an old friend of mine." Each time they turned his eyes went back to the stairs. The urge to go after Celia was very strong, surprising him. With difficulty he tried to concentrate on Eliza. "Have you thought over my proposition?"

"Yes, but I haven't decided yet." Her dark eyes were outlined with smudgey grey, her face very pale. He liked the scent she wore but his attention was with Celia, trying to remember every expression, to think why she had become angry so suddenly.

"Did you like the offices?" Eliza said, with an edge to her voice because she sensed his preoccupation.

"I had to change the appointment. I'm seeing them on Tuesday at five. Would you like to come too?"

"I'm going to Rotterdam with David tomorrow morning. We get back some time on Tuesday. If I can come, I will."

Robert smiled. "Good, because if you come and work for me you'll be spending much more time in them than I will." He touched her face lightly. Then with slight pressure he moved her closer to him so that they danced against each other. Eliza was very thin, long-legged, her body moving easily under the long black dress that was like an extended T-shirt. They didn't speak for some time.

When they sat down with a drink each and Robert lit a cigar Eliza said mischievously, "Shouldn't you be chatting up some of these shipping people?"

"I've been doing that for hours."

She put her head on one side, eyes dancing. "Yes, I noticed. I'd love to know what Celia Otterwood was confiding in you?"

Robert laughed and picked up her hand and put it to his lips. "One minute you tell me to chat up shipping people and the next moment you complain. You're a difficult girl to predict, Eliza."

"Good. I like to have your complete attention."

"At this moment you have it. I promise. One hundred per cent." He put an arm along her shoulders. "But I think you are being approached by someone else."

Eliza stood up as the wife of one of David's guests came to discuss the alteration of train tickets for the following morning. She wanted to leave after lunch. Robert watched Eliza being patient and polite. She was good at her job. He wanted her to work for him very much.

It was just after midnight. Robert watched Eliza for some time, occasionally meeting her eyes. They were joined by two other women who also wanted to alter their travel arrangements. An elderly man brought Eliza a drink and stood beside her, listening intently. Robert finished his drink. He waited another fifteen minutes but there was no sign of Eliza escaping and, catching her eye as he waved a brief goodnight, he went up to his room.

Eliza watched Robert leave with a feeling of intense disappointment which she hid carefully as she waited for these maddeningly muddled women to make up their minds what time they wanted to go where the following morning.

Chapter 10

Robert had an appointment with Michael Copper the following Tuesday morning and he left Michael's office at ten thirty, full of optimism. He felt he knew how to handle Michael now. He had arranged to see the Holborn offices at five and he was beginning to think that as he was spending so much time in London, he should also look for a flat.

It was a fine morning. He caught the tube at Monument and got off at Sloane Square, coming up into the thin sunlight of early October. Some of the girls he passed still wore loose layers of summer clothing. The world was warm and clean and pretty and he was in a triumphant mood. Everything was going right. Almost without planning the action, he stepped into a telephone box by Peter Jones and rang Celia Otterwood's number at the Flood Street house.

Celia was making lists for Scotland, of friends, of clothes, of food that should be ordered. Although there were other people who would see to it all, she needed to reassure herself that she still had a unique part to play and to try and counter her steadily increasing unhappiness. She wanted to see Harry. She wanted to try and talk to David again. Days went by and neither of these things were accomplished. The weather was so fine that she longed to be back in Hampshire. Because there had been last-minute things to buy in London before Josephine and Julia went back they had left Hampshire in early September. The London house was very quiet without the girls but it was not worth going home for the few days that were left before Scotland, however much she yearned for the view across the watermeadow to the deep-set little river or to watch autumn transform her garden. She was sitting in her bedroom at her desk and when the phone rang she picked it up eagerly, wanting distraction. "Hello?"

"Celia?"

"Yes. Who is it?" The voice, although she didn't at once realise who it was, gave her pleasure and aroused intense curiosity. There was a short pause.

"Robert Stoner. You remember, the mad man who asked you to lunch."

She thought, *I knew who it was, really.*

"Will you change your mind and have lunch with me today?"

A variety of excuses rushed through Celia's mind.

"Well?"

"I'm thinking, Robert."

"Thinking of a reason not to come?"

"No. Thinking of a reason why I should come."

"Are you doing anything else?"

"No."

"Well then?"

She laughed at the simplicity which he implied. Perhaps he was right. A simple invitation to lunch. What could be more harmless? How absurd she had been in Hull. "Where would we meet?"

"There's a small restaurant in Chelsea Green called Carter's. Do you know it?"

"Yes."

"We could meet there at one."

There was another long pause during which Celia told herself it was ridiculous to invest so much drama in a lunch invitation. She had no one to see today unless she deliberately rang one of her friends. She had planned to go shopping. She needed some warm pretty clothes for Scotland to wear in the evening but there was nothing essential that she had to do.

"Do you want to come?" Robert asked, almost impatiently, because he wanted to see her so much.

"Yes."

"Good. One o'clock at Carter's."

She put the phone down and sat very still for some moments, drawing circles with her pen and turning them into flowers. She laughed at herself. How absurd to feel guilty. Nothing but lunch with a friend. Not really a friend but an acquaintance. It was nothing and yet she was worrying about what she should wear.

Robert came out of the phone box and looked at his watch. He had a sense of intense pleasure and of apprehension. He thought how stupid it was to risk antagonising David Otterwood and, even as he thought it, he knew it somehow added savour to the whole idea. He wanted to see Celia very badly, to have reality fill out again the indelible impression she had left in his mind.

Celia walked out of the Flood Street house at half past twelve, nervous and exhilarated and every now and then she would turn on herself and a wave of embarrassment would kill the exhilaration. She intended to walk. She enjoyed London in the autumn when the tourists were leaving and it became a big, familiar town once again until the glittering horror of Christmas stained the shops and streets. The pavements were dry and clean. She tucked her hands into her pockets and walked fast, her long, heavy cotton skirt swinging, a big loose bow at her neck, and she was at Chelsea Green by ten to one. She wasted time in a shop of wallpapers and materials, thinking about Josephine's room in the London house which badly needed decorating, thinking about Josephine's miserable letters. "Why can't I come to Scotland? You could say I was still ill." Celia made herself wait until five past one and then she went to Elystan Street, into the small restaurant.

It was fairly crowded but she saw Robert at once because he stood up. As she came across to him he moved the table slightly so that she could step past it and sit with her back to the wall. Robert sat down, facing her.

"I'm very glad that you came. I was almost sure you would but I felt you could have changed your mind and left me sitting here all afternoon, feeling ridiculous."

"I had to come because I wanted to hear more of how you were getting on. I have decided that as it was my fault you met Michael, I must take an interest." She smiled. "David was rather annoyed. He hates me to interfere with his arrangements."

"Do you often interfere?"

"Oh yes, often. I look round the room and pick a new face, someone that I want to sit next to, and juggle the names around. It was nothing special, you know."

Robert nodded. "So Michael Copper told me. He warned me you were always chasing men." Robert's eyes were laughing. He made her feel very young again. Untouched. "What would you like to drink?"

"Some wine, please. Where do you stay when you are in London?"

"At a small hotel near the Cromwell Road, but I'm starting to think I should get a flat now that I'm in London so often, although I'm reluctant to commit myself to living somewhere that I dislike so much."

Celia frowned. "You can't dislike the whole of London. It has so many different parts. It's like a small country."

"I hate all cities. I hate the noise and the smell but most of all the people. So many people. Unfortunately, I have to deal with some of them and it is so much better to see them in person. A hundred times better. You pick up so many subtleties when you go and see people."

"David often says that. Especially when he's expecting trouble. If he goes, in person, he can very often defuse a situation." She thought, *Why did I have to talk about David again? Can't I leave him behind for an hour? Am I so irrevocably married?*

"I can imagine that," Robert said dryly.

He poured Celia a glass of cold white wine. Celia leaned back, sighed slightly, smiled a little.

"You look tired."

"Don't start that again. Unhappy. Tired. It makes me think I look old and soon I shall be at a sensitive age." She drank some wine. "Actually, I am rather tired. It's just the end of the summer holidays, getting the girls off and things."

"Things like Harry?"

"Harry and David. It's only the men in my life who cause trouble. The girls are easier." She put her elbows on the table and leaned forward. "I know this restaurant very well. When I was first married I used to lunch here every week with David's grandmother. She was eighty then. She knew everything. They all listened to her. She told me to stand up to David. She told me that the men in her family were not easy to live with. I hardly understood, I was so in love. I couldn't imagine that David would ever do anything that I didn't absolutely agree with. She died while I was pregnant with Harry."

She looked up at Robert, her speckled eyes full of memories, and he reached out and covered both her hands with his, and as she let her hands lie under his everything dissolved except the face opposite her and the way her body responded, sloughing off layers of reserve in such a swift sequence that it was almost instantaneous. The feeling was so strong that it made her laugh.

The moment lasted for a few seconds and then she withdrew her hands and it could not be put into words. Robert was watching her so gently. A waiter came to take their order and they had not even looked at the menu.

"I had forgotten that we came to eat," Celia said. "I don't want very much. Melon and a bit of fish and a salad please."

"I want a lot." Robert read the menu. "Soup of the day and lamb's liver. What sort of bit of fish? Dover sole or turbot or trout?"

"Dover sole with no bones in it so that I don't have to work at it."

"I see why you don't get fat. Food obviously doesn't matter much to you."

"Sometimes it does. Not when I'm worried." She had been going to say miserable but caught herself in time. "Where would you look for a flat?"

"As usual, I shall be entirely ruled by cost. Except that

there is no point in looking too far out. I'd like to be reasonably near a station. Pimlico would suit me quite well. I'm looking at some offices in Holborn this afternoon."

Part of it, Celia thought, *is that sense of haste and energy and optimism. I remember it in David before it hardened into ruthlessness. I used to feel David could do anything. Now I can feel Robert's excitement about his life.*

"What's happening about Harry, or would you rather not discuss it?"

Celia leaned back, picking up her glass. "Nothing's happening. He thinks he has solved everything by merely announcing he has dropped out. David is just waiting for the right moment to snatch Harry back. He will bribe or frighten or shame him into the company. David honestly believes that Harry could be successful working for Otterwoods. I think about it so much. Harry has a lot of charm. He needs friends. He enjoys the way of life he has been brought up to and I suppose David thinks he could work for Otterwoods and continue with his way of life; the sad thing is that David thinks nothing of Harry's honesty. Harry won't take a job he can't do. He would be humiliated. But if he was allowed to find himself, to have time, it would be different. Instead he is living away from home, doing nothing and probably drinking too much. The only good thing that has happened to him this summer is Alice, Eliza's sister. Have you met her?"

"Yes."

"I found her enchanting. The first time I saw her I thought of some lines from *The Blessed Damozel.* 'The wonder was not yet quite gone from that still look of hers.'"

"So you did learn something at that hopeless school you spoke of ?"

"Only poetry."

"Can't you persuade David to give Harry some time?"

She shook her head. "Nothing that I say influences David now. He used to listen to me but somewhere along the way he has decided that because I have become exactly what he wanted me to be, a woman who lives exclusively for him, my opinions count for nothing. Isn't that ironic? Even two or three years ago he would tell me what was happening in Otterwoods and when I gave him my opinion he would check himself and soften and listen, almost against his will. Now, if I ask what happened about something or other he tells me shortly and I know it is irrelevant, that there is some quite new problem."

Robert shrugged. "He must be mad," he said simply.

Celia drained her glass. "Robert, I'm sorry. Is there anything more boring than listening to husbands and wives complaining about each other? I'm sorry."

"I get the impression that you hardly ever say what you have just said to me. I don't think you complain enough."

Celia smiled and shrugged her shoulders slightly. "I never talk like this. I don't know why I should inflict it all on you."

"Perhaps you sense that, however strange it may seem, from the first moment I saw you, I was concerned about you. I was very angry about other things, that's why I probably seemed rude, but I wanted you to be different, I didn't want such a vulnerable woman to be married to David Otterwood. I wanted him to have some bright, hard, brittle woman who was living her own life."

There were tears in Celia's eyes but she blinked them away, holding out her glass for more wine. "I see I have a friend."

"You could say that."

"What did I think about you? I thought that you couldn't be put into any of the usual categories. That you were original and that if you went on looking at me as you did you would start some awful rumours! I still don't know anything about you. Are you quite self-contained or do you need someone to listen? Have you got someone? Have you got a wife?"

He shook his head. "I don't need anyone, but it would be a pleasure to talk about myself if you were interested enough to listen."

They were both smiling. The food came and was eaten or not eaten and plates taken away as they talked, coffee cups filled and refilled and a second bottle of wine drunk and it was three o'clock when Celia said she should go.

"Don't invent an excuse."

"I wasn't going to. It's just that I feel it's enough for now."

Robert smiled and paid the bill. He walked with her out into the brightness of the afternoon, into a real world which was bewildering for a few moments. He walked with her as far as the King's Road and on the corner of Jubilee Place, as she put out her hand to touch him and say goodbye, he kissed her cheek.

"Can we do this again?"

"I'm going to Scotland in a few days."

"And I'm going to Venezuela tomorrow. But when we both get back?"

Celia smiled. The idea of seeing him again enchanted her. It was something in the bleakness of the next few anticipated weeks. "Yes."

He watched her walking away, narrow figure, brisk long-legged walk, smooth dark head.

As Robert braced himself against the movements of the tube, he tried to think that it was useful to see her. That he could learn things. He tried to fit her into the normal pattern of the women in his life. But he knew the truth was that he wanted to see Celia despite, not because, of who she was.

He was a little late meeting the agent at the Holborn offices but Eliza had been right. They were ideal. He agreed to take them for five years. They walked down the stairs and emerged into the street, and as the agent turned and walked away, Eliza came running towards him, her pale face flushed with running, hair coming loose from its combs. She stopped, panting and smiling and trying to catch her hair back again. "The train was late but I hoped I'd be in time. Any good?"

"Very good. I did suggest to the estate agent that perhaps Miss Marland might get some commission on the deal but he was out of earshot or pretended to be."

"Come and have a meal at my flat tonight?" Eliza said.

"Thank you. I'd like that." He put his arm through hers. "But first we'll have a drink. I need one."

"Why? What have you been doing today?" Eliza asked, watching him intently, her eyes as dark and shining as molasses.

Robert shrugged. "Nothing unusual. I saw Michael Copper early. Walked for a bit. Came to see these offices. And in between time I lunched with a friend."

Chapter 11

For three weeks after the night they saw *Evita*, Alice tried to find an opportunity to tell her mother that Harry wanted her to spend a week in Scotland. She had discussed it with Paddy and Alice was afraid that Paddy and Jane might meet one another by chance in Brighton and that Scotland might be mentioned. The weather was wet and business had been very bad, with little impulse trade and none of the browsing customers the good weather brought out into the streets. With his mind finally made up for him by very small takings, Paddy had actually put the shop on the market and it wore a large For Sale sign defiantly in the street of buildings which were all contentedly owned, a divorcee among happily married women. Alice had begun to sort out the stock. It was a massive job. There were trunks full of things that had never been unpacked. She saw much less of Harry but he rang every day to tell her that he was negotiating to buy the house in Pembridge Gardens and to ask if she had told Jane yet. The telephone conversations were long and comfortable, as if they were in the same room, the sort of conversations Alice had never had before.

"My parents leave on October the seventh. I think we should go up a few days later, on the twelfth. It's a Monday. We can put the car on the train overnight and we'll arrive in time for lunch on Tuesday. Tell her today, Alice."

"I will. I will."

But Alice didn't know where to begin. Jane knew nothing about Paddy selling the shop, about the London house, about the idea of Alice running her own business. *A few weeks ago,* Alice thought, *she knew about everything in my life, as I know about everything in hers. As if we touched even when we were apart. No space between us. Now there are secrets and things that are not secret but that I haven't told her because I don't know where to start and the week in Scotland is the most difficult thing of all.*

There had been only one holiday since her father died. Her aunt and her mother and herself. Eliza had either not been asked or had refused to come. They went to France on a coach and saw Paris and were away for five days in October. They had been afraid of getting lost. None of them spoke much French. Alice had longed for Eliza's confidence, for Eliza to laugh with. Her mother and her aunt were vastly amused by everything to try and disguise their terror but their laughter could not be shared by Alice, at thirteen.

She walked home on this damp evening in early October. The sea wore a layer of mist and a row of late swallows sat along the wire like clothes pegs on an empty line. Alice walked down the path at Seagull Avenue and went into the kitchen. She found Jane sitting at the table, with a cup of tea, trying to sort out the never-ending nightmare of accounts.

Happy to be distracted, Jane looked up and made a face and Alice pulled out one of the chairs and sat down, thinking how extraordinarily different her mother was from the severe façade she projected. Only with Alice and with her sister, Molly, could she be soft and funny. What would happen to Jane if Alice ever left?

"Dempseys out?"

"Yes. They don't want a meal tonight or tomorrow. They go on Friday and then we have no one until October the eighteenth when we have two elderly sisters from Derbyshire, the Misses Winter." Jane sighed. "How I hate these sums."

"Why don't we go to a film tonight?" Alice suggested, "and get away from it all?" She dropped her chin into her hands. "We could see *The French Lieutenant's Woman*."

Eliza had told her, "Meryl Streep is my ideal. You must see it. I love it when angular, strange-looking women are hailed as great beauties. I'm going to buy a cloak this winter."

Alice smiled as she remembered and then, as if prompted by the thought of Eliza to face up to things, she forced herself to speak. "I've been meaning to tell you for some time now that Paddy has decided to sell the shop. I shall have to get another job. Also, Harry has asked me to go to Scotland for a week and stay in the castle." She made a face, trying to make a joke of it. "When I told Eliza on the phone she said, 'Just like the fairy tale. Sleeping beauty, the handsome prince with his castle, substitute dirty red sports car for white charger.'" Jane smiled very slightly and Alice saw her mistake, admitting that Eliza had known first. She went on, quickly, "But Harry says the castle is not at all fairy tale. It's Victorian. Enormous and hideous and warm and comfortable and in the most beautiful place you can imagine, with a river hurtling by and a big trout pool and the hills all round. Miles from anyone else. And he wants me to go up on Monday and stay for a week."

Jane looked down at the page of figures, took a cigarette from a packet and lit it, before looking up at Alice again. "Do you really want to go? Have you thought about it? Do you want to spend a week with his family and a lot of other people you don't know? You haven't got the right clothes, you don't know the right people. You won't know what to talk about. You haven't even got a warm coat."

"Harry says they have masses of clothes to lend, boots and socks and things, and he will borrow some of his sister's tweed knickerbockers for me and we'll go stalking."

"Stalking what?"

"Stags."

"To kill?"

"Well, some of them have to be killed otherwise there are too many."

"You could apply that reasoning to people." Jane inhaled deeply. "You'll be lost up there, Alice. They will all know each other, or each other's families." Her voice became exaggerated and sarcastic. "Who are you? Alice Marland? From where? Where did you go to school? Hove High School? Who did you say you were?"

"Well I should be used to it. I've never known who I am, have I? It doesn't make any difference where I am. I don't know anything about myself and you won't tell me what little you know."

"You don't need to know. You live here. You have a mother and a home. Isn't that enough?"

"In some ways." Alice spread out her hands, helplessly. "Why do you make it so difficult for me? I am nervous enough without you pointing out more difficulties. It isn't the end of the world if they don't like me and I am shy. I won't die in a week. I'm not a plant." She was trying to make Jane laugh. She turned back to one of the endless anecdotes, knowing it would make Jane smile. "I'm not one of Granny's cuttings."

Jane smiled, reaching out her hand to touch Alice's. "Lavender and buddleia and camellia, those brown paper parcels, year after year we tried to make them grow here and every time they died and she told me what I'd done wrong. Too sheltered, too open, not enough muck, too much fertilizer. But they were almost dead when they came!"

"And then when the lilac finally survived those cats fought and broke it."

"Yes. Those bloody cats. And from then on I lied about it and it grew into a tall, strong imaginary bush that flowered its second summer. A pretend white lilac." Such safe memories. Alice had been smaller then. Easier to keep.

"I really want to go," Alice said, into a softer silence. "He needs me to go. His family are going to try and force him to go into the company."

"So I should think. What else can he do? Nothing." Jane thought, *What do his needs matter? He has no rights.*

"Let's go to the film now. We can buy a pizza on the way back." Alice leaned down to her mother, trying to lift her mood. "I want to see *The French Lieutenant's Woman* so badly."

There was a long pause and then Jane pushed back her chair, allowing herself to be persuaded and Alice understood that the agreement to come to the film also indicated that there would be no obvious opposition to Scotland.

Although she tried not to let her mother's doubts

depress her too much, Alice rang Eliza the following afternoon from the shop. When she got through, Eliza was speaking in a crisp working voice.

"It's Alice. Can you talk?"

"Yes. But not for very long. I'm trying to get Harry's car booked on the overnight train to Aberdeen. It was bad enough getting a place for Celia's Alfa Romeo last week. I can't think why they need so many cars up there. Have you told her yet?"

"About Scotland but not about the idea of the shop in London yet. She wasn't too bad but she's got me worried about not having any winter clothes. She's made me realise that I only have cotton dresses. In the winter I just wear more layers and a shawl or my tweed jacket. Can you lend me a coat or some money to buy one, Eliza?"

"Yes. Either. Come to London by train tomorrow evening. Come and have supper. You can spend the night if you want and go down early Friday morning. I've got a tweed coat but it might be very long on you and I've got some thick trousers you could roll up. And some sweaters."

"Of course, Harry says it doesn't matter about clothes, that they have lots to lend."

"Well he's completely wrong. Of course it matters. I am sure he can lend you clothes to stalk and fish but not for the evenings."

"Will it be smart in the evenings?"

"Yes. I flew up last year with some vital document David wanted and spent a night there. It is smart but it's wonderful and you'll love it. Don't let her stop you going." Eliza paused, suddenly wanting to see Alice very much. "Do come up tomorrow. There are things I want to tell you. I may be changing my job." Happiness danced in Eliza's voice. She had felt happy ever since Robert came and had supper at her flat. She believed they would be lovers soon.

Jane made no effort to stop Alice. She pretended that nothing was happening. She expressed no interest. She spent the days before Alice was due to go cleaning her house and throwing things away. She spent her time cooking ahead for the Misses Winter. On the Monday afternoon, Alice waited in the kitchen for Harry to collect her, dressed in a heavy yellow cotton boiler suit of Eliza's, drawn in to fit her small waist by a wide leather belt. She carried Eliza's tweed coat and in the suitcase Eliza had lent her were more of her sister's clothes; Fair Isle sweaters; a pair of leather boots a size too big and two long, full Viyella skirts which, on Alice, nearly reached the ground. She had gone through the trunk of her father's clothes when Jane was in the garden and taken the silk dressing-gown to wear over her white Victorian nightie. She kept lifting the suitcase to test its weight. In her basket lay two white, lace-trimmed Victorian handkerchiefs for Celia. Eliza had suggested the present. "It's pointless taking her drink. They buy everything on the company. I know she doesn't eat chocolates and flowers wouldn't survive the journey. Take something from your shop." Alice was ready an hour early and she sat in the kitchen. Her mood swung from terror to excitement and back through a middle stage when she merely wished she wasn't going.

When Harry arrived, Jane was nowhere to be seen and Alice searched the house for her, desperate to say goodbye.

Harry was impatient, eager to remove Alice in case Jane staged a last-minute scene. "Come on, Alice. We can't miss the train. We've got to get to King's Cross through all the rush hour traffic."

In desperation, Alice ran out into the garden and found Jane digging.

"I'm going. I'll be back in seven days and I'll telephone tomorrow night."

Jane nodded and kissed her stiffly. "Enjoy yourself."

I must be mad, Alice thought, crouched in the front of the car as Harry drove frighteningly fast. *What am I doing? It's just because I want to see him that I agreed to go. I'd much rather see him at home or in London.* She became aware that Harry was speaking.

"It's all coming on well. I've been to see one of the trustees. He's moaning a bit because the house is not freehold and it's a fairly short lease but I convinced him that I wouldn't spend very much money on it. The owners have accepted my offer. Funnily enough they are friends of cousins of mine so it's all very civilised and they've let me keep some keys so I can take some builders round and get estimates for decorating it and putting another bathroom at the top and a loo in the basement. It would be fun to paint it ourselves but it would take so long and also apparently there's some damp in the basement which has to be sorted out."

Alice said nothing.

"If everything goes smoothly, contracts could be exchanged in a few weeks but I wish I could have got it all signed before Scotland. Then my father couldn't have stopped it. I would have felt armed. I've never done anything like this before, Alice. It's not that difficult to deal with solicitors and estate agents and things. It all helps to build a wall between myself and Otterwoods but the pressure won't really lessen until we are actually running the business."

They were at King's Cross by eight and they loaded the car onto the train. Two sleeper compartments had been reserved, the single ones, with names on the door. They installed their luggage. There was an air of echoing excitement about the station in the evening, an atmosphere of holiday, and for longer and longer stretches Alice forgot her guilt. When the train started she was as pleased about it all as Harry. They had dinner in the dining car and it was the first time Alice had ever eaten on a train. Everything delighted her. Harry had two whiskies before they began on the bottle of wine and he talked so expressively about Scotland that his words drew pictures for her.

"It's wonderful there. It's my mother's favourite place. She'd like to live there, I think. I've been every autumn since I can remember even if it was just for half-term and sometimes in the earlier summer and occasionally at Easter. The people up there are charming. The same families for generations. Most of them worked for my grandfather. In Scotland I feel different. There is always a sound of water, the meals are enormous and we go out whatever the weather. We don't count the weather like we do in the south. You might catch a salmon, Alice. You can use Josephine's rod. I asked her." He ordered more wine and they drank the second bottle between them and everything they said was funny. They swayed back down the passageway, thrown from wall to wall by the movement of the train, and had difficulty finding their compartments.

Alice slid open the door of hers and almost fell in. Harry was thrown in after her and they collided and laughed as they flopped down onto the bunk. Harry slid the door shut and put his arms round her, his face in the warm hollow of her neck and shoulder.

The wine had changed her, and the darkness and the train and being in this little secret place with nobody to interrupt. Changes in her body. It seemed to have come alive. Harry moved farther onto the bunk and she was pressed back against the wall. His hands explored her body, at first over the boiler suit and then seeking a way in past the zips and buttons. "God, what is this garment? How does it work? It's full of false entrances." Her body grew warmer, making movements on its own. The only light in the sleeping compartment came flickering erratically through the window. A lighted station roared by, making them leap apart and then laugh. Harry began to get rid of his clothes. He slid under the thin blanket beside her and she registered for the first time the absolute rightness of another warm naked body against her own. They kissed and touched each other for an immeasurable length of time.

"We have all night," Harry whispered. "Isn't that wonderful? All night with you."

"Harry, we can't make love."

"We must. When you have me, you won't need the family you are curious about. The two of us will be enough. We won't care about anyone else. They won't be able to touch us. We must."

"Not yet. I never have."

"Don't you think it's obvious?"

"It's too soon."

Harry propped himself up onto one elbow and the

flickering light showed that he was smiling. "When we're over the border?"

"I don't know when."

He sighed. He looked at her face in the erratic light. It was smooth, fascinating, eyelids heavy. He closed his eyes and tried to reverse the insistence of his body.

Alice thought how different he seemed without his clothes. He looked right. The thought that he was hers, if only temporarily, was overwhelming. They were squashed together in the narrow bunk and Harry wriggled an arm under her shoulders and she turned towards him so that they could almost lie side by side. He stroked her breasts. "I knew you'd be beautiful all over."

"Have you had lovers, Harry?"

"A few." She felt him tense. "I wanted us to be lovers by the time we got to Scotland. To arrive as a pair. I'm afraid of being like my father. I despise his behaviour and yet I understand. I used to think of nothing but sex. I was obsessed with the idea of girls' bodies, of making love. I couldn't believe it would happen and then suddenly it did, with someone I hardly knew. It was so easy. She wanted me to. She was older than I was. And then it seemed as if, once I'd started sleeping with women, they all knew. I had thought about it and imagined it for so long and in the end it was easy. So frighteningly easy to move from one to another." He laughed. "Josie knew. She looked at me in that funny way she has and said, 'You've slept with someone, haven't you?'"

"What did you say?"

"I told her it was nothing to do with her and threw her in the pool." He looked serious again. "I never want to be like my father. I want one woman to be enough."

They lay in silence for a long time. Alice said nothing because she had no idea how to answer. His vehemence both scared her and made her feel very serious and very honoured. Gradually his breathing deepened and she realised he was asleep. Then a great wave of love for him possessed her. A strong, protective love that she had never experienced before. It was impossible for her to sleep in the noisy vibrating train with the sudden flashes of light through the darkness and the shock of Harry and the love she felt. She was uncomfortable, alternately too cold and too hot and she lay so stiffly that her body ached. When Harry woke, after a period of time she could not estimate, she pretended to be asleep. He made a few gentle attempts to arouse her and then slid out of the bunk and took her father's dressing-gown from the hook behind the door. He gathered up his clothes from the tangle round his feet and went quietly next door to his own compartment.

In the end Alice must have fallen asleep because she was woken by tapping on the door and she snatched the white blanket up round her shoulders as the attendant brought in morning tea and plain biscuits. Outside the window she saw farmland and black cattle, streaky clouds and the grey light of a cold sea as the train moved onto a bridge. The iron supports criss-crossed past the window and there was a loud knock and Harry came in, still in her father's dressing-gown. He sat on the bunk, putting his arms round her, his face nuzzling into her tangled hair.

"This is the Tay bridge. You can see both ends of the train at once because it is so long and the bridge curves. We loved it when we were children. We'll stop at Dundee next." He kissed her. "I love you, Alice."

"I love you, as well." The shock of the truth of the words made her need to do something and she knelt, blanket all round her, and poured out tea from a fat little brown pot and added sugar lumps. She settled back to drink it. The biscuits were delicious.

Harry yawned enormously. "We'll have breakfast at Aberdeen. I want to show you everything that I like best. Breakfast at Aberdeen is one of the things."

Jane was right. It was much colder in Scotland. Alice enveloped herself in Eliza's tweed coat and followed Harry into the station hotel where he ordered an immense breakfast which he put on the Otterwood bill.

"The company use this hotel constantly," he explained as they ate hot buttered toast and kippers.

"Did the company pay for the train too?"

"Yes." He frowned, putting down his knife and fork. "I know what you're thinking, that if I really want to cut myself off, I shouldn't let it pay but as far as I'm concerned, I am owed quite a bit. The family has had so much of my time and attention in the past, a few train tickets and breakfasts will even the score."

At ten they drove away from the station, through the centre of this town which had been so dramatically changed with the coming of oil. They drove up the long centre streets, crowded with people and shops and then turned west, following the long green valley of the River Dee to Ballater and then turning north across the Highlands on narrow roads, climbing and falling through spectacular scenery on a perfect October morning; they crossed narrow stone bridges and came into high open spaces, winding through Tomintoul and Aviemore and up to Inverness. Oil rigs stood knee deep in the water of the Moray Firth and after Inverness the roads became narrower and even more twisted in the last hour it took to reach Glencardine.

The castle stood at the end of a long drive and behind it the hills rose up smoothly and were so high that the scale of it all seemed quite wrong to Alice. A huge grey stone building with Victorian turrets and towers and beside it a complication of cottages and stables and a clock tower, it was perfectly reflected by a still pool in the front. There was a constant sound of water. Harry left his car beside numerous other cars and took their luggage from the boot, pushing open the inner glass doors of the porch and leading the way into a hall hung with stags' heads and salmon in glass cases. A cluster of people, most of them in stockinged feet, stood round an immense log fire, pink-faced from a morning spent outside.

Chapter 12

Alice forgot to telephone Jane that first night and remembered guiltily the following evening. She forgot everything beyond this place which was so different from anywhere she had been before. Celia, who could remember how it felt to stay away amongst so many strangers and who liked Alice, made a special effort to include her in the conversation and to make her feel at home. Celia liked Alice's calmness and the gentle face under the halo of honey-coloured hair. The borrowed clothes made Alice look smaller, like a child, but there was nothing childlike in her intelligent eyes. The liking Celia felt appeared to be reciprocated. Alice would come and seek Celia out. She was interested in Celia's tapestries and admired the older woman's skill and they talked about fabrics, about tapestry, Alice describing some of the things she had come across in nearly four years of working in the shop and attending sales.

"Had you realised that our names are anagrams of each other?" Celia asked as the thought occurred to her.

"No, but I know we are both Pisces, Harry told me when your birthday is."

Celia shivered and made a face of mock horror. "Don't remind me!"

Celia's fingers were never still. More and more she needed things to make and they must be difficult enough to demand her concentration, to move her thoughts away from the conviction she had that, as far as David was concerned, she lived behind a glass wall. David was so remote from her now that it felt wrong that he should be in her bed at night, that he should wander in and out of her bathroom when he chose.

Because David loved Glencardine as much as she did,

because it was like coming home to be here amongst all the Glencardine people again, they had both tried, for the first few days, to let the atmosphere smooth over the jaggedness between them and they had partly succeeded until David's first guests arrived, two Australian couples Celia had never met before, both shipping clients. Stella, the younger Australian woman, was very tall and sunburnt and she talked to David as if she had known him for years. Celia listened and wondered if they had been lovers, if everyone else knew and she did not, but she had almost moved past the stage of minding about feeling a fool. She tried to like Stella. She made another attempt to approach David. They went stalking together and the intense enjoyment they both felt as they walked steadily behind Donald, the stalker, across the highest and loveliest mountain in the area, pausing to savour the breath-taking view, made a bridge between them. David shot two stags and they opted to walk back to the castle and arrived home with a faint undertone of affection between them. There was just a ray of hope, Celia felt, until the following day when Harry arrived, bringing with him the biggest problem of all. Himself.

That first day Harry took Alice fishing. They spent some time sorting out Josephine's rod and practising casts on the lawn at the side of the castle and then walked half a mile down a narrow valley where the river had washed out steep sides and water the colour of tea swirled past the tumbled rocks. Wooden fishing stages had been built and Harry stood Alice on one and showed her how to cast into the fast-flowing water. Then he established himself a few hundred yards above her. She found it enthralling, every cast a new opportunity, letting the fly float down with the current; aiming each time for the far side of the river and every now and then getting her fly caught up in the steep heathery bank behind her head. So totally engrossed was she that she was surprised when Harry came and suggested they go in for lunch. They walked up to the castle and after a morning spent outside Alice felt different. Almost as if she belonged.

* * *

The first evening went by with no awkwardness and under the attention of Celia and Harry and the Australian husband, Mike, Alice was not really shy at all. She wore one of Eliza's long skirts and a fluffy jumper and shuddered when she thought how strange the cotton dresses would have looked.

The following morning at breakfast it was decided that Harry and Alice should go stalking. It was a fine, cold morning. They took packed lunches and met Donald outside the castle. They drove in the Land-Rover for two or three miles into the hills and then stopped while Donald searched the distance with his binoculars. They drove on a little way and stopped again and this time spied the beasts, a herd of six or seven stags and fifteen hinds.

They walked in single file and the mountains that looked so smooth from a distance were, in reality, uneven underfoot with tufts of heather and boggy places. They went round the bottom of the hill so as to approach down wind, walking for nearly two hours at a steady pace and almost in silence. Then, as they drew nearer the herd, it was time to crawl and Alice was put at the back as the men edged their way down through a damp, muddy hollow and then, inch by inch and in absolute silence, up towards the rim of a ledge. At the top they could look across a small valley at the grazing stags. Alice wriggled forward, damp heather pricking her chin, smelling earth and bracken, heather and grass, wind pushing at her face if she lifted it. The sky above them was blue but finger-printed all over with clouds. She listened as Donald selected the stag Harry was to kill, a large male with a set of lethal-looking antlers without the branches that made them desirable. This male, Harry explained later, had an unfair advantage in a fight and they did not want him to pass on his antlers to offspring. Harry settled himself into position and took the rifle from its case and loaded it. He looked through the sight and there was a long pause. The stag, oblivious of its deadly, crouching enemy, raised its head and sniffed the wind and then, at the same instant that Harry pulled the trigger, staggered and crumpled and the others in the herd flinched and then ran. Everyone stayed motionless for thirty seconds lest the stag should move and then Alice followed the men, running down the steep hillside and up the incline to where the dead stag lay. They clustered round it, breathing heavily after their run.

The stag's death seemed so strange. Like a mistake, Alice thought. Strong honey-coloured body, head thrown back, eyes surprised. Donald crouched and felt along its ribs. "Straight to the heart. A good shot."

Harry had forgotten Alice in his exhilaration. He turned to her as Donald took a knife from his belt and began to gralloch the stag, sawing through the tough hide all up its stomach and letting the intestines spill out onto the clean heather. There was a strong smell, Alice took a step backwards.

"Don't look if it revolts you."

"It doesn't. It just seems unreal. An extraordinary thing to do."

Harry shrugged.

"Do you enjoy it, Harry? A few minutes ago it was standing with its head up, sniffing into the wind, part of all this beauty and now it's a pile of meat."

Harry looked at her seriously. "I do enjoy it. I enjoy the stalk. It doesn't always go this well, you know. The wind changes and they scent you and they run and you must start again. I'm pleased that I shot well. I've missed a few times but I'm glad to say I've never wounded anything. If that happens you have to follow it and kill however long it takes."

Donald wiped his knife on the ground. He straightened. "I'll come for it later. Shall we go down and eat our pieces now?"

Celia fished alone that morning, up by the falls, high above the water, looking down and seeing the salmon as they struggled again and again to get up the side of the falls, casting out into the far still pools where they would gather their strength. She loved this place. The taste of the air and the sound of the water. Best of all when the children were here. Her mind turned back and she remembered holidays when David had fished here with her, when they had come to this place to reassure themselves about one another. It had been possible before to blot out bad patches. Now so much was bad, could it ever be healed? Did she want it to be healed? She reminded herself how much went with David. *All this,* she thought. *It would be the end of all this. How many of our friends are just his friends? Where would I live? In London? Somewhere near here? Is there enough of me to function on my own or am I the weaker half of Siamese twins and would David take all the vital organs with him?* She stood very still. Gentle rain fell, like a cloud, and a question she had never considered before hammered in her head. *Why have I never challenged him? I have always let him get away with it, terrified and trying not to believe it the first time, always looking the other way after that. Is it because I have so much to lose or has it already gone and will I have to stand up to him now, for Harry's sake?*

The atmosphere in the drawing-room that evening was loud and happy as they assembled for drinks. Everyone seemed to have had a good day. Like an evening in a ski resort, Celia often thought, everyone pleased with themselves or, if not, with a dramatic story to tell. They drank champagne. They looked well. As Celia stood by the fire, David moved across and stood beside her and for a little while they stood in a silence which had an air of truce.

"How was the fishing?" David asked. His eyes were interested. She had forgotten that intense, questioning expression.

"I didn't see many salmon but I had one definite bite, a big one. I lost it after about a minute."

"Long enough to be exciting, though."

"Yes."

"Remember the first year? Your first salmon?" He smiled. "You kept shouting for me to come and look before it got away but it never did."

She felt like smiling too as she remembered but she was too wary. Why was he doing this? He was standing close to her. She could feel his concentration like warmth. When she did smile it was not for now but because she was remembering two people she had known long ago who had loved each other.

"A long time ago," David said, reading her thoughts as he often had when they were close.

They went into the dining-room rather later than usual, at nine, and everyone sat where they happened to be and Harry found himself one place away from his father, with Alice between them as a buffer.

At first David talked entirely to Stella, who was on his right, but later in the meal he turned towards Harry and Alice.

"Was it a good day, Harry?" he asked.

"Very good," Harry said stiffly.

"And did you enjoy yourself, Alice?"

"Yes, I did." Alice sat straight, quite determined to talk and conceal the nervousness David made her feel. "I was surprised how warm you get when you keep moving for so long and I thought the deer looked wonderful against the skyline. It seems terrible to kill them but I suppose it is satisfying to make a good shot and Harry says some of them must be culled."

"Yes. On some estates where they have tourists paying for a day's stalking, they often go for the beasts with magnificent heads so they can have them mounted, but we aim to improve our herd all the time by taking out the switches. Have you tried shooting?"

"No. But I like fishing."

"I hope you catch a salmon before you go. How long are you staying?"

"Another four days, I think."

David nodded. He looked past Alice towards Harry. "And what then, Harry?"

Harry sat back a little. "I have a few ideas."

"Are they confidential or can you discuss them?" David said and although his voice was pleasant Alice shivered slightly.

"I can discuss them if you want." Harry became aware that conversation at the rest of the table was slowing down, that people sensed the tension and were listening. Celia stopped eating and picked up her glass of wine.

"You should think about coming to Australia for a while, Harry," Mike said. "You could work with us in Sydney."

"I did think about it once."

"A year ago," David remarked, "going to Australia was the summit of your ambition."

"That was a year ago. Things have changed."

"So, what are you going to do?"

There was a silence round the table.

"Alice and I are going to start a small business in London."

"What sort of business?" David asked.

"A shop. We will hire out props for photographs. We will specialise in the hire of linens to begin with, for cookery shots. So many photographer's stylists come into the shop Alice works in at the moment and hire old lace bedspreads and shawls and Victorian pillowcases that there is obviously a big demand."

There was total silence until David said, "You're going into the second-hand clothes trade, then?"

"In a way." Harry made himself look at his father.

"Quite a new venture for an Otterwood," Mike said, and if it was meant to be funny, no one laughed.

"Have you got any premises yet?" David asked. "Or will you be operating from a barrow?"

"I am about to sign a contract for a house near Notting Hill, quite close to the Portobello Road. We can use the ground floor and the basement for the business and I shall live above it."

"I see. And will you set up all your girlfriends with little businesses all over London?"

Harry flushed. "I don't give a damn how unpleasant you are about it. You can't stop me."

"It's hardly worth bothering about, is it? I should think it will last six months if you're very lucky. You might like to have a sort through some of the cupboards here. I'm sure you'd find some suitable stock for your venture."

"Stop it, David!" Celia said from the opposite end of the table, her hands clenched.

Mike's wife, who never liked to be out of any conversation for long, said loudly, "Do you mind if I smoke, Celia? The tension is killing me."

Celia pressed the bell. "I don't mind what you do, Stella. Which is probably just as well."

David turned to his German friend who sat beyond Stella and began to discuss the plans for the following day as if nothing had happened, while the plates were removed and lemon mousse and Stilton and celery were brought to the table. Alice took little sideways looks at Harry but he did not respond. Alice looked back at David and she remembered Eliza saying, "He has to win, doesn't he? In everything. The more difficult it is, the more he enjoys it and if by any chance it seems he will lose, he will try to destroy the prize so that at least the other man hasn't won either."

David turned suddenly and met Alice's eyes. "What are you thinking about, Alice, watching me so closely and with such narrowed eyes?"

"I was thinking that all my life I have had a craving to know my real family. I have felt incomplete. I believed that if I found them I should be a part of them all. Tonight you have made me wonder if I am wrong. Perhaps it is better to have no family than a family that is against you."

David laughed. "How dramatic, Alice! Don't take it all so seriously. You will get used to us in time. Everything that I say is for Harry's good. I am not against him. He is tremendously important to me."

Alice dropped her head helplessly. She couldn't say any more. David laughed at her again, almost affectionately and she looked down at her plate and hated him with tears in her eyes.

He has ruined everything now, Celia thought. *Even this place. Harry will go now. Why should he stay? Shall I go too?* Misery paralysed her. She made a few automatic answers and longed for the meal to end.

* * *

Harry did not go at once but the atmosphere between himself and his father poisoned the following days. "Why did I let him goad me into mentioning the shop?" he asked Alice. "I wanted to keep it quiet until it was safe. I'm such a fool!" He seemed more angry with himself than with David, but he sat as far as possible from David at meals, trying to be down his mother's end of the table. He was subdued and he drank so much through the evenings that not long after dinner was ended, Harry would excuse himself and stumble off to bed. Alice knew he was only staying for Celia's sake. The fifth day of their stay they took a picnic up to a loch that was situated, like a lake on the moon, in a high heathery bowl in the hills and they lit a fire to try and defeat the icy mist and fished for trout from a small rowing boat. They were late starting for home and came back in the dark, to find Celia waiting anxiously for them in the hall, her narrow fingers stabbing the needle into her canvas and dragging through the coloured threads. Alice had seen that expression a thousand times on her mother's face but Jane's fears were normally without any real foundation. To be out in the darkness on these cold, damp mountains seemed to be a reasonable cause to worry.

"I didn't mean to worry you," Harry said gently, bending to kiss her.

"I was not afraid of you getting lost out on the hill. I was afraid you might have gone somewhere else entirely."

Harry stood and kicked at a log in the fire, hands deep in his pockets. "I wanted to go after that unpleasantness at dinner the other night but it seemed so childish. Anyway, I love it here and I know you want me to stay. But I can't stand the atmosphere much longer. We might go tomorrow, a couple of days early. I am so eager to get things settled in London and I'm half afraid that now I've told him, he'll try and do something to stop me."

Celia put down her tapestry. "That's what I wanted to tell you. One of the trustees rang this morning shortly after you left, either returning a call of David's or checking things with him. I happened to answer the phone."

Harry sat down on the opposite side of the fire from his mother. Alice was forgotten. "I'll have to go then."

"I doubt if you'll get the car on the train tomorrow."

"Then we'll drive. We'll start early. Don't tell him."

Celia sighed. "It's all so sad, Harry, and so silly. We must make it better."

"We will. Once I have my own thing going, however small, it will be better." He turned his head and gave Celia one of his enchanting smiles. Alice felt like a spy standing so awkwardly and listening. She walked quietly towards the stairs. Beautiful as the castle and its surroundings were it would be such a relief to escape in Harry's car and drive back along those twisting roads towards Inverness and the south.

Harry woke her at five and she dressed quickly and took her suitcase down the massive staircase into the hall which was lit only by the embers of the fire. Somewhere a dog barked half-heartedly. Harry came soon after. On the long refectory table was a basket with flasks and packets of food. Harry went towards the big double doors and unbolted them and, following him, Alice looked round as Celia came down the stairs, like a ghost in bare feet and a long white dressing-gown. She ran across the stone floor and kissed Harry.

"Ring tonight if you can?"

He nodded and then Celia turned to Alice and put her arms round her and kissed her cheek. "I'm glad I've got to know you a little."

Then they went out into a bitter morning with steady rain and hurried into the car. Harry revved it defiantly and accelerated out of the tall gates, scattering gravel. He was silent for a long time and Alice had no words to break into the silence. The dawn began at six thirty and by seven the sky in the east was made of brilliant layers of pink and grey.

"What a fool I was to think I could settle it all just by saying. It's only just begun." She watched him hunch his shoulders up and then drop them down. "What an arse."

"How long will it take, Harry?"

"About twelve hours. But we can always stop somewhere. No one expects you for two more days, do they?"

"No." She yawned. "I could drive some of the way if you like. I'm slow because I don't get much practice but I passed my test two years ago."

Harry smiled. "I bet you passed first go."

"As a matter of fact, I did."

"We'll go straight to Pembridge Gardens. I've got a key. We'll spend tonight there. I've brought some sleeping bags." He took swift glances at Alice. "Don't say you won't do it, Alice. We must. It's like staking a claim. It will be ours. Don't you start telling me things can't happen."

Alice said nothing. They drove all day, stopping twice, and arrived in London at seven. Harry turned off the ignition and leaned forward wearily, head on his hands. "God, I'm tired." He unlocked the front door and they went into the damp darkness of the house, shivering, and found the master switch for the electricity and lit the ancient gas fire in the first-floor bedroom. Since Alice had last been here, Harry had hung a pair of curtains at the tall windows. They were too narrow and so long that they lay in folds on the floor. *Like a child in an adult's clothes*, Alice thought.

Harry brought up the luggage and went out again for hamburgers and chips and a bottle of wine and they sat and ate, wrapped in the sleeping bags with just the light of the gas fire. The only other light in the room, a naked bulb overhead, made them feel they were about to be interrogated and the darkness outside was so much friendlier when the room was dark inside too. There was a little coffee left in one of Celia's flasks.

A white full moon rose, shining through the gap in the curtains. A wide stripe of light. They had hardly spoken since they finished eating.

"She will think it's terrible if I stay here alone with you."

"She need never know." Harry was shivering. "You must stay." He went into the bathroom.

Alice stood in the stripe of moonlight and took off her

clothes. She put on her nightgown and was so cold that she took the silk dressing-gown which Harry had adopted since the train journey to Scotland, and pushed her arms into the sleeves. It smelled of Harry. She tucked her hands into the pockets which were very low down on her and took out a handful of pieces of paper, thinking they were Harry's. But they were old bills of her father's, tucked into his pockets to be forgotten or hidden from Jane. Memory flared suddenly, bringing tears to her eyes; he had worn this dressing-gown so much, especially at the weekends, sometimes infuriating Jane by keeping it on all afternoon as he sat and watched the racing on television; if he won he would dress in a suit and a tie and take them all out for supper; she remembered his untidiness, her mother constantly running after him, sweeping after him, and he would guiltily tuck into his pockets the pieces of paper that seemed to appear all around him. She looked down and tears blurred the bills in her hands. Eight-year-old bills. A wine shop. A garage. A letter in his handwriting with a cheque for fifty pounds made out to R. Vesey that had never been sent.

"What are those?" Harry said, coming across to her. "Why are you crying?"

"I was remembering. In the pockets I found some of my father's things." She put them back. "You'll keep this, won't you, Harry? I like to see you in it."

"I like to see you in it," Harry said, putting his arms round her, rocking her.

"There's so much of his stuff. She never gave anything away. It's all neatly packed in trunks and boxes as if, one day, he will come back."

Harry sang softly, "So up she went to her grandfather's chest and bought him a coat of the very, very best . . . " until she smiled.

Harry decided to zip the two sleeping bags into one and he struggled in the narrow patch of moonlight and the zips got stuck on the material. Alice sat cross-legged and watched him get angry and tried to help and in the end they had made one big soft bag to sleep in.

They lay and faced each other.

"How can anything that makes us so happy possibly be wrong?" Harry said seriously and the stripe of moonlight ran across his head and down his bare shoulder.

We're going to make love, Alice thought. *It's so simple. Harry's right. All the fuss and the rules are irrelevant.* The stripe of moonlight fell across them both like a wide ribbon and she remembered Jane telling her long ago that it was lucky to lie in moonlight. That it made you beautiful.

"Anyway," Harry said as they moved towards one another, "we'll probably get married in the end. I can't imagine feeling like this about anyone else. I can't bear the thought of being without you. We'll live here and run the shop and get married and none of them will be able to touch us. We need never see anyone we don't want to see." His hands began to move over her body.

"Harry, I don't want to get pregnant."

"Do you take me for a complete fool?" he said gently.

"You've got something to use?"

"Lots of things!"

"I'm telling you because I believe I was conceived by two people who loved each other but never thought about having a baby and when they realised about me they were horrified and panicked and my birth must have been just a nuisance. A terrible nuisance. Perhaps my mother wanted an abortion and couldn't get one. I shall never have a child that isn't deliberate."

He remembered her voice in the garden on the first hot afternoon, the seriousness of her face. He tried to understand her feelings but he was so impatient for her.

"It won't happen. I promise you. Anyway, I love you. I would love your child." His face grew blurred as it came close to hers and even as she let herself slide into the joy of kissing him, the exquisite pleasure of his hands on her body, Alice was aware of a new fear. Was Harry to be everything to her? Was she to move from Jane's protective love into his overwhelming need with no space in between for herself at all? Then her body surprised her, responding, moving with Harry as if she had known all along how it would be. She was swept up onto a plateau of sensation from which she slid down again and again to register intense surprise only to be drawn back up. She was aware of Harry's exultant laughter.

The night was a series of little nights and days and sometimes she was awake and thinking very clearly and sometimes drawn out of sleep by Harry's mouth and hands. When she woke properly it was only just light. Harry was sleeping deeply. *I have a lover.* She moved gently up onto one elbow and looked down at him and the extraordinary words rolled over and over in her brain. *Harry and I are lovers.*

Chapter 13

Throughout October, Eliza saw very little of Robert and when she did see him there were always other people present and the meetings gave her no satisfaction. At the end of the month he left England to be away, he told her on the phone, for about three weeks. "I'll ring you about once a week in case there are any messages," he said.

"I'll look forward to that," Eliza said dryly but her indifference was quite false. He came into her mind constantly. The thought of him disrupted the satisfying order of her life. She felt disturbed. Eliza had always been a planner. From early childhood she had considered and arranged her life and the people in it, even if her impatience and fierce temper caused her to ignore her plans later, but this preoccupation with Robert and trying to decide whether to go and work for him or not obsessed her. She weighed the idea of seeing much more of him, of demonstrating her considerable ability to him, against the risk of disaster. Her job with Otterwoods held great potential. Was it asking too much to expect Robert to provide both work and love? Because love was what she wanted from him. His company was so new and so risky and it was only the confidence he projected that gave her any hope for his success. One day she would decide definitely that she would not leave Otterwoods and the next, thinking of the opportunity of seeing Robert all the time that he was in England, of using her efficiency to the hilt and being in a position of power, would change her mind completely.

A week after David returned from Scotland he told Eliza that his secretary had recovered and would be coming back at the beginning of December. "But it's obvious that you are extremely capable, Eliza, and rather wasted in personnel. Stephen McNeil needs a P.A. There would be a lot of travelling and an increase in salary. I'd like you to think it over for a couple of weeks."

"Would there be an eventual chance of doing his job?" Eliza asked quietly, heart beating too hard.

David looked up, surprise in his face for a moment. "His job? There's always a chance. It would depend on you, I suppose. You are ambitious, aren't you, Eliza?"

"Yes, I am." Eliza took a deep breath. "There are always rumours among the female staff that you won't tolerate women above a certain level in any of your companies."

David sat back. His eyes were wide and innocent, his expression amused.

"That's absurd. That would be blatant discrimination. In Otterwoods everything is decided on ability. Perhaps you could intimate that when the discussion next comes up."

Eliza coloured slightly. "I enjoy working for Otterwoods. It has so many different aspects. I would love the travelling and I'm confident I can do the job, given time to settle in. But I don't want to find myself in a dead end, however well paid and stimulating." She took a deep breath. "I have been offered another job with a very small company which I think I could virtually run."

"Have you? Well, I can't make up your mind for you but we would be very sorry to lose you and I suggest you think very hard before leaving us. I won't rush you but perhaps you could give me your decision by the end of the month." He handled the large leather-bound volume of Kipling poems he kept on his desk as he often did when he was thinking. "I hope you decide to stay with us, Eliza."

Think very hard. Eliza lay stiffly in bed that night. She had been to a play with married friends and a man who had been carefully selected for her. He might as well have been made of cardboard for all the interest Eliza felt. She had struggled to talk enough to be polite but the evening had dragged agonisingly when they went on to eat afterwards and in her boredom she had drunk far too much wine. Her head pounded. *Think very hard*. She got out of bed and went into the bathroom to take some soluble aspirin, dropping the pills into a glass of water and watching them fizz and frowning at her reflection. Eliza hated her own face without the disguise of make-up to colour and change it, hated the hard dark eyes. Snake eyes. White skin. Why couldn't she have taken the good bits from her parents? As people had remarked endlessly when they were younger, Alice was more like Gerald Marland than Eliza had been. "But they try and match up the looks, don't they?" was another remark often repeated. And occasionally Eliza had overheard, "Does it worry Elizabeth that Alice, who is adopted, should be so pretty?" Many things had bothered Eliza, who had been an intense and passionate child, as wild as a hawk, her father had often said, but she had never felt jealous of Alice. Rather she felt proud. Possessive pride. Everyone wanted Alice's love. *Think very hard before leaving us.* She drank the water with all its little white gritty bits and went back to bed. *I wish I could stop thinking so hard.* She made a determined effort and put the problem out of her mind to make way for sleep but she knew that, in the morning, it would be waiting for her as surely as daylight.

Alice telephoned Eliza frequently throughout November, eager to confide the changes in her life that she could not tell Jane. She came and spent a night at the flat. Alice was different. She was more definite. The round eyes were alert and sparkling and far less dreamy and she looked so pretty that Eliza wondered if she and Harry were lovers but thought it crude to ask. Alice would tell her in time, she was sure. Alice told her everything else.

"Harry has signed the contract. He says the trustees will have to pay now he's signed it. The completion day is mid-December. The builder's estimates have come and they could start as soon as we complete. Because the owners are friends or relations or something, they say we can start storing things there if we want to. Harry is so optimistic about it all, Eliza. He expects so much. But at the beginning it will be very slow and very small."

"Tell him all that, Alice, not me."

"I try. He just laughs. He says that anything which comes between him and Otterwoods is bound to be a success. He's so happy that after a while I give up. As I do when I try and tell Mum about it. I've started a dozen times. She knows I am looking for another job but that's all."

"Just come straight out with it."

"I'll have to. On Saturday we're going to spend the day buying stock. I have made enormous lists. We'll probably be in London. Can we come and see you later on?"

"Yes. Come and have supper." Eliza welcomed the thought of a diversion at the weekend. Everywhere she looked now, the first signs of Christmas threatened and, despite what Robert had said, he had telephoned only once since he had been away. She had not spoken to him since David had offered her the new job and she was anxious to discuss Robert's offer in detail before she answered David.

As the days passed Eliza's impatience steadily increased and when, one Monday in late November, Michael Copper wanted to get in touch with Robert quite urgently, having tried for two days without success, Eliza rang the Nigerian number, glad of an excuse. She got through on the third attempt. A deep, educated woman's voice answered. Something in the woman's confident manner worried Eliza and made her realise just how little she knew about Robert's life.

"Robert? Actually, he's on his way back to London," Eliza was told. "He should arrive in a few hours."

This information changed Eliza's day suddenly and completely. At lunchtime she bought a silver shirt that glistened and shimmered when she moved; she was back in the office by two in this, her last week with David Otterwood, the week she must give him her decision, working fast so that she should finish by five-thirty. Robert rang at three.

"I'm in London. I'm bloody tired but I have to have dinner with a South African tonight because he goes home tomorrow and he particularly wants to see me. His wife is over too. I'd be very pleased if you would come. I'd love to see you and if he wants to talk business, perhaps you could divert his wife."

"Thank you," Eliza said dryly, wondering if she would ever have an invitation from Robert that didn't have strings, thinking of the film she had promised to go and see with her only genuine girlfriend, who had just become disentangled from the man she had hoped to marry. Much as she longed to see Robert, she badly wanted the strength to refuse such an invitation and to demonstrate her loyalty to Kate.

"Thank you yes or thank you no?"

"Thank you yes."

Robert yawned. "I'm going to sleep for four hours. Ring me at seven, will you, and I'll pick you up at eight."

"Sleep well," Eliza said, abandoning Kate with the thought that, in the same position, Kate would probably have done the same to her.

It was exactly eight when Robert stepped into her flat. She moved towards him and he smiled admiringly at the silver shirt as he kissed her. He had hardly thought about her in the past few weeks. "Wonderful, like something out of a pantomime." He went on kissing her. He was still tired and it felt good to kiss her. "Eliza," he said softly and drew back. "What a pity we have to go out."

Eliza made a prim face. "Not at all. I'm hungry. I forgot to have lunch when I heard you were coming back."

He frowned. "How did you hear?"

"God!" Eliza blushed, ashamed of her uncharacteristic forgetfulness. "I'm sorry. I should have told you earlier but your gracious invitation confused me and then I completely forgot. Michael Copper wanted to speak to you as soon as possible so I rang the Nigerian number and a sophisticated female voice told me you were on your way back to England." Eliza watched him closely. "Who was she?"

"Probably Sophia M'habela. A very old friend. Can I ring Michael now?" He was already lifting up the receiver and after a few moments, he spoke into an answerphone.

"Would you like a drink?" Eliza asked when he had finished.

"We'd better go. I said we'd pick them up at their hotel around eight."

Bernard and Mira Van Ryn were in their forties. It was obvious that Robert had not met either of them before. They had been in London for eight days and, as it was Mira's first visit to London, she and Eliza discussed the shops and museums she still wanted to visit. Bernard had booked a table at Wheeler's and as they ate the exotically cooked fish, Eliza sensed a certain wariness between Robert and Bernard and she wondered why this meeting mattered. Bernard was nothing to do with shipping. He owned a large South African property company and it was almost as if he and Robert spoke in code to one another.

"How is business, Robert?"

"It's going well enough. I've bought a small tanker and we're carrying crude oil from Venezuela to Nigeria and taking light Nigerian oil back again. The small tanker can get in and out of Venezuela easily. It's going well." Robert lit a small cigar. "Of course, I hope this is just the beginning."

"Of course. You've got some good contacts in Nigeria, I suppose?"

"Yes."

"Particularly Michael M'habela. Since he became a minister last year he has become a very powerful man." Bernard paused. "Michael and I have known each other for a long time."

"I couldn't have run the Lagos deal without him. Taking the cement cargoes off in many small consignments made the bills of lading complicated."

"What is a bill of lading?" Mira asked.

"It's a vital document which the master of any ship must see before he will part with his cargo. He holds the document of title to cargo and the bill of lading has to match. Michael issued me dozens of bills of lading for

Cement Nigeria, a company he runs, and we got round the problem."

Bernard nodded his balding head. He, too, lit a cigar. "Will you continue in Lagos?"

"The cement business is almost finished. It's a very small operation and so many other people are in on the act it's not so worthwhile."

"You had some trouble with the competitors, I understand?"

"Just one unfortunate incident. My engineer objected to being threatened. It was smoothed over."

"Because of your friendship with Michael M'habela?"

"It helped. You have taken quite a lot of trouble to find out about me."

Bernard nodded. "A little. One more question. Now that you have begun to carry oil, will you expand that side of your company at all?"

Robert lifted his head sharply. Suddenly he understood why this man had taken the trouble to seek him out. He sensed M'habela's hand in this somewhere. There was a long pause in which both Eliza and Mira looked expectantly at Robert. "Certainly. If things are favourable."

"Perhaps we could talk some more one day. It's always interesting to meet a man with a small, flexible company and good friends."

Robert nodded. "It's always interesting to meet a man with a good idea."

For the rest of the evening they discussed London and the price of air fares and dabbled round South African politics. The two men drank a lot of Armagnac and it was after one when they dropped the South Africans back at their hotel.

"I wonder what that was all about," Robert said, as he stopped his car outside Eliza's flat. "Wait and see, I suppose."

"What are you talking about?"

"I don't really know."

"Robert, I want to talk to you. I have to decide

whether to stay on at Otterwoods or not. They've offered me a new job."

Robert yawned enormously. "Can we go in? If I sit here much longer I'll fall asleep."

It was warm in Eliza's flat. She made some coffee while Robert plunged onto her sofa, lying with his legs extended straight out in front of him, eyes closed. He tugged irritably at his tie.

"Do you really want me to come and work for you?" Eliza said softly, looking down at him.

He half opened his eyes. "Yes. As soon as possible. We can take possession of the offices on the fifteenth of December. How much notice do you have to give?"

"A month. But I haven't decided yet."

He folded his arms behind his head. "When I suggested it before it was rather unreasonable as the business didn't exist. Now it's quite different. Venezuela is steady trade. And there is something else in the wind which is really interesting. That will happen early next year if at all. And if that doesn't happen, there will be other opportunities." He sat up suddenly and reached out and put his arms round Eliza's waist, drawing her down onto the sofa. "If you don't want the job you must tell me now and I'll start looking for someone else. Yes or no?" His fingers traced the straight lines of her collar bones inside the silver shirt. "Such white skin," he said, almost to himself. "Yes or no, Eliza?"

A longing to make love to him invaded every part of her, every bone and muscle, every particle of skin was hungry. *So this is how it feels,* Eliza thought. *To want someone, adult to adult and no games. Body craving body. No choice any more.* As she thought the words she was moving her face down, closer to his, so that when she finally said, "Yes" her mouth was almost touching his.

Robert was smiling as they drew apart. "I'm very glad that's settled. You can give in your notice tomorrow so there will be no turning back." He kissed her lips again briefly and he felt a small but sweet satisfaction that, in this at least, he had taken something that David Otterwood wanted. Eliza sat and looked up at him, dark eyes narrow.

"I would love to stay, Eliza, but I haven't slept for twenty-four hours. I got involved in a party in Lagos that got out of hand and I virtually crawled onto the plane, only to find myself sitting next to a chap who is setting up his own insurance company. We talked for hours. Sleep is what I need and if I stay here I won't sleep." He crossed the room, turning at the door and blowing her a kiss.

"Nobody asked you to stay," Eliza said softly but she had the satisfaction of hearing Robert's laughter as he closed the door.

When he was back in his hotel, Robert sat on the bed and lifted the telephone and every trace of exhaustion had left him. He dialled Bernard Van Ryn's hotel.

"It's Robert. I hope you weren't asleep."

"Not yet."

"I think we may have more to discuss."

"Yes. Michael intimated you could be in a very key position."

"When could we meet again?"

"Our flight is not until six, tomorrow. Could we have lunch somewhere quiet?"

"Yes. There's a little Italian restaurant across from your hotel. I'll be there at twelve thirty."

"It might be a little too public. Mira will be doing last-minute shopping. Why not come to this hotel and we'll have a sandwich in my room?"

"Fine."

"By the way, Robert, how much a barrel would you pay for Nigerian oil?"

"Twenty-nine dollars."

"In South Africa we buy for thirty-three plus the cost of shipping."

December sunlight streamed in the tall hotel windows as Bernard and Robert sat each side of a small table, drinking beer. Open suitcases lay on the bed in the adjoining room.

"I presume I have Michael to thank for this idea."

"Yes. If we are able to do business, Michael will profit from the introduction."

Robert nodded.

"As you know, we are extremely eager to buy oil. Life is made difficult for us by sanctions and the attitude of most of the oil-producing nations. I was bemoaning this fact to Michael when your name came up in the conversation. Can I speak openly?"

"Of course."

"If you were to ship oil from Nigeria on a regular basis in a tanker of at least a hundred thousand tons we would, as I said last night, be prepared to pay four dollars over your purchase price plus the cost of the shipping."

"And the bill of lading?"

"Officially you are sailing for Singapore. You leave the port of Lagos and sail towards Singapore and once out of Nigerian waters you paint out the name of your ship and the funnel is painted black and you sail for Durban."

"Let me have a turn. One and a half miles off Durban we pick up a pipe at a single buoy mooring in deep water and discharge our oil. That takes twenty-four hours, during which time we keep radio silence. The harbour master at Durban has no record of us. We are invisible."

Bernard smiled. "Exactly."

"It takes twenty-three days to sail to Singapore, unload and sail back to Lagos. It takes eleven days to sail to Durban, unload and return to Lagos. We have a lot of time to fill in."

"That's your affair. Just make it look good. Keep out of sight. Arrive in Lagos at a suitable time and you are ready to make another voyage the following month. At the end of a year, Robert, you would be a very rich man."

Robert pushed back his chair and took a packet of small cigars from his pocket. He offered one to Bernard who shook his head.

"Obviously I need time to think about it. It is very risky. If anyone in Nigeria found out I was trading with you, there would be real trouble. The sort of trouble even Michael couldn't handle."

"Obviously."

"So the farther away I keep from South Africa the better."

"Yes. In a month I will get in touch again. Shall we have some coffee sent up? How about an Armagnac?"

"Why not?" Robert said. "Yes, in a month my office will be established here. Everything will be easier then."

Shortly after the coffee and Armagnac was delivered to the room, the door opened again and Mira Van Ryn came in, arms full of carrier bags. The two men stood up and raised their glasses to one another in a silent toast.

Chapter 14

Jane Marland parked her car in the street opposite Paddy's shop and looked across at the big brightly-lit window behind which she could see a coloured blur of people. She lit a cigarette, settling down slightly into the seat. She had known something was coming. Alice was bad at secrets. She had known there was something for weeks before Alice told her about Scotland and for the past few weeks it had been the same. She had watched Alice circling, trying to find the right time. She was sorry. She hated to see Alice worried but she could not help. Whatever Eliza said, however happy Alice seemed, Jane did not want Harry for her. She and Alice were all right as they were. In the end Alice would obviously find someone but not yet. Too soon. And not Harry. Jane knew all about extroverts, all about charm, that extraordinary gift which opened the world so effortlessly to the possessor of it but which, in return, required that the possessor should not belong to any one other human being. She knew about presents, spread like ointment over a wound, about drinking, about the kind of face and smile which drew an automatic response from the whole world. She had recognised all this in Harry from the beginning. Not for Alice. So unfair. She knew that Harry and everything that went with him would damage Alice and so she watched Alice floundering and waited, believing, as she always had done, that, if things were not actually put into words, they might just go away. And eventually, three days ago, Alice had told her in the darkness, waiting for sleep, had told her everything. About the shop in London, about Paddy closing down on the twelfth. "There is going to be a small farewell party. He wants you to come," Alice had ended, desperately. "Please try and understand how happy I am. Please come to the party."

Well, I've come, Jane thought, stubbing out the cigarette and opening the car door. *And I don't know why. Perhaps it can be different this time, if I try hard, if I don't just stand and watch, helplessly.* Or was it to escape for a few hours the tidy silence of the house without Alice. Without anyone. She crossed the street and stepped into the shop and Paddy saw her at once and came, smilingly, to draw her in. He put a glass in her hand and filled it from the flowered china jug he carried. He introduced her to his neighbour who ran a bookshop but after the initial effort, Jane spoke very little. She seemed to be always on her own although Paddy brought a steady stream of people to meet her.

"For God's sake drink faster, Jane. You're a constant worry to me."

"I don't know why I came. I hate parties. I always did. You can't talk naturally even to people you know well. Alice seems quite unreal. So do you. Harry is coming, I suppose? He's very late."

Paddy sighed. "Well, I'm glad you came even if you hate it. When Alice is working in London you'll have to get out more." Then a look of horror flickered over his face. "My God, she has told you? I haven't blundered, have I?"

Jane smiled at his expression. "She's told me."

He put a hand on her arm. "You must try to see more people."

"Why? I have more than enough to do at home with the garden and the cooking. I'm going to paint some of the bedrooms. Why should I get out more? What is worth seeing and doing?"

Paddy shrugged and kept her glass full. He wondered, as he had so often in the past, what kind of man Gerald Marland had been, what kind of woman Jane had been before she turned in on herself? Had their lives together been so perfect that his loss had crippled her or had the marriage caused her to withdraw long before his death?

"You might as well live in the world while you can. You're a long time dead, as they say."

Jane drank deeply from the wine cup which was heavily reinforced with Pimm's. She seldom drank more than a couple of glasses of wine and this harmless fruity liquid began to attack her before she realised what was happening. She looked at Paddy's concerned and friendly face and spoke her thoughts aloud.

"It's because she's adopted, I suppose, that it's worse. I think if she once moves away, why should she come home?"

"You are the only mother she knows. Of course she'll come home."

"Eliza doesn't."

"Who's fault is that?"

Jane leaned towards him and spoke very quietly, as if confiding a secret. "Alice and I are so happy together, Paddy. It's always been like that, ever since she came. She was lovely. A smiling baby, enchanting me against my will. She was perfect. Despite everything, I couldn't help loving her. Such a pretty little girl. Very small. Full of original sayings and affection while Eliza would glower at me, challenging me, scrape at my feelings with that brutal honesty she has, always wanting to change things. At times the irony of the situation would overwhelm me."

"I don't understand. Despite what? Why shouldn't you have loved Alice?"

Jane flushed. "I had Eliza."

"But presumably you chose to adopt a second child? She wasn't thrust upon you? Or are you saying that you felt guilty because you loved your adopted child more than a child of your own flesh and blood?"

"It's not so simple, Paddy. Life is not like a play."

"Surely you could care for both of them? There is nothing in the rules to say you can love only one person."

"Only one person ever loved me," Jane said simply

and she drank again. She sat down and put her hand on Paddy's arm in a confiding way.

"Harry is so shallow. He has been brought up in a series of castles, not just one. Castles of privilege. He has always been liked. People like that, who give themselves to everyone, aren't capable of a deep relationship." She laughed, spitefully. "If you frown at him, he's lost. He panics. No wonder he can't stand up to his father. He doesn't understand about money. He doesn't understand anything." As she was speaking, someone backed into a tall china vase which rocked sedately and spilled its top-heavy arrangement of peacock feathers on the floor around Jane's feet. She shuddered as she felt the lightness of the feathers and she stood up sharply. "They are so unlucky. I hate peacock feathers. I've told Alice. Paddy, I should go. I promised to call in on Molly on my way back. Tell Alice I've gone, will you?"

Paddy held her arm for a moment. "It hurts Alice to see you unhappy. How about repaying some of the good times she has given you? Don't make her choose. Stay for a bit. Have something to eat. The food is wonderful. I did it all myself."

Jane shrugged but the moment Paddy's attention was claimed elsewhere she put down her glass and took up her coat and went very quietly out of the shop door into an icy night, thinking she had talked far too much.

Alice waited anxiously for Harry as the party unravelled and by ten, when she finally saw his figure in the doorway, people were sitting and eating with plates on their laps and the noise was a steady roar. Alice crossed the room to meet Harry and she knew at once from his expression that he was drunk. Very drunk. More than she had ever seen him. He stood still, swaying a little, and she took his arm and led him unsteadily to the stairs where she had been sitting and went to get him some food.

"And a drink," he called after her and sat, frowning, rubbing his forehead gently with one hand.

Alice came back but he didn't eat the food she had brought him.

"What's happened?"

"A lot. You know we were due to exchange contracts today and pay. They rang this morning to say they had decided it was an unsound investment, that I should not have gone ahead without getting their clearance, that I must withdraw." He drank the glass of wine in one mouthful. "Where were you when I rang?"

"I have been out a lot, buying food and getting glasses and I wanted to give Paddy a present. He never said you'd rung."

"I never got through. There was no answer." He sat upright. "Anyway, I've fixed it. I have some money which my godfather left me. It's in shares. I used to have the income to spend. I've sold them. I was ten thousand pounds short. I've borrowed some of it at an appalling rate of interest and I've sold my guns. My grandfather left them to me. They were Holland and Hollands. I got six thousand pounds for the pair. And to hell with the bloody trust!" He turned to Alice and held both her arms, his fingers digging into her flesh. "It's ours now, Alice. The builders start on Monday and it's ours!"

That Saturday, because Paddy wanted to move out of his shop the following week, Harry borrowed a horse lorry and they transported all of the contents of the shop in big plastic bags to London and stacked them in the biggest room which was to be painted last.

"The builders said it will take five or six weeks to treat the damp, install a new bathroom, improve the kitchen and paint the house," Harry said as they drove. "I talked to my mother for a long time this morning. They are selling one of the farm cottages. There is an almost new bed we can have and a few other pieces of furniture and we went up into the attic at Flood Street, and found some more curtains and a big, brightly coloured Spanish rug. She suggested that if the floorboards in the big room are in reasonable shape we could hire a sander and then polish them. She wanted to lend me some money but I won't let her. I want to do this entirely on my own."

Eliza rang and came to tea with two pottery-based lamps which she had bought and never liked and a small armchair. She spent a little time in the small paved garden with Alice, trying to imagine how it would look when the bare branches of the plane tree, which now stretched in a lattice pattern against the grey afternoon sky, were in leaf, and deciding what could be planted in the bare patches of earth. She crouched down and poked about with a stick. "I think this is a rose. I'd love to have a garden."

"I never thought I'd hear you say that," Alice teased her. "You hated the garden at home. You never would help." She laughed. "Are you getting broody?"

"Don't be ridiculous," Eliza snapped, annoyed that Alice should so plainly see the change in her. She shivered as a very cold wind disturbed some of the dead leaves. "I think it's going to snow," she said, more gently.

"Let's go out and eat," Harry said, when Eliza had gone, warming his hands by the gas fire. "And talk about when we can open for business and shall we have an opening party and what to put on the invitations or announcements."

"Will it be done by February the twenty-first?"

"They say so. Why?"

"It's my birthday. I shall be twenty."

"In that case, we'll get it done. You have a list of people to send the invitations to?"

"Yes. But it needs to be more a brochure, setting out what we do, than an invitation."

"Perhaps we should print both." Harry slammed the front door behind them.

"Or just have the brochures printed on a big card, on both sides, and leave a white space and write in that about the party."

"Okay." He tucked his arm through hers and they hurried towards a small bistro they had noticed in the past. A light flurry of snow came down and Alice shivered in her woollen shawl. Harry put his arm round her. "Why do you never wear your coat?"

"Because I borrowed it from Eliza."

"You must have a coat."

"No. At school I had a mac. I've got a short jacket but no coat."

"I'll buy you one for Christmas."

"I think my mother is giving me one," Alice said quickly.

"I thought you said, before, that she was short of money."

"Well that's a constant thing. She is always short of money. She spends too much on our guests. She gives them such good food and she hates cheap soap and thin towels. There is never enough money, Harry." She looked up at his face as they waited to cross the road. "Can you imagine what it is like to have nothing to fall back on? If we get into debt there is no one who will help us."

"What about your father? When he was alive was it different?"

"Not really. He earned quite a lot but he spent far more. He loved good things. He was always changing his cars, trying to get something better but they were never new; he bought a lot of presents but my mother hated them because she said they were bought with credit cards and he could never pay off the whole amount."

"How ungrateful! How awful for him to have his presents constantly frowned on."

"I suppose it was, but nothing depressed him for long. He and Eliza were so alike, full of enthusiasm and energy. Sometimes, watching them together, I felt sad that I was not like them, had nothing of them in me. They were wild, really. They laughed about everything. They would get furious and then, in a few moments, it was forgotten. He hated work. He dived from job to job. My mother started taking in the PGs a couple of years before he died. He liked most of them and they loved him. He played cards with them in the evenings. When he died, Eliza didn't cry. It was as if she was paralysed by her feelings. When he died there were terrible debts. It's not going to be like that with Pembridge Gardens is it, Harry? And what did they say about selling the guns?"

Harry laughed. "For once in my life I really made him sit up and take notice. He is furious. My mother said he went on a lot about family tradition and inheritance. I expect he'll buy them back. I don't feel guilty. They were mine. I was quite entitled to sell them. I'm just sorry because they were such lovely guns to shoot with; I was asked up to Yorkshire this weekend to go shooting. It would have been fun." He shrugged.

They walked round the corner in silence, but as they approached the door of the small restaurant in the next street, Harry stopped her suddenly. "I've just thought, if you know when your birthday is, there must be a birth certificate and that must have the name of your real parents on it."

Alice shook her head. "If there is one I've never seen it. I only know it's my birthday because it's always been celebrated on the twenty-first of February."

They sat at one end of a long table and chose from a blackboard what they would eat.

"I can't believe that Paddy's shop is really closed," Alice said. "It's Monday tomorrow and for the first time in nearly fours years I don't have to go in. But no work means no money. I thought I might try and get a temporary job in Brighton just until Christmas."

"Don't do that. There is so much to do in London. The builders start on Monday and they have to be supervised. We've got to buy more furniture and things for the kitchen and Christmas presents." Harry filled their wine glasses. "I don't know what to do about Christmas. I really can't face going home."

"Well, come and stay with us then? It's always just my aunt and my mother and Eliza and me. It's the same every year."

"Your mother would hate me to come."

"She hates Eliza to come, so it won't make much difference. Perhaps you would cancel each other out?"

The door opened bringing with it a gust of cold air and a small crowd of people who bore down on Harry, exclaiming his name loudly. They squashed onto the long table and Alice was introduced to them all. She sighed quietly and made herself narrow. Harry seemed to have hundreds of friends. He changed in their company. More wine was ordered. News was loudly exchanged. And Alice sat quietly in the middle of it all and wished they had gone somewhere else. In the end they all came back and looked at the house, tramping from floor to floor, and Alice made coffee in ten paper cups and someone had brought brandy and beer. It was after one when they left.

"It's so late," Harry said, "And it will take hours to get back in the lorry. Shall we stay? We can spend tomorrow getting organised here. We'll go out for breakfast. Did you say you'd be back? Ring and tell her I've drunk too much to drive."

She weighed the thought of being with Harry here, of making love to him and waking with him tomorrow in this house which was becoming more familiar, against the thought of Jane. "I said I'd be back. How did it get so late? I didn't think about the lorry."

"Ring her."

"She will know I am staying with you."

"Tell her you're at Eliza's flat."

"Lie to her, you mean?"

"Well, if it makes her happier, does it matter?"

"I never know about that, about white lies. Sometimes they're worse."

"Do we have to have a discussion about moral values now," Harry said, smiling, "just before we make love? Could we discuss it in the morning?" He stood behind her, rubbing his face gently against the side of her head, his arms round her so that, for the moment, she could not move.

Jane answered the phone so quickly that Alice knew

she had not been asleep. She pictured her mother, sitting up in bed, hand ready to pounce on the phone.

"We met some of Harry's friends and everything went on rather and now I think I'll stay with Eliza and do some work on the house in the morning and come down tomorrow afternoon."

"I see." Jane said dully. "Good night."

"See," Harry whispered, "how easy it is?" He turned off the lights. There was still a gap between the curtains but tonight there was no moon.

Chapter 15

Otterwoods' annual Christmas party was held on December the eighteenth. David stood in the centre of the huge hall with a glass of whisky in his hand and watched them come in, the management and their wives, the personnel officers, visiting employees from foreign branches, established secretaries and office juniors; messengers and drivers and acquaintances. There was an abundance of drink and cold food on a buffet and the party, he knew, would go on and on and on. Some people would get very drunk and cringe for weeks afterwards when they remembered what they had said or done. Babies were conceived after Otterwoods parties and rocky marriages finally dislodged. David looked round, a frowning lion of a man, and those who would have approached him hesitated because he seemed so preoccupied. He drank deeply from his glass, experiencing a weariness which surprised him. David very seldom thought about how he felt. There was always some Otterwood problem to absorb him, or something more personal, and if he did find himself bored on a long flight or train journey he would test his memory by reciting from the many Kipling poems he knew by heart and then checking in the Kipling books he carried everywhere, like so many Bibles. He drank some more whisky and he stood with his back to the immense Christmas tree and knew that, although he still felt excitement and pride in it all, Harry's absence saddened and angered him. He realised with surprise that Harry's defection and Celia's lack of support had hurt him more than any other event in his adult life, since the death of his baby son.

It was Eliza's last week with Otterwoods. She had changed in one of the comfortable ladies' cloakrooms into a red and silver dress which fitted her slender body like a skin and attracted considerable attention as she came down the wide stairs into the hall and the roar of voices, thinking how strange it would be not to attend this party next year. She paused on the bottom stair and was surprised to see Celia's tall figure. Celia had not come to one of these Christmas parties since Eliza had been with Otterwoods. Eliza saw the flushed faces of the juniors who had drunk too much already and the group of serious drinkers strategically placed by the long white-clothed tables which served as bars. For one panicky moment she thought of telling David she had changed her mind, that she wanted to stay with all this, but almost at once the feeling was countered by the thought of Robert. He was coming here later to meet her. Merely thinking his name filled her with exhilaration. Although she did not show it outwardly, her emotions were extreme at the moment, swinging wildly from joy to apprehension. Stoner Shipping would officially open its London office on January the fourth. The rooms were being decorated and Robert had found some second-hand office furniture and filing cabinets. He had bought two new typewriters and had told Eliza he intended to hire another girl who would work for her.

"I'll come on to Bishopsgate and get you when I finish talking to the electricians," he had told her on the telephone earlier that day. "We'll have dinner somewhere. From what I remember of previous Christmas parties, you'll be fairly drunk by then and it would be too flat to go home alone."

"What makes you think I'd go home alone?"

"You're a difficult girl to ask out, Eliza."

"Perhaps you don't try often enough!"

He laughed. "Do you want to see me or not?"

"Of course I'd like to see you later." Each time he suggested a meeting she was reassured that it was not only that she was useful. "But it's so far to the City. I could meet you somewhere."

"No. I want to come. I'd like to have a nose round an

Otterwood party again." Eliza had pulled a wry face, thinking she should have realised.

As Eliza stepped into the throng and made her way towards the bar for a drink, she paused close to Celia, who was standing with her two daughters. Celia smiled at her and introduced Julia and Josephine.

"I understand you're leaving, Eliza?"

"Yes. In four days' time."

"David is sorry you are going."

"I'm flattered, but much as I've enjoyed working for Otterwoods I think I will have more opportunities in the small company I am going to."

"Because of my father's attitude to women in the company?" Julia asked.

"That's part of it, I suppose."

"Are you going to another shipping company?" Julia wanted to get all the facts for her case.

"Yes. Stoner Shipping."

Celia looked surprised. "So Robert has got as far as setting up an office?"

"Yes."

"Is he here?" Celia asked casually.

"He's coming later." Eliza met the older woman's eyes. "To fetch me."

Celia smiled but her speckled eyes were wary. "Well, if I don't see him, wish him good luck for me. I hope you have great success. But not so much success that you have to have parties like this. I haven't been to one for eight years and now I remember why."

Robert came at eight thirty. Some people had left and most of the food had been eaten. But the hard core were settling in to make a night of it; the waiters circulated more slowly but the roar of voices and laughter was daunting. He came into the warmth and took off his overcoat, exchanging it for a small white ticket, and he pushed his fingers through his hair, to smooth it, and stood for a few moments, looking into the mass of people. He saw Michael Copper, who raised a hand in greeting, and David; he saw Celia and approached her before she saw him so that when he touched her arm she turned and was unable to hide the smile of pleasure, the instinctive slight movement towards him as if they might have kissed. In a second she had remembered and rocked back again. She had expected to feel embarrassment if she saw him, certainly awkwardness. Not this exhilaration which she was afraid might show.

"How nice to see you, Robert. Do you know Charles and Prue Baker? Charles is our financial director."

Robert nodded but surprisingly he didn't want to make the effort to talk to them. He wanted to look at Celia.

"You haven't got a drink, Robert." She attracted the attention of a waiter and Robert took a whisky.

"I haven't really been invited."

"But you've come to fetch Eliza. She told me. I understand she will be working for you. She seems very pleased about it all. I'm sure she'll be marvellous. David is sorry to lose her."

Robert nodded.

"How did you manage to lure her away? David pays his people very well. I'm surprised if you out-bid Otterwoods," Celia said, longing to hear that Eliza's move was purely for money.

"I didn't try. She wants more opportunity, not more money, and I think the idea of a small company interests her."

Celia looked down into her glass for a moment, experiencing jealousy so acute that it scalded. The Bakers had drifted away. She raised her eyes and she and Robert were alone in the centre of this loud mass of people.

"How are you?" Robert asked gently.

She shrugged, "I've got a cold. I wasn't going to come."

"I've been away most of the time since we last met. When I got back I wanted to ring you but I wasn't sure of your movements and I had no real reason to talk to you. I just wanted to ask about things."

"It's all much the same. Scotland started all right and ended badly. Harry is starting a shop!" She laughed unhappily. "I dread Christmas. I ask more and more people to stay. Far too many. We'll be in Scotland.

Christmas there is usually wonderful. The same families have worked at the castle for generations and no one minds working over Christmas. My parents are coming up and my sister and her family and David's sisters. There will be twenty of us."

"And Harry?"

She frowned. "I don't know. I doubt if he'll come. I wouldn't, in his position."

"When do you go to Scotland?"

"A few days."

"Any chance of lunch tomorrow or the day after?"

She could not really believe what she remembered of their last meeting and at the far side of the room she saw a patch of scarlet which was Eliza's dress. "Oh no. I'm sorry. You know how it is before Christmas."

He narrowed his eyes slightly. "I don't take much notice of Christmas. I have rather lost touch with my family." It was impossible for him to be cold towards her. He was quite sure she had been pleased to see him initially but something had caused her to withdraw. "You have my number if you should find you do have time. Same hotel. I'm always there in the mornings till about nine thirty." He smiled. "Happy Christmas. I hope to see you afterwards."

Celia turned away and Robert searched the room for David and then made his way towards him, pausing on the edge of the group of people David was talking to until David looked towards him.

"I thought I'd better come and make myself known as I wasn't actually asked," Robert smiled.

David gave a small shrug. "Nice to see you. I understand from Michael things are progressing well."

"Yes. And, on that subject, I was hoping to come and see your chartering manager after Christmas. I understand you'll be in Scotland for a while."

"Yes. We come back on the second but everyone else will be working from the twenty-eighth."

"Then I'll make an appointment for that week. I'm interested in taking an option to charter a tanker."

"Well, we have several available. We'd be only too happy

to discuss it with you." David thought, *He looks different already. There is more confidence about him.*

When Robert finally found Eliza she had surrounded herself with a circle of admirers. She had been watching Robert's progress round the room with steadily mounting impatience. She hadn't expected him to seek her out at once but he had been in the room for nearly three-quarters of an hour, and for the last thirty minutes Eliza had wanted to go. Her circle laughed raucously at anything she said. Several of them were very drunk indeed. Robert stood slightly behind her and put his hand round her arm. "Can you bear to tear yourself away?"

"If you can spare the time to talk to me," she said crisply.

Robert looked amused. "You knew I wouldn't waste an opportunity like this."

"I knew you wouldn't have offered to come and take me out afterwards if the idea of getting in amongst this lot hadn't appealed, but a simple hello would have made me feel less used."

"I'm sorry." They were facing each other. He saw that Eliza had drunk quite a lot. Her pale cheeks were slightly flushed. "If I had been able to find you earlier I would have said hello but you were lost in the throng and apparently having a good time."

Eliza shrugged. "I had to do something while I was waiting. Have you finished now? I'm hungry and there are a lot of things I want to discuss with you. Can we go?"

As if he hadn't heard her, Robert said, "That tall balding man by the fireplace. I've met him before. He's quite high up in the Navy, isn't he? D'you know him, Eliza?"

"Yes," Eliza said through tight lips. "John Spurrell. He's got a desk job now with the Admiralty. Why?"

"Like to meet him again if I could." He grinned at her, holding his glass up to his mouth. "Any chance?"

"No chance. I'm hungry."

"Sorry. Can't go yet. A Navy contact is always useful."

"Bastard," Eliza said under her breath and swung round and made her way with difficulty across the still-crowded hall until she reached the tall figure by the fireplace. She had known him since her early days at Otterwoods, had gone out with him once or twice before he married. He saw her approaching and smiled down at her with pleasure, leaning to kiss her as she drew near.

"Eliza. I thought I saw you in the distance. Heard a rumour you were leaving Otterwoods."

"I am, in a few days. I'm going to work for Robert Stoner." She introduced Robert and the conversation turned, under Robert's skilful control, to the Navy and the government cuts. Eliza listened, fascinated at the way Robert could steer the subject in the direction he wanted.

"How do you repair and support your ships at sea if they should be on long engagements?"

"God knows. We have no supply ships capable of going any distance. In the event of a conventional war we would have to charter, quickly, if we could. We could be in a very bad way, as I never stop pointing out. Her Majesty's Brokers would be in a frantic scramble."

"Well, don't forget Stoner Shipping if you should need supply vessels. I'm sure we could undercut a lot of people."

"I'll keep you in mind, but just at the moment we're not anticipating a war."

"It needn't be a full-scale war. You could find yourself in the position of having to send a few war ships merely to make a point and even then you'd need support vessels."

"You're preaching to the converted," John Spurrell said. "Try and convince the government!"

Eliza was tired. Her head ached and she excused herself and went up to the ladies' cloakroom on the first floor. She drank some cold water and checked that she looked all right. *Face of a stoat. Face of a bad pixie. Ugly dark eyes like pebbles.* She leaned in close to the glass until her breath fogged it and then she smeared a clear place and reapplied red lipstick. She wanted to leave. She wanted to be in Robert's car, to eat with him somewhere and laugh with him, to make plans with him. She hunched her shoulders, stiffening her body. She wanted to make love to him.

The lethargy left her. She was in a hurry as she went down the wide passage and turned onto the staircase, pausing to seek out Robert's dark red head and seeing him still with John Spurrell. She made her way across to them more easily now as the room was beginning to clear.

The two men acknowledged her arrival. "John and his wife are joining us for dinner," Robert said, tucking an arm through Eliza's, and she could do nothing but smile. Smile and pretend. Gather her coat, smile at Jo Spurrell, smile her goodbyes. While inside a broth of disappointment and anger simmered and she knew, of old, that it would boil over before too long. *And this,* she thought, *is before I have even started to work with him!*

It's not too late, she thought. *I can change my mind. David would take me back. Working for Robert will be one long frustration. I know that I want too much from him.* She took her arm from his. *How ironic. Always in the past they have been the ones trying to pin me down and I have been elusive. Now I know how it feels to try and take hold of someone who will not be held.*

"Robert, I'm tired and fed up with talking to people I don't particularly like. I want to have dinner alone with you."

He was reclaiming his coat and he put it on and then rested an arm along her shoulders, leaning over to whisper into her ear, "All part of the job, Eliza. It's important, believe me. You damn well have to work for your ten per cent and a lot of the work will be outside office hours. Starting now. Be nice to that plain woman. I want them to remember us. By the end of the evening I want him to feel he could lift the phone and ring us without a moment's hesitation."

They stepped out into the wide porch and Eliza stopped so suddenly that Robert had to turn and look at her. She smiled slowly. "All right. For my ten per cent. But you can bloody well make up for this tomorrow. Just the two of us tomorrow night. Promise?"

"It's a deal," Robert said and then they were out into the blustery December night, ducking their heads against the rain as they ran towards Robert's car and behind them, under a huge black umbrella, came the Spurrells.

Shortly after nine, David's driver took him and Celia and his daughters to a restaurant in Walton Street where he had booked a table. Julia and Josephine settled themselves with their backs to the wall, facing their parents, while David ordered wine and Coke for Josephine who hated alcohol and had become, over the last six months, a sort of vegetarian, refusing to eat what she referred to as "bloody meat". This dinner had been Julia's idea and it had taken some skill on her part to organise. When she suggested it the previous evening, David had been non-commital. He still did not know how to react to his elder daughter.

"You can leave the Otterwoods party about nine thirty, can't you?" Julia had said. "Josephine and Mum and I could come to the party and then we could have dinner somewhere. I would be very interested to come, and Josephine likes to go to any restaurant so she can tell her friends, and I think Mum is rather depressed and needs diverting."

"I usually take some of the senior staff out with me."

"Is it already arranged or could it be different this year?" She looked up at him with her round, steady blue eyes. They were uncomfortable eyes. They seemed to pierce through to his thoughts. Josephine was a daughter he could understand, feminine and pretty and vulnerable. Julia, standing so still, round-faced and square-bodied and wearing one of Harry's discarded rugger shirts, fitted no category.

"Yes, it could be different this year." He decided to respond to Julia's appeal. "If you really want us to go out, we will. Have you consulted your mother?"

"No, but I think she'll agree."

"She hasn't been to an Otterwoods party for years."

"When did you last ask her to come?"

"I can't remember. Seven or eight years ago, I think."

Julia shrugged. "Then it's time she tried again. You can't always go alone. You can't keep on doing the same things year after year. Habit is a wicked wasteful thing."

David laughed a little. "Is it?"

"Yes. Like preconceived ideas." She turned and went towards the door and said, as she was leaving, "Neither Harry nor I can fit into your preconceived ideas of a son and a daughter, can we? Josie's okay. Has it ever occurred to you that you were probably not exactly what Grandpa wanted?"

David looked at Julia now and recalled the conversation. Julia spread her table napkin on her lap, examined the restaurant and the people with her round curious eyes, with an air of confidence which was very disturbing in a girl who was just eighteen. *Was I like this?* David thought. *As bumptious as this? Just asking to be put in my place?* Josie, by contrast, was excited and nervous, aware of almost nothing but herself. Although she suspected that she was very pretty, she had no proof yet. Restless, long-fingered hands, changing expressions. She was so like Celia had been when David first met her. David met Celia's eyes and he smiled, raising his glass to her. He intended things to be better. It was just that his fury at Harry's rejection of Otterwoods and all that it stood for was thrown at Celia instead. Warily she returned his smile, understanding that an effort was to be made, determined to try and enjoy herself.

They drank white wine with their first course and talked about people at the party, about Christmas, and David was benevolent, apparently enjoying himself and being amusing about the office juniors and the state they would be in the next morning.

"We always try and have the party on a Friday but this year we couldn't as I have to go to Washington tomorrow."

Celia looked at her daughters, watched their laughter, and, utterly different as they were, they both seemed to her barely finished adults, untouched and perfect and vulnerable and she was torn between pride and fear for them when she thought of them taking on the world as adults.

"We met Eliza Marland this evening," Julia said as they began on the main course. "She is not a bit as you described her."

"I didn't know I had described her."

"Yes, you did," Josephine said. She was eating grilled lobster; it hung over the plate, primitive and evil-looking and, to Celia's mind, far more revolting than a harmless piece of meat. "You said she was flat-chested and thin and quiet and boring. I thought she was amazing-looking. I'd love a tight red and silver dress like that!"

"You'd look ridiculous in it, like a pencil," Julia said.

"Well I'd rather look like a pencil than a pillar box."

There was a pause and then they both laughed and Julia returned, doggedly, to her subject.

"You said she was very efficient indeed and intelligent. You must be sorry she is going."

"Yes, we are. I offered her a job as PA to Stephen McNeil but even that couldn't keep her out of Robert Stoner's clutches."

"Well you'll probably start losing a lot more clever women now that women have higher expectations," Julia continued. "She just wasn't content to be a glorified secretary. She wanted to go into management, I expect, and she knew in Otterwoods she couldn't. She was dead-ended!"

"Don't be ridiculous, Julia," David said coldly. "She could have had a very good career with us."

"Up to a certain point. After that your blinkers come down. Habit again. Woman. Must be diluted by husband and children. Must be a bit soft and probably not capable of ruthlessness. Not – "

"Julia, I'm bored with this subject and so, I imagine, are your mother and Josephine. Now you suggested this family dinner party, don't ruin it."

Julia's face coloured. "Why will it be ruined if we have a discussion about something that matters instead of just talking about Christmas and skiing?" She put down her knife and fork and her face was fierce. "I have noticed that you completely change gear when talking to Mum or Josie or me, you begin to talk down. You pause for a moment and think; in fact you're bloody patronising most of the time. When I got the results of my A levels you almost patted me on the head; the impression I got was that you thought it was rather a waste really. I worked bloody hard for those exams. I was the only girl in my year to get into Cambridge. Now, if it had been Harry you would have killed the fatted calf."

"Julia, we were thrilled with your results, you know that," Celia said quickly.

"Stop it, Mum. Stop always putting yourself between him and us to calm things down. Things can't be calmed down. They have to be fought out. That's what's gone wrong about Harry. He should have stood up to you long ago. Harry's very good at a lot of things, mostly practical things, making things. Not just slightly good at it but so good that it's a terrible waste that he should be bumming around and drinking too much. Do you know how much he drinks? You've made him feel useless because you only ever asked one thing of him, that he excel in exams and step into the place you have carved out for him." Her eyes blazed and she was sitting forward, small hands gripping the edges of the table. "Well, unlike the others, I'm not afraid of you."

"I can't understand how you did manage to pass those exams so well when you apparently think in such muddled circles," David said coldly. "I presume you have a good memory and learn things by heart. Well you have to start understanding as well as reciting other people's thoughts, Julia. It is too easy to blame one or other parent for everything, to heap all the problems on them."

"I don't blame you for everything. I blame you for putting far too much pressure on Harry and for not taking me seriously enough." There was a silence and when she spoke again, Julia's voice was low but very clear. "But above all else I despise the way you play around with other women and that is probably directly responsible for your attitude to women in general. To quote from your beloved Kipling, 'I'm tired of the hired women. I'll kiss my girl on her lips! I'll be content with my fountain. I'll drink from my own well. And the wife of my youth shall charm me–an' the rest can go to Hell!'"

Celia got up. She was trembling. "I can't stand any more of this. I'm going home. I'll send the car back for you if you want to stay." Josephine was already beside her mother, tears in her eyes, aware of the curious glances from neighbouring tables.

"Well I'm not leaving yet," Julia said. "I'm not like Harry. I haven't finished."

David went silent for a moment and then he said, "Send the car back. Julia and I will come later." As Celia and Josephine went towards the door and were handed their coats, he picked up his knife and fork and said in a voice that managed to convey fury although it was soft, "You succeeded in hurting your mother then, not me. Also you got it slightly wrong. It's 'sick of the hired women', not 'tired'. Tired and hired would be too trite. I didn't know you knew *The Mary Gloster*."

Julia gave a long sigh. "I've been reading avidly since I was five. I've probably read everything in the house at least once and the poetry a lot more times. I'm sorry that I upset the others but I have to start somewhere."

"I can't see that a personal attack on me which also insults your mother is a very good way to start making me respect you."

Julia pushed her plate away. "I wasn't going to say that. I got angry. I'm sorry about that bit but not the rest and do you really think we don't know what's going on?"

"I don't care whether you know or not. It does not affect my family. It's not your affair."

"God what an awful pun," Julia said and waited until, after a few tense seconds when she wondered if her father might hit her, David laughed.

"Of course if affects us. Everything you do affects us."

For the first time ever David looked at his elder daughter as a person in her own right. He felt the fury lessen. He could see the determination boiling in her.

"What an extraordinary girl you are. Now that you have managed to get me alone here you may as well tell me what your plans for the future are. I'm sure you have some."

Julia relaxed visibly, sitting back, suddenly looking much younger as the relief coloured her face, eyes shining as she said, with an air of calmness, "Yes, I have."

Chapter 16

"Yes?" Robert said, into the insistent telephone, and the impatience in his voice was magnified by the instrument. "Yes. Who is it?"

"Celia."

"You sound quite different."

"I am different. Robert, can we have lunch together?"

For a moment his surprise silenced him and she took the pause to mean he was seeking an excuse.

Quickly, she said, "Of course if you're busy today it doesn't matter."

"I'm not very busy and even if I was I would still have lunch with you."

He could hear the smile in her voice as she said, "Carters, at one?"

"One thirty. I have the keys to my new offices. I'll take you to see them."

It had taken her an hour to gather the courage to ring him but now she was impatient, cringing from the ashen reflection of her exhausted face, pulling a brush through her hair, dragging on a new brightly-patterned sweater which had cost so much she had thought it was a mistake. A long raincoat, a tweed hat on her head, calling something vague up the stairs to the girls about Christmas shopping, back at two thirty or three, unable to talk to either of them naturally; she was aware that the scene of the previous evening, which had so devastated her, appeared to have left Julia untouched and even Josephine's misery seemed to have been forgotten this morning. As she thought this, Celia was walking towards the restaurant half an hour too early with the fine rain on her face. At Carters she sat at the table Robert had reserved and ordered a gin and tonic. She shook her damp hair, thinking how flat and straight it would look, thinking she would probably get pneumonia and that she didn't give a damn. She gulped down the drink and the cold had taken her taste away. She ordered another.

Robert was earlier than he said, coming in with a gust of wind, collar of his raincoat turned up, seeing her and smiling at once and bending to kiss her hello. They met as old friends. This time there was no difference of age or situation and all the crushing complications that hung about Celia, like puppet strings, were temporarily severed.

"If I was unfriendly last night," she said, "it was because you surprised me and it made me nervous. I hate those huge parties. It seemed so long since I last saw you. I thought I had invented what I remembered when Eliza started talking about coming to work for you in that enigmatic way she has."

"It is a long time. Five weeks and two days," Robert said, taking her hands, and wondering what Eliza had said.

"And I didn't expect to see you. It confused me." She took her hands back. "Why am I lying? I only went because I thought you might be there. David was amazed when I said I was coming. Julia suggested she and Josie come too and that we all go on somewhere for dinner afterwards. I know David expected me to say no. It was the first party I had been to for eight years. When I began to lose touch, I admitted to myself how much I hated those parties. Otterwoods is David. I stopped going when I felt I had nothing to offer him. As I stood in that vast hall and listened to it all, I knew why I had hated them so much and suddenly you were beside me. You weren't invited, were you?"

"No. I came to meet Eliza."

Celia nodded. "I really can't think what I've done since I last saw you. Nothing very much. I live in a shell. David avoids me now. We are polite but there is no kindness between us and sometimes he is deliberately hurtful as if he feels like hurting me all the time but only occasionally does he lose control. Everything between us is disintegrating. We never mention Harry but I know David is making plans all the time. In the spring he'll have another attempt to get Harry back, when he thinks this shop idea is beginning to pall. He tried to stop it. He influenced the trustees but somehow Harry raised the money himself. He sold his guns. David was absolutely furious." She tore a roll into little bits but she did not eat them.

"What has happened?" Robert said quietly. "What's wrong?"

She was silent for a moment and then she said, "David's away. He went this morning to Washington. He comes back on Christmas Eve. I didn't sleep at all last night. Dinner was awful. We took the girls out and both David and I were trying to hide the stiffness between us but they know everything. They read our silences and our false laughter; they see how we avoid each other's eyes. I can remember the sensitivity of that age. Nothing escapes you. They are so clean, Robert, all dressed up and wanting life to go well, expecting it to go well. In Julia's case, demanding it. It was all right for about three-quarters of an hour and then Julia began. I should have guessed she had an ulterior motive when she suggested we all have dinner together. She is so like David." Celia drained her glass. "It was horrible. I sat there and saw the pathetic pretence of a normal family that I try and maintain crumple up. She told David she despised his infidelity. Josie and I left them in the restaurant. When we got home Josie and I talked for a long time. She is terrified that we will split up. I lied to reassure her. I drank so much coffee. For hours I couldn't sleep and when I did David and Julia woke me. I heard them talking in the hall. Laughing. I will never understand either of them. David came in and I know he wanted to talk but I couldn't. But even last night I didn't take myself to another room. How can I protect Josie? In the past, David has never treated me badly. I have been able to push aside whatever he was doing. But now I think he hates me. I thought about Harry and then about you. It rained all night. At last it was morning." She dropped her head abruptly. She let her breath out in a long sigh and covered her eyes with her fingers, running them along the dark brows. "He left this morning without speaking to me. I feel desolated, half-mad."

"Come back to my hotel and sleep. Just sleep." Robert

stood up and spoke to the waiter, paying for the drinks, and gathering Celia's coat. She followed him like a sleep-walker into the drizzle and it took a while to find a taxi. She leant back against the seat, eyes closed, Robert's arm along her shoulders. She went with him into his small hotel, up in the lift to his room, and no one saw them. Robert took her raincoat and she lay on the bed. He put a quilt over her and came and sat beside her so that her head rested against him. They sat in complete silence until she slept.

Robert sat and thought, frowning, checking over events, thinking about John Spurrell and Bernard Van Ryn, amazed each time he looked down at the woman sleeping beside him under the quilt. She coughed occasionally as if reminding him of her presence. At four, she woke suddenly and half sat up. The room was almost dark.

"I should go, Robert."

"Why? Who is waiting for you? We'll have dinner somewhere. I want to show you my offices." He stroked her hair. "How do you feel?"

"Guilty. As if we are lovers. As if I have known you all my life. But not as if I am going mad any more." She knelt on the bed, pushing back her straight hair. "What the hell am I doing here?"

"Nothing," Robert said. He wanted to kiss her so badly that he made himself wait, prolonging the moment.

"Celia, do you have to go back yet?"

"Not really. I could ring. The girls are going to a party." She smiled. "You'll get my cold," she said as he moved his face towards hers. She watched him until the last moment, only shutting her eyes when their mouths touched.

"I want it. I want anything of yours," Robert said, just before he kissed her.

Not me, not me? Celia thought as the shock of another man's mouth against hers made her stiffen defensively before she responded. *Other people do this. Not me. I can't be drawn into the preliminary stages of an affair. I hate it. I despise it in David. I'm coldly prim and disapproving when friends confide in me. And yet Robert and I seem to have nothing to do with other people at all. I feel as if I have been born again.* Robert held her against him, enveloping her. He seemed immensely powerful and gentle. *I have forgotten everything and yet I remember everything. Could I start again? Is this how David feels?*

At the thought of David she pulled herself roughly away, shaking her head.

"Ring them," Robert said, putting the phone into her hand.

She shook her head. "I must go, Robert. This is ridiculous."

"It's ridiculous to go. Tell them you are spending an evening with a friend. First of all we'll go and have tea somewhere. What could be more harmless? Would you have tea with a lover? Then we'll go and see the offices. I'm longing to show off to you. Then we'll have a drink and a meal and we'll both forget everything else for a few hours and at eleven I'll take you home and no one will ever know except us." He leaned forward and kissed her mouth again, very lightly. "Ring."

She dialled the number of the Flood Street house and Julia answered:

"Julia, I'll be some time. I don't seem to have got anything yet. Then I'm meeting Susie for a drink to listen to her troubles. Can you girls get yourselves to the Macphersons' party and ask Henry to bring you home?"

As Robert listened he thought, *It is utter stupidity to get involved with David's wife. At this moment in my life the last thing I need is a complicated woman like this. Surely I have learned something from these years with Sophia? And yet she fascinates me. And it's much more than that. I care about her happiness. She is without self-interest. David doesn't deserve her, has never deserved her.* He knew that, in Celia, he had someone to whom he could confide his surprise in his own moderate success and his fears that it would not last, someone to whom he could present a quite different face from the attitude of extreme confidence he had to display to the world.

Celia put the telephone down and looked up at Robert. "I've never lied to the children before. I can't do it again, Robert. Not to them. Not even to David, I don't think."

"Doesn't he lie to you?"

"I don't think he does. I'm careful never to ask questions. I overheard someone saying once that I didn't mind, that I just looked the other way and lived my comfortable life. That's not true. I didn't believe it the first time. I couldn't see why he should possibly want another woman when we loved each other, when we had everything. I should have stood up to him then, shouldn't I, that first time? I should have brought it all out into the open. But it finished. He was back and I thought it would be forgotten, that it was just once." She stood up and looked for her shoes. "When I found out about the next one, I thought I would let it run the same way." She shook her head, and pushed her arms into her raincoat as Robert held it out for her. "The irony is, I don't think he has a lover at the moment."

"To hell with him," Robert said roughly. "He's never had to abide by the rules, that's his trouble." They stepped out into the passage. "Forget them all for the moment. Where shall we go for tea?"

"Actually I couldn't care less about tea. Can't we skip that stage and move directly to your office and the drink?"

"Only if I pick up a sandwich somewhere. You may be able to forget about food but I can't." He tucked his arm through hers and they went down the flights of dimly lit stairs and out of the back entrance to Robert's car.

It was after midnight when he put Celia into a taxi to go home.

"I'm sorry that I'm going away again."

"Don't be." She touched his face. "Just thinking about you and knowing that I have a friend is enough." She sat back and Robert closed the taxi door and went back to his car. It was not until he was back in his hotel room that he remembered Eliza.

The phone drilled into the silence and darkness of Eliza's night. She was not asleep. She rolled over and felt for the receiver. "Yes."

"It's Robert. Eliza, I'm sorry. I forgot and that's all there is to it."

"Forgot what?"

"Dinner."

"Did we arrange anything?" Eliza said coldly.

Robert laughed admiringly. "Nothing definite. But I was hoping we could for Friday. We must talk before I go back to Lagos. You will be in charge from the second."

"Friday then," Eliza said. "Goodbye." She sat up in bed, arms round her knees, swearing at him with every dirty word she knew and then getting out of bed to make herself tea. It was not going to be easy but she knew there was no question of giving up. She was committed.

Chapter 17

On January the fourth, Eliza let herself in to the Stoner Shipping offices in Holborn at ten to nine and went up the flight of rather dusty stairs, carrying two plants and a suitcase which contained new mugs, teaspoons and a small filter coffee maker. She unlocked the glass-panelled door and went in to the first room, which she would occupy, and through it into the room which would be Robert's, just to look at it all again. Exhilaration throbbed through her. At last it was starting.

The previous two weeks had been an ordeal. At first, when Robert left, she had thought she would ignore Christmas as some of her friends did, meeting a few people for lunch perhaps and treating it like any other bank holiday, like a Sunday. But as it drew nearer she knew she would take the alternative course and would be drawn back to Seagull Avenue, to see if this time it would be different; to try again for three or four days to ignore Jane's remarks, to tolerate her aunt's stupidity, to escape with Alice for some time on their own, only to be hunted out; to endure the extraordinary annual pilgrimage to church which Jane insisted on although she had no belief in God. It was, Eliza knew, just part of her superstition, like crossing fingers, the midnight service in the icy ugly church where all the decorations seemed to make no difference, where there were tiny islands of heat round the calor gas stoves and the carols were visible as clouds of breath; the organist pounded out the familiar tunes in impossibly high keys and the congregation struggled unsuccessfully to stay in touch, like exhausted long-distance runners.

It had been different this year, because of Harry. He arrived on Christmas Eve, his car full of presents, a Stilton and bottles of claret and champagne. Even Jane's coldness and her remarks about the wine she provided obviously not being good enough, could not dampen Harry's enthusiasm. He watched Alice all the time, touched her whenever he could. The love between them was obvious, surrounding them like an aura and making Eliza feel more isolated than usual. This year, even Alice was shut away from her. Eliza walked along the seafront, morning and evening, watching the December winds whip the usually flaccid waves into an imitation of real sea; she loved the wet wind in her face. She had had her hair cut very short just a few days earlier and it pleased her that she could go bare-headed in the rain; she felt she was taking a breath, gathering all her resources for a new stage of her life and she was as mild as she could be and let many a barbed remark go unchallenged.

The first morning in the new office was surprisingly busy. A lot of stationery was delivered and two filing cabinets brought noisily up the stairs and installed. Michael Copper rang and six agencies answered the advertisement for a secretary; a computer salesman tried to persuade Eliza to buy an Apple computer and there was a long list from Robert of people he wanted her to write to or ring. At lunchtime, armed with the company credit card, she went by tube to a second-hand furniture shop and bought more bookshelves and a small table and an armchair and came back with them in a taxi. She was visited by a receptionist from the advertising company which occupied most of the first floor and when she was finally alone, she made lists of things which she had always taken for granted before: cleaning equipment, loo paper and washing-up liquid and some pictures for the blank cream-coloured walls. Blinds, too, for in the afternoon the brittle winter sunlight streamed through the tall windows of this west-facing office and was blinding.

It was very strange, though, to be on her own with no other people coming and going, no sense of urgency. Strange but also comfortable. She relished the thought that she could do everything her own way. She began a filing system, organising the letters which related to Michael Copper and Copperline, all the correspondence about the first Stoner ship. In the late afternoon she had an agitated call from Lagos which she eventually understood to be from the captain of the *Stoner Herald*, as Robert had named his ship. And the gist of the call was that the crew's wages had not arrived.

"Robert is not here," Eliza repeated. "I expect him back in a couple of days. I think he is in Lagos. I have a phone number."

"That's okay. If he's here, Sophia will know where. I thought he was in London. Are you Eliza?"

"Yes."

"Robert told me he had found someone to run the London end. I hope to meet you some time. I'm Rolfe Petersen. Okay, I'll stall the crew until I find him."

"All I know is that he left here just before Christmas to fly to Singapore and that he intended to come back via Lagos to London in early January but I've only opened the office today. I haven't heard from him since he left. He has an appointment here on the sixth.

"Singapore? What's he up to now, I wonder?" Then the line crackled and the voice was lost.

I am like Alice, playing in her shop, Eliza thought the following morning, laughing to herself as she watered the plants and dusted the windowsills. *I am like my mother in some ways although I hate to admit it, but I will get someone else to come in and clean. There may be time now but we will be much busier soon.* She was to interview three applicants for the secretarial job that morning. "I leave it to you," Robert had said. "As long as you don't pay them too much."

Of the three, Eliza preferred a large, capable woman in her forties whose family had grown up. She was free to start the following Monday and as Eliza saw her out, pleased with her choice, Alice and Harry came bounding up the stairs.

"Do you mind if we visit you? Are you too busy?" Alice asked.

"Have you an appointment?"

"We've brought a lot of sandwiches and some wine. We thought we'd all have lunch here."

"Do you stop for lunch?" Harry asked.

"Every other day."

Eliza brought forward the new armchair and the two office chairs and they sat round her desk and ate the sandwiches and drank the wine from china mugs. Harry tilted the chair, feet on her desk and sun on his back, content, making Eliza laugh as he described how Alice examined various damask tablecloths.

"It doesn't seem possible that it could take more than five minutes because they all look identical and cost a fortune. She feels the cloth like some old tailor, virtually smells it, looks at the pattern which is only woven in another sort of white anyway, unfolds another half dozen and then decides none of them are good enough and we have to go somewhere else and go through the whole process again."

Robert stepped through the outer office door into a room full of laughter, briefcase and small roll bag in his hands, and they stopped as he came in.

He smiled. "You all look guilty, as if I've caught you out at something, especially Eliza," he said as she stood up. He put an arm along her shoulders, almost before he thought what he was doing. "This looks very efficient."

Harry handed him a mug of wine. "It was until we came but we're going soon. We have a few hundred damask tablecloths to sniff."

Robert helped himself to a sandwich as he went through into the room which was his office, putting his bags down on the desk. Eliza followed him with her notebook.

"Rolfe Petersen rang yesterday. About the wages for the *Herald*."

"Yes, he got me just before I left."

"He said Sophia would know where you were." Eliza watched his profile intently as he looked out of the window.

"She did."

"I confirmed the appointment with Otterwoods' chartering manager for the day after tomorrow and I've taken on a secretary and so far, so good!" Her large mouth stretched into a wide smile and the dark eyes sparkled and Robert let his gaze rest on her for a few moments. Alice and Harry leaned through to call goodbye. The outer door closed behind them and Eliza and Robert were alone.

She experienced a surprising moment of shyness and went to make Robert some coffee, giving herself time to let the feeling lessen. She took it into Robert's office. He was standing by the window.

"Did things go well in Singapore?"

He turned from the window, hesitating for a moment before he answered. "Yes. Surprisingly well. I was just trying to organise it all in my mind. I find it hard to believe that it's finally started." He turned slowly, taking the mug from her. "I can appreciate how much you've done in just a couple of days, Eliza. It all looks so businesslike I can't really believe it's anything to do with me. Does this tiny place seem unreal to you after Otterwoods?"

"I'm getting used to it. It seemed extraordinary yesterday. But I like doing things on my own. I've always hated the filing system they use at Otterwoods. It's clumsy."

Robert sat on his desk. "I want to find a flat, Eliza. I hope to spend much more time in London. We will do all the wages from here and avoid cock-ups like yesterday."

"How many crew will there be if you charter a tanker from Otterwoods?"

"About thirty. A master and eleven officers, probably Scandinavian, and Rolfe will be the supernumerary master. The crew will be made up of Filipinos but it will be an Otterwood crew. It's not a bare boat charter. If it trades profitably, we may charter a second tanker in the summer. I shall take an option on the second when I see the chartering manager. What's his name?"

Eliza went back to her desk and looked in the diary. "Kit Secombe."

Robert had followed her through. She sat at her desk and looked up at him. She rested her chin in her hands. It was enough, for the moment, to have him to herself. She could wait. Instinctively, she tried to make him laugh.

"I know what's coming. You hate women with elaborate names who eat prawn cocktail and have very short hair."

Robert smiled. "Quite wrong. I like it very much. It suits your pixieish face and women's necks are so delicate." He stood behind her and put one hand round the back of her neck, like a collar, and moved the fingers slightly. "Would you ring some estate agents for me, Eliza? I want a flat with two bedrooms, somewhere I can park a car, within half an hour's drive of this office. I don't really care where it is as long as it doesn't cost a ridiculous amount."

At five, Robert came through into Eliza's room and waited until she had finished speaking on the telephone.

"There should be masses of particulars for you to look through tomorrow morning."

"Good. Now, let's go home. I'll give you a lift."

"It's only five," Eliza said severely.

"So what? We've finished. I don't believe in sitting around for the sake of it." He went back into his office and switched out the lights.

Eliza said very little as he drove. It was in her mind to offer him dinner but something prevented her. Some instinct told her it was too soon and there had been so many unsatisfactory meetings, she did not want to risk another. She would rather wait. Robert was obviously preoccupied, whistling some tune quietly to himself, and he would have swept past her turning if she hadn't reminded him.

"I'll get out. I can easily walk from here." She opened the door and stepped out into the street. "See you tomorrow."

"'Night Eliza," he said after a short pause, as if concentrating with difficulty. "Yes, see you tomorrow."

She stood in the street and watched him drive off and although she was apprehensive about the future she was in no doubt at all that she had done the right thing.

Two days later, Kit Secombe and Robert met at four in Kit's office in the Otterwood building. They had not met before.

"David tells me you were with us for a long time?"

"Yes. Fourteen years. I was master on the *Peacock* for three years. That's how I got to know Nigeria so well." Robert left one of his pauses, looking intently at this small, fair-haired man. "I mentioned to David before Christmas that I would need a ship and I'd like you to find me a good one. A hundred thousand tons. I have a contract to ship oil from Nigeria to Singapore, initially for one year, which will run from early March; I have just returned from Singapore, via Lagos, and I'm all set to go ahead."

Kit nodded. "Right. A hundred thousand tons. I can offer you the *Otterwood Endeavour*. She is due to discharge her cargo in Rotterdam on February the fourteenth. She could be in Lagos by March the first. We will want payment monthly, in advance, and if you commit yourself to a year's charter," he paused and tapped his pen against his lip while he considered, "we will ask fifteen thousand dollars a day. If the charter is to run from March the first, the initial payment should be no later than February the twentieth." He looked at Robert expectantly.

"That all sounds fine except the price," Robert said without a moment's hesitation. "I have been in this business a long time and when I set up this deal, I expected to pay thirteen thousand a day."

Kit Secombe raised his eyebrows.

They haggled for some minutes and finally settled, as both had expected, at fourteen thousand dollars a day. They shook hands across the desk.

"And I would like to take an option to charter a second tanker from June. I will confirm that by early April." He stood up and the two men approached the door.

"Is David here?" Robert asked as he went out, as if they were old friends, as if he would have liked to put his head round David's door and said hello.

"No. He was in Scotland over Christmas and he flew to New York yesterday. He should be back at the end of the week. Did you want to see him?"

"Not really. I thought he might want to see me but obviously he is satisfied."

"Michael Copper seems very content with the arrangement you have," Kit Secombe said and as Robert left he thought what a cunningly interwoven network he was binding himself into. For the first time he saw some significance in Sophia's spider folklore. The world of business was a web.

Robert walked back to Holborn, coat collar turned up against a bitter wind. The sky was threatening snow. He thought about Celia, wondering if she was still in Scotland, and he walked more slowly, hands deep in his pockets. By the time he neared his office it was snowing steadily and his feet left prints on the pavement and snow on the stairs. He walked into the warmth of Eliza's office, shaking the snowflakes from his hair.

"Bernard Van Ryn telephoned to say that the funds have been transferred."

"Good." Robert hung up his coat and went through to his office and Eliza followed him.

"And there were calls from Rolfe Petersen and a man called Connelly who is apparently due to take over from Rolfe as master on the *Herald*."

Robert nodded. He picked up the heavy bronze armlet which he had brought in that morning to use as a paperweight and traced the spider motif which stood out in strong relief.

Eliza looked at it with interest. "Did someone really wear that? It looks far too heavy and the spider is gruesome."

"It was certainly worn once. It was probably made by a Senoufo of the Ivory Coast. Some West African peoples believe that spiders can talk and act like humans and tell a man how to become rich."

"If you wish to live and thrive, let a spider run alive," Eliza said. "Seagull Avenue is a virtual spider reservation as we were never allowed to kill one. Some were so big they made rustling noises as they walked but I never heard them talking among themselves about making money." As Robert laughed she went on, "I thought you didn't have any time for luck, anyway."

"I don't. Which is why I use it as a paperweight. It was a present. It's a beautiful object and such castings are rare. Most of the artists in West Africa who work in bronze today are too busy producing items for the tourist trade to take the time to make something like this. The ancient smiths of Benin developed the skill. I was told that the wax process began in the ninth century and reached West Africa from the north, along the trade routes of the

Sahara. This is probably three hundred years old and it was certainly made by that ancient wax process." He slid the heavy bronze armlet over Eliza's narrow hand and it rested on her arm, stretching from her wrist halfway to her elbow. "Rather impractical, I admit. But it suits you. When I have time to wander round the markets I'll try and find one of the carved ivory bracelets for you. They are not so heavy and not quite so big."

Eliza slid her hand out and replaced the armlet on Robert's desk. She didn't like to tell him that she found the spider, standing out from the background of the armlet, repellent.

"There are two flats to look at this evening, one at five and one at six."

"Okay. I'll try and speak to Rolfe and Connelly and then we'll go flat-hunting."

"Do you want me to come? It will mean leaving the office empty."

"I want your opinion. I know nothing about flats in London. Since my childhood, the only house I've ever lived in was in a suburb of Lagos and I shared it with Mick. Apart from that I've lived in cheap hotels or stayed with friends or been at sea. I thought when I saw your flat how much I liked it and I've been trying to work out why ever since."

"Simple. It's a very nice flat," Eliza said.

He grinned. "It was more than that. On that Sunday, the first time I saw it, I remember thinking how light it was and the room was a good shape and everything was compact. We're looking for something like that, Eliza."

Eliza was looking at him enigmatically. The curiosity he had felt about her in the very beginning he felt again now. He remembered that Sunday with pleasure. *In the beginning,* he thought, *I was still occupied by Sophia. And then Celia unexpectedly filled Sophia's space and women can only inhabit a certain portion of my life. It will be a long time before a woman comes first.* He followed Eliza down the rather dark flight of stairs towards the street which was transformed by snow. She turned a delighted face to him.

"Isn't it lovely, Robert? Quite unexpected and lovely."

Some snowflakes settled on her hair as he took her arm and they walked towards his car and he wondered, as he saw through her eyes the wide, rather dull street and solid buildings quite changed by the snow and was infected by her delight, what would have happened if he had never met Celia? If he needed a woman to love, Eliza would be the right choice, but he never really needed women. It was only when he could not resist that he became involved.

Chapter 18

Harry had made no New Year resolutions. Waking in the New Year with an appalling hangover, cowering from the light, he had felt no need. He believed in 1982. And a week into the new year he was still optimistic that the shop would succeed. It had to, he thought, as he stood waiting for the kettle to boil, arching his bare feet away from the cold of the basement's tiled floor. He cleared a space for a mug and pushed the unopened white and brown envelopes into a heap. In the past few weeks he had developed a technique of ignoring bills until they turned red or actually presented themselves on the doorstep in human form and demanded to be paid. He rubbed his face. Where had he been last night? There had been so many parties this week. Why hadn't Alice come with him? Why did she have to spend the evening with her sour old mother? Four or five of them had begun the evening in a restaurant and gone on to a party but after that the night was vague. Friends. He remembered Alice saying, wonderingly, "You have so many friends, Harry. Where do they all come from and why don't they leave you alone?"

It was true. He did have an army of friends; people he had been at school with, friends who were now working in London, friends of Julia's, friends of his mother's who constantly asked him to their daughters' parties. There was always someone coming or going from the house in Pembridge Gardens, or a group of people drinking coffee or wine, especially in the evenings.

"Friends aren't meant to leave you alone," Harry had answered after a pause.

"They can still be your friends if you don't see them every day. How can you stand them all?"

"I like them. Don't you like them?"

"I don't know them and they don't know me. Some of them I quite like but it's an ordeal for me to have people here all the time. Don't you ever want to be alone, Harry?"

Harry shuddered. "I hate being alone. I like the way I am with friends."

"Well, alone with me, I mean? Or just quiet. We need to talk about things."

"We're alone at night, when you stay here. Stay more often, Alice. Stay for ever. Let's get married. I despise the way my father has allowed his sexual instincts, or whatever he calls them, to interfere with his life with my mother. I am a one-woman man."

He had first mentioned marriage just before Christmas, when they were setting up their shop like children playing house, and it had seemed to Alice that for some unknown reason her life had been touched by magic and was perfect. Harry pretended fantastic pasts for her, weaving stories about Gladstone bags and princesses who misbehaved.

Some nights she stayed with him in the rooms above the shop, officially with Eliza, thinking she would never get used to the joy of Harry, never wholly believe he would go on wanting her. She did not stay very often. It was so quiet at Seagull Avenue in this, the wet season. The house was big and sombre without the irritation of guests and her mother, trying so hard to involve Alice, offering an alternative to London and Harry, was so brusque and touching that she made Alice feel she was being pulled in half. Harry and Jane both asked so much of her in their different ways. The brilliance and amazement and responsibility of being with Harry was shot through with concern about Jane and a certain longing for silence and solitude. But the old safe rightness, the comforting smell of the house in Seagull Avenue, the good feeling of being with Jane became spotted after a few days with the need to reassure herself about Harry and the shop. And every time she went to London she took a few more of her things from her side of the bedroom she shared with Jane. Little things, one or two at a time, so that perhaps Jane wouldn't notice at first and then she would see one morning that another of the old Victorian dolls had gone, another little china bowl had been taken, another silhouette, and she took to checking through all Alice's remaining collections one by one, like beads on a rosary, to reassure herself. Such a very gradual move, Jane thought, hurt almost more than Eliza's swift hacking off of the past.

Alice could not believe the shop unless she was actually there. All through January she and Harry worked on it, nagging at the painters, addressing the large oblong cards that had been printed and writing in the date of the opening party; Celia came to see them and brought two armchairs in the back of the car. Along one whole wall of the big room, Harry had built shelves. The methodical way he worked amazed Alice. Previously, she had seen only the disorganised side of him. They went to a wood yard after he had measured up and wandered the tall warehouse full of different-sized timbers and the smell of sawdust; light filtered through the slatted walls into the dusty cold. They tied the wood onto Harry's car and Alice sat astride it all to hold it on as Harry drove slowly back through London; a bright silk scarf fluttering on the long pieces of wood that stuck out behind. He produced an electric drill and saw and a neat box of tools. "I loved carpentry at school," he said, and for three days he built the shelves and then sanded and primed and painted them.

In the small rooms at the top of the house, Alice had established a neat little apartment. Two white-walled rooms and a tiny new bathroom were hers to arrange as she felt like with all the Victoriana she had collected over the past six years. Harry's area on the first floor wasgchaotic, strewn with clothes and cardboard boxes and books which moved from room to room as the painters worked. When the painters finally left in mid-February, Harry and Alice had five days in which to sort out the shop and prepare for the party.

On the new deep shelves which Harry had made they folded the tablecloths and napkins, graduated in colours; the cushions were heaped on a small wicker sofa, and lengths of cloth and scarves and big tablecloths hung from hangers on a clothes rail. Every item was marked with a ticket giving its number and value.

"And the hire charge is ten per cent on the risk," Alice said, "the risk being the replacement value."

"Why can't we charge more?"

"Because why should the stylists pay more? Especially as we're new and we have got to get them used to us."

Alice was unpacking a trunk of saris in jewel-coloured silks. She stood up and wound one round her body and Harry took another and wound it round his head like a turban. He bent to kiss her and she could smell the whisky on his breath.

"Harry, it's only ten-thirty. When do you start drinking?"

"When I need one."

"But why do you need a drink?"

"Because I like it, for God's sake!"

"That's not the main reason. Is it more bills?"

"Just one particular bill," Harry said with a bitter little laugh, "from my father's company asking me to repay the cost of two rail fares to and from Aberdeen plus the car and breakfast for two at the station hotel. Kippers were listed, I think." He shrugged. "It's so bloody petty. And it hurts. Also it comes to about two hundred pounds."

"And there's nothing left?"

"Less than nothing, if that makes sense. A considerable overdraft."

"I still don't see how drinking can help. Will you stop it, when I'm here more often?"

"When you're here all the time, you mean. You are going to live here, aren't you, Alice? You can't commute from Hove. It would be ridiculous."

Alice appeared to be busy, folding and smoothing the saris, holding them up to admire the colours.

"You haven't answered my question," Harry said softly and he sat down on the floor beside her and put his hand on the saris so that she had to stop.

"I'm not sure yet what I'll do," she said, unhappily.

* * *

On the day before the party, while Harry went to collect the glasses they were hiring and the wine, Alice came down into the showroom and turned on the lights and the miracle of it all overwhelmed her again. It was an Aladdin's cave. On a table she had arranged tea-cosies and oven-gloves and a fan of bright table napkins; the antique section of the showroom held white lace-edged bedspreads and damask cloths and delicate pillows and handkerchieves; the 'ethnic' shelves were filled with more coarsely woven fabrics in neutral colours; buttermuslin and silk and voile in long soft streams like brides' veils and rolls of plain, differently coloured cloth in specially placed wine racks. She even had ribbons and lace, coiled into neat spots in a big, flat wicker basket.

At a small desk the accounts books stood waiting hopefully. This side of things was ready. Alice shivered. Tomorrow she would be twenty. There would be a party and a cake and Harry, so exhilarated at the moment, wrapped in all this, full of energy except on occasional mornings when she would come in and find him weighed down by the drink he had consumed the night before.

The telephone interrupted her and she lifted the receiver.

Her mother's voice said, "Alice?" rather tentatively.

"Yes, it's me."

"You are coming home tonight, aren't you? Aunt Molly's coming to supper. She has a present for you. She particularly wants to see you."

Aunt Molly was punctilious about Alice's birthday, never forgetting; Alice's birthday was a ritual. She looked at her watch. "There still seems to be a lot to do here but I did tell Harry I was expected home. He's gone to collect wine and glasses but he said he'd drop me at Victoria at six thirty. I should be home by eight."

"I suppose that will have to do."

Alice thought of Harry's fierce opposition to the idea of her returning home that evening. How difficult it was to be the one in the middle. Perhaps, she thought wryly, rather than disappointing both it would be better to commit herself wholly to one or other.

"She's had you for twenty years," Harry had said last night in the darkness. "The next twenty are mine."

They had asked people for seven. Alice had begged Jane and Molly to come and they drove up together in the afternoon and they hardly spoke at all on the way. Alice experienced a rather sick-making blend of excitement and apprehension.

"Strange to think," Jane said, as they parked her ancient Rover, "that if you had been a little later home last summer, you would have missed Harry. He would have stood around for a bit and then, presumably, gone home, and our lives would be untouched instead of shaken up like this. Such tiny particles make up the whole."

"It was really the Bramsdens' car breaking down that caused it. If they had been coming, I could never have given Harry a room for the night."

She led them into the small house, pride in the organised beauty of the showroom with all its stock overriding all other feelings, showed them the whole house and her small apartment upstairs. Jane made tea while Alice changed into her latest 'best' dress, a nineteen-twenties beaded flapper's dress, and wondered where Harry was. Not until six when she was beginning to get anxious did he come bursting in.

He swept across the room and took Alice's face in both hands, kissing her. "Happy birthday. Sorry I wasn't here when you all arrived. I was arranging your present, Alice." He put an envelope into her hands and she opened it slowly and took out a single piece of paper. She read it without understanding, feeling Jane's and Molly's curiosity.

"A holiday?"

"Skiing. Two weeks in a chalet. Most marvellous bit of luck. Josephine's best friend's elder sister is cooking in a chalet in Verbier all season and it's very cheap because they've had cancellations. You'll love Verbier. We go on

March the twentieth so we've got four weeks to get what you need and find someone to look after things here."

Alice stared down at the piece of paper. "Harry, it's a lovely idea but I can't go away four weeks after we open. We will hardly have started."

"Exactly. So what better time to go away?"

"How can I leave it to someone else? The first weeks are vital. If we don't get going from the very beginning our reputation will suffer. 'No point in going there. There's a temporary girl and she doesn't know the stock.' You have to know everything, help people find things."

Jane stood motionless, her eyes bright with excitement, a mug of tea cupped in her hands, watching Harry's face, seeing the expressions change from bewildered surprise to disbelief.

"Skiing is one of the very few things I'm any good at," Harry said quietly. "I love it; I want you to love it too."

"All right, I'll love it, but not this March!"

"We'll postpone the opening."

"Don't be ridiculous."

"Well then, we'll close for two weeks."

"When we've just opened? You might as well throw the whole thing away," Alice shouted, "and I know what you're going to say next. That it's your shop. All yours to do what you like with."

"I wasn't going to say that at all!"

"But it's what you are thinking, isn't it? You don't take it seriously because you don't understand about money. You have the means to live anyway. To you this is just something to try and keep your father quiet. To me it's everything. More important than anything else."

"That's obvious," Harry said and went swiftly up the stairs to his rooms and slammed the door.

For a few moments Alice was frozen and then she looked at her mother's eager face, at her aunt's embarrassment, and she ran up the stairs after him. She pushed open the door to the living-room. Harry stood by the window. She approached him slowly and touched his back.

He turned and put his arms round her, holding her so tightly that her feet came off the floor.

"I want to be more important to you than anything else. Much more important than a bloody shop."

"I'm sorry. I feel so nervous about everything." Her voice was muffled against him. "Of course you are more important. You are the most amazing thing that has ever happened to me, Harry. I still can't believe it. But let me make something of my own, too. I am so afraid you will change. I have nothing to offer you. You are free to go wherever you want. I am not." She leaned away from him. "I am afraid that this is temporary for you. That you will drift away from me. If I don't establish the shop I have nothing."

Harry sighed. "I understand. Skiing was such a lovely idea, that's all. There are so few things I do well. I wanted to show off to you."

"You go anyway, Harry. Why shouldn't you go?"

"Maybe I will. Although I don't know how to pay for it." He put his hand in his pocket. "I have one other present for you but I couldn't give it to you in front of your mother. There is something called the National Organisation for the Counselling of Adoptees and Parents. They call themselves NORCAP. This is the address. If you want to find out who you are, they will help, but they told me that only about five per cent of adopted adults seek to meet their birth families." He put the piece of paper into Alice's hands. A single white sheet of paper. Her hands trembled.

"It's not easy, Alice. To trace your natural parents you have to approach the agency which handled your adoption but it's possible there was no agency. If you can discover the name under which your birth was registered you can then trace your original birth certificate. But your real father's name would not necessarily be on it. They said perhaps you would just like to talk."

She held the piece of paper in one hand, staring at the address. She said nothing. The idea she had thought about for so long terrified her in reality. Although she wanted to know the truth, while she didn't know she was safe. Her parents could have been evil people, hopeless people, not the sophisticated, gentle people she imagined. She pretended she had been wrenched from her mother by devastating circumstances but in reality, she could have been merely discarded. She looked from the paper to his face.

"Don't you want that either?" Harry said desperately. "When we first met you spoke so passionately about finding out. We sat in that suffocatingly hot, scented garden and I was half-drugged with no sleep and misery and whisky and you leaned forward and talked like someone half-mad with curiosity. I watched you and listened to you and everything about you fascinated me. Don't tell me it wasn't true."

"Of course it was true. I do want to know. I have wanted to know so badly and for so long that I'm afraid of knowing." She folded the paper in half once. "Thank you," she said stiffly, and carried the piece of paper upstairs to the rooms she thought of as her own.

The party was a strange mixture of people, of trade people Alice had known well or slightly, Paddy and some of the other shopkeepers from his street, a mass of Harry's friends and later, Eliza. Celia came at seven thirty, without David who was in Boston, the guest of honour at a dinner there. The clash of dates had been extremely fortunate as Celia knew Harry would not have wanted his father to come. She looked round curiously for Jane Marland and asked Alice to introduce her.

"I thought you must be Harry's mother. You look exactly like him." Jane reacted to Celia's beauty with the same hostility that Harry's charm aroused.

Celia smiled. This stern woman made her nervous. She saw, in Jane's manner and expression, a distorted reflection of herself as a rich, spoilt woman. "The shop looks well organised, doesn't it?"

"I just hope they can make some money. Harry seems to think it's all so easy." Jane sipped the wine without enthusiasm.

Celia tried again. "In the past things have come easily to him but this is different. He has done this on his own."

Jane looked sceptical. For a few minutes she stood while Celia struggled to talk to her and then abruptly excused herself and went up two floors to the comparative peace of Alice's rooms. She couldn't go on talking to Celia. It was like talking to Harry. She sat down on Alice's bed and breathed more freely, looking round at all the familiar things Alice had brought here. Over the fat little armchair lay a man's silk dressing-gown with a dark paisley pattern. She touched it, bringing the soft silk to her face. The male smell seemed to make her hollow, brought a profound sense of loss. As she let it drop, her eyes fell on a sheet of paper on the bedside table, lying flat. The words of the name leapt out at her: National Organisation for the Counselling of Adoptees and Parents.

Celia had not seen Robert since the extraordinary day after the Otterwoods party but he had written to her and she had answered his letters, pouring out on paper all the frustrations of her life. His letters, in return, were factual and interesting, describing the places he visited, the people he met, describing his own feelings in a very straightforward manner. He repeated, in each of the five letters he had written in the six weeks since they had met, his distrust of the way things went so well. "Hard to believe in it all." His letters were her lifeline. He had said he would come to this party. She waited for him with hammering impatience, hardly listening to the people she was supposed to be talking to, eyes always on the door. And when she finally saw his wide figure, the dark red hair, she caught her breath and hesitated for long enough to see him touch Eliza's arm as she stood near to the door, saw Eliza turn and smile. Celia hesitated for a moment and then made her way firmly across the room which had become tiny now that so many people were crowded into it.

Robert saw her coming. He took a drink from a tray that Harry held and started towards Celia and they met in the centre of the room. They smiled at each other for too long,

Celia thought, and yet she couldn't keep the expression from her mouth. She felt lightened by seeing him, changed. But still she felt she should speak warily.

"How are you? I understand things are going well? David told me that you are chartering a tanker." She kept her eyes on his face.

"Yes. Is he here?"

"No. He's gone to Boston. He is guest of honour at some dinner."

"Have dinner with me later? I am longing to talk to you."

"Can I, without it showing?"

"Of course. Have you got a car here?"

"Yes."

"I've just got myself a flat. I moved in last week. It's in Hyde Park Mews. Seventeen. We could meet there later?"

"Yes." Celia was beginning to back away. "Now I want to go and talk to Harry. I'll see you at nine."

"Happy birthday, Alice." Eliza put a small package into her hands. Alice opened it and took out a pair of hair combs, edged with mother of pearl, and smiled her pleasure. "I thought you'd like them. They reminded me of you as soon as I saw them," Eliza said as Alice wriggled her way towards the large looking-glass they had hung over the mantel and pushed the combs into her hair.

"I love them, Eliza, thank you. You'll come with us later, won't you? Harry's booked a big table at the Crocodile and anyone who wants can come." She turned round to look at Eliza. "Will Robert come?"

"I don't know. He's been out of the office most of the day but I'll ask him later." Eliza pushed her way towards Paddy's corner and he embraced her fondly. She liked him and his friends and she stayed with them, discussing the chances of this shop succeeding, discussing Paddy's latest pantomime.

"So lucky we only do matinées on Tuesday. Couldn't

have missed this. You're coming on afterwards, aren't you, Eliza?"

"Yes," Eliza said, and looked at her watch and thought it was time to find Robert again. She burrowed into the centre of the room without finding him so she went up to the first floor, where the rest of the party had overflowed and Celia came past her on the stairs.

"Goodbye, Eliza. It's most impressive, isn't it? I'm sorry I can't stay and have dinner with you all."

Eliza found Harry, sitting in an armchair. He was surrounded by a group of his friends who all talked across him and Eliza crouched down.

"It's a lovely party, Harry."

"Thanks. Shop looks good, doesn't it?"

"Very good."

"Hope it's all right." He frowned, as if thinking deeply.

Eliza touched his arm. "Have you seen Robert?"

"He's gone. He said goodbye a few minutes ago."

"Are you sure?" Eliza frowned, standing up, feeling all the elation drain from her, feeling the evening go black and white.

"Quite sure. Gone." Harry got unsteadily to his feet and went in search of more wine.

They finally reached the small restaurant in the adjoining street at ten thirty, sweeping down the stairs to the basement dining-room where Harry had reserved a table for twenty. Eliza watched the people who were already there flinch at this invasion. She found herself sitting between Harry and Paddy and tried very hard to shake off the melancholy which possessed her but she longed for Robert's presence, the amount of wine she had consumed dissolving her usual strict censorship of her feelings. In the daytime and coldly sober she never would have allowed herself to indulge in such longing.

Harry ordered champagne and the party grew louder. Somehow food was ordered and they shouted happily at each other and the basement was hot and thick with smoke. Harry had arranged a birthday cake which arrived just after midnight. A whole day late, Harry announced, and then sat down abruptly and Eliza imagined Jane being here and was thankful that her mother and Molly had gone home. The coffee cups were filled and refilled and at one, when a few couples had left, there was a move to go on to a club and dance but no one could decide where.

Eliza stood up and went round the back of Alice's chair.

"I think I might go home, Alice."

"I wish I could," Alice said. "It's been lovely but Harry never knows how to stop and they all use him to get them in to places. I keep trying to tell him that we have to open on time tomorrow but he's untouchable when he's drunk this much."

"Don't let him drive home."

"I won't. I know, I'll pretend we're going to wherever they arrange and just drive back to Pembridge Gardens instead." She kissed Eliza. "'Night."

"What about paying for all this?" Eliza said.

"I don't know. Harry will put it on one of his plastic cards, I suppose."

Eliza took out ten pounds and put it into Alice's hand. "Give him that."

"He won't take it. It's pointless."

"Make him." Eliza said goodbye to Paddy and went up the narrow stairs, retrieving her coat and stepping out into a bitter February night. She walked quickly to her car and got in, sliding down in the seat and lighting a cigarette and then putting it out almost at once. She had expected this evening to have great significance, the first party she had known Robert would be at since everything changed. She had deliberately worn the silver shirt. Anger and impatience made her clench her hands, and then, despising herself for her childishness, she drove towards Marble Arch and turned left into the narrow mews where Robert had taken his flat, pausing opposite it for a few moments to look up at the lighted windows. It was reassuring to think of him in there.

Whatever he had been doing he was home. She looked across to where his car was parked and then her eyes were drawn in this well-lit mews to a car that was parked facing Robert's, nose to nose, and a shock wave of recognition hit Eliza. She turned off the engine and got out of her car, running across the cobbles to make sure. There was no mistaking Celia Otterwood's white Alfa Romeo. After the trouble she had had booking it onto the Aberdeen sleeper, Eliza would never forget the distinctive numberplate.

"I feel I have no one at the moment," Celia said. She sat on the floor, legs folded beneath her, a glass of brandy cradled in her hands. "And when I think that I am filled with terror at being so isolated. Harry is shut away from me by the gulf between him and David. I am part of David as far as he is concerned, even if I am a sympathetic part. I miss Harry terribly. He used to phone me, often." She drank some brandy. "He has Alice now and doesn't need to. Julia and I have never been very close. Her self-possession builds a wall round her. She is so sure of herself. David all over again. And Josie worries so much that with her I have to pretend everything is all right. I want her to be happy. To protect her. With my friends, even close friends, I have pretended for so long that David and I understand each other that I can't change now. I don't want their sympathy because first I have to admit to the failure." She looked up at Robert. "I live with David and yet we are separate. It is a desolate feeling, this nothing where there was once so much. That's why being with you and talking to you is so wonderful."

"It's a luxury for me to be able to talk, too. I have never felt, before you, that I could trust anyone absolutely. Not even Sophia." He spoke her name deliberately. He wanted Celia to ask.

"Who is Sophia?"

"Sophia M'habela. She is the daughter of the notorious Chief Michael M'habela, the Nigerian minister who gets himself into the news now and then."

Celia frowned. "I have heard of him. In fact, I even know what he looks like. He came to London not long ago, didn't he? And there were some demonstrations against him. He's very black and very good-looking."

"And very unscrupulous. Sophia has inherited her father's looks but nothing else. She was educated in England, at Benenden. Her voice is rather like yours, but deeper." He smiled. "Like you, she has an inborn confidence, nothing to pretend about. That openness is very attractive. Sophia qualified as a solicitor in England and went back to Lagos six years ago. I had known her father for some years. We met soon after she arrived and we lived together until shortly before I met you, although, for the last year, things have not been too good."

"Why not?"

"Because, all the time I have known her, Sophia has been trying to make me into what I am not, to succeed with me where she has failed with her father. She has dreams for Nigeria. Impossible dreams of changing the whole order of things, of stamping out corruption and replacing people like her father with people like herself. I have no interest in the country apart from its potential for business. To me, the success of Stoner Shipping and my own personal comfort and survival come above all else. I have never pretended otherwise but Sophia believed she could change and inspire me. Because we were such successful lovers, she wanted us to think alike. Until eight months ago everything I was doing was so insignificant it didn't count. But last July there was an incident at the landing stage where a man was killed. I wasn't even in the country but Sophia feels that the men who worked for me were protected by her father. She wanted me to make sure they came to trial." He laughed, bitterly. "It is hardly surprising that I wouldn't go out of my way to cause trouble for my own men, especially when it was all neatly smoothed over, but it was the end as far as Sophia was concerned. She finally admitted to herself that I will never be what she wants. We are on different sides. I am not dishonest but my chief concern is to make myself a lot of money as soon as possible and that means that sometimes I won't be as scrupulous as I should."

Celia sat up, hunching her shoulders tightly, putting down her drink and folding her arms round herself.

"I hate it when you talk like David. You must be careful. You need more than success in your life. David is the most purely selfish man I have ever known."

"But you loved him?"

"Yes, I did. And he seemed to love me. He enveloped me. I was a child when we met. I loved the attention, his importance, the power he projected although he was so young. My uncertainty was lost in his confidence. We were happy. He was delighted when Harry was born. In fact, every time I have been pregnant, he has treated me with a most touching reverence and deep respect. I think, when I was carrying his children, he really loved me. In between times he loved other women." She rocked slightly. "Not long ago, he suggested we have another child. I was amazed. Appalled that he should think it is possible when there is such a distance between us. But perhaps it was our only hope and he knew it."

Robert moved down onto the floor beside her. Absolute stillness fell between them as he touched her, putting one hand on the side of her face until she leaned her face down. They moved together, agreeing without speaking, into the small bedroom. It was lit only by the overflow of light from the living-room and it was cold. They sat on the bed and Celia shivered and moved close to Robert's warmth.

Robert wrapped the duvet round them both and they lay on his bed and as his hands began to touch her body she rolled suddenly away from him, dragging the duvet with her, and sitting on the edge of the bed.

"I can't make love to you. However empty our marriage is, I still feel married. If I behave like David he will have changed everything about me."

"Don't think about him at all. He doesn't matter. You and I matter. And I'm bloody freezing."

Celia turned, half-laughing, apologetically spreading the duvet back over him.

"That's not enough. I want you to make me warm."

She hesitated and then slid back into bed, into Robert's arms, and there was not another chance for her to change her mind.

Chapter 19

Celia woke very early the following morning after three hours of fragmented sleep. Her head ached and she moved nervously and restlessly, as if she had a temperature. She longed to speak to Robert on the telephone and dignify their love-making by arranging further meetings and yet she felt it would be so much better if she did not see him again. She wanted to hide from the thought of all the complications to come, the joy as well as the pain. *I have taught myself to live on a level plane. I don't want to feel shaken up like this.* At six thirty she went down to the kitchen and made herself a mug of tea which she carried back up to bed. It was not until eight thirty that Robert rang and by that time she was beginning to feel the whole thing was a terrible mistake.

"I felt I had to wait until a reasonably respectable time in case someone else answered your phone," Robert said. "I'm in the office now. I shall expect you to meet me for lunch at one."

"Do you really want to see me?"

"Of course I bloody well want to see you. Last night may have been fairly routine for you but it was fantastic for me and I want to see you as soon as possible. Half past twelve, not one!"

Celia laughed. "You know it wasn't routine. It was so amazingly out of character that I can't really believe it happened."

"Don't talk in the past tense," Robert said. They talked for ten or fifteen minutes and Celia was surprised at how easily they could talk. Then, quite suddenly, his voice altered. He named a restaurant and Celia guessed that Eliza had arrived.

If Robert noticed a distinct strangeness about Eliza that

morning, he did not analyse it. He met Celia as arranged. She was early, arriving fifteen minutes before Robert and watching the door nervously as she waited for him. When his solid figure appeared, standing in the distinctive way he had, she felt a moment of absolute panic and she half rose, as if to leave, until he caught sight of her. As their eyes met the panic evaporated and a feeling of inevitability took its place.

She could hardly be bothered to look at the menu. The thought of food was uninteresting, almost revolting. She wanted to talk and talk and talk, she wanted to explain her delight to him.

"Everything has changed, Robert. I have thought so much in the past few hours. I have had to face up to things and, whatever happens, I can't go on living with David now. I shall gradually gather my strength and break away."

"Just like that?" Robert said, taking her hands. "I must be even better in bed than I thought."

Celia felt warmth in her face and body as she remembered their love-making. "It was special, wasn't it?"

He lifted her hand up to his lips. "Very special. I spent most of this morning planning how I could get you to myself somewhere for a few days, not just an evening."

She let the pleasure of being wanted lap over her like warm water. Being with him, touching him, looking across into his face, quite simply made her happy. Robert ate hungrily as they talked, and listening to him and having her opinion considered, being involved in his ideas and ambitions, delighted and alarmed her at the same time. "It's just that first break. Once you start, however small the start is, it's enough. If you are determined, you can make it."

He was silent for a few moments and Celia shivered.

"What is it?"

"You are talking like David again and it scares me. Nothing really matters in David's life but himself. You must care about people and things beyond yourself."

"I care about one person beyond myself, although she is

the last person I should get myself involved with," Robert smiled. "Will that do?"

When they left the restaurant in mid-afternoon and came out into the street Robert put his arms round her and kissed her.

"Robert, you're mad. I have friends all over London."

"Tell them I'm your long-lost cousin."

"Why should I bother? I don't care. Let them talk!" She leaned against him, her face close to his, and kissed him back.

"I wish I could see you tomorrow but I am flying back to Lagos. I take possession of the ship I am chartering from Otterwoods on March the first and it is due to sail five days later so I want to be around to make sure everything goes as it should."

"It would be difficult to see you, anyway. David is flying back on Concorde. Tonight we have a business dinner at Flood Street and tomorrow I am lunching with my sister and David has tickets for the ballet." She made a face. "It's my bloody birthday. I shall be forty. I can use it as an excuse, can't I, for my imprudent behaviour? A fear of old age."

"Not looking as you do. Now I want even more to be with you tomorrow but, as I can't, I'll bring you something back from Nigeria."

He embraced her again and she broke away and walked quickly, laughing, to the corner where she turned and waved and blew him a kiss. The King's Road was transformed, gilded by weak February sunshine. Even the fat, dusty pigeons and the punks were beautiful. Nothing could touch her now.

By midnight the last guests had gone and Celia sat in the deep chintz sofa, a glass of brandy cupped in her hands, and at last allowed herself to think about Robert, to wonder if he was asleep or if he was thinking of her.

David's voice broke into her thoughts. When she had looked at David that afternoon she had felt nothing. No guilt, no anger, just nothing and it had shocked her. Is this how he feels about me when he has a lover, that I am irrelevant?

"Celia."

She wanted to ignore the words and stay with her thoughts, the way she sometimes tried to hold on to a good dream, but he spoke again and reluctantly she forced herself to concentrate.

"Happy birthday," David said.

"I don't want to think about it."

"Don't you want your present now?"

She shook her head, without looking at him. "No thank you."

David raised his eyebrows. Then he said, "I talked to Geoffrey for a long time tonight."

Celia concentrated again, with difficulty. "Geoffrey?"

"Geoffrey Masters. He runs the Hong Kong office. He's a shrewd man. I trust his judgment. We discussed Harry. He thinks Harry will come round if he is given time and I agree, as long as he drops all this ridiculous talk about marriage. The last thing he wants is to tie himself up to that empty-headed girl who will instantly produce children."

"She isn't empty-headed," Celia said. "She is intelligent and calm and lovely to look at and quite charming. She could be exactly the right person for Harry. He is not a stable person. Sometimes I'm afraid for him. You must not corner him, David. It's true, what Julia said about him drinking too much. Alice could be just what he needs."

"That's fine as long as he forgets about marrying her. How can anyone seriously talk of marriage at nineteen?"

"I was nineteen when I married you."

"And I was twenty-five. A boy of nineteen doesn't need any one girl, he needs lots of different girls."

"At what age does that rule change?" Celia asked coldly and had the satisfaction of seeing the surprise on David's face. She sat forward a little, emboldened. "When are you going to accept that Harry will never run Otterwoods and admit that Julia probably could?"

"I can see just as well as you can how clever Julia is and

how tough she pretends to be, but, even today, a woman cannot run something as large and complex and essentially masculine as Otterwoods."

"A few years ago I would have agreed with you but then, a few years ago I always agreed with everything you said. Now I am sure you are wrong. Obviously she may not last the course but she must be allowed a chance and, if she can successfully work her way up through the company, she could, in the end, run things just as well as you do."

"Over my dead body."

"Probably," Celia said dryly. "Not even you will live for ever!"

David looked down at her. Celia had changed lately. There was more bite to her. There had been a time when her gentle but perceptive comments had meant a lot to him, a time when she had been involved in Otterwoods, involved in his life. Whatever situation he had been in, he had felt Celia's unwavering loyalty and belief in him. Had he lost that now? He wondered at what point they had drawn back from one another. Celia even looked different, he thought. She had some new clothes that were brighter and more daring than the normal expensive but very classical things she bought. Tonight she was dressed in leather trousers and a brilliantly patterned silk shirt, a wide belt round her waist. The large eyes shone angrily in her face. She seemed to be aware of her body in a way that was new, almost arrogant. She looked lovely.

David sat down on the sofa beside her and put a small leather box into her hands.

"As I won't last for ever, would you open this now while I'm still around?"

Celia lifted the hinged lid very slowly and took out a diamond and emerald ring, the stones encircling the ring entirely. She put it on her finger in complete silence. David took her hand and looked at it. He caressed her fingers gently, thoughtfully, and lifted them to his lips.

"The woman who sold it to me said it was an eternity ring because the stones are set in a complete circle."

Celia took her hand back, some habit of politeness

making her murmur, "Thank you." She turned and looked at him. "Why do you give me this now when everything is so awful?"

He shrugged. "To try and make things better. To demonstrate that you mean a lot to me, whatever impression I may give sometimes. Don't pretend you don't know me, Celia. You know exactly how I am. When I want something badly enough I tend to forget about other people. It's not deliberate."

"Isn't it? How convenient to hurt people absent-mindedly. Not really your fault. You forget and ignore 'other people' completely until they are forced by their desperation to react and then, suddenly, you remember and think you had better make some small move towards 'other people' to get them on your side again. Well it's not so easy. As you said yourself, I know exactly how you are. And the things you have done and are still doing cannot be undone by all the rings in the world."

Celia stood up abruptly, put down her glass and went out of the room, running up the stairs, snatching her nightgown from the bed and taking it into one of the spare rooms. She felt strong and resolute. Robert's attention, Robert's body, had left their mark. She no longer felt she was facing David entirely on her own. She pulled the ring off her finger and went back into the bedroom she shared with David and put it on the dressing- table.

Five days after the charter began, the *Otterwood Endeavour* was fuelled and loading. Rolfe was installed as supernumerary master in an advisory role and the tanker was due to sail on the evening of March the sixth. That afternoon, as Robert drove down towards the docks, the road took him past Sophia's office. She had left a message with Mick that she wanted to see Robert and a combination of habit and curiosity and the urge to talk about his success made him stop. He went into the large air-conditioned room where she sat, frowning down at a pile of letters.

She raised her eyes as Robert came in, her face

impassive, but before she had time to control her feelings the sight of him, unexpectedly like this, affected her strongly. Her face became stern as she suppressed the emotion but she kept her eyes on his face. It had been months since he had come here.

Her voice was cool. "I heard you were back."

"Not for long. Just to watch my ship sail."

"So things are going well?"

"Very well indeed. I have taken a small office in one of your father's office blocks and Jenny Patricks is going to work for me part-time. I thought you might have grown tired of being my messenger girl in the circumstances."

"Actually, I rather liked keeping track of you."

"Well it will be even easier now. Just lift the telephone and ask Jenny."

"Yes. I realise you have deliberately chosen someone as gossipy as she is to prove how incredibly honest and open your whole business is!"

"How astute you are," Robert said dryly, and smiled.

"Well, is it?"

"What?"

"Honest and open and above board?"

"Of course." He came towards her desk and sat down, folding his arms and leaning forward. "Is that what you wanted to ask me?"

"Yes. There are so many rumours. My father is being watched. I am worried about you."

He shrugged. "There is no need."

"Can I come down to the Terminal with you and watch the ship sail, just for old times' sake?" His voice and the way he sat, his familiar smell as she leaned towards him, all these things weakened her.

"You never asked to come and watch the landing craft unload cement or to watch the little Venezuelan tanker set sail."

"This is different."

"It sure is. This baby costs four hundred thousand dollars a month. This is the real thing." He tilted the chair slightly so that he leaned backwards. "Do you really want to come and watch, Sophia? I thought you detested the whole idea of my selfish obsession with becoming rich."

"I do. But that doesn't mean I don't want to come and watch."

He stood up, as she did, feeling, as he had so many times over the past five years, that her mind was a maze he would never reach the heart of.

They drove towards the docks in Robert's car, passing through the conventional dock area with its mass of wharves and warehouses, containers and lorries. The scale of everything was different here. Sophia looked up at the huge slanting sides of the ships standing aloof from the activity of dockers and seamen. Tall cranes stood out against the hot blue sky and then they moved into a different landscape of oil tanks and pipelines, parking the car and beginning to walk the half-mile-long T-shaped jetty to where four tankers were loading. Robert pointed out the *Otterwood Endeavour* proudly, an enormous black ship with a distinctive green and orange funnel at the stern, her sides festooned with ropes and hoses and chains.

"Rather a distinguished-looking ship, isn't she?"

There was a smell of hot oil in the air as he led Sophia up the slanting walkway onto the lower deck and through a series of passageways and steep stairs until they reached the bridge where Rolfe Petersen greeted them warmly and Sophia was introduced to the master, Per Yversen, an enormous blond man who was also Norwegian.

Rolfe rocked on his heels as if enjoying some secret joke. "We're ready, Robert. We sail at six. Have you come to wish us luck on our first voyage, Sophia?"

"Yes, I have. Good weather, is that what I should wish you?"

"Just an uneventful voyage."

"How long does it take to sail to Singapore?"

"Ten days, three days to unload and ten days back, with slight variations for weather."

"I've never been to Singapore. Maybe I'll come with you some time."

The three men laughed. "I don't think that's a good

idea. There are a lot of quicker and more comfortable ways to get to Singapore and your presence on board might be a little unsettling," Rolfe answered.

Just before six, Robert and Sophia left the ship and watched as the last ropes were drawn back on board and as the immense bulk of the *Endeavour* was gently eased away from the jetty by a tug and taken out towards the open sea. "Rolfe could handle the *Endeavour* himself without a tug," Robert said scornfully, "but it doesn't do to throw your weight around too soon." They watched for some time and then turned and wandered slowly back along the jetty.

Exhilaration pulsed through Robert. "Drink?" he said, taking her hand lightly.

Sophia hesitated. He seemed to move so effortlessly in and out of her life, either without knowing or without caring that each time she saw him the top was scraped off the wound. She could sense his exhilaration. It was irresistible.

"Well?"

"For old times' sake, I suppose."

They drove back through the derelict area which surrounded the port into the richer suburbs where many of the white workers had their houses and Robert turned his car in through the tall gates of the Ikoyi Club. They sat on a wide verandah, watching and listening as the African night made ready to pounce, staring out at the rough scrub that constantly threatened to engulf the well-kept grounds.

"You are very different," Sophia said after a long silence with half a large gin and tonic inside her.

"Of course I am different. I am beginning to get what I want. I am exhilarated and I can't stop thinking. My brain races on ahead of me." He paused, surprised that he should still speak so openly to her. He found it difficult to know how to respond to Sophia now they were no longer lovers. The intensity and passion they had shared for five years did not easily water down into friendship.

"It's more than that. It's not just that you are at last

achieving the success you crave. Will you tell me about her?"

"How do you always manage to read my bloody mind?"

Sophia shrugged.

"She is the wife of someone I particularly don't want to antagonise."

Although she had pressed him, to hear it admitted in words was shocking. Like a cell door slamming shut. Reality.

"How unlike you to be so rash," she said glibly. "Can I come to the wedding?"

"There won't be any wedding. It is just an interlude. You know that the only thing which really concerns me is the success of Stoner Shipping and everything hinges on this first voyage."

"I desperately want you to succeed too. I want you to be able to cut yourself off from my father and his deals. Get free of it all." Sophia finished the gin. "Can I have another drink, please?"

"I think I can afford that."

She ignored the flippancy, her face stern and serious. "Promise me one thing, Robert. Promise me that this shipping of oil to Singapore is not one of my father's dubious schemes."

Robert laughed. "And if it were and you found out about it, would you throw us to the wolves, Sophia?"

"I wouldn't have to. As I said earlier, he is being watched all the time. He has so many enemies. General Lugamo came to see me last week. He has wanted to get something on my father for years. Any small excuse would do."

"How can you even see that man? He is completely unstable and very dangerous."

"He may be a Hausa but he wants the same things for this country as I do. He is volatile but he is also sincere."

Robert held up his hand and indicated he would like more drinks.

"I think you are straying into bad company, Sophia, without my calming influence."

"You don't know that man at all. You can't have met him more than twice."

"Once was too much."

"You never gave him a chance, Robert."

Robert raised an eyebrow. "Can I come to the wedding?"

"Don't be ridiculous." She narrowed her eyes, angrily. "If I ever marry I want a man to myself. I don't intend to join a family group." She sank down in her chair slightly, long legs entangled round one another. "As usual, you have distracted me." She sat forward, looking into his face. "Robert, will you promise me that there is nothing dishonest about this oil you are shipping to Singapore?"

"I promise you. As far as Singapore is concerned you have nothing to worry about." He took the second drink and as Sophia took hers he said, impulsively, "Come and eat somewhere? I don't want to eat alone tonight. I'm too happy. And you are not happy and I don't like to see you disturbed." He leaned towards her. "Just friends?"

For a moment she thought of all the evenings in the past when they had eaten together and drunk a lot of wine, laughed and fought and lost the night in love-making. It would all be changed. Because of the woman in England, would the night end with Robert leaving her politely at her door? She shook her head. "I really don't want to. I have been so careful to put you out of my thoughts and my life. I can't be just friends, Robert. I'm sorry. When are you leaving?"

"In two or three days but I'll be back at the end of March when the *Endeavour* prepares for her second voyage. I'll see you then, perhaps?"

"Probably not. I'll be away. An old school friend wants me to be godmother to her baby daughter. Marie-Clare lives in Kenya, in Nairobi, so I thought I would take a couple of weeks and have a holiday. I hardly know Kenya."

As she stood up, Robert did the same, taking her arm.

"Can I drive you back into town?"

"I'd rather take a cab. I have someone to see on the way

and then I'll pick up my car. I have a lot of work to do tonight. I am in the middle of a very complicated case." She looked into his eyes and gave a rueful smile. "Life goes on. Goodbye, Robert."

He raised his hand in a little salute. "My regards to your father," he said.

He sat down again and watched Sophia walk across the short grass, thinking what an extraordinary blend of cultures she expressed: African tribal instinct and English public school education bound together by a daunting intelligence.

Chapter 20

Five days after the *Otterwood Endeavour* set sail, ostensibly for Singapore, it approached Durban. The radio officer contacted SASOL and was instructed to approach a single buoy mooring one and a half miles off the coast. The distinctive green and orange funnel of the *Endeavour* was now black and the ship's name on the bows and stern concealed. The large ship was manoeuvred skilfully through the deep water towards the floating island and they picked up the oil pipe and began to discharge oil, estimating it would take twenty-four hours to unload the one hundred thousand tons. The radio was silenced. The harbour master at Durban would have no record of the unnamed ship's visit and the South African coastguard made no contact. It was a nervous twenty-four hours for Rolfe. Although Bernard had done his job well and the unloading was accomplished without a hitch, it was still with a sigh of relief that he left the mooring twenty-four hours later and turned towards the open sea, to anchor in a secluded spot off the West Coast of Africa for a few days and spend the time they had to spare before they could legitimately sail back to Nigeria.

The *Endeavour* was seldom far from Robert's mind through those early days in March but he knew that silence was a good sign and he didn't expect to hear from Rolfe unless there was trouble. He just had to wait it out.

Two days after he returned to London, Eliza came in with some letters for him to sign and an invitation from Kit Secombe.

"He rang and asked if you want to go to a lunch next Wednesday. David has arranged a lunch for some of their clients. He won't be there himself. He's going to Japan." She looked thoughtful. "He's never at home for more than a few weeks at a time, is he? I know he likes to fit in some shooting and fishing here and there and the odd skiing trip. The talk was that Celia hardly ever went with him. She doesn't like skiing, does she?"

Robert looked up from the letters he was signing and studied Eliza's expression. "I've no idea." He was continually impressed by the efficient way Eliza ran the small office. There were no mistakes, no lost messages, and after years of having to type his own letters he appreciated the way his letters were presented. And yet he was aware of a distinct change in Eliza. He frowned. "Eliza, I've hardly spoken to you since you came to work here."

"Since I joined the company, you mean."

"Okay, since you joined the company. I really am very pleased with the way things are going. How about dinner tonight to celebrate our first few months?"

"Why? Are you entertaining someone I can help with?" Eliza said. Once the remark would have been followed by the paisley-eyed smile and would have drawn a smile from him in return. Now it merely sounded sarcastic and she regretted it.

"I just want to know if you're content," Robert said patiently.

She thought for a moment, choosing her words with great care. "Content, yes, but not fully extended and I have a great many more ambitions."

Robert smiled. "Tell me about them tonight. We can go back to my flat when we finish here, have a drink and eat quite early."

"I'd like to change."

"Why? I like the way you look now. I nearly always like the way you look, in fact." He put his elbows on his desk and smiled at her.

"I'd rather come to your flat about seven-thirty. I prefer to have a bath and a little time between work and going out."

Robert shrugged. "As you wish."

In the early days, each time Eliza anticipated an evening

with Robert she imagined that it would change everything, that somehow they would cross the gulf between mere attraction and becoming lovers. Now she was not so sure. Many times she had imagined they were lovers. They should have been together after the launching. A simple, wonderful night. In the early morning she would have gone back to her own room to wake on home ground. She had thought of it so much that sometimes it seemed they had made love. Often when she looked at Robert, it was as if she remembered his body. Did he think about her? It would have been so different, she was convinced, if it had not been for Celia.

In the last few months, Eliza had watched Robert as closely as she had once studied David. She knew him now. The sparkle in his eyes and the change in his voice when he was in difficulty, the relish with which he approached a problem. It must be difficult for him, she thought, to have to maintain such an air of confidence. He must need to relax with someone, to trust someone and talk. He must have doubts. Although this first voyage to Singapore appeared to be going smoothly, Eliza knew they operated on a knife edge. Sometimes he must worry. Was it to Celia that he talked? When Eliza got back to her flat she bathed and changed and drove to Hyde Park Mews, leaving her car outside in the very spot where she had seen Celia's white car parked. She wanted to arrive in a different role, to separate the evening from the day. *This time*, Eliza thought, *this time*. But without conviction.

Robert poured her the glass of wine she asked for. His flat was untidy, with newspapers and unwashed mugs; he treated it like a hotel room, Eliza realised.

"You need someone to come in and clean. Shall I try and fix it for you?"

"Yes, but in the afternoons. If I am here in the morning I don't want to be disturbed." He sprawled on the sofa, a drink in his hand, and Eliza sensed his thoughts were elsewhere. He looked up apologetically and smiled.

"It's going to be all right, isn't it?" Eliza said, sitting on the arm of the sofa.

"As far as I know. I want two or three runs to Singapore under my belt. I want to charter that second tanker. Also I have an option from a Swedish company to charter two supply ships very cheaply indeed. But that's rather a long shot." He stood up. "Let's go and eat, Eliza, and this time I'll give you a chance to look at the menu." He held out her coat and as she pushed her arms in she brushed against him. An imperceptible shiver passed through Eliza.

He must feel it too, she thought. *It is never one-sided when the feeling is as strong as this.* But although Robert laughed a lot through dinner, as hard as Eliza tried she still felt he was behind a glass wall. Twice it was on the tip of her tongue to mention Celia and twice she bit the words back. It was still far too soon.

She turned the conversation back to Stoner Shipping, genuinely wanting to know everything about the company and thinking that it was a subject Robert wanted to talk about.

"How dependent are we on the Singapore charter? Is it essential?"

Again there was a hesitation before he answered, as if he were considering how much to tell her. "The Venezuela run is viable in its own right. If we lost Singapore it would be a blow but something else could come up."

"And what if the *Endeavour* went unserviceable?"

"We would charter another tanker as quickly as possible. There is no shortage of available tankers at the moment."

"And we pay month by month."

"Yes."

"So you can't pay for something you haven't had. If anything went wrong, I mean?"

"No. But I have chartered for a year so, in theory, Otterwoods could hold me to that and still demand their money even if the trade disappeared. However, that would be extremely vindictive. With something as small as Stoner Shipping they would be trying to get blood from a stone and they'd know it."

Eliza nodded.

"Why so many questions?" Robert said.

"So that I understand it all. So that I can run things if you are away, take decisions if necessary. I have worked with a shipping company for seven years but I had very little to do with chartering. I want to know all I can. I want you to take me much more seriously and discuss everything with me."

Robert leaned towards her across the small table and for the first time she felt the full weight of his concentration. "Why this earnest career woman act, Eliza? You have impressed me anyway. You don't have to keep proving how serious you are and the slightly aggressive air is completely transparent. It makes you seem vulnerable. It's rather touching, but why do you need to do it?"

Eliza narrowed her eyes furiously. She felt the familiar pulse of her anger in her swift, hard heart-beat. "Don't patronise me, Robert. I'm just as intelligent as you are. I want to know how things work so I can run the company. What is so extraordinary about that?"

Robert folded his arms. "Why do I always get tangled up with ambitious bloody women?" He sat back. "Look, Eliza, all day long I think about shipping and worry about it and plan the next move. I really don't want to talk about it all evening too. Can we discuss it again tomorrow?"

"So that's Celia's appeal, is it? Her total lack of interest in shipping despite having been married to David for a hundred years. You'd think that kind of naïvety would get boring. Perhaps that's why David misbehaves? Perhaps, although she looks so lovely, she is very dull?"

Robert straightened his shoulders and his face stiffened. His eyes narrowed and his voice was soft. "What exactly are you getting at, Eliza?"

Eliza knew she was about to go too far. She drank deeply from her wine glass. "I'm getting at you, that's who I'm getting at." She held onto her control with extreme difficulty and managed a rueful smile. "I told you about my temper a long time ago. I am also very jealous and possessive person even if I don't have the right to be. But take me seriously, Robert."

"I might say the same, Eliza. If we're going to work happily together and you are going to achieve all you want, you will have to respect certain confidences."

Eliza searched his face for some trace of anxiety and found none. "You know you can trust me absolutely as long as I am not required to do anything dishonest," she said primly and had the satisfaction of hearing Robert laugh. He drove back to his flat where Eliza's car was parked and offered her a drink but she refused. The evening had gone so strangely that she wanted to go home and think.

For the first few weeks in the shop in Pembridge Gardens there was very little trade and Harry was hounded by bills. He pushed them into heaps. Sometimes he opened and shuffled them and paid very small ones.

Alice would spend her mornings arranging and re-arranging the stock and perhaps, towards mid-afternoon she would be visited by a stylist but more than half a dozen customers in a day was unusual. The most constant visitors were Harry's friends.

For the first week Alice commuted from Hove, leaving Seagull Avenue in the darkness of early morning and catching the seven twenty-eight to Victoria. She was at Pembridge Gardens just before nine but it cost her nearly four pounds a day.

"Why?" Harry asked, coming down into the shop in her father's dressing-gown. "It's such a waste of time and energy and money."

"Just this first week, Harry. To make it gradual. I can't move out so quickly."

"You don't want to, is that it?"

"Of course not," she protested but there was some truth in it. Much as she loved being with Harry at Pembridge Gardens, she needed time to herself, Harry demanded constant attention. She urged him, again and again, to go skiing without her. "I want you to have a holiday and I want to be here on my own for a short time, to feel that I am running things." In the end he agreed to go for a week, more to get away from the bills than anything else.

"I could never have paid for two of us to go for two weeks, anyway. I must have been mad." He caught Alice's arm. "You must stay with me for a few days before I go. I must store you up for the week I am away."

In the end she agreed and they spent a week together in mid-March. The mornings were a desperate struggle for her to open the shop by nine, with Harry full of love, holding her like an octopus, and full of reasons to stay in bed.

"What is the point of opening a shop which has no customers?"

"It will have. It must be open." She made a prim face at him. "I am older than you Harry. I only hope you will develop a sense of responsibility when you are twenty." She slid out of his reach and stood, lost in one of the big white nightgowns she wore, looking so appealing that Harry would spring at her and roll her back into bed again but she always managed to be dressed and down by nine, to turn the sign to open and unlock the door with a feeling of satisfaction and pride. And the morning before Harry was due to go skiing she was rewarded by an early visit from a girl she knew slightly who was selecting the props for a large cookery book and wanted some different accessories. She and Alice spent two hours selecting linens for twenty different shots and they were hired for two weeks. When Sally finally left, Alice went running upstairs to show Harry the cheque, waving it at him and bouncing on the bed.

"And she's coming back on Monday for more. Our first big contract."

"Hurrah," Harry said, throwing aside the newspaper and leaning forward to look at the letters Alice had brought up. "So your faith has been rewarded." He opened a long white envelope and stiffened as he read the contents. "From my father. He wants me to go and have lunch with him and discuss matters." Harry leaned back. "Luckily I'm away on the day he suggests. I'll pretend I went before the letter arrived. Now I suppose I'd better pack. Hugh and the others are picking me up at six tomorrow morning. Our flight leaves Gatwick at nine." He opened the second letter and went very pale. "Great news, Alice. The bank had bounced one of our cheques."

Harry spent the morning silently making lists or throwing clothes into a big nylon bag but by lunchtime he had managed to put the bank letter out of his mind and announced he was going to Flood Street to get his skis and boots. He was back at two thirty, with a long canvas bag hooked over his shoulder. He leaned it against the wall in the entrance passage.

"My mother is a bit odd," he said thoughtfully. "I had a bowl of soup with her. She seemed jumpy. As if she was waiting for something and when the phone rang she didn't sound natural. Funny how, when you know someone really well, you know every note of their voice and you can tell exactly how they are feeling. She looked different, too. Very pretty." He shrugged. "Whatever is making her happier, I'm glad. She asked how you were and I told her you couldn't wait to have the shop to yourself. She said she'll come round and see you one morning."

They went to have supper with Eliza the night before Harry left, coming up the dark, cold stairs into the warmth of Eliza's flat and a delicious garlicy smell. Eliza had left the door slightly ajar and she looked out of the kitchen, her face unusually pale and clean of the vivid make-up she usually wore. She was dressed in baggy jeans and a big sweat shirt and her very short hair stood away from her head as if it had been ruffled.

"How's business?" she said, coming out to pour drinks.

"Suddenly, yesterday, very good. A big order. And today was quite busy too." Alice went to the window and looked out into the evening, into tall lighted windows opposite. Some melancholy guitar music was playing quietly. Everything felt different.

"Is Robert coming?" She took the glass of wine Eliza had

poured her and sat on the arm of the chair Harry had dropped into, a large tumbler of whisky in his hand.

"I didn't ask him." Eliza tucked her mouth in thoughtfully at the corners and drank deeply from her own glass.

"But how is Stoner Shipping going?" Harry enquired.

"Very well. The Venezuelan ship makes a decent profit even after we've given Michael Copper his substantial cut and the first voyage to Singapore seems to be okay. The bank balance looks healthy."

"Do they come back empty when they have discharged their oil?" Alice asked.

"No, they are full of ballast. It seems rather a waste but they can only carry oil. The Venezuelan ship carries light oil one way and heavy oil back again but the Singapore trade is one way."

"But still profitable?" Harry said.

Eliza sat forward on the chair. "Yes. There are huge sums of money involved, Harry. When I was with Otterwoods it never seemed like real money because there were so many people between me and it. We'd talk of a five-hundred-thousand-pound insurance claim and it really didn't seem to count but in Stoner Shipping it is all frighteningly real. I do almost everything. Today I was getting out the monthly figures. We could be wiped out by a single disaster because we have no reserves. Everything we make will be needed to cover next month's charter. I don't understand why we seem to have been paid for the next voyage before it has happened. I must ask Robert. I want to know everything. I love the feeling that what I do matters and that I have a share in it all. And that we seem to be making money!"

"Don't talk about money," Harry said. "For the first nineteen years of my life when I had it, I never gave it a thought. Now, suddenly, everyone is asking me for money I haven't got!" He stood up and refilled his glass. "When I get back from Switzerland I'm going to sell my car."

"You could always go to work at Otterwoods through this temporary crisis," Eliza said gently.

"Give in to him? You must be bloody mad! I'd never get away."

"It might not be so awful. You have made him think, over the past few months."

Harry laughed bitterly. "It's more a case of he has shown me!"

Eliza went back into the kitchen and put on water for new potatoes. "Do you leave early tomorrow, Harry?"

"Yes. Six. And Alice can't wait to be rid of me." He went into the kitchen and came out with knives and forks and laid the gate-legged table in the window for three. "She is longing to have the shop to herself."

"Anything to get rid of the packing." Alice laughed. "There are huge boots and thick socks all over the house and he keeps losing the ticket and . . ."

"Jesus!" Harry said abruptly. "Passport! It's still at Flood Street. We got it out of the desk where they keep everything and then we were talking so much we must have left it there." He looked at his watch. "I'll go round for it later. Can we all go and have a drink somewhere?"

They went at ten thirty, driving in Harry's car to Flood Street and parking outside as Harry ran up the shallow steps and let himself into the house. He was out again in a few moments.

"I wonder where my mother goes in the evenings when my father is away?" he said thoughtfully. "She's not expected back until very late."

Eliza bit her tongue. A wave of misery passed through her, leaving her cold. What was the point of saying anything? Harry wouldn't know. And Celia could be anywhere. She knew, from the time she had worked for David, how much time Celia spent at private views and at the theatre. If she chose to, she could go out every night. Still an instinct told Eliza that Celia was with Robert and she ached with jealousy but said nothing. *I must be getting old*, she thought. *I am learning to keep quiet.*

"Does any one wonder where you are?" Robert asked Celia, rolling onto his side and looking at her in the semi-darkness.

"I don't think so. We have a housekeeper in the

basement flat at Flood Street but if I am out or away, once she has given the dog his run and put him in the kitchen she goes down to her flat. I always tell her if I'll want breakfast or not in the morning."

"Don't you dislike having to make such trivial plans in advance?"

"I suppose in the beginning I may have found it difficult but now I am so used to it." Celia touched his face, moved close to him, kissing his lips and his bare freckled shoulder. His skin was warm and smooth. "I can't really believe in this, Robert. I don't want to. Just a day at a time. Like a holiday from life. That's how I think of you." The heavy bronze bracelet he had brought back for her from Lagos slid up towards her elbow as she raised her arms. "But Josie breaks up in ten days. Then I shall see much less of you for a time."

Robert put his hands each side of her face. "I don't think I like that. I don't want to have to fit in with your children's needs. I want to be a permanent part of your life." He moved his hands down her body and she closed her eyes and drew in her breath.

"You can be whatever you want."

Harry and Alice lay in a warm tangle, bodies still linked together.

"I shall miss you, every day and night of this week," Harry said. "I'm afraid that someone will come into the shop and impress you and carry you off. You are my lifeline, Alice." He sat up in the darkness, hands round his knees. "Before I met you I had this feeling of horror growing in me. A sort of helplessness. I suppose I mean failure. It was so strong. Could be again if I didn't have you and this place as a reason. The drink helps. I'm afraid you won't be here when I get back."

Alice sat up beside him, hand on his arm. "I was only half alive before I knew you. I need you just as much as you need me and no one could make me leave this shop."

He smiled. "No, I don't think they could. But I'll ring

you, anyway, and see how you are. It will be a very long week. I really don't want to go that much, Alice."

"You must go. It's all arranged. I want you to go. If we can't be separated for one week, if we can't function on our own, it will be hopeless."

"Will it?" Harry said softly. "I rather thought that was what loving someone meant."

Chapter 21

It was strange at Pembridge Gardens without Harry. Alice had expected to relish the silence, to be poised for every customer, to live without distraction and finally come to believe in it all – but she had forgotten Harry's friends. It didn't seem to matter if Harry was there or not. They came and talked and sat about and helped themselves to bottles of wine and when it was all gone, although Alice was careful not to buy any more, they weren't discouraged. They drank coffee instead.

The decorators called and asked, politely, to be paid.

"Harry's away," Alice said desperately. "But I'm sure he sent you a cheque last week."

"It was one of those rubber ones that don't work. It bounced, Miss."

"Well he gets back on Saturday."

Eliza came for lunch on Tuesday with a carrier bag full of food. "It only took me fifteen minutes on the tube. I thought it would be longer," Eliza said, restlessly pacing the shop and eating little of the food she had brought.

"Robert has gone to Hull today and he's going away again as soon as the *Endeavour* docks." Her voice was dull. "He's flying to Lagos to arrange the second voyage to Singapore, which you would think Rolfe could handle. But apparently Robert has to be there as well. And then he's going on to South America. There have been some rather mysterious phone calls. They won't talk to me." She sighed and walked to the tall window, then she rocked forward abruptly and held back one of the heavy curtains. "You've got a surprise visitor. It's Celia!"

She stood back rather quietly by the big fireplace as Celia came in, silencing Alice for the first few moments because she looked so lovely. Almost unreal. Her face was thinner and the speckled eyes were exaggerated with more make-up than Alice had seen her use before. She wore a green loden coat and a large woollen shawl was thrown round her shoulders. She greeted both girls warmly, as if they were old friends.

"I told Harry I'd come and visit you. I wanted to see you in action." She became aware of Eliza's expressionless face and tried to make her smile. "Have I caught you out, Eliza? Do you often come for lunch when Robert is away?"

Eliza tilted her head slightly to one side. "How did you guess? Especially as he only decided to go last night." Her dark eyes were hard, giving Celia a feeling of apprehension.

Celia laughed and coloured a little and turned to look at the draped lengths of butter muslin. "It was just a guess. He travels so much, doesn't he? Almost as much as David." She moved on to examine the old lace pillows, throwing back the folds of the tweed shawl.

What a bad liar you are, Eliza thought. *When you have to lie to survive you will be hopeless. I think I am good at it if I have to be.* She felt stronger now, storing the knowledge.

"These pillows are lovely. Do you only hire things, Alice, or would you sell them?" Celia turned towards Alice, holding one of the pillows, and Eliza, looking at her hands, saw the dull sheen of bronze on Celia's wrist.

"I could sell some and replace them," Alice answered.

"Would you like some coffee, Mrs Otterwood?" Eliza interrupted brightly, surprising Alice.

"Yes. I would. Please call me Celia."

"Shall I take your coat?"

"Thank you." Celia slid out of it, turning towards Eliza who took the heavy garment and now saw, quite clearly, the deep bronze bracelet, with a pattern of long-legged deer, round Celia's narrow wrist. Eliza's pale face became momentarily flushed. Her stomach turned over as if she were on a roller-coaster.

"That's a Benin bronze, isn't it?" she said.

For only a second did Celia hesitate. Then she held out her wrist. "I don't think it's as old as that. It's probably a copy."

"But several hundred years old?"

"I believe so. It's very heavy. I don't often wear it."

"Have you had it a long time?" Eliza asked.

"Yes. A very long time. Years." Celia looked down at Robert's birthday present to her, a small smile on her mouth.

She loves him, Eliza thought, turning away and murmuring about going to make coffee. *She is not just bored and angry with David. She loves Robert.*

When Alice and Celia were alone together, Celia was forced to say what was in her mind quickly, before Eliza returned.

"Alice, is Harry all right? I am desperately worried about him. I have been all year in fact. He has changed so much and sometimes he seems so unhappy. Is he all right?"

Alice looked at Celia steadily.

"Well, when we first met he seemed quite desperate. He sat in the bedroom and drank whisky. He was like someone hunted. He is happier now, except sometimes when it seems to come back."

"What is it?"

"He calls it failure. Not being what you wanted him to be. When I told him I was adopted he said he envied me more than I could possibly know because I would never let my family down."

Celia let out her breath in a long sigh. "Are we that terrible? Did David ask so much? I never did. I love Harry as he is. All I want is for him to find his own way."

"He still feels threatened." Alice came towards Celia. "There are so many bills. The trouble is, he says, that having sold his shares to pay for the lease on this place he has no income at all. The painters need paying. And the telephone bill is rather high. He uses the phone as if it were free. I am afraid that everything will go so wrong that he won't want to stay in England. That he will feel he must get right away."

"It could happen," Celia said gently. "Perhaps he will need to go for a while, but he would come back."

"That's why I'm so desperate for this place to succeed. So we can pay the rates and things. He had to borrow some of the money at a very high rate of interest. If only his trust had agreed to pay. Harry is sure that his father got at them. We could have looked for somewhere else but they might have objected to that too and I couldn't bear to discourage him. Any form of opposition, even if it's because I want to help, frenzies him. He's so volatile. And yet he can be determined."

"You love him, don't you, Alice?"

"Yes."

"Some people meet the person they should spend their lives with when they are very young. In a way it's bad luck. It is easier if you have some years to yourself first. I wish I had been older when I met David, but I wasn't and you can't stop, can you? There is no holding back time. I knew I was too young, but David was not the sort of person you could send away for a few years and I thought, why throw everything away just because it has happened a few years too soon. It all seemed inevitable. A kind of natural timing like the phases of the moon." She thought, *And now it is happening again.*

"I've always thought that. That I couldn't change things. That I must just wait and it would happen."

"That's a coward's way out," Eliza said, coming back up the stairs with a tray and three mugs of coffee. "You can change things if you want to. Or you can certainly try. And if you know you have tried your utmost then you can accept failure if it is inevitable."

She held the tray out to Celia and their eyes met and Celia was almost afraid to let Eliza look into her eyes. She felt as if Eliza could read her thoughts and feelings, her joy and her guilt. She drank the coffee too quickly, burning her mouth, and she cursed herself for being so stupid as to wear the bracelet and then reassured herself that Eliza couldn't possibly know where it had come from. Just before she left she said again to Alice, "Can I buy the two lace cushions?"

"Yes. I know where I can replace them." Alice looked

them up, rather importantly, in her stock book although she knew the price by heart. "They are fifteen pounds each."

Celia wrote a cheque which she handed to Alice. Alice had wrapped the cushions in brown paper. As she handed them to Celia she glanced down automatically at the cheque in her hand. A look of amazement touched her face.

"This is wrong, Celia. They came to thirty pounds. You've put on an extra nought."

"Have I?" Celia said with the smile that was so like Harry's. "That is a bit of luck for you. Put it towards the bills."

The following day at lunchtime, Alice closed the shop and went to the address that Harry had given her on her birthday, walking past the sedate-looking office a number of times with her heart pounding. She would probably have used up the entire half hour she allowed herself if two girls hadn't come out. They looked so ordinary that their normality gave Alice the impetus she needed to go up the steps and through double wooden doors into an area like a dentist's waiting-room: polished wooden floor and ugly assorted chairs and ancient magazines. She approached the glass window with the *Enquiries* sign above it and was asked, kindly, to wait. Five minutes later a middle-aged woman took her into a small office.

After an initial hesitation, Alice explained about herself, about her curiosity, her voice so calm it concealed her real feelings.

"I don't know anything about myself. My adopted father arranged things; he died some years ago. My adopted mother won't discuss it."

"To trace your natural parents you have to contact the agency which handled the adoption, but until a few years ago it was quite legal not to use an agency. The first step is to trace your birth certificate, but before we start I think you should talk to your adopted mother again. Explain how you feel. Tell her you have been here. She may know much more than you think and to hear it from her would be so much better for both of you."

Alice left at two, extravagantly hailing a taxi to take her back to Pembridge Gardens, and leaning back with her hands tucked deep into the pockets of the heavy army greatcoat Harry had bought for her. How could she talk to Jane yet again?

When the *Endeavour*, back in its normal colours, docked at the Terminal exactly twenty-three days after she had departed, Rolfe came ashore with a feeling of satisfaction and relief. He rang Robert that afternoon, getting through to London on the third attempt. Eliza put the call through to Robert's office.

"Safely back, Robert. Very smooth voyage. No trouble from crew or any nosey authorities. The bill of lading looked good. Your friend Bernard seems to have things very well organised."

"And the timing?"

"Perfect. Anchored for a while and went for a cruise on the way back. Seems a bit of a waste, that's all."

"I've been thinking exactly the same thing myself. I've been looking out for a neat little charter that would take a few days in the middle and I've come up with something. You will be two days loading and refuelling?"

"Yes. We're due to sail again on March the thirty-first, in the early evening."

"That's fine. I'm booked on tomorrow evening's flight. I'll see you on the thirty-first and give you details."

"Good news?" Eliza said, looking round the door when Robert finished the call.

"Very good. The first shipment went smoothly and Rolfe is back at Lagos and should sail again in two days. I'll fly out tomorrow, Eliza, and just take a look round." He grinned happily. "Another two or three runs to Singapore and we could probably charter that second tanker we have the option on. Rolfe seems happy enough, which is good. When Rolfe is unhappy he tends to drown his sorrows, with disastrous results, but when he's sober he's superb."

Two days later, Robert strolled out along the wide walkway of the oil Terminal towards the *Endeavour*, the midday sun blazing and the flat water shimmering blinding. The *Endeavour* was due to sail in three hours. Bernard Van Ryn's second payment had been in Robert's Swiss account for ten days. Otterwoods had received their payment two days ago and the fuel had been paid for this morning. Satisfaction made Robert hurry. Despite the heat, he almost ran up the unstable steps.

"Rolfe."

The tall Norwegian turned and smiled.

"You look as if you bring good news, Robert."

"I do. I heard on the market that AGIP needed a ship to take eighty thousand tons from Egypt to Mombasa. I've chartered to AGIP on a voyage charter basis." He lowered his voice slightly. "Four hundred thousand dollars. You sail to Durban as planned, discharge and then sail to Shukeit. You load there on April the tenth, discharge at Mombasa on April the fourteenth and all being well you should make it back here by the twenty-third or twenty-fourth. A couple of days won't matter but for God's sake don't attract attention anywhere you shouldn't be." Robert grinned. "There's a substantial bonus in this for you, Rolfe, and anyone else who needs it. This is the document of title to the AGIP cargo. Good luck."

"Thank you. We should have no problem if Durban works as smoothly as it did last month. This will be much better than skulking about for ten days."

"I'll try and fix trade for each voyage," Robert said and remarked, as he turned to leave. "There are some very odd rumours in South America, Rolfe. Might be worth following up. What do you know about the Falkland Islands?"

Rolfe shrugged. "In the South Atlantic. The Argentinians are constantly talking about having them back. In seventy-seven I remember, the Royal Navy mounted an exercise in the South Atlantic. I was on a tanker then.

Apparently the military in Buenos Aires were threatening action but it didn't come to anything."

"We also stationed nuclear submarines off the principal naval bases, I remember. But nothing's been happening for the past three or four years, has it?"

"Not that I've heard. Why?"

"There's a lot of talk in Venezuela, that's all."

"They're always threatening in that part of the world. Nothing'll come of it."

"Probably not," Robert said. "But if there was any trouble, it's a long way from England."

"You haven't brought Sophia to see us off this time?" Rolfe said dryly.

"No." Robert said. "I haven't seen her for some time. I think she told me she would be away for a couple of weeks, having a holiday in Kenya."

Chapter 22

Alice had not left Pembridge Gardens for nearly four weeks. It had become her home and her other life, in Seagull Avenue, seemed remote and unreal until, as on this wet Friday evening in April, Jane telephoned, trying to disguise the urgent loneliness in her voice. She ended the conversation, as usual, by asking when Alice was coming back.

"This evening," Alice said. "I'll come tonight."

When Harry first came back from his skiing holiday he was as happy as Alice had ever seen him. He was very suntanned and full of stories and he proudly showed her a hideous bruise on his left shoulder caused by a collision with a rather solid marker post during an inter-chalet slalom race. His happiness had lasted until Monday morning and the arrival of the bills, followed, shortly afterwards, by the painter. By the end of his first week back Harry was changed beyond recognition. The coldness of reality and London was far worse after a break when he had not thought about any of it. Every day brought more bills and, as the early weeks of April were wet and quiet, very few customers. Harry's bursts of optimism were short-lived. He was drinking steadily and Alice watched helplessly, sensing that things would come to a climax whatever she did. She was unwilling to leave the shop or Harry, afraid of what might happen; she felt, as always, that there was no choice in her life, that she must just wait. And as she waited, Harry steadily withdrew from her, sinking into himself, becoming a stranger. On this wet Friday Harry had been drinking heavily for most of the day. Alice looked at his sprawled figure and went quietly upstairs. She packed a small case and as she came down, Harry turned to her, staring at her incredulously, leaning forward.

"How can you possibly go home now? Everything is falling apart here."

Alice stood by the door, suitcase in one hand. Harry lay back on the wicker sofa, legs straight out in front, his eyes half closed. The familiar wine bottles were lined up in the fireplace.

"You had it all to yourself for a week. You didn't do much with it. The shop has been open for a month and the money we are taking is pathetic. It's a game, not a business. It's a charity. And instead of staying here and helping me try and find a way to keep going, you go back to Seagull Avenue to see your bloody mother who will tell you how hopeless I am, how hopeless this whole thing is, and she'll be right! You'd better stay there."

"I haven't been home for a month. I'm only going for one night," Alice said, her voice shaking. "I'll be back tomorrow." She had no idea how to treat Harry in this mood.

"There won't be anything to come back to. Don't bother." As she turned towards the door, Harry made a low moaning sound and sprang towards her, grabbing her arm. "Don't go, Alice."

Alice turned and pushed him with all her strength, amazing him so that he let go of her and rocked back unsteadily.

"What's the point of me staying when you are so hopelessly drunk? You can't think straight, you can't even speak. This shop is doing very well. It has good weeks and bad weeks but over all it's fine. If you stopped crouching pathetically and blaming everyone else we might be all right." She could feel tears running down her face but she ignored them as Harry sank back onto the wicker sofa, head falling into his hands. "If it collapses, Harry, it's because you always expected it to. There must be other ways of keeping going for a few more months if you really want to, but I don't think you do. I think you've made your great grand gesture and now it's real and it's difficult you want to go back and give in."

"That's a bloody lie," Harry said, voice muffled, and a

moment later Alice had crossed the room and was holding onto him. She never did go home that night.

Eliza was always early in the office, usually getting in by eight thirty and reading the newspaper with her first coffee, stunned and fascinated by the extraordinary events in the South Atlantic, the Argentinian invasion of South Georgia and the Falklands and the subsequent news of the British task force. It was so strange to read and talk about a war at all. It gave her some understanding of what it must have been like in the early forties. There was an atmosphere of patriotism and apprehension but most of all surprise, which she had never experienced before. People talked about historic battles, D-Day and Dunkirk. And it was something to balance against the obsession which occupied her like a malignant disease, the obsession to find out the truth about Robert and Celia.

She would use any excuse to drive to Robert's house, frequently bringing him messages which could have been relayed easily by telephone. On the first occasion Robert had asked her in but on subsequent evenings he answered his door impatiently. Some nights, when she knew he was away, Eliza sat in her car outside his mews house for an hour or so, looking across at the friendly white building and trying to predict the future, telling herself that she had time, that Celia would never have the courage to leave David and her life with him. *Anyway, from the very beginning, from the first time I heard about Robert, I knew he would be significant in my life. I felt he was mine. I still feel it. I must keep the faith.* But it was much more difficult now.

Throughout the early weeks of April, Eliza could see that Robert was in love. He had a soft expression in his hard blue eyes. He laughed a lot, his strong, humorous face constantly alive. There were telephone calls when he would laugh and then pause and his voice would drop away to nothing. Once Celia phoned and gave an absurd false name, enraging Eliza as she put the call through, but in mid-April Robert had a new line installed in his office and Eliza was cut off. During those early weeks of spring, with the dark backcloth of the Falklands unrolling but still difficult to believe, Eliza paced like a tiger in a cage, telling herself to wait; that it could not last; that she was in a position to wait years for Robert if necessary and that Celia would eventually disperse, like so much smoke. But still she seized opportunities to visit Robert's house and raged inside.

On April the twenty-sixth, a fine Monday morning, Robert came into the office half an hour after Eliza. He too was absorbed by the war, and ready to talk about it at length. He sat on the edge of Eliza's desk, drinking a mug of coffee, and reading the account of the loss of a Sea King helicopter. He was anticipating a call from Rolfe to announce that the *Endeavour* had docked at the Lagos Terminal after her second voyage. They were a day late. Rolfe should have docked on the twenty-fourth and Robert was aware of mild concern.

"Have you booked me on Thursday's flight to Lagos?" he asked Eliza without looking up from the newspaper.

"Yes."

Robert lunched with Michael Copper, spent an hour with his insurance brokers, and came back into the office in the late afternoon.

"Any word from Rolfe?"

"No."

Robert frowned. "I'll probably stay here for some time. If you want to go off early, Eliza, that's okay." He found the intense concentration in Eliza's penetrating eyes made him uneasy and he wanted to telephone Celia with no danger of interruption. It seemed that Celia was gathering her strength to leave David, poised like a diver on a high board.

Eliza looked at her watch. It was four-thirty.

"David Otterwood rang while you were out and asked if I had time to go down and see him this evening. He said he'd be in his office till six-thirty but I could go earlier."

"I hope he's not going to try and get you back," Robert said, smiling.

"I don't think so. He hinted it was about Harry."

Robert nodded and then, as the telephone rang, almost snatched up the receiver.

He had expected it to be Rolfe. It was not. Eliza knew the changing expression on his face and in his voice. He paused for a few seconds. "I could come now," he said. Then he listened again, his face serious, before he said goodbye.

"Something's come up, Eliza. I expect Rolfe will try me at home but I won't be there till around five thirty. Perhaps either you or Carolyn would wait here till then?"

Eliza finished the letter she was typing and then sat with her hands curled round a cup of tea, not drinking it but watching the patterns of the steam as she wondered what David Otterwood wanted. She thought of the quiet weekend she had spent, of the way her life had narrowed down to one single aim of Robert and she thought so deeply that when, some fifteen minutes after Robert had left, the telephone rang, she jumped violently. She answered it and, recognising the strange internal noises of the Nigerian telephone system, expected it to be Rolfe.

It was not Rolfe. A deep female voice asked for Robert.

"I'm afraid he has left the office. Can I take a message?"

There was a short hesitation. "This is Sophia M'habela."

"Yes, I recognised your voice."

"Eliza, isn't it?"

"Yes."

"How are things at Stoner Shipping?"

"Flourishing," Eliza said crisply.

"Especially the transporting of oil from Nigeria to Singapore? Is that going smoothly?"

"Yes. Perfectly."

"No complications on the way?"

"None at all. Rolfe is due to dock today after the second voyage." Eliza wanted to impress this deep-voiced, confident woman with her knowledge of Stoner Shipping. "The *Endeavour* is a couple of days late at Lagos, due to unpleasant weather on the way back from Singapore."

Sophia laughed. "Really? Well the *Endeavour* is back

now, I assure you. I've been waiting for it too. I have a very important message for Robert. Where can I reach him?"

The implication that she could not be trusted with this message infuriated Eliza. "I don't know where he is at the moment but I do know where to find him later. I could call by on my way home."

There was a hesitation. "It is really important. Could you tell him that I have just returned from my holiday in Kenya. While I was there I drove to Mombasa and went sightseeing. I visited the docks. I took some photographs of ships."

Eliza frowned with irritation, the vagueness and personal nature of the message angering her even more. "Is that all?"

"I think it will be quite enough. You will be sure to tell him?"

"Of course," Eliza said coldly.

She said good night to Carolyn, asking her to lock up, and went down to her car. Something in Sophia's tone had made her spine prickle. She turned out into heavy Holborn traffic and drove towards Robert's house, fingers drumming impatiently on the steering wheel. It was a radiant spring evening, the trees just beginning to show traces of green and blossom falling in a light wind. It took thirty minutes to shake off the tangle of cars and taxis and turn into Robert's cobbled mews with its bright window boxes. She drove to the far end and parked in a space almost opposite Robert's house. There was no sign of his car but she rang the bell anyway and stood for some time on the doorstep. Then she got back into her car, content to wait for a time. She turned on the PM news programme and listened to the latest bulletin of the war. A gentle evening sunlight warmed her through the glass of the car window and she was pleasantly drowsy so that when Robert's car turned into the mews and pulled up outside his house Eliza made no sudden move to get out. Instead she watched as, almost in slow motion it seemed, the tall, dark-haired figure climbed out of the passenger seat and walked to Robert's scarlet front door. Like players in a silent film, she saw Celia put out her arms to embrace Robert, saw him drop his head onto her shoulder in a gesture of familiarity and affection, a gesture of love; saw them open the door and go into Robert's house. The whole episode had lasted perhaps thirty seconds. For another thirty seconds Eliza stared at the front door and then she started her car and drove out of the mews.

She drove into the park, acting automatically, circling round for five or ten minutes while she tried to think what to do. It was not as if she hadn't known. But she had always been able to argue against the knowledge. Not any more. A sense of absolute hopelessness possessed her, something she had not felt since her father's death. Desperately she clutched at distraction, turning her car towards the City, thankful to have somewhere to go.

It was ten to six when Eliza stopped by a row of telephone boxes. The third had not been vandalised although there were obscene childish rhymes written in felt pen over the list of dialling codes. They weren't funny. The box smelt of urine. All the world was dirty, her fingers stiff as she dialled Robert's number.

Robert swore softly, got off the sofa and picked up the phone.

"Hello? hello?" His voice was impatient.

Eliza had not thought what she was going to say. His tone made her flinch. She imagined that he had been in bed, that he had reached for the telephone with reluctance. Or on the sofa, a drink in his hand. She could not make the words come. She thought of Sophia's message, the urgency and sarcasm in that deep voice. "Hello?" he said again, this time angrily, and Eliza put the telephone down. She leaned her head forward so that it touched the cold plastic of the instrument. She shuddered. She wanted to stay with her eyes closed. It was hopeless, wasn't it? Eliza lifted her head and took several deep breaths. "To hell with her and her important message." She pushed open the door of the telephone box sharply and got back into her car.

* * *

"I expect you think I'm going to offer you your job back, Eliza?" David joked as she came in.

"No." She tried to smile as she shook his hand but her mouth was stiff.

"Well, thank you for coming." He looked at her intently as he always had. "Is something wrong, Eliza? You look strange."

Eliza sat in one of the deep leather chairs and crossed her legs. She shook her head. "I don't want to talk about myself."

David frowned. "But you look absolutely miserable." An expression of genuine concern changed his face. Only once before had she seen it, when she gave in her notice. "Seriously, Eliza, there would always be a place here for you if you wanted to come back. I never expected you to leave. Why did you leave Otterwoods?"

It was extraordinary to talk to him as another human being, not just as a man she worked for. She had had very few real conversations with David. He was watching her so sympathetically. She sat forward, her face pale, eyes compelling. "I enjoyed working here. I think I would have got on well. But Stoner Shipping appealed to me in a lot of ways. To be honest, the biggest appeal of all was Robert himself. I had been intrigued by him long before I met him. All that excitement about the boat people. I had wondered about him, admired him. When I met him he fulfilled all my expectations and I went to work for him not only because the idea of helping run a new, small, optimistic company appealed to me but also because I wanted to be near him." She moved nervously, uncrossing her legs, feet side by side. "He's made a success of it and we work well together. Everything was going to be all right."

"Until?" David said softly, intrigued at the extraordinary confidences this previously very self-contained girl was disclosing.

Eliza didn't answer. She sat back in the chair, mouth a tight line.

"Until this happened?" David pushed across the desk towards her a sheet of newspaper, a gossip column. He indicated a few lines headed *Stoner's Progress*. "This is edited by my friend who wrote the article about Harry. She has gone from strength to strength. She rang me to tell me the part she was leaving out. Is it true, Eliza? Is she talking about my Celia?"

Eliza sighed deeply. "Not really your Celia any more. She is Robert's Celia. I thought it would just go away, that she would get tired of him even though she doesn't seem the sort of woman to take an affair lightly. But I really think she loves him." Eliza gave a small desperate laugh.

David sat motionless, his face completely without expression. He did not need to protest or ask for proof. She merely confirmed what his instincts had told him. A hundred little things suddenly sprang together, like iron filings to a magnet, and formed a whole.

"What will you do?" Eliza said simply.

"I don't know. I need time to think."

"I'd rather they didn't know you asked me."

David smiled slightly. She felt a pang of pity for him and for the first time she understood what a difficult man he would be to reject.

"Does it really matter? In a few days my informant won't stop at hints. I don't want any details. I just needed to ask if it was true."

"I don't know any details except silly things like the bracelet she wears and her car outside his house. Until tonight I could pretend it wasn't happening."

"What happened tonight?" David asked, against his will.

"I drove to Robert's house with a message. I saw Celia arrive with him in his car and they embraced in the street. They are together now."

Chapter 23

"Three phone calls," Sophia said aloud to herself.

She was sitting in her office and it was almost dark. On the desk in front of her was a tall glass of whisky.

"The newspaper. The General. The secretary. They sound like Tarot cards." She drank deeply from the glass and spun her chair, dropping her head.

Ever since the afternoon at Mombasa docks, she had lurched from fury to despair. She had approached the holiday so eagerly. She needed some time to herself. Two whole weeks with no work, no anxiety about her father, time to think about Robert. Robert had occupied five years of her life. Was there to be any future? The peaceful and happy week of the christening, spent on a coffee plantation outside Nairobi, had been followed by an invitation to spend a few days in Mombasa. The drive down was breathtaking. Sophia was calmer than she had been for months. There was time to think. Time at last to face the truth.

Night after night, stretching her long body in the darkness and reaching only emptiness, she knew how difficult it was going to be to replace Robert. The men she had tried to put in his place had been quite unable to match the instinctive rapport between Robert and herself or the effortless, infinitely satisfying love-making.

Have I been unfair? I certainly forced the break between us. Could he change? If this oil trading with Singapore gets him the start he needs, the success he craves, he could become aware of the things in life that really matter. Isn't it worth one more try? If he is still there to go back to, if there is still time, I must try. The decision brought such impatience and yet such peace.

Everyone who visited Mombasa was taken to see the fifteenth-century Fort Jesus; almost everyone leant on the coral-pink battlements and looked over the shining lagoons to the Dhow harbour and along the coast to the docks; some people watched the container ships coming and going and the tankers, vast unmanoeuvrable dinosaurs, just a couple of miles off the coast.

The photographs were spread out in front of her. A dozen of them. Even now, each time she looked at them she felt the stinging sense of betrayal, the humiliation of being lied to. A reporter was on his way. Lugamo had just left.

"Such an absurd risk to take," Lugamo had said, his voice rippling with satisfaction.

"At first I thought I was mistaken. The name was different. The *Otterwood Avo*. I wanted, so badly, to believe it was a sister ship. God, what fools they take us to be. It took ten minutes to drive to the docks to get a closer look. I didn't need to get very close. There was no mistaking that enormous blond-haired Norwegian captain. I took a dozen shots of the ship with the name clearly visible and, in the background, the distinctive shape of Fort Jesus."

The photographs were developed in two days. It had taken a week and several thousand pounds to establish the truth about the *Endeavour*. Then she had forced herself to wait. If she exposed the *Endeavour* too soon, it would not come to Lagos. She wanted the tanker trapped in the Nigerian Terminal. Agonising, furious waiting until this afternoon, at last, the *Endeavour* had docked.

"Such arrogance." Lugamo had looked across at Sophia and moistened his lips. Excitement always made him feel like sex. She was obviously done with Robert Stoner now. "I suppose he thought to shelter in your father's shadow should anything go wrong, or perhaps it was pure greed? The South Africans pay extremely well I'm told."

"Does it matter why? All that matters is that we stop it. This endless laughing at the rules, lip-service to the laws and then turning round and laughing in our faces. He actually told me there was nothing illegal about the voyage."

"You realise, Sophia, that even your father may find this hard to explain."

"Oh we have no proof to tie him in with it. It will be coincidence, merest chance."

"I don't think so," Lugamo said. "I want Stoner here, back in our country to face charges. I would like to set them one against the other."

Intense dislike for the man made Sophia say sharply, "Robert would hardly be such a fool as to come back when this story breaks."

"Perhaps he will come back before he realises. On both previous occasions he has been in Lagos to supervise the loading of the *Endeavour*."

"It doesn't sail for five days," Sophia said flatly.

"So you have timed your disclosure neatly? But perhaps we could sit on this information for a little while?"

Sophia shook her head. "What a pity I didn't think of that, General. I have already informed the press."

Lugamo looked at her with a small, unpleasant smile on his lips. "I think, Sophia, that before all this finally breaks you are going to have to work out exactly where your loyalty lies."

"With Nigeria," Sophia said sweetly. "And I try very hard to keep personal feelings in second place."

"Where does he think you are?" Robert asked. He lay on his back, one arm behind his head, and Celia lay beside him, chin on her hand which rested on his bare chest, looking into his face.

"I didn't say. I don't tell him anything. And now that Josie has gone back to school, I can do as I please."

"So why the urgent summons?"

"Because of that foul gossip column. How can people spy like that and hint? I needed to see you so badly. Last night we had another argument about Harry. He is terribly in debt. I think David is destroying him. I want him to stop. He has made his point; he has humiliated Harry. It's enough." She sighed. "Today I was so sad. And then that awful woman's sly hints."

Robert stroked her straight dark hair. Absolute peace filled him. He had never felt like this with a woman before, this timeless contentment. How many times had she been here? Five or six? And yet everything that had happened before was relatively unimportant. "I didn't know I was capable of feeling like this. I would change the whole course of my life to go on seeing you, Celia."

"I hope you won't have to do that."

"Well, we can't go on living like this all summer. Not now. I hate creeping away for a night at a time. I hate the feeling that I am skulking about, waiting to move in the moment David goes away. I want things in the open. I don't care if they print it on the front of every paper there is."

She dropped her head, her cheek against his chest. "At first I didn't think farther ahead than the next day. Now it is different. I hate the pretence too. I feel ashamed and I hate lying. I can't understand how David did it for so long."

"I suppose it was necessary," Robert said. "But it isn't necessary for us, is it? Why don't you leave him? Come here."

"The only thing that has prevented me is the fear of what he can do to Harry and the girls if I am not there as an intermediary. I am so worried about Josie. She is desperately unhappy. She hated going back. She rings me all the time from school. I feel I can still protect them."

"From their own father?"

"From his ambitions for them." She sat up and rested her weight on one elbow, looking down at Robert. "Just coming here for a night at a time, as you put it, has made the whole difference to my life, Robert. I will break away from him."

"When? I can't see what you're waiting for, unless it is that you feel you have too much to lose?" Robert said coldly.

She flinched. "Not in the way you mean it. Not in material things."

"Then leave him." Robert pulled himself into a sitting position, resolution making his voice harsh.

"I will leave him. This week." They were such extraordinary words that when she had said them she was paralysed for a few moments.

Robert enveloped her, his voice muffled against her. "I'm afraid that you'll change your mind. I am due to go to Lagos on Thursday. You can come with me."

"I can't, Robert. Just for a few weeks, while Josie is so unhappy, I must stay in England. I must explain to her myself."

"Then I'll change the flight and go tomorrow morning. I have the voyage arranged. I can see Rolfe on Wednesday and be back by the end of the week. I want to be here for you to come to. You musn't come to emptiness."

"How can I tell him?"

"You said yourself that David forewarned is far more formidable. Just leave him. I'll fetch you as soon as I get back. In the meantime do what you want about Josie." Robert got out of bed and walked across to his chest of drawers. She watched his naked body with pleasure, possessively, and wondered if she was unusual that, in all her life, she had only known two men's bodies. He seemed to make everything so simple.

"What time will you go tomorrow?"

"I'll ring reservations now; if I can change my ticket I shall leave here at six thirty tomorrow morning."

"I'll be late this evening," David had said to Celia that morning as he kissed Josie goodbye and slipped a ten-pound note into his daughter's hand. "Have a good term and do try and stop this constant telephoning." Celia wondered if it was to be a woman. There was no official dinner planned for this evening, but there could be visiting ship-owners to be entertained. She had shivered violently, anticipating the drama of taking Josie back, the way Josie would start the drive quite normally and grow more and more silent as the miles passed.

"Stay the night," Robert said, when he had finished telephoning. "I'll drop you at Flood Street as I leave tomorrow morning."

Celia thought of the silence of the London house. No

Josephine. No David. What was there for her to go back to? How could the chilling loneliness of her room compensate for the live warmth of Robert's body and his love?

David stayed in his office for a long time after Eliza had left. At some stage he was aware that Sheila said good night. It was automatic for him to think through any problem but under the careful consideration he was aware of intense shock, of disbelief. He had not felt it since the baby died, this amazement that something should occur so absolutely against what he wanted. For some time he let himself imagine life without Celia, thinking deeply into the detail of it; not only would it be awkward domestically and difficult for the girls, Celia was also essential to him. All his affairs were conducted from the beginning with the understanding that he would never consider a divorce. In fact there had been no one for months. Ironically, beneath his fury about Harry had been a desire to get closer to Celia again. His thoughts spiralled inwards, circle after circle, and at the end, as he lit a small cigar and let his shoulders relax and realised that he had been sitting quite rigidly since Eliza left, he allowed himself to admit that he loved Celia. He dipped back into the complications of the past, skimming through the years. Odd, unimportant memories surfaced. He had come to love Scotland through her feelings for the castle; he remembered when they first found the house in Hampshire, wandering from one damp, deserted room to the next, and her excitement about the house; the children and all the rituals that went with them, birthdays and school speech days and the illnesses and holidays. Celia and Otterwoods were his real life. The other women counted very little. *The hired women . . . The wife of my youth shall charm me – an' the rest can go to Hell!*

It was a long time after Eliza left that he allowed himself to think of Robert Stoner. Stoner must be totally destroyed. He must be humiliated. Perhaps Celia was reliving, through Robert, the early days when she had been part of

Otterwoods? He convinced himself that she had turned to Robert as a temporary comfort while their marriage had been through a cold, hard patch. With his small success stripped from him Robert would appear ridiculous. A failure, Celia would not relish the thought of life with a merchant seaman, would she? His mouth hardened. Or was he putting too much into it? For the first time he wondered if it were true or if Eliza was unbalanced by jealousy? She had always seemed to him a strange, intense girl. Slowly he got up, turning out the lights and leaving his office. He drove home through the deserted City and parked outside Flood Street at nine. He let himself in to the silent house and Mrs Wickham came up from her flat with mild surprise on her face.

"I understood you were going out this evening, Mr Otterwood. Can I cook you something?"

"No, thank you. Everything finished earlier than I expected."

As she turned he said, "Is Mrs Otterwood going to be late, did she say?"

"Yes. Very late, she said." Mrs Wickham paused at the top of the stairs. "And Josephine rang at six and at seven. She sounded upset. She said she will ring her mother first thing in the morning."

David poured himself a glass of brandy and sat in one of the deep armchairs in the small study. The room was quite warm although there was no fire. Some of Celia's sewing lay on a low table, a tapestry he had been aware of for months. So she had not left home. Perhaps Eliza did exaggerate. He thought back to Robert again and began to plan an intricate and deadly strategy.

At several stages during the long night David got up and refilled his glass and then returned to his chair. He made notes in the small leather book he carried everywhere. He thought through Robert's destruction as carefully as he would have thought through a major new project for Otterwoods. He slept a little but he was awake at five, beginning to think he was wrong, that she had gone after all. It was with relief that he heard Celia's key in the lock just after six thirty.

She let herself in quietly, standing for a few moments in the hall, and turning in amazement as David opened the door to the study, her eyes moving down from his face to observe that he was fully dressed in a dark suit and then darting up to his face again.

"I've been waiting up for you."

"Since when? You said you would be late but have you waited all night?" She stared incredulously, making no move to come towards him.

For the first time he remembered where he should have been. Extraordinary that yesterday he had anticipated the evening with pleasure.

"I didn't go."

Celia seemed not to be listening.

"Will you come in here? I don't want to talk in the hall."

"I'm very tired, David."

"I think we should talk. I had a visit yesterday evening from someone who works at Stoner Shipping."

"Robert?" Celia asked, wondering why David should be so obtuse.

"No, not Robert. Eliza."

Celia walked past him into the study. The curtains were drawn although it was quite light outside. The friendliness of the room enveloped her. It was her favourite room in the London house. She could not sit down. Her heart hammered in her chest as she watched David's face. Was this it? Was this how it felt when something came to an end? She was cold. She felt like a prisoner awaiting sentence, knowing what it was going to be and yet dreading the actual words.

"Are you in love with Robert Stoner?"

"Yes. I am."

"I don't want you to leave."

"Why not? Am I useful?"

"Much more than that. I love you and I don't want everything destroyed."

"You began the destruction, long ago. It has taken me twenty years to react. You have had twenty years, David."

"What is it you want from him?"

She sighed. "I can't talk about it to you. I want everything. I want to feel loved. Important. That he needs me even if it's only temporary. That he considers my feelings and above all, that I am enough for him. I have never been enough for you, have I?"

"The others never mattered."

"They mattered to me."

"They were irrelevant."

Celia flinched. "He asked me to leave you. He's always asking me. I know he's right. There is absolutely nothing left for me here."

David touched her arm. "I don't want you to go. I love you Celia, I always have. You knew what I was when you married me."

"I didn't know you. I didn't know anyone. But I know you now." Even through her fury she was aware of a strong feeling for David that she had never experienced before. A deep concern. Pity? She thrust it aside. She didn't want to feel anything for him. She ran upstairs and pushed a few clothes into a case. When she came down again, David was standing in the hall.

"Celia, you must think about what you are doing. You can change your mind. At any time you can come back, especially if things go wrong. I've been where you're going and you'll find it's not that different. I can't bear you to be unhappy."

Celia barely heard him as she pushed open the front door and ran out to her car.

Chapter 24

"My dear General," Michael M'habela said, getting up slowly from behind his breakfast table and holding out his hand to the much smaller man. "How nice to see you. And so early in the morning. Would you like coffee?"

Lugamo shook his head. Suppressed excitement made him keep his hands tightly interlocked. He sat down, his eyes fixed on the other man's face. He had waited so long for this moment that he hovered over his prey like a hawk, wondering where the shock would touch M'habela's face first. In the long, cold eyes perhaps? Or would it attack that wide confident mouth and snatch away the smile.

"What can I do for you, Joshua?"

"I don't think you can do anything for me. I have come to inform you of an extremely serious situation which has come to my attention."

"You're being very pompous." Michael's eyes danced maliciously.

General Lugamo ignored the remark. "You have for some time been associated in business with an Englishman named Robert Stoner, I believe?"

"I have certainly known Robert for a number of years. He and Sophia have been very close, as you well know, although lately I think they have drifted apart. It is probably for the best. I don't really approve of mixed race marriages, do you, Joshua?"

"I have no strong feelings on that subject but I do care passionately about the downfall of the South African regime, as do the rest of the government." He bounced his chair forward with a small leap of triumph. "If you were to drive down to the docks this morning , Michael, you would find them in a state of chaos. The dockers are on the verge of a complete strike. From your face, I take it you haven't read the morning papers. I have brought one to show you.

They are all much the same. They all show this photograph of the tanker *Endeavour* which has been chartered to your associate Robert Stoner for the past two months." He put the paper carefully on the table and Michael lifted it slowly and raised his eyebrows.

"I expect you are curious to know where we got the photograph and what significance it has."

"As you are obviously about to tell me I won't be curious for long."

"Your daughter supplied it. It seems that the *Endeavour* has not, as its documents stated, been carrying oil to Singapore but oil to trade illegally with South Africa. The visit to Mombasa was by way of filling in time, Sophia discovered, so the ship could arrive back at the Terminal after the correct number of days." He paused, playing his trump card delicately, his voice almost affectionate. "I think I should tell you that we have known about your friendship with Bernard Van Ryn for some time."

"That's unfortunate. I do hope you won't interfere in any way. I am making steady progress." Michael crossed the room and lifted his telephone. He had the satisfaction of seeing surprise in Lugamo's face. The action was made with not a moment's hesitation. Michael dialled, speaking to Lugamo as he did so. "I can't tell you how pleased I am that you have come to me with this, Joshua, although I realise it must have been a difficult decision for you. I won't disappoint you. Although Robert Stoner has been a friend of mine in the past, and a close friend of my daughter, it is obvious that the man has laughed at all our regulations. I want him detained for questioning the moment he arrives in this country."

"And your own part in this matter?" Joshua Lugamo said coldly when he had recovered from the counterattack and when Michael had finished speaking on the telephone. "You will, of course, be asked a lot of questions yourself. You will make yourself available?"

Michael looked irritated. "Don't be ridiculous. Of course I'll be available. I shall be in my office trying to get to the bottom of it all."

When Joshua Lugamo had gone, Michael sat motionless for a few moments, thinking rapidly. He did not trust this telephone any more. As he was about to leave his housekeeper came in. "A Mr Rolfe Petersen wants to speak to you, sir."

"I haven't time to talk to him now but you can give him a message. Tell him we take a very serious view of breaking the trade sanctions against South Africa and I intend to see they are all prosecuted."

He left his house and went out to his car and gave the address of Sophia's office. The action would seem perfectly understandable if he were being followed. On the way he stopped at a main post office and used the telephone, going through the operator for a credit card call to London.

Eliza had hardly slept at all that night. The misery she felt, and the apprehension, kept her pacing her small flat. Once she went down the stairs, intending to drive around London for a while, but it was cold in her car and after a short time she went back inside and made herself a mug of tea. Should she have lied to David? Would it have made any difference and was he the sort of man you could lie to convincingly?

When she eventually slept, it was so deeply that she didn't hear her alarm and for once she was late into the office. April sunlight splashed the pavements but it would not touch these tall windows till afternoon. Eliza put the kettle on. There was a message on the answerphone from Robert. He would not be in. He had caught the early morning flight to Lagos to supervise the third voyage of the *Endeavour*, he said. Eliza was both relieved and disturbed. She needed time but why had Robert altered his plans? She had booked him a seat on Thursday. His trips to Lagos concerned her. Why couldn't Rolfe handle the turn-round? Was there a great deal that Robert hadn't told her? She suspected that Robert needed to talk to Rolfe before each voyage and was unwilling to trust this conversation to the telephone. Robert had been extremely busy over the last few days, fixing a voyage for a ship he had not named.

Eliza wandered into his office and straightened the few papers left on his desk. She collected a coffee mug to wash. It was just after nine thirty. Carolyn was always late, full of wordy explanations, but she worked well and seemed to be content. Eliza had just sat down at her desk with her coffee, pulling her chair in slightly and trying to let the order she had created here calm the chaos in her mind, when the telephone rang.

"Eliza, it's Rolfe. We have big trouble. Where's Robert?"

"He took the morning flight. He'll be in Lagos this afternoon. What's happened?"

"Just about everything. The dockers are refusing to load us and I think the whole port will be out on strike shortly. Every newspaper in the city has the same picture on the front of the *Endeavour* at Mombasa. I rang that bastard M'habela and the bloody hypocrite told me he took a very serious view of trading with South Africa and he was going to throw the book at us!"

"South Africa?" Eliza said. "Why South Africa?"

"Never mind if you don't know. Why did Robert change his flight? He was due to be here on Friday. Did he have any warning?"

"I don't know why he changed. There is just a message on the answerphone. Can I do anything, Rolfe?"

"Not really. If Robert's already left it's too late. I just hope M'habela is bluffing to make it look good, but if it's a question of saving his own neck, he'd let anybody go under. We'll be all right. We are just a crew following orders. But God help Robert if they get him. Say nothing to anyone, especially not the press."

For the next half hour, Eliza wandered the office, tormented with worry but trying to present a reasonably normal façade to Carolyn. When the phone rang again at ten, she snatched at the receiver eagerly.

"Hello. This is Michael M'habela. Is Robert there?"

"No. He's left for Lagos. He caught the morning flight."

There was a short silence. "That is a great pity. I'll have to see what I can do. Goodbye."

"What's going on?" Carolyn asked, her comfortable face wrinkling with the question.

"I wish I knew." Eliza answered the telephone again and it was a reporter. "I know nothing about it. Mr Stoner is on a routine business trip to Nigeria. He goes every month." She put the phone down hard.

Sophia stood up as her father came in and motioned her secretary to leave. Michael closed the door.

He sat down and lit a cigarette. "Why did you do it?"

"I warned you not to lie to me. I told you Lugamo was watching you."

"But why now?"

"Because I believed you were changing. No, I didn't. I made myself believe it. Because Robert promised me that there was nothing illegal about shipments of oil to Singapore!" Her voice trembled with fury. "No oil ever went to Singapore, did it? You'll never get out of this one."

"Of course I'll get out of it, Sophia, but you have offended me very much. Although we hardly knew each other when you were a child, I thought that through the past few years we had grown fond of each other. Obviously I was wrong. Is there not enough of your ancestry in you to know that the family is everything? I will get out of it by using my wits and money, by using the very channels you profess to despise, but I will never forgive your disloyalty. Whether Robert will get out of it is another matter. I have given orders for him to be detained as soon as he arrives in this country."

"He's not stupid enough to come here now, is he?"

"Unfortunately, he's on his way. I hope I can persuade Lugamo that he is still in London and keep him out of sight on the aeroplane."

"But he's not due here for three days. He always comes just before the *Endeavour* sails. I checked his reservation."

"He altered it. Something in London made him want to

come early. Some woman, is it? Is that the cause of it all? Some other woman? Is it jealousy, Sophia?"

"You will never understand the way I think. It is a waste of time explaining to you."

Her father looked at her coldly. "On the contrary, I understand you perfectly. We are exactly the same, you and I, but unfortunately, we are on different sides. And Robert is with me."

"Robert is with no one but himself."

Michael stood up. He put out his cigarette in the ashtray and reached into his pocket, taking out a handful of small coins which he threw down on Sophia's desk.

"Your pieces of silver, Sophia, in case you haven't already been paid."

The stewardess moved down the left-hand aisle of the aircraft and paused at Robert's seat.

"Mr Stoner?"

"Yes."

"A message has been radioed through from Chief M'habela. He advises you to leave the flight at Kano. He will send a driver for you. Do not go on with the other passengers to Lagos."

"Thank you," Robert said, and a pulse of apprehension began to beat steadily in his temple. What the hell had happened?

When Celia let herself in to Robert's empty flat she went up the narrow flight of stairs and through the living-room to the bedroom, dropping her case and lying on the unmade bed, burying her face in the pillow that still bore traces of his distinctive smell, pulling the bedclothes over herself. Exhaustion overwhelmed her but not the exhilaration she had expected, no sense of release. Just questions flicking through her mind like birds past a window, passing too quickly for any answers to be formed. The questions turned into a headache. She burrowed further down the bed and the pillow over her head brought silence and gradually the throbbing and the questions stopped, levelling out into the steady rhythm of breathing. And the image that kept pushing through the silence was of David's face, wearing an expression she had never seen before. He had not known quite what to do or what to say. She could seldom in their lives together remember seeing David show uncertainty.

When Alice closed the shop that evening, she went very slowly up the stairs to the living-room in search of Harry. She knew something was terribly wrong. Although they had talked for so long on Friday night the weekend had been disastrous. On Saturday night Harry had gone with friends to a party that Alice refused to go to. "I can't go to a party, Harry. I can't pretend to laugh and talk to people when everything is so awful."

Harry had looked at her uncomprehendingly. "What better time to go?"

He came back at four on Sunday morning and slept most of the day. Sunday evening was miserable and yesterday they had hardly spoken. Today, Harry had left Pembridge Gardens at two thirty, looking unusually respectable in a shirt and tie, but ever since his return at four he had been drinking. Now it was just after six. Jane had telephoned twice over the weekend and Alice had promised to make the long-postponed visit home this evening.

"Harry, I'm going to catch the six forty-five. I'll be back tomorrow morning."

"Why do you keep going away?" Harry said desperately.

"I haven't been away yet. If you remember, I never got there on Friday. I have to talk to her, Harry."

"But you never do."

"Well, it's so difficult to find the right moment."

"I don't think that's it at all! I don't think you really want to know about yourself."

He poured the wine remaining in the bottle into his glass. With his foot he kicked at a pile of bills. "Why can't we make any more money? Can't we advertise?"

"I keep telling you," Alice said defensively, "that every

week there are more customers but I have to use some of the money we take to buy new stock. And the telephone bill is ridiculous. Why can't you wait till cheaper times to ring people?"

Harry shrugged miserably. "I mean to. But it's all so petty and squalid, worrying about telephoning before one or after one. The cheque for the rates has bounced." He sighed. "I thought I'd sold the car but the man's changed his mind." He stood up, and began to wander the room.

"At least the painters have been paid," Alice said into the restless silence.

"Oh great! So we don't have to worry about them any more. But what about the electricity and the rates and four hundred pounds for a table for twenty at the Crocodile?" He sat down in the fat old armchair and his voice was different. Very subdued. Far more frightening than his anger. "I know that none of it is your fault. I hate myself when I moan at you like this. It's just not going to work, is it, Alice? I have the same feeling that I had before my exams. Hopelessness. It could have worked if the trust had bought this place. Then there would have been enough to live on until we became properly established. As it is, it's hopeless."

Alice stared at him in absolute horror.

"I feel terrible about it," Harry said in the same dull voice. "I have dragged you into my misfortune. But I just can't see a way out. I began it all with one vital misconception. I thought I had money to use, but I didn't."

"Your mother? Couldn't we ask her?"

"I don't think she has a lot of capital of her own. She has a big income but she hasn't got nine or ten thousand pounds to spare. We need to pay off that absurd loan and have enough money to live on for the next six months. D'you think I haven't gone through it all a million times?" He looked up at her. "I went to see the bank manager this afternoon."

"Why didn't you tell me?" She was trembling. This subdued misery was so much more frightening than his bursts of short-lived rage.

"Because he was so discouraging I couldn't bear to repeat it all. He told me the only thing I can do is to try and resell this place. That we have probably improved the value. Look for smaller premises." He sighed. "He suggested I look for a job. He didn't suggest what as. I can't do anything. I'm nearly twenty years old and completely unfitted for anything except a place in Otterwoods, working my way up." Harry reached for another bottle of wine and opened it.

"Will we have to close down, then?" Alice said, her voice shaking.

"Yes. We can go on for a time until we find a buyer, I suppose. We could try and find a flat." He lifted miserable eyes to Alice's face. He wanted to exaggerate the horror. He wanted more reaction from her. Her stillness goaded him. "I could go to Australia. Mike would find a job for me. That's what I'll do. I'll go to Australia and you can go home to your mother. At least one person will be happy. She can tell you again and again, that she knew how it would be!"

His speckled eyes were fixed on Alice's face. She narrowed her eyes in agony. She turned without a word and went down the stairs and out into a warm April evening, walking very slowly and deliberately towards the tube station.

Her legs and arms felt so heavy that it was impossible to move at a normal speed. Seagull Avenue was soft with blossom trees and a warm sea breeze shook the trees slightly. Seagulls screamed as Alice was screaming inside. If only she had never left here, never known him. She had been all right in her isolation. To escape, to love him and be with him and then to have it all snatched away was unbearable.

Alice let herself into the kitchen. It was just before eight. Jane was putting helpings of steak and kidney pie onto four plates. The smell of the food and the absolute normality of the scene made Alice feel sick but automatically, without a word, she took off her heavy cardigan and picked up two of the plates, carrying them through to the dining-room; she came back and took two others. Then she closed the door and sat down at the table and dropped her head onto her folded arms. She was trembling.

Jane came and stood behind her. She put a cautious hand on Alice's back. "You've got so thin in the last month, Alice. Do you want some supper?"

Alice shook her head. She lifted her face and tears poured down her cheeks. It was quite extraordinary to see Alice cry. She was so patient, so passive, if things went wrong she just waited.

"The shop has to close. We can't pay the bills. We have to sell the house."

Jane let out an explosive breath. "I knew it would happen. If it was a profitable business, Paddy wouldn't have sold up. It was obvious. And Harry has no idea at all about money. No idea." She took a cigarette and lit it, inhaling deeply. "To be fair, I think it is brutal of his father to give him everything all his childhood and then snatch it away when he wants to start up on his own. But at least he knows what it's like now, to have nothing. He'll be all right in the end. They'll bail him out when they have got him where they want him."

Alice's shoulders shook. Her face was covered by her small hands. "He's going away."

Relief, swift and sweet, poured through Jane. Now it would be all right again. Alice and herself, living here. Alice would find another job. And someday there would be someone for her. Quite different. Someone ordinary. Someone she could claim absolutely as her own.

Alice raised her face, smearing away tears like a child.

"Tell me now. Now that everything has gone wrong for me, tell me about myself. I went to a place called NORCAP."

"I know," Jane interrupted. "I saw the address in your

room in London. You left it out for me to see, didn't you?"

"Of course not. I never thought. I was so unhappy that night about the skiing."

"You see how it is?" Jane said, her voice low and passionate. "And how it would always be with someone like Harry? Expecting his charm to get him everything. Bewildered if people don't fall at his feet. Well the world hasn't fallen at his feet, has it? It doesn't, you see. It didn't for your father either. He thought he was immortal, but he wasn't." Eliza's voice rang in her head on that appalling night after the funeral. "Now you needn't be jealous any more. Now he's dead you've got him all to yourself!"

"I went to see those people," Alice said doggedly, "and they told me to ask you." She sat upright. "Please tell me what you know about me. At least let me have that much."

Jane moved out through the kitchen door. She returned with empty plates and carried back a tray bearing bowls of trifle, decorated with bright green Angelica and halved red cherries and rosettes of cream. When she returned, she put the kettle on the hot plate and picked up her cigarette from the ashtray. Her hand shook.

"The woman I saw asked me if I had ever been abroad. I told her about the holiday in France. She said, then I must have a passport. I said I was on yours. In that case, she said, there must be a birth certificate."

"There is." Jane watched the expression of absolute amazement possess Alice's face. She stood across the table from Alice, her voice quite normal but her eyes extraordinary, hands so tightly interlocked that the knuckles were white.

"I have it all. All the papers. I keep them in the bank. There is even a little money, a few thousand pounds. Your mother left it to you. She had no relations. I suppose that was one of the reasons your father picked her up in the first place. He was always intrigued by that sort of thing. Outward vulnerability. A certain rather charming hopelessness. Probably contrived. But she was a lovely-looking girl. You are very like her. She was eighteen or nineteen, I suppose. Tiny little thing. I only met her once. I came back here unexpectedly and found them. Just talking. I suppose she was telling him she was pregnant. She needn't have been so worried about me. I was used to it. Twice before it had happened. They had abortions. He couldn't help it. He was drawn to them, the more helpless the better, and they could never resist him. She wouldn't have an abortion. She believed in the sanctity of life but not, apparently, of marriage." Jane lit another cigarette. "She was killed in a car accident, hitch-hiking back from a pop concert about two months after you were born. She had left you with the landlady. He was very unhappy. I suppose he loved her. I tried not to hate him for it. He brought you here." She stubbed out the cigarette. "Haven't you ever realised how like him you are? Couldn't you see how much you meant to him?"

"Why didn't you tell me before?" The tears had dried in stripes down her face.

"Because I couldn't admit to anyone that I had taken in a child he had by another woman ten years after he married me. To say you were adopted was so much simpler and it saved my pride."

"Did anyone know?"

"Only Molly. I had to talk to someone, sometimes. You'd think that once I'd done that for him, he would have changed, wouldn't you? But he didn't. He couldn't. New jobs, presents he couldn't afford. Once he came back with a Shetland pony for you. Eliza is so like him, except that he could control his temper and she never could."

"Eliza is my sister?"

"Half-sister."

"And she doesn't know?"

"Of course she doesn't know."

"But she loves me anyway."

The kettle boiled and Alice stood up and made cups of coffee and carried them through to the dining-room. She brought out the empty bowls. Then she sat down again and drank some coffee herself.

"What was my mother's name?"

"Rosalyn Vesey." Jane said the words with difficulty.

"How much money?"

"Not nearly enough to help Harry. It was three hundred. Now it's about two thousand. I never touched it, even when I was desperate after he died." Jane sat down. "What do you feel now I have told you? I knew I would have to, some day."

"Didn't he want to tell me before?"

"Often, but I wouldn't let him. It would have shut me out, you see, if you'd known. You and he and Eliza would have all been related and I would have been shut out."

"And instead," Alice said softly, "you were shut in."

Alice got up very early the following morning and walked to the station. It took three-quarters of an hour but she needed to walk; changing her light bag from shoulder to shoulder. She caught the seven forty train but she went, not to Pembridge Gardens but to the Stoner Shipping offices, arriving just after ten. She went up the stairs to Eliza's office.

Eliza was standing by one of the windows, a mug of coffee in her hands. She turned in surprise.

"I tried to get hold of you last night, Alice. I was desperate to talk. God knows what is happening here." She looked very pale. "There are constant phone calls. The press have been here. A telex came from Robert, instructing me to contact Kit Secombe and cancel the charter on the *Endeavour* but I can't get hold of him."

"Perhaps it's to do with the war," Alice said. "Perhaps they've sunk one of Robert's ships. The *QE2* is sailing next week. It's on all the news stands." She was staring at Eliza, struggling to believe that some of the same blood ran in both their veins.

"This is nothing to do with the war." Eliza sat on her desk and tried Kit Secombe's office again. This time she got through.

He listened in silence as she repeated Robert's message. "I'm afraid Mr Stoner didn't give an explanation but he seemed anxious that I contact you at once. Of course, I'll put a letter in the post today."

"I'm afraid it's quite impossible," Kit said slowly, looking down at the memo on his desk marked *Urgent*. "The charter was for a year. There is no question of cancelling it, especially in these rather unsettled circumstances."

Eliza laughed uncertainly. "But if he has lost the trade for it, he will not be able to meet the costs."

"That's his problem, I'm afraid."

"God Almighty," Eliza said as she put the telephone down. "Everything is coming apart. Where the hell is Robert?" She looked back at Alice. "Why are you watching me so oddly? What did you come here to tell me so early in the morning, Alice?"

Alice stood with her back to the tall windows. After a long pause, she said, "Last night Harry told me the shop is hopeless, that he has to sell the house and that he is going to Australia. He wasn't really furious with me but with everything, I think. I love him so much, Eliza. In the beginning it was just that there had never been anyone else but now it's different. When he said he was going I was desperately unhappy. I went home. I told her and she was thrilled. And I asked her, again, who I was and this time she told me." Alice was like a sleep-walker, eyes dull; like someone drugged. Tears sprang into her eyes.

"Gerald was my father, too. My mother was a girl of eighteen he met somewhere. She died two months after I was born."

Eliza lurched forward awkwardly and embraced her for a long time. There were tears in her eyes too. Neither of them spoke until they turned, disturbed and embarrassed when Carolyn came in. They moved awkwardly apart.

"I'll go now," Alice said. "I just wanted to tell you, that's all. I hope things calm down here."

"Have you read the papers?" Carolyn said, bustling towards them. "D'you know I'd never heard of the South Atlantic before this started. I thought there was only one. And when those Argies landed at first I couldn't think what the fuss was about. Look at it now!"

It was after eleven when Alice reached Pembridge Gardens. She found a customer on the doorstep and let her in guiltily, full of excuses, and opened the curtains and put away the coffee mugs. For half an hour she was busy. Then she went upstairs, looking cautiously into Harry's bedroom. There was a suitcase on the unmade bed, an empty wine bottle on the floor; the cupboard was wide open and some of the clothes were lying on the armchair. Alice sat down on the edge of the bed and felt sick. Then, just for something to do, she tidied the room until the bell summoned her down again.

She had a busy morning. At one thirty she went down to the kitchen to make a sandwich and try to eat it. She thought it might make her feel less shaky and unreal but she had just taken her first bite when she heard the bell again and she climbed wearily up the stairs.

Harry stood in the narrow hall. He looked so different that for a moment she didn't recognise him. He wore a dark suit and his hair was combed rather flat. He wore a bright red tie. He walked towards her and put his arms round her, holding her so tightly that he lifted her off the floor. He held her for a long time.

"I never meant any of what I said last night. I was desperate. After you'd gone, I sat for a long time, thinking about what you said. About me giving in to it all. I thought of everything I could possibly do to keep going and in the end I rang Julia. It took ages to find her. She told me that I was behaving like a child. That I was perfectly capable of doing a normal job. She said, 'Why don't you use him instead of letting him flatten you. Go and do his bloody job. Take the money and use it to keep Pembridge Gardens going. Get a foothold. I'll get in somehow and between us we'll do pretty well.' I told her she was changing sides. I was furious with her. And then I thought of the alternatives. The only thing that matters is being with you. So I went and bought this suit. I had to use a credit card!" He grinned at Alice. "I rang him and made an appointment. I am meeting him for lunch on Friday. It's the first day he can manage."

Chapter 25

The evenings at Flood Street were quite extraordinary without Celia. The house seemed dead. David cancelled three engagements three nights running. It had never occurred to him that, although he was so often out without her, Celia very seldom went out leaving him at home. Nor did she go away very much. The evenings were long and desperately quiet, punctuated only by Josephine's phone calls.

"It's even worse this term. Where is Mummy?"

"She's gone away for a few day."

"Where to? She never told me. She isn't ill, is she?"

"Of course not, Josie. She's gone to Devon for a few days to stay with an old friend," David lied. "You must stop this constant telephoning and try to settle down. When are you next allowed out?"

"On Sunday. For lunch. Will Mummy come? She said she would."

"You've only just gone back but I'll tell her. Now, I don't want you to ring again until the weekend."

By day he was unable to concentrate on the normal business events, so obsessed was he with the effect he could have on Robert. Michael Copper came to lunch.

"I can't argue with you, David. I am realistic about the situation and you can make life pretty difficult for me if I don't fall in with your plans but what has the man done? It's a nice little operation in Venezuela. It's profitable for me. I hate to see it fold up."

"If you demand the repayment of your capital, I think I can put a far more lucrative investment your way."

Michael shrugged. "I really have no choice. How's Celia?"

"She's away," David said crisply.

* * *

For two silent, miserable days, Celia had been alone at Robert's flat, doing nothing, eating almost nothing, desperately missing her tapestries but feeling she could not go back until she had at least heard from Robert. She rang the office several times to be told, stiltedly, by Eliza that Robert had disappeared. She watched the news in bewildered horror when they related a strike at the Lagos oil Terminal, and talked of breaking sanctions with South Africa. No word all day Wednesday, nothing on Thursday. So much time to think, swinging from one conclusion to another. Suppose Robert never came back? David, what of David now?

On Thursday evening, she sat on the edge of the sofa in Robert's flat watching the news on television, watching the destroyer *Sheffield* abandoned and burning and screwing up her face in pity at the horrific wounds of the victims; so engrossed was she that for the first few moments she didn't register Robert's footsteps on the stairs but when he spoke her name, she sprang to her feet.

He put his arms round her, holding her for a long time and letting his breath out slowly. Then he raised his head and glanced over her shoulder at the television screen. "Poor bastards. I bet they didn't expect anything like that." He moved across to the small table where he kept the drink and poured himself a very big whisky.

"Where have you been? What's happened?"

"I'm so sorry I wasn't back yesterday. I tried to ring. I hoped you'd be here. How long have you been here?"

"Since early Tuesday morning. When you dropped me at Flood Street, David was waiting up for me. He knew." Celia stood with her arms crossed over her body as if to protect herself. "He had seen the newspaper and Eliza told him it was true. But how can she have known?"

Robert stared at her, the brief expression of amazement being replaced by one of anger. "God knows. But what the hell has it to do with her?"

Celia uncrossed her arms and opened her hands.

"That's easy to answer. Because she loves you and I have ruined things."

Robert stood with his head bent, feet slightly apart, deep in thought and Celia watched him and felt a wave of love and of hopelessness. It was so extraordinary to be here now that he was back. For the past silent days and nights she had thought far more about David than about Robert, trying to picture his life without her and thinking with agony of the destruction of their home.

"I suppose I should have thought about it more." Robert rubbed his forehead wearily. "What a strange girl she is. Hasn't she heard of loyalty? What does she expect me to do with her now?"

"David is a difficult man to deceive and she only told the truth. But how did she know it was true?"

Robert shrugged. "At least now there is no going back."

The words chilled her. She was trembling. "Please tell me what has been happening? I was nearly going mad with worry. They have mentioned Stoner Shipping on the news and the strike at Lagos docks but the Falklands gets nearly all the coverage."

"The strike is over. I knew it wouldn't last. It was that bastard Lugamo whipping up ill feeling."

"Who is Lugamo? I don't know any of these people you talk about. What had the dock strike to do with you?"

Robert poured himself another drink. "Come and sit down and I'll explain." He looked at her gently, the expression replacing for a moment the grimness of his face. "Thank God you're here."

Celia came and sat beside him. "I have hidden here. I've hardly been out. I don't know what David has told people. I don't think he knows the address of this flat although I suppose he could easily find out. I haven't been back for any more clothes. I've just waited. Tell me everything, Robert."

Robert drank deeply and reached out for her.

"It's painfully simple. I took a risk. I set up a deal to trade with South Africa. The potential profits were enormous but it went wrong and I'm bloody lucky to be here at all. If I'd gone on to Lagos I'd never have got out. Luckily M'habela got me off at Kano and hid me until I could get into Morocco. I came back by a very devious route."

"But how did it go wrong?"

"I can hardly believe it myself. It's absurdly unlucky. Sophia went to Mombasa on holiday and at the docks she recognised and photographed the *Endeavour*. Although they had done a little art work on the name it wasn't very difficult to work out it was the same ship." He laughed, bitterly. "I took her to see it myself before it sailed the first time. I even pointed out the distinctive colouring on the funnel."

"I still don't understand."

"If we had genuinely been trading with Singapore, as everyone believed, we could not have been at Mombasa. There wasn't time to get there." He was silent for a moment, remembering Michael M'habela's sarcastic voice on the telephone. "You seem to have underestimated Sophia's feelings considerably, Robert. Surely you could have stopped her?"

"Sophia was furious with me. I had assured her Singapore was genuine. When she found out it wasn't she told everyone, especially the press. And she timed the disclosure to do the maximum damage. The dockers went on strike. Bang goes the contract with Van Ryn and any other contract with South Africa. Luckily I was able to telex Eliza and tell her to cancel the charter."

"Eliza has telephoned here several times. She is desperate to talk to you. It seems Otterwoods are refusing to cancel the charter."

"Jesus," Robert said softly.

"What will happen?"

"God knows. Venezuela certainly won't bring in enough to cover it. I shall have to find some other trade for the *Endeavour* bloody fast. Look, I think I'll go down to the office now. I've got a lot of phone numbers there. I'll be about an hour." As he spoke he was walking towards the door.

"I'll come too, shall I?" Celia said, standing up.

"No, don't. I'll be on the phone all the time. I'll be back for you and we'll go and eat somewhere." He kissed her absentmindedly.

When he had gone and his flat was silent again it was as if he had never been back.

Robert ran up the stairs to the office three at a time. It was seven thirty but the door was unlocked and he went in.

Eliza was sitting at her desk. She looked very pale. As Robert entered she pushed her chair back sharply so that it almost fell over. She stood up, her arms rigidly at her sides.

"What the hell have you been saying, Eliza?"

She ignored the question, almost running round the desk to stand in front of him. "Where have you been?"

"It's a long story," he said coldly, wondering why, when he looked at her, he felt such a complex set of reactions.

"I've been desperately trying to get hold of you. Otterwoods won't cancel the charter."

"So Celia told me."

"John Spurrell is screaming for supply ships. He rings all the time. He left a home number."

Robert nodded.

"And Michael Copper wants to speak to you urgently."

"Him too?" Robert said. "Has the bastard got to him as well?"

"David is out to annihilate us." Eliza said.

"Not just David, it seems. You made a pretty good start yourself, Eliza. Do you still consider yourself part of it?"

Eliza was very white. "Yes. I do. And I am. Robert, I had no idea what would happen when I went to see David. I honestly thought he wanted to discuss Harry.

By the time I got there, I was so miserable I could hardly think straight and when he showed me the article and asked me if it was true, I couldn't deny it. It is true, isn't it?"

"Yes. But you couldn't have known for certain."

"Don't you understand what happened? On Monday afternoon, just after you left, Sophia rang. She said it was very important. She said to tell you she had just got back from Mombasa and had photographed some ships. She said I must tell you. I drove to your house. I wanted to tell you in person. I have been several times before when I could have telephoned." She met his eyes defiantly. "You weren't there but Sophia had been so insistent I thought I would wait. So, like the loyal employee I am, I sat patiently in my car opposite your house. I waited for half an hour. When you arrived with Celia and got out I saw you hold her, laugh with her and kiss her. I wasn't hiding. I was sitting there in broad daylight but you were both much too engrossed to see me. I drove away. After a time I rang to give you Sophia's message but when you answered the phone I couldn't talk to you. You sounded so impatient. I went on to see David. I was going to give you Sophia's message in the morning but in the morning you had gone."

As he listened, Robert experienced a strong feeling of relief that Sophia had tried to warn him. So the past did count for something, after all?

"What perfect timing," he said and his voice was icy. "Absolutely perfect. What a pity I didn't make it back to Lagos. Then between the two of you, you would have really screwed me." He looked into her ashen face. "And for what? I can understand Sophia's fury, but what have I done to you that you didn't give me the message? I offered you a job, Eliza, nothing else. Everything else you wrote in for yourself."

As he watched the colour came into her face. Her body stiffened and the apologetic air vanished to be replaced by fury.

"You bloody hypocrite! I don't give a damn what you

said, you implied a lot. You must have known how I felt. Don't pretend. That night when you told me to make up my mind about working for you, you knew how I felt and you used it. Over and over again you've used me. And why didn't you trust me with the truth about South Africa? All I did, Robert, was exactly what you do in your life. You told me yourself that you see something you want and do your utmost to get it." She was shaking with fury.

There was a long silence and then Robert sighed, shaking his head. He sat down. "I implied nothing that I didn't genuinely feel. I wanted you to work for me very much. If I had stopped to think seriously, I probably wanted a lot more. I didn't know how Celia would affect me. What I said just now was unfair. But it's all irrelevant. What the hell are we going to do now to survive?"

Eliza shrugged helplessly. "God knows." She felt the anger drain away and as she softened she knew she was going to cry. She snatched up her bag and her jacket and ran out of the office, stumbling slightly at the bottom of the stairs.

Josephine came back into the dormitory from matron's room, holding the two aspirins she had been given in the palm of her hand, her cheeks still flushed from the woman's sarcasm. She did feel ill. Everything about this place made her feel ill and miserable. It would have been all right if only she could talk to Celia. Why hadn't her mother rung? She had left dozens of messages, ringing Flood Street in the day in case her father answered the phone. She had rung Julia but it was impossible to find Julia.

She sat heavily on her bed, tracing with one finger the pattern of the flowered duvet. There were five other girls in the dormitory and they were coming up from supper. It was just before eight. They treated Josephine this term with a certain amount of irritation. She was attracting unwanted attention to the dormitory.

Josephine sat with her head bent, hand still clasped round the pills.

"I'm going tonight," she said, in a perfectly normal voice. "Will you help me? Cover for me?"

Quite suddenly she had everyone's attention.

"You can't. They'll throw you out."

"I don't care what they do."

"It would be much better to wait till the weekend. Go on Saturday, at lunchtime. Write a going-out letter and pretend it's from your mother. No one will miss you till Sunday night."

"I can't wait. Something has happened at home." It was easy to let the feeling take over, to let the panic seep into her, into her face and voice, to let herself believe it. "My mother must be ill or dead. Or they've split up. She's gone away. I know something has happened."

They were with her now, drawn to the excitement and conspiracy. Josephine was the eldest in the dormitory. They all sat on her bed, clustered round her, and the seriousness of it gripped them all.

"After she's been round for lights out I'm going down the fire escape in the corridor. I shall walk to the station and get the last train to London. It's the ten fourteen, I checked. If she asks in the morning, tell her I'm in the bath. Then, at first class, say I'm in the san. It's History. Gillies won't be surprised. I was ill so much last term. That should give me until lunchtime. I'm going home, that's all. I just want to know what's going on. If they are angry, say that I made you do it. I am the senior in this dormitory. But I hope you'll be able to play dumb."

"Haven't you just been to matron?" Melanie said.

"Yes."

"Then all we have to say is that you came back and told us you were going down to the san."

"Yes. Perfect." Josephine smiled. "Thanks."

Much later that evening, after he and Celia had eaten and come back to the mews, Robert got hold of Michael Copper at his home.

"I'm back. I gather you've been trying to get me."

"Yes. Come in to the office early tomorrow, will you, Robert? I have to talk to you about our arrangement. Something has come up and I want my capital out."

"Now?"

"Yes. As soon as possible." There was a short silence. "I'm sorry, Robert." His voice had an unmistakable tone of genuine reluctance. "I really am sorry. It's the last thing I want to do but I can't go against David. My business depends on managing four of his ships. If he takes them away, I'm buggered."

"I'll have to sell the ship to raise the capital to repay you."

"I know. Believe me, it's the last thing I want to do. It's a neat little business."

Robert put the telephone down and dropped his forehead into his hands. Vaguely he was aware of Celia standing behind him, putting a tentative hand on his shoulder. He stifled an impatient impulse to shake the hand off and instead covered it with his. He turned slowly in his chair.

"He is out to annihilate me, Celia. And it's so bloody easy for him. This fiasco couldn't have happened at a better time for him. Without Venezuela and South Africa there is nothing left unless I am extremely fortunate and find trade for the *Endeavour* for the next ten months."

He stood up. He thought much better on his feet. Celia watched him pace the room and she knew he would be easier without her, that she could not contribute anything. She had watched David go through similar crises.

The telephone rang again and Robert answered it swiftly.

"Robert?"

"Yes."

"John Spurrell. Eliza called in earlier and told me you were back. Do you remember before Christmas we discussed supply ships?"

"Yes."

"Her Majesty's Brokers need to charter at least four. Keeping the task force supplied is a major problem. The *QE2* leaves on May the twelfth. Have you got any supply ships available?"

"Definitely two. Possibly more. I'll be in your office at nine tomorrow morning with the details."

Robert put an arm round her. She could feel his tension and his excitement and she knew that, dangerous as it was, he was relishing all this. She had seen David in a similar situation perhaps a dozen times in their lives together. It was all familiar. She had been there before. Robert and David were becoming entangled in her mind.

Robert bent his face down and kissed her. "Come and make love to me," he said.

Celia did not sleep at all. Their love-making left her body subject to frequent violent echoes as if the sensations were being replayed again and again. Robert slept deeply. For a long time she lay and watched him, needing time to realise and store the power and the tenderness which he could unleash, still amazed at her own uninhibited response. But it was underscored with deep sadness, with hopelessness. She simply did not believe they would be together for very long. She lay and thought through the whole sequence of the last nine months, from the moment Harry made his announcement; she thought of Alice and Eliza; of Josie and that terrible dinner after the Otterwoods party. All her thoughts led her, eventually, to David. It was impossible for her to sever the strings. Of the nine months she had known Robert, he had been out of the country for at least half of the time. Could she go with him, confined to hotel rooms, watching the television in languages she couldn't understand, reading yet another lurid book? In some of the places she would be able to wander the shops but she would need friends to see and how many of the Otterwood friends who covered the world would want to see her? And how could she be away from Josie for months at a time? She could not think of the castle, of her garden; all of that brought her back to David.

Then she would turn and look down at Robert and try and balance her feelings for him against all the massive problems and when, in the early morning, he woke and reached for her again, it seemed he had won.

She cooked breakfast for Robert, using the new frying pan she had bought and the little coffee filter machine but he was in a hurry and was gone by half past eight, leaving Celia to sit and pick at pieces of bacon she didn't want. It was Friday, she realised, and on Sunday, Josie could come out. She felt a great wave of guilt that she had not been at home to receive Josie's calls. Also she wanted some thinner clothes. Robert would obviously be gone all day. She bathed and dressed, did some shopping and drove to Flood Street, ignoring the questions in Mrs Wickham's eyes as she met Celia in the hall.

"Has everything been all right, Mrs Wickham?"

"Not really, Mrs Otterwood. Josephine rings all the time. She kept asking for your telephone number. I didn't know it or I would have told her. I asked Mr Otterwood and he said you wanted to remain undisturbed for a few days. Julia rang too. And Harry has been round several times. They all seem very agitated."

Celia sighed and went into the small sitting-room. She sat down and closed her eyes and was almost asleep when Mrs Wickham brought a tray of coffee. She smiled her thanks. As she sipped it the telephone rang.

"Mrs Otterwood? Thank God I have found you in. It's Miss Longridge. Josephine was reported missing this morning. It turns out she left the school last night, after lights out. She walked to the station intending to catch the last train to London but she missed it. The station master found her asleep early this morning and rang the police. As I rang them half an hour later, we have her safely back but I'm extremely concerned about her. Could you come to the school today and talk to me?"

* * *

Harry came into his father's office at twelve thirty. David motioned him to sit down. He was frowning as he spoke on the telephone. "Thank you, Michael. Don't give him any leeway. Have lunch with me on Monday?"

Harry leaned back in one of the deep leather chairs. David watched him in silence for a few moments. Then he said, "I'm very pleased that you're here, Harry. We can at least talk about things."

"I suppose so," Harry said dully.

"Let's go and eat. I thought you would rather eat out than in the dining-room here." David stood up. "It's been quite a week, one way and another." His father looked grim, Harry thought, and tired.

They walked down several flights of stairs and through the glass-walled atrium and were silent for the few minutes it took to reach the small Italian restaurant where David had booked a table. At first they discussed the effect of the Falklands on Otterwoods. It was a safe subject and Harry was intrigued by the thought of war and fascinated by the nightly television coverage.

"I thought of joining the Air Force," he said, watching his father's face closely. "I've always wanted to learn to fly. I had a few lessons at St Andrews."

David's expression did not flicker. He knew when he was being wound up. "That's not a bad idea, learning to fly I mean. I would be perfectly willing to pay for your tuition. I let my PPL lapse about ten years ago and I'm rather sorry."

"This business about Stoner is rather odd, isn't it?"

"Very odd. My original instincts about the man were right. He's unsound."

"But surely Otterwoods have played a few games with sanctions in their time."

"Certainly, although I would never admit to it. The great crime is getting caught out. I'm rather glad to see Van Ryn get some adverse publicity. I've never liked him."

"Do you know them all?" Harry said.

"Yes, I think I do. Anyone who matters." David ate his

hors d'oeuvre in silence for a few minutes and then he said, "Harry, since I last spoke to you, I have spoken to Ronald Tobin. Tobin's are nearly as old as we are; they are competitors but we respect each other. Ronald has offered you a job in their insurance department. You would get a good training with them, moving round to different departments, and if you choose to come into Otterwoods later on, you will be well placed. Also you will have a broader view than if you started with us from the beginning. I thought it might be better for you."

There was a long silence. The amazement was plain on Harry's face.

"If I choose to come into Otterwoods?"

"Yes."

"Why have you changed your mind? I thought it was essential that I come into Otterwoods?"

"I've changed my mind about a lot of things over the past few days. I still want you to come into the company in time."

"I see," Harry said stiffly.

"Well?"

Harry edged forward in his chair. "I could start next week. When would I get paid?"

For once in his life David could barely conceal his amazement. After a few moments, silence, he said, "You will have a monthly salary cheque like everyone else in the company, I imagine. You can go and see Ronald at four this afternoon. Ask him."

"I suppose there's no chance of getting an advance from him?"

"I doubt it." David drank some wine. Then he leaned forward. "However, if you were to go into your bank manager and explain that you will be starting work very shortly at a salary of ten thousand a year in the insurance department of Tobin UK I think you will find he will give you a little more time."

David smiled and Harry looked down at his plate and wondered if it would ever be possible for him to like his father. He thought back to what Julia had said. "Use him, Harry. You can't win outside but you can inside. Take the money."

"How is your other business going?"

"Quite well. Unfortunately I had to borrow some money at very high rates of interest. It's those repayments which make it so difficult."

Something in Harry's expression, the tucked-in corners of his mouth, made him seem a child again. David's voice was gentle. "But you intend to carry on?"

Harry shrugged. "Alice may carry on. I hope she will." He looked up as a waiter approached their table and spoke quietly to David.

"There's some drama at home, Harry. Your mother wants to speak to me. Order yourself a pudding if you want."

Harry ordered coffee and a large brandy and sat at the small table wondering why he didn't feel either depressed at having signed his life away or elated at having saved Pembridge Gardens, and he realised, as he had last night, that it was not Pembridge Gardens he cared about, or his independence. It was Alice. And he wasn't at all sure how she felt now. He needed to get out and think. He swallowed the brandy very quickly and stood up, and he met David in the small hallway.

"Thank you for lunch. I have to go now. I'll go and see Ronald at four." He hesitated awkwardly and then moved up the stairs out of the small restaurant.

Chapter 26

Robert came into Kit Secombe's office two hours later than the arranged time. He didn't apologise. He sat down heavily in the chair opposite Kit's desk.

"So you won't cancel the charter?" he said flatly.

"I'm afraid not. If we abandoned all our charters the moment any client had some difficulty, all our ships would be idle."

"You know perfectly well that, in the present circumstances, it would be comparatively easy to find trade for it."

"If you're so confident of that, why not find trade for it yourself?"

"What the hell do you think I'm trying to do?" Robert said.

"I'm sorry, Robert. We will expect the third month's payment by the end of the week at the latest."

Robert raised an eyebrow. "All you will get is a court case with nothing at the end of it. You might point that out to Otterwood," he said and he stood up and walked out of the office.

He walked back to Holborn and he was hot when he arrived. He sprang up the stairs. There must be a way out. He had taken up the charter on the two Swedish supply ships and John Spurrell had mentioned a figure of twelve thousand pounds a day. As Robert would be paying four thousand, even after crewing there was a considerable profit but no way would it tide over the payments on the *Endeavour* and initially the arrangement was only for three months.

As he entered the office Eliza looked up anxiously. He nodded briefly to her and Carolyn and went through to his own room and a few minutes later Eliza came in, carrying a mug of coffee. She closed the door behind her.

"Well?" she said, impatiently. "What happened?"

"The supply ships will be chartered to go to the Falklands. I shall start assembling crew this afternoon. We'll have to pay special rates, of course." He sat down. Eliza put the coffee in front of him. "Thanks."

Eliza stood with her fingers interlocked, her dark eyes seeming to burn in her face. She swallowed. "I have a little money. A few thousand pounds. I was left it by a great-aunt after whom I was named. An unpleasant old girl. She liked to be kissed a lot. Anyway, if it helps you can have it. Well, borrow it without interest."

Robert sat forward. "You never cease to amaze me, Eliza. We are on the brink of annihilation. The chairman of one of the biggest shipping companies in the world is determined to ruin me, no matter what it costs him. Stoner Shipping is collapsing like a card house, you may be out of a job in a few weeks, and you offer me your savings. Why?"

"Because it's partly my fault and because I believe in you and I am desperate for you to survive."

"Despite Celia?"

"Yes. I will take things one at a time."

There was a short silence after which they both, at the same instant, started to smile. Robert stood up and walked round his desk. He put his hands on Eliza's shoulders. He touched her mouth with his.

"Thank you for the offer. I'll let you know."

David double-parked his car outside Flood Street and ran up the few steps to the front door which opened inwards as he reached it. Celia was standing in the hall. She moved back, anxiously, into the study.

"David, why didn't you tell me she'd been ringing?"

"Because it's been going on for months. I didn't think there was any greater urgency in the calls. I was angry with her. She's too old to play this game and I thought, with you away, it gave me a chance to be tough. She's just getting her own back."

"Don't be absurd," Celia shouted. "She's desperately unhappy about us. Don't you understand that? She can sense what's happening. That night after the Otterwoods party, I sat and talked to her for hours. She was distraught. She told me it was easy to tell the children of divorced parents at school. They fall into two categories, she said, those who are painfully extrovert, anything for attention, and those who are just silently worried. You can always recognise them, she said."

"Why didn't you tell me?"

Celia opened her hands in a gesture of helplessness. "I haven't been able to tell you anything for months, have I?"

"What do you want me to do?"

"Come to school with me and reassure her."

David gave a loud, bitter laugh. "Reassure her about what? Exactly what she feared has happened. You have left. Are you going to lie to her, because I won't?"

"We could pretend. Just for a little while until she has grown up a bit more. Just to give her a year."

"No." David said flatly. "There has been far too much pretence. I can see that now. Far too much looking the other way. If there is anything left it has to be absolutely open and honest."

"I could tell her the truth but be with you all in the holidays." Even as she said it she knew it was absurd.

"And what is Stoner going to think of that? I don't think he's the kind of man to take kindly to having you when your children don't need you." His voice changed, became gentler. "I think you have to choose, Celia."

Almost before David had finished speaking, Celia was conscious of a sense of agonising loss, like a deep inner sigh. Somewhere inside her a door closed.

"There is no choice," she said.

"So Josephine comes first?"

"Of course."

David took two steps towards her and reached for her

hands. They were very cold. "This is absolutely ridiculous, Celia. I am prepared to make radical changes in my life if you will come back. These past few days have been quite terrible. I just can't believe you will allow everything to be broken. I have thought a great deal about what I would say to you. I was going to tell you that, if it's sex that you want, you don't have to leave me. I was going to say, go on sleeping with him but stay with me. But I can't. I think I would kill him in the end. You say I've had twenty years and it's true, I have. But what about the next twenty? We have come through all the worst of it. They are virtually grown up. Otterwoods is far more successful than I ever dreamed it could be." It was extraordinary to see David so intense, without the mask of indifference. "There will be much more time."

"Do you want to spend it with me?"

"Yes. I want you to come with me much more when I travel. Not all of it is my fault. You used the children and the houses as an excuse. You hardly ever came with me. You lost interest in everything I was doing."

"Surely it was the other way round entirely?"

"The crucial thing is, do you still want to live with me?"

She stared at him for a long time. There was no simple answer.

"When you talk like this and I remember how it was in the beginning, then I want to live with you. I have thought about you so much in the past few days. It was ridiculous. I thought about you much more than about Robert. I wanted to help you get over my not being here. For the first time ever you seemed uncertain. But I cannot come back unless things change."

"What things?"

Celia took a deep breath. "You must let Harry go. He must be allowed to find his own level. Buy the house for him. Give him a chance and let him come to you if and when he's ready."

David let out his breath slowly.

"You don't know what you're asking, Celia. He had

lunch with me today. I could have forced him to come into Otterwoods but, over the past few days I have been doing a lot of thinking. I have arranged, instead, for him to start with Ronald Tobin. He will gain valuable experience. He will be on the ladder and he can come into Otterwoods in five or six years with a well-rounded view of the City. To have Harry back means almost as much to me as having you back." He paced the room. Celia had never seen him like this. She felt there was no barrier, that he was speaking his thoughts without the normal careful consideration. "I think you are wrong, Celia. If I agree to this we may look back on the decision in ten years' time with great regret. He could still be bumming around, drinking too much, starting incessant hopeless schemes. At nineteen he can come in at the bottom and work his way to the top. At twenty-nine it will be very different. I honestly believe that at Harry's age it is better for him to be coerced. In the long run he will thank us." He poured himself a glass of brandy.

"Just give him a free choice, David."

"Who else has a free choice? People work for money."

"It will matter so much later on that you didn't compel him."

"I think you are wrong, but if it's the only thing to make you come back, I'll agree. Is there more?"

"Let Robert off the hook. Cancel the charter. Free Michael Copper from whatever obligation he has to you." She stood in front of David, her speckled eyes wide open as she waited.

His voice was very soft. "D'you think I give a damn about Stoner if you come back? He'll hang himself soon enough, anyway."

Celia moved swiftly towards the door, picking up her bag. "Let's go now. It will take us at least two and a half hours at this time of day."

"Christ, what a waste of time. I always said it was bloody silly to send her to school in Malvern, anyway. Perhaps she's right. Perhaps she should be at school nearer home." He caught at Celia's arm. "Is that it? Is that finished then, the discussion about our whole future lives and the lives of our children?"

"Of course not," Celia said impatiently. "We can talk in the car, can't we?"

Robert was on the telephone most of the weekend, trying to fix the *Endeavour*, without success. Celia had left a message in the office on Friday afternoon to say that there was a family drama concerning Josephine and she would be spending the night in Malvern. Eliza relayed the message with an expressionless face and such clamouring joy inside that she could not meet his eyes. Robert received the news just as blankly but, although he felt a sense of betrayal, one part of him was glad to be on his own. It freed him to spend his time on the telephone. Celia rang him late on Saturday night.

"What the hell are you doing?" Robert said gently. "Where are you?"

"I'm in a hotel in Malvern with Josie. They've let her out for the weekend but we thought it better not to go home. She ran away. I think it's going to be all right. We've told her she can leave at the end of this term, and take her A levels in London."

"We?"

"David and I. He's here too. We had to come together."

Robert grimaced. He had the feeling of something infinitely precious slipping through his fingers. "Come back to me as soon as you can," he said.

On Monday morning he was in the office as early as Eliza. They met at the bottom of the stairs.

Eliza touched his arm, concern on her face. "You look exhausted."

"You look pretty terrible yourself. That was a damn good move going to see Spurrell. That, at least, is going to work."

"But no luck with *Endeavour*?"

"Not yet. I tried to get a loan out of Van Ryn but he's not interested. M'habela can't speak to me because that lunatic Lugamo has everything bugged. I've tried just about every contact I know but word is out that I'm in a corner and the price has dropped accordingly. My only option now is to fix the *Endeavour* at an absurdly low rate so that at least my losses will be partially covered. The money is due on Friday."

Eliza made coffee for them both. She carried it into Robert's office and sat in a chair. There was no sense of constraint between them now but a shared feeling of desperation.

"It was horrifying to watch the Harriers dropping bombs, to see live war on television. Really terrible. People being killed while you watch."

"You don't have to watch."

"I can't help it." She sat forward, the short dark hair standing away from her head, mouth bright; she wore a striped dress with a wide leather belt. The dress was very long, almost reaching to her narrow ankles. She picked up the spider armlet and put it on her hand. "What's going to happen, Robert?"

"I think we've had it."

"Can't Celia do something?"

"I've no idea. I haven't seen her since Friday morning."

Hope surged into Eliza's eyes and she dropped them quickly before Robert saw. Her voice was subdued. "I wish to God I had lied to David. If only I had given you Sophia's message in time, you could have done something." She shook her head. "It's this bloody awful temper of mine, Robert."

Robert came round his desk and ran his hand down the back of her head, down the dark silky hair. "Forget it. It wouldn't have made any difference. I had persuaded Celia to leave David so it would all have come out in a few days anyway."

"But a few days would have made all the difference. You could have cancelled the charter."

Robert shrugged. "We're not quite dead yet. Something may come up."

Just after nine thirty the telephone rang.

"Kit Secombe for you, Robert," Eliza said, watching his face through the open door. At first it was wary and extremely hard. Over the next few moments his expression changed to one of elation. When he put the phone down he came into Eliza's office, put his arms round her and kissed her.

Michael Copper rang an hour later.

By eleven thirty Stoner Shipping was afloat again.

Celia was waiting in her car for him in the mews. When he drove up she got out at once and came across, stumbling on the cobbles. He got out of his car and embraced her, his mouth against hers; his hands encircled the back of her neck, thumbs under her chin, the pressure hurting her.

She went ahead of him up the narrow stairs, turning at the top to speak before he could touch her again.

"Is it all right? You look triumphant."

"I feel it. They've agreed to cancel the charter."

"And Michael Copper?"

"Him too." He looked intently at her. "You did it, didn't you?"

She backed away. She looked pale. She looked more beautiful than he had ever seen her look before but delicate and untouchable and immaculate. Hard to believe she was the woman who had been in his bed. She looked almost transparently fragile and her eyes were desolate. She didn't answer.

"Don't tell me you're going back to him? Not now, the moment you are free and I am alive again. If it is part of some bargain I would rather go under."

"I am not free, Robert. David has grown into me after all these years. Like ivy into a wall. If I root him out I will destroy whole areas of my life."

"I don't believe that. Just leave. You left once."

"Not really. I took a little time for myself. You gave me a chance to be everything I have never been because I married so young. I thought David and I had nothing left. I didn't realise I was capable of hurting him so much. For the moment I have all his attention. Perhaps it will last. Perhaps he will change." There was agony in her eyes.

"Don't go back," he said gently. "Don't waste it. It's not a thing I'll find again in my life, the way I feel about you."

Tears in her eyes. "You were too late for me, Robert. I knew all the time. I am not just one person any more. They are all grown into me." She looked at his face and then the image shook as the tears overflowed. She blinked and then closed her eyes.

"You're condemning yourself to the same life. He won't change. Oh, you'll go with him on a few trips and be bored and long to be at home; you'll watch him at parties and wonder who and how many, has it started again? He'll push you into the background. Soon even your children will have entirely separate lives. Do you want to grow into a withdrawn, self-sacrificing, garden-obsessed, dog-obsessed, English lady?"

She almost smiled. "There are worse things to be."

"Don't go back."

"I never really left."

"Why do you say that?"

"Perhaps because I know him so well." She walked down the stairs and out into the mews, turning to look up at Robert's window before she got into her car. They were going to Scotland at the weekend. "Just try it." David had suggested. "It could be like the beginning all over again." But how to get through the time from now until then?

She sat in her car for a long time. There were so many things she could have said to Robert, so many ways of explaining, but how would words change anything? She sensed that this initial parting, like realisation of death, was not too hard to cope with. It was the gradual acceptance of the truth, the full horror of loss, that would increase so agonisingly until, looking back, it seemed in the beginning one had been half-asleep. As she drove back to Flood Street she gathered round herself, as preparation, the good things. Harry and Alice, Josie's face when they told her she could leave at the end of the term and come to London. David's attention. Those were the good things she would use to arm herself against the sense of loss.

Alice still felt unreal, days after Jane told her the truth. To be given Eliza as a blood relative was an incredible gift. To be given the memory of her father as a real father was almost unbearably poignant. Coupled with her elation was the most bitter sense of injustice that she had never been told when he was alive, but she countered this. Would it really have been any different? Could she have loved him any more?

She moved in a daze. At night she had dreams in which she was trapped in situations of agonising frustration and she would wake, sweating, and realise that it was all right. That everything was saved.

Harry was being good. It seemed to Alice that, having been forced to take the decision to start work, he was almost relieved; music that he liked sang from his cassette player constantly; he bought Alice small presents; he got up in the mornings and staggered down to sit in the shop as Alice opened it, coffee cup clasped in his hands; he drank nothing but coffee until the evenings. His best behaviour made Alice smile but she was uncertain of him and when he went out and bought two half barrels to put in front of the shop, to attract attention, he said, she was very careful to show pleasure. She went to the flower shop and bought petunias and little white daisy plants and she dug up soil from the little back garden to fill the tubs with. Eliza rang, often, just to talk. There were enough customers, neatly spaced, and between times Alice washed and ironed linen that had come back from hire.

On Sunday she and Harry went to Hove. Alice felt stiff with her mother, felt that somehow Jane had cheated her, but she hid the feeling. She had not known what to expect from Jane but she found that her mother, after a first few anxious moments, relaxed into comparative normality. There was a change in Jane. She received the news of the shop's reprieve calmly. It was as if, with the truth, she had somehow severed the strings and had lost her intense anxiety. She laughed once or twice at something Harry said and then afterwards caught herself, as if she had made a mistake. And she amazed Alice by replying, when Alice asked how the bookings were for this summer, that she had decided to leave July empty. To have a holiday and do some serious garden visiting with Molly.

"What did you expect?" Harry said teasingly as they drove back. "Nothing will make her like me. But I suppose she will come to tolerate me in the end. She'll have to when we're married. She will never change, though."

"But she has changed, somehow. There is a feeling of relief, I think."

On Monday morning, Alice came down at seven thirty to collect the newspapers and the post. Harry was shaving, humming to himself, not at all like the condemned man on his way to serve a life sentence.

Alice gathered the letters from the mat. She opened all the letters now because Harry would not; to Harry, every envelope was a potential threat. Alice carried them downstairs as she went to make coffee, glancing through them, putting personal letters in one pile and bills in another. The Monday morning batch were fairly normal apart from a long white envelope. It looked familiar. The paper was stiff and expensive. There had been a few letters like this before, the black ink shaping neat and confident handwriting. Alice tore it open and unfolded the thick paper. There were a few lines of writing in the middle of the large sheet. It was from David and she could not stop herself from reading the letter.

Dear Harry,
As you may have realised, your mother and I have had some problems over the last few months but I am happy to say we have sorted them out. However, she is extremely anxious that you should be allowed to choose your future freely. As you know, I am equally anxious for you to start work with Tobin's and eventually come into the company. As a compromise, which she suggested, I have persuaded your trustees to buy the lease on Pembridge Gardens for you. Therefore, if you go to work on Monday as I expect you to, it will be willingly.

Alice held the sheet of paper for a long time, aware of the sounds of Harry upstairs. She imagined Harry freed from the torment of the bills. What would he do? How long would he be content to live here, doing nothing, drinking endless cups of coffee and glasses of wine with the friends, ready to seize a suggestion of amusement at a moment's notice. If he read this letter he might not go to work at all. Just a few weeks. Let him try for a few weeks, Alice thought, and with her hands shaking, she put the letter back in its envelope and put it in the drawer in her desk.

Harry came down to the kitchen at eight, tidy and clean and very good-looking in his grey suit, his dark hair smoothed flat. He kissed her as he passed, sitting on one of the chairs and looking up at her with his speckled eyes. He sighed. "D'you know, Alice, it really doesn't seem so bad now I've done it. Or said I'll do it. After I had lunch with him, I just walked. Miles. And thought about things. Julia's right. I'm not a fool but I am not a person who finds it easy to organise my own life satisfactorily. I like making things but I'm never going to concentrate enough to do it for money and I can't be bothered to learn. I don't do any one thing particularly well. I like my friends, I like to go skiing, I want to live this sort of life. Most of all I want to marry you and live here with you. If it means working at Tobin's, even with

Otterwoods, it's probably worth it. All my father did was to make me start at the bottom with nothing, the way most other people start. So I'll try his way unless it becomes intolerable." He smiled, the wry enchanting smile. "I don't know if I'll ever like my father. He's too good at everything and much too calculating. But he does treat me with more respect now. Julia said that too."

Alice kissed him, standing on the doorstep to watch him go with a sense of relief and hope. She went back to the drawer and read David's letter again. In hiding it she had taken an extraordinary step. She had sought to change things, not just to sit back and wait. Because she thought it would be better, she would hide this. It occurred to her then, and the thought was amazing, that this was just what her mother had done all those years ago. Taken a view and acted upon it, hidden the truth. For the first time since Jane had told her who she was she felt some sympathy and understanding.

Just a week, Alice thought, wandering the silent shop with its rich fabrics, straightening some damask cloths, loving the look and feel and smell of it all. *A week or two.*

Sophia stayed late in her office that evening although, for once, she had no work to do. Lugamo had been here earlier, raging about Robert's escape. "He was actually in this country. He landed at Kano. Somehow your father got him out. It must have been him, I think, although some people suspect it was you. They feel, after so many years of being lovers, you would never let him be caught. Some people wonder if you, too, are laughing at us. Somehow your father has cleared himself of suspicion. This time. But he will be much more careful now. I watch every move he makes. I want us to work closely together in the future, Sophia."

She had watched him go with a sense of relief. She got up and poured herself a drink and went to the window, remembering the early days, the first ecstatic days. They seemed to be part of an earlier lifetime.

"What have you achieved in the end?" her father had said. "Nothing. Robert will never want to see you again; it will be a long time before he ever comes back here. I resent the loss of such a good friend. I will never be able to trust you again, and no one really takes those sanctions seriously because they do no good. You have stirred up a lot of mud, Sophia, that's all. What can you do now?"

"I am going into politics if I can," she had answered. "I am going to do my best to change this country."

Michael shrugged as he left. "Don't expect any help from me."

"I don't," she said aloud into the silence. "Not from you or from anyone. I shall do it on my own."

Robert's letter was on her desk. It had been waiting for her that morning. He had written to her a great deal in the first years when he was at sea, long, interesting letters which she had kept but thrown away last summer, shortly before he left for England.

This short letter said very little. "I suppose it was irresistible, Sophia. I even understand why. Be careful. You have stirred up a hornet's nest."

She half closed her eyes and the brilliant orange of the flowers in the bed outside the window blazed and danced like flames. Like Robert's hair. Sophia, always a lawyer, sought a word for her feeling but no one word would do. A sadness shot through with disillusionment? Waste, she thought, that summed it up best of all. A pity. A pity beyond all telling.

Chapter 27

Eliza sat at her desk and thought briefly, and miserably, of the weekend to come, looming like an iceberg in her imagination. The silence of her flat, once so comforting, was now an intolerable contrast to the extremely busy days. In the past four weeks, she had supervised the crewing of two more supply ships and dealt with Venezuela and again tonight it would be seven thirty before she got home. Stoner Shipping had not only survived but was riding high on the opportunities presented by the war. A terrible little war that was now over. As it seemed to Eliza that a whole section of her life was over. She had given up struggling. She felt exhausted and numb and for the first time in her life she had abandoned her future into the hands of fate. Summer had come but she felt so isolated she could not even take pleasure from the gentle weather.

Robert had been in Aberdeen and Rotterdam, South America and Japan, and on the few occasions when he had been in the office during the last month, he had treated Eliza with a distant politeness which had devastated her. During the crisis they had shared a feeling of desperation, a sense of working together that had given Eliza hope. Why then, since their salvation, had she felt this frozen awkwardness? She had certainly achieved her ambition to run the company in Robert's absence. What she didn't know she had learned very fast. She sat forward in her chair and finished typing the letter of resignation she had begun half a dozen times and the irony of the situation made her pen shake in her hand as she signed it. Although she had achieved the position she wanted in Stoner Shipping, it was impossible for her to stay on. She could have faced Robert's anger but his indifferent politeness was intolerable. She sealed the letter into an envelope and wrote his name on the front and she was so deeply immersed in her thoughts that when the telephone rang it was several seconds before she answered it, anticipating as she did so some new complication which would eat further into her evening.

"Eliza? It's Robert. I'm glad I caught you."

She wondered if she would ever hear his voice without experiencing that flickering, joyful apprehension.

"I'm at home. On Monday I left all the correspondence about the *Endeavour* on my desk and I want to go through it this weekend. Would you be able to drop it in on your way home tonight?"

"Yes." She closed her eyes, knowing she would take the letter too. Why wait any longer?

"How long will you be?"

"About half an hour," she said.

Tonight there was a space outside Robert's front door and as she got out of her car, she wondered if things might have been resolved differently had she parked here on the night when everything fell apart, had Robert seen her, had she delivered the message? But such conjecture was pointless and it hurt. She no longer wanted to pretend. Pretence would never again be enough. Robert's door was open and she went up the steep stairs into the empty sitting-room, standing for a few moments and looking around as she wondered if it was the last time she would come here.

"Robert."

He came out of the kitchen holding a bottle of champagne, twisting the wire as he walked, and as the cork hit the ceiling he aimed the white froth of liquid at two waiting glasses and filled them. He handed Eliza a full glass.

She stared at him, his actions so contradictory to the way she felt she couldn't speak at first. "Has something happened?"

"Yes. A lot of things. We have survived for a start. I had a very successful time in Japan and I've decided to stop behaving like a fool and face reality. We are drinking to the future and the continuing success of Stoner Shipping."

"But why tonight?"

"Because I'm home. Because you've been doing a bloody good job and I've missed you and because I'm tired of trying to observe a decent period of mourning. You know the song *Clementine*? 'Then I kissed her little sister and she promised to be mine.' I didn't want you to feel like that."

Eliza sat down. She drank and sighed and allowed herself to register a feeling of extreme exhaustion. She closed her eyes briefly and when she opened them, Robert was looking at her with a serious expression. The very tight hold she had on herself began to soften but she did not want to let the feelings come through again. Not again.

"I've got rather a lot to discuss with you," Robert said. "Shall we go out somewhere?"

She didn't answer. She looked down at the brown envelope lying on top of the file.

"Just the two of us," Robert said, smiling slightly. "No clients to entertain. No information wanted. Just a celebration."

She stayed very still for a long time, slightly bent forward as if she were getting her breath after a long, uphill climb, as if she were recovering from temporary paralysis. Very gradually the old optimism and relief began to filter through, but they were tempered with caution. It could never be like the beginning all over again.

"Why are you so quiet? It makes me nervous. Are you going to fly into a rage and shout at me?"

She shook her head. "Have you really got a lot to discuss with me?"

"Yes. Percentages and things." He crossed the room to fill her glass and he picked up the *Endeavour* file from her lap and threw it in the rubbish bin. The envelope fell with it.

They walked to a restaurant a few streets away. They sat opposite one another at a small square table and Robert told her every detail of his last trip. As the time passed Eliza stopped stamping on the happiness every time it rose up like a wave. But she needed proof, dignity, things to hold on to and Robert sensed the need.

"You've never asked me why I waited for you outside Otterwoods on that first afternoon."

"I assumed it was because I was David's secretary and could be useful."

He took her hand. "I remember coming out of the lift, totally involved in what I would say to David, thinking of nothing but the meeting and the money I wanted very badly and as I walked across that huge, rather forbidding office I looked up and saw you behind a desk that looked far too big for you, sitting very straight with a bright yellow dress on and looking at me anxiously as if I had to pass some kind of test. Then you smiled, as if I had passed. And you wished me good luck. I came out of his office disappointed and infuriated and you wouldn't come for a drink, which annoyed me, but I kept remembering the way you'd looked at me so I waited, because I wanted to see you and because I had nothing else to do." He leaned forward and touched her pointed chin. "I'm still waiting, in case you hadn't noticed."

"What about Celia?" she said very quietly.

"Celia took me completely by surprise; if things had worked out differently perhaps I wouldn't be here now, but I have a feeling I would have been here in the end. Celia realised before I did that it was too difficult. I don't expect to feel like that in my life again and I don't really want to. I would rather be with someone who is quite capable of telling me to go to hell and then offers me her life savings; someone who wished me luck months ago when she didn't know me and runs my office better than I could ever run it myself."

It was after eleven when they came back into the mews. Robert had his arm tucked through Eliza's. He unlocked the door and stood aside slightly for Eliza to go ahead of him, giving her a gentle push as she hesitated.

"I hate to leave a bottle of champagne unfinished, don't you?" He began to whistle *Clementine*.

Eliza turned and looked up at him and the corners of her eyes and her mouth tilted upwards into the wide smile.

She couldn't sleep after they had made love. She lay against Robert and tried to believe in all this, listening to his breathing, looking at the grey patterns of streetlight and moonlight on the ceiling and the wall. She had to keep touching him to reassure herself because she had imagined being with him so many times. But reality, as always, was nothing like imagination. She could not have imagined his strong, freckled body, the way they had touched each other, curiously, delightedly, the conviction that it wouldn't matter what happened after this triumphant laughing love-making. She had never been able to imagine the feeling of being loved which she had craved for so long. Robert had made her feel loved. But how to believe in it? How to trust the love? It had never lasted before. As he slept all the doubts came back, all the agony, until she began to slide away from Robert very gently, moving her body with infinite care towards the edge of the devastated bed and putting one bare foot on the floor.

His arm tightened around her waist and he pulled her back. "God, you're skinny. Where are you going?"

"I was going home."

"Why?"

"I never stay all night. I wouldn't know how to be in the morning. I have to wake on home ground."

Robert laughed and pulled her tightly against him.

"This is home ground," he said.